TRAINING COMPLEX

LETA BLAKE

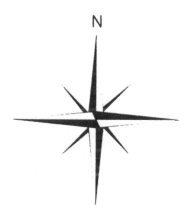

ISBN: 9781626227286
Print Edition

Cover design Copyright © 2015 by Dar Albert at Wicked Smart Designs
www.wickedsmartdesigns.com

Editing by Keira Andrews
keiraandrews.com

This is a work of fiction. Names, characters, businesses, places, events and incidents are either the products of the author's imagination or used in a fictitious manner. No figure skaters or former ranchers, living or dead, were harmed by the writing of this book. Any resemblance to any actual persons, living or dead, or actual events is purely coincidental.

Other Books by Leta Blake

Any Given Lifetime
The River Leith
Smoky Mountain Dreams
Angel Undone

The Home for the Holidays Series
Mr. Frosty Pants
Mr. Naughty List

The Training Season Series
Training Season
Training Complex

Heat of Love Series
Slow Heat
Alpha Heat
Slow Birth
Bitter Heat

'90s Coming of Age Series
Pictures of You
You Are Not Me

Co-Authored with Indra Vaughn
Vespertine
Cowboy Seeks Husband

Co-Authored with Alice Griffiths
The Wake Up Married serial
Will & Patrick's Endless Honeymoon

Gay Fairy Tales
Co-Authored with Keira Andrews
Flight
Levity
Rise

Leta Blake writing as Blake Moreno
The Difference Between
Heat for Sale

Leta Blake writing as Halsey Harlow
Stay Lucky
Stay Sexy
Omega Mine: Search for a Soulmate
Bring on Forever

Audiobooks
Leta Blake at Audible

Free Read
Stalking Dreams

Discover more about the author online:
Leta Blake
letablake.com

Gay Romance Newsletter

Leta's newsletter will keep you up to date on her latest releases and news from the world of M/M romance. Join the mailing list today. letablake.com

Leta Blake on Patreon

Become part of Leta Blake's Patreon community in order to access exclusive content, deleted scenes, extras, bonus stories, rewards, prizes, interviews, and more.
www.patreon.com/letablake

Can Rob help Matty defeat his inner competitor for good?

It's summer in the city and figure skater Matty Marcus is still desperately in love with Rob Lovely. Although he misses the thrill and pressure of competition, he couldn't be happier in their new life together, so he doesn't understand why he's secretly indulging in his eating disorder again and requesting harder, more intense BDSM scenes. Matty's scared he's losing control, and he has to believe that Rob, as always, will save him.

Rob is equally crazy about Matty. He finally has the vivacious man he adores in his arms every night. But taking it to the limit has always been the name of Matty's game, so Rob's love must be stronger than Matty's self-sabotage. Even when Matty's inner demons try to take control, Rob is committed to find their way back. Together.

Loving Matty isn't always easy — but for Rob it's always worth it.

Training Complex is an MM romance about a feisty, self-sabotaging former figure skater and the steady, strong man who loves him. It features opposites attract, hurt/comfort, domestic discipline, chastity play, and a heartfelt and epic happy ending. No cheating, no threesomes, and no breakups — just two amazing men fighting for their love!

Content warning for disordered eating, misapplied BDSM, and mental health issues.

*Dedicated to everyone who struggles
to find their place in the world.*

Disclaimer

"Depiction does not mean endorsement."
~ Kathryn Bigelow

Sometimes what's sexy in fiction can be—and sometimes is—injurious or even deadly in real life. This novel depicts a number of kinky sexual acts, including breath play. I cannot stress it strongly enough: *please don't try this at home!*

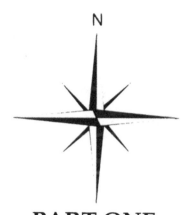

PART ONE:

CONTROL GOES DOWN THE RABBIT HOLE

CHAPTER ONE

THE THUDDING OF Mr. Wegman's footsteps on the floor above woke Rob from a dream of snow-capped mountains and brilliant sunlight. In the dream, Rob had sat astride a horse and watched Matty skate his old Olympic program on a frozen-over pond surrounded by daisies. Blinking his eyes open, Rob drifted in the space between the dream and their small New York apartment.

At the sound of Mr. Wegman's boots coming off in a one-two thump as he tossed them on the floor, Rob willed his mind back to the image of Matty leaping into the air, dark hair twirling, smile radiant and strong thighs taut with effort. Mr. Wegman coughed loudly, and his unsteady bed made a grating groan. Then it was quiet. The sounds of the city at night were held at bay by the white noise of the standing fan, and Rob pulled Matty's warm, naked body closer. The darkness of their ground-floor bedroom tugged at him, urging him back into the liminal place that promised more of Matty's sunshine-smile.

The smell of evergreens lingered, and he rolled his head, sleepily recognizing that the scent wafted up from his pillow. Oh, yes, his shampoo. Still new. He'd purchased it with Ben a few weeks before because it'd reminded him of home. And Matty had liked it too, calling him his cowboy and riding him hard. Rob's dick stirred at the memory, and he slid his hand down Matty's side, dragging him flush against his own naked body. He pushed his hips against Matty's muscled ass, and felt him respond in his sleep.

He didn't know what time it was. If Mr. Wegman had just come back from his bar, it must be after eleven but probably before two in the morning. The clock by the bed had a book propped in front of it to block the glowing numbers. He'd put it there the night before to block out that little bit of extra light, trying to get the room as black as possible in the city. Matty stirred against him, arching his ass back to push against Rob's cock.

"Sweetheart?" Rob whispered, reciprocating the thrust. "You awake?"

"The stomp-monster woke me up." Matty's voice was sleep-blurred and warm.

Rob snorted softly, tucking his nose into Matty's hair and breathing in. "You smell good."

Matty's soft giggle caressed Rob.

He opened his mouth to press a wet kiss to Matty's throat. "Yummy."

Matty shivered under the thin green blanket and pushed his ass back again, a hint of amusement under his next words. "Oh, no. I hope I'm not yummy enough to eat."

"Mmm. I think you just might be."

Matty's cock was hard in Rob's hand, curving perfectly against his palm. "I hope you aren't the Big Bad Wolf," Matty whispered, his tone playful and falsely earnest. "Here I am, a poor lost boy in the evil, bad city. Can you help me find my grandmother's house?"

Rob laughed against Matty's shoulder, kissing his soft skin, and running his hands up and down Matty's back, feeling each dip of muscle and bone, each inch familiar and *his*. "I'm always happy to help a lost boy find his way," he said gruffly, his cock sliding between Matty's ass cheeks. The friction was wonderful as he rubbed it up and down Matty's warm crack.

"So you won't eat me?"

"Well, I can't promise that."

Matty sighed and moved his hips to work Rob's dick between his cheeks more. "Will it hurt?"

"Maybe. But only if you like it to hurt."

Matty turned in his arms, Rob's cock sliding free from the warmth of his cleft, and pressed their chests together. Rob reached to hold Matty's cock in his hand again, treasuring the rightness of it. In the soft, ever-present city light that slipped under the blinds, Matty's smile glinted. "Oh, Mr. Wolf, I like it to hurt *so much*."

Rob kissed him hard, holding his jaw and rubbing his fingers against the growing stubble. Pulling away, he pressed his forehead to Matty's, feeling his breath against his lips. He slid his fingers down Matty's neck, touching the place where his pulse beat so firmly.

"Do you love me?" Matty asked quietly. "As much as I love you?"

"Yeah. More."

"No, I love you more." Matty kissed him again and Rob let himself fall into it, reveling in their bodies moving together, their cocks pushed side by side, and their gasps and sighs filling each other's mouths.

Matty broke away, kissing a line by Rob's jaw. "You're not so mean, Mr. Wolf. I thought you said you were going to eat me and make it hurt." He bit gently at Rob's earlobe. "But I don't feel any teeth."

"Still want to play, huh?"

"Yeah. That okay?"

"That's fucking great, sweetheart. You want the Big Bad Wolf to eat you up? Use his sharp teeth until you cry? Hmm, poor little Matty lost in the city?"

"Fuck, yes."

"All right." Rob took hold of Matty's hips and rolled him flat on his stomach, sliding beneath the covers to spread his ass and breathe on his asshole. "This looks delicious. Have you ever let anyone taste it?"

"Oh, no! Oh please don't!" Matty laughed softly as he said the words, unable to stay in character. "It's not right, Mr. Wolf. It's a naughty place."

"Naughty places always taste the best."

Matty caught his breath as Rob licked his hole. "Don't do it again, please. Please, Mr. Wolf."

Rob drove his face between Matty's ass cheeks, closing his eyes and pressing his tongue to Matty's hot asshole. He pushed Matty's legs apart and rubbed his own cock against the soft sheets as he continued. He opened Matty's hole with his tongue, chewing at the tender skin with his teeth.

Matty bucked beneath him, stifling his sounds with his pillow before lifting up to say over his shoulder, breathless and eager, "Oh, Mr. Wolf, that feels so good. Fuck, eat me harder. Bite me. Make it hurt."

Rob plied Matty's cheeks even farther apart, biting harder than usual. Matty surged back, crying out, "More! Again! Please, please, Rob. Oh, please bite me hard."

Rob bit the apple of Matty's right butt cheek and then hauled himself up, covering Matty's slim back with his chest and sliding his cock into Matty's spit-slick crack, stroking over his hot hole again and again. He lowered himself fully and kissed Matty's neck, biting at his shoulders and clasping both of his hands in his own.

Matty gripped back. "Love feeling you, Rob. Love you on top of me like this. Feel so safe with you." He sounded strained, like it was harder to breathe, but he wrapped his ankles back over Rob's calves, holding him there. "Want you to come for me. Are you gonna come for me, Mr. Wolf?"

"How does a lost boy like you know about dirty things like that?" Rob whispered and Matty laughed again.

"Maybe I'm going to eat you instead," Matty murmured. "Maybe my ass will devour your cock and make you come so hard you forget everything else in the whole world. And you'll be my love slave forever."

"Mmm, how would that work?"

Matty lifted his ass up as much as he could with Rob's weight against him. "Fuck me and I'll show you."

Rob stretched over Matty far enough to get the lube from the bedside table drawer, and then kissed him, messy and sideways, while he slicked his dick and rubbed lube over Matty's asshole.

"Yeah, I'm ready. Please, just—yes, oh yes. Fuck." Matty moaned, and Rob let out a low groan as he pushed the head of his cock against

Matty's asshole and the ring of muscle gave around him.

"Not so dangerous now, huh, Mr. Wolf?" Matty gasped, but he sounded strained and his asshole was tight on Rob's cock.

"Oh, I'm plenty dangerous, sweetheart." He plunged in harder, and Matty writhed under him. "Feel that? Enough bite for you?"

"Fuck, Rob, so good."

"Yeah?"

"Oh, fuck yes."

Rob smiled. In their safe room, darkness curving over and around them, Rob breathed in the scent of a no-longer-sleepy, fully-aroused Matty, and held him tightly as he fucked him hard. Each gasp, each jolt of pleasure, each touch a reminder of their love and connection. His heart bloomed with love as the game fell away and it was just him and Matty, just their pleasure and affection, their kissing and tender touches.

"I love you," Matty whimpered.

"Can you come for me?" Rob muttered, rolling onto his back and pushing Matty off his cock. "Ride me. Come on my chest. Hold my hands and don't touch yourself."

"Fuck," Matty said, clambering onto him and seating himself eagerly on Rob's dick. The heat of his ass swallowed Rob's cock and he groaned, biting his lip and gazing up in the half-light to watch Matty's beautiful body writhe and twist. He gripped both of Matty's hands, twining their fingers together, and watched as Matty worked, angling himself for the most pressure on his prostate, the most pleasure from his cock bouncing as they fucked.

"Show me. I want to see it. Shoot for me."

"Oh God…"

Matty tossed his head back and then dropped his chin down again, staring Rob right in the eye and saying with radiant intensity, "This is how I love you."

Rob opened his mouth to say he loved Matty too, just like this, on him, over him, taking his cock like the beautiful champion he truly was. But before he could, Matty's asshole gripped him tightly, the rhythmic pulse of his orgasm starting there. Rob's balls drew up, his pleasure drawn aching and tight, and he stared up at the shadows of Matty's face as they came together. Matty crooned, his eyes on Rob's, and his stomach and thighs convulsing. Hot splashes of come spurted against Rob's chest as he pumped his release into Matty's tight, clenching body.

"Yes, Rob," Matty moaned. "Yeah, yeah."

Matty squeezed Rob's fingers and then released them to grab his own cock to prolong the last of his cresting pleasure. When Matty started to quake, Rob drew him down for a kiss. "Love you," he whispered against Matty's soft lips. "Love you so much."

"I've captured you now, Mr. Wolf. You'll be my love slave forever."

Rob laughed and held Matty to his body, still trembling. "Isn't that the truth?"

The city carried on around them, but they were quiet, safe, and tired. Matty left the bed to get a wet washcloth and cleaned them both up, and then Rob pulled him over to his side of the bed, away from the windows and the dawn that would come too soon.

"G'night," Matty whispered. He yawned, curling his back against Rob's side and pulling the extra pillow between his knees the way he liked it. "Was it good for you?"

"Loved it, sweetheart. Always love it with you."

Matty smiled sweetly and made a soft, sleepy sound. The darkness and the groan of the pipes slowly lured Rob back to sleep, and though the snow-capped mountains never returned to his dreams, he rode in a forest wearing a wolf-fur coat, looking for Matty in the trees.

***

MATTY'S IPHONE READ twenty minutes after four in the morning and played Miley's "#GETITRIGHT" through its tinny little speakers. He danced around their little Brooklyn bathroom while he touched up his face, adding a hint of glossy lip shine and a touch of color to his cheeks. Dancing through his favorite part, he swung back around to the mirror, lip-syncing and batting his eyelashes.

Still shaking his hips, he picked up the eyeliner and mascara, preparing to brighten his dark eyes and darken his long lashes. But as Miley faded out and a heartfelt ballad began, he remembered he'd be teaching Sabrina for what was probably the last time. He took a deep breath in and slowly let it out. He set aside the eye makeup. He'd be a big enough mess when he said goodbye without the added drama of eyeliner and mascara running down his cheeks.

He pressed skip on iTunes until he found something upbeat again. Running cold water over his fingertips, he dabbed them against his hot eyelids. Then he evaluated himself in the mirror, twisting a piece of his dark hair down over his forehead for a rakish, windblown look that would soon be made real enough. The hot summer breeze that tore down the corridors of the city had left him a frizzy mess the day before.

After checking for runaway makeup on his black running shorts and white tank, he paused the iPhone music, snapped off the bathroom light, and headed into the bedroom to grab the rest of his things for work.

Fragile near-dawn bled through the window over the bed. Rob's blond head was half hidden by the thin green sheet wrapped around his body. Matty carefully clicked on the desk lamp to keep from tripping. Rob made a soft snuffling sound, and Matty smiled tenderly, tiptoeing closer to get a better look.

Rob might be five years older and wiser than when they'd first met, but he was also five years more handsome as far as Matty was concerned. Blond stubble grew on his strong jaw line and his lashes lay like small, gold fans against his cheek. The upturned edge of his well-proportioned mouth was made to fit perfectly against Matty's own. *Beautiful.*

"What time is it?" Rob murmured, his eyes still shut and voice creaking sleepily.

"Four-thirty. You don't have to get up yet. I just wanted to look at you before I left."

Rob flung an arm out and dragged Matty down against him.

Chest hair bristled against Matty's cheek, and Rob's warm, sweet-smelling skin felt so good under his hands that he wanted to crawl back in and make a morning of it. He kissed Rob's chest and collarbones, resting his face against Rob's neck and taking in slow, deep breaths. The peace and gentleness of Rob's arms seeped into him. It was a balm against the tough world outside their door—against the demanding voice in Matty's own head.

"Stay with me."

Matty reluctantly pulled away. "I've got ice booked."

Rob made a sad little sound but released him. "Missed you last night."

Matty's stomach did a silly little flip. How was it possible that Rob still made him feel so squirmy inside? "You had me in the middle of the night. Remember?"

"Oh, I remember." Rob winked. "Don't get lost in the city today."

Matty grinned.

"But I meant yesterday evening. We barely had time together before we hit the hay."

"Then you shouldn't have stayed out so late playing with your ex-wife," Matty teased, running his hand through Rob's hair and down the side of his face to feel the stubble along his knuckles.

Rob snorted. "We were having so much fun talking finances I just couldn't bring myself to break away."

"Money. My favorite."

"When it means you get to spend it, sure." Rob sighed, his mouth hardening a little and tiny stress lines appearing around his eyes. "Which reminds me, I need to talk to Bing about the goats. If we aren't going to get some kind of payout soon, I may need for him to buy me out of my investment."

"No!" Matty squeezed Rob's shoulder. "We'll figure something else out." He had a call in to Julien Alban asking about the possibility of skating some shows with him in Asia at the end of the summer. If he was lucky, he'd be able to bring in somewhere between three to six thousand dollars a show. Not enough to bring them up in the world, but it'd be a nice little bundle to help tide them over. "The

10

goat farm will pay off eventually. We just have to be patient."

"You? Patient?"

Matty punched his arm gently. "I can be extremely patient."

"I know you can, sweetheart." Rob rubbed knuckles over his tired eyes, which didn't look green so much as gray in the low light. "You're right. The goats are going to pay off. After all, it was a brilliant idea."

"Your idea." Matty chuckled.

"Yep. By the way, Anja sends her love."

"Did hearts come out of her eyes? You always promised me hearts from her eyes, and I've never seen it yet."

"They'll come eventually."

"It's been a hard sell."

Rob chuckled again. "Well, you did break my heart. But she's almost over it."

"Jeez, it's only been three years, but okay." Matty rubbed away the lip gloss trail on Rob's chest, shoulders, and neck.

"She's just overprotective. You know that."

"L-oh-L. Understatement. At least she's nice to me."

"She's coming around. Oh, and she wants to take us out to dinner for our anniversary."

Matty swallowed down the objection that rose immediately to his lips. Anja's idea of a good place for dinner was vastly different from his own. Everywhere Anja liked served plates with ten thousand calories per bite and so much extra fat cooked in that it made his arteries ache just thinking about it.

"Sounds good," he murmured, not wanting to get into it with Rob. He trailed his fingers down Rob's chest, smoothing over his crinkle of chest hair and tracing down to his morning wood. It was hot and hard, and Matty rubbed the backs of his fingers against the rigid, velvety length.

Rob captured his hand and held it in place. His cock swelled even more under the combined pressure. "She's thinking next week or the one after. Speaking of, you haven't tried to trick me into telling you where we're going on our trip lately."

"Are you going to tell me now?" A zip of curiosity almost overpowered the frisson of apprehension about the proposed dinner. Matty pried Rob's hand free, and then teased the head of Rob's dick with the tips of his fingers. Wetness welled up at the slit, and Matty felt an answering thrum in his own body. He slid his thumb over the pretty, mushroom head, smearing the drops around.

Rob's voice was sandpapery with drowsy desire as he murmured, "No. It's a surprise."

Matty left off teasing and wrapped his fingers around Rob's dick. He squeezed, eliciting a soft, encouraging noise. It was almost distracting enough to shatter the whirl of awakened anxiety, but not quite. Hopefully Anja's dinner plans weren't also a surprise. He needed to be able to plan in advance what he was going to eat. "Where's Anja planning to take us?" Calorie counts whizzed through his head and he bit down on his inner cheek to try to silence them.

"She mentioned Otto."

You will not have pizza. You'll have salad.

"Oh."

"You love Otto." Rob frowned.

Matty took a slow breath and let it out, smiling and trying to shake off the intrusive thought. "No, it's fine. You're right. It'll be great."

You'll have a salad and, if you're very good, some of the olives.

Matty pulled his hand away from Rob's dick and wiped his fingers on the bed clothes, moving to get up. Rob stopped him with a hand on his leg.

"Do you want to go somewhere else?" Rob offered, squeezing Matty's thigh and sliding up farther. Matty grabbed hold of Rob's hand and lifted it, kissing his fingers.

"It's fine. I was just thinking about everything I need to do today."

"Right." In the low light, Rob's eyes went sea-water soft. "Sabrina leaves for Colorado when? Tomorrow?"

"Yeah."

"You going to be okay?"

12

Matty shrugged. "I'm always okay."

Rob lifted his brows. Tweaking Matty's tight tank top, he said, "You look hot. Jogging in?"

"No, walking to the station and taking the train the rest of the way." He leaned down and kissed Rob's eyebrow, then his other eyebrow, and then his mouth. Pulling away he wrinkled his nose. "Ugh. Morning breath."

"You love it."

Matty rolled his eyes. Admittedly, if he was going to get back in the bed to stay, it wouldn't matter that much. As it was, he suddenly had other, very amusing plans. Matty pulled back the sheet to reveal Rob's treasure trail slipping down to his thatch of pubes and his beautiful, still-hard dick below.

Rob took it in hand and aimed the fat, rosy head at Matty. "Too bad you have to go. Up for another round?"

"Can I be the wolf this time?"

"Sure."

Matty licked his lips and bent down, kissing the head and taking it into his mouth, letting Rob's slowly jacking fist bang softly against his lips as he suckled.

"Mmm, take control, sweetheart," Rob murmured.

Matty grinned. "Okay. Roll over."

"Hmm?"

"Just roll over for me."

Rob complied, casting a saucy look over his shoulder, and Matty knelt between his slightly spread thighs. "Well?" Rob asked, rolling his hips against the bed, making his ass flex beautifully under Matty's kneading fingers.

"Shh. I'm enjoying myself. And plotting dirty, naughty things for your hot ass."

"Plot faster." Rob lifted his hips, offering his hole. "It's been a long time. Going to fuck me?"

Matty snorted as he ran his finger down Rob's crack, sliding in the moist heat until he reached the soft, crinkled skin of his asshole. He pressed against it gently. "Don't get your hopes up." Matty glanced at the clock on the nightstand. "I've got to leave in exactly seven minutes if I'm going to get to the train on time."

Rob chuckled and relaxed against his pillow, spreading his legs even farther. "Oh well, if you're just having a free look at the goods, I'm going back to sleep." He closed his eyes and went limp.

Matty slapped his ass. "You've only got a few minutes before your alarm now anyway."

"Mm-mm. We're having employee training this afternoon. I get to sleep in."

Matty rubbed Rob's asshole, feeling the muscle relax under his fingers. "Lucky bastard. I never get to sleep in."

Rob grinned, his smile wide and shining even in profile. "So are you going to do anything with this seven minutes? Or is this hole teasing all I get?" Matty slapped his rear again, and Rob laughed. "Ow! I'm not the one into being hit, sweetheart. So if you're trying to turn me—oh!"

Matty spread Rob's ass cheeks wide and dove down, licking wetly over his asshole. Rob groaned and pushed back for more. He smelled a little musky, but otherwise he was still clean from his shower before bed. Matty nuzzled the peach-fuzz of hair on his ass cheeks, licking his hole sweetly. When Rob reached back to hold him in place, he went to work really eating him out. Teeth, tongue, suction.

Deep, wondrous grunts and growls of encouragement drove Matty on harder and faster. His own cock demanded attention. He didn't touch it, though, or do more than concentrate on making Rob's universe shrink down to the tongue in his asshole—until the clock said he had two minutes to get out of the apartment.

Slapping Rob's ass one last time and wiping a hand over his face, Matty climbed off the bed and adjusted himself.

"No," Rob moaned. "Come back. What the hell was that?"

"It's a new game I made up. It's called—" Matty darted into the bathroom again, calling over his shoulder, "Good morning, starfish, my tongue says hello!"

He brushed his teeth quickly, washed his face and mouth with his creamy cleanser, and swiped the moisturizer and makeup bag from the counter. He'd re-apply on the train or at the rink.

Rob had rolled to his back when Matty returned to the bedroom, his dick hard and his chest heaving as he moved his hand over his erection. His eyes burned hot as he gritted out, "You're not going to stay and see this through?"

Matty chuckled. "Sorry. Gotta get the train. I have faith in you. You can handle it."

Rob's hand worked faster over his dick, the head popping through his fist over and over. "Jerk. Tease," he gasped. "Should never have plowed your drive in Montana."

"Oh, sexual innuendo. My favorite." Matty laughed.

"Brat."

"You know it." Matty opened the closet, which housed most of his shoes. He pulled out the pink and black Mr. Hare summer sandals he'd picked up on eBay for beyond super cheap and bent to put them on. "You must love brats."

"Well, I love you, yeah," Rob said, moving his hand up and down his cock, his voice gritty with desire. "So it stands to reason that—God, bend over again."

"No time. Sorry." He grabbed his pink tee, pulling it on over his tank top and picked up his duffel packed with his skates, a black thermal shirt, and leggings. He jammed his makeup bag into it. "I'll make it up to you later."

"Hey!" Rob said as Matty leaned in and kissed his mouth quickly. "Just—give me..." Rob made a half grab at Matty's legs with his free hand, his fingers brushing against the hairs and sending a thrill up Matty's back.

Darting away from the bed so he couldn't be dragged down again, Matty winked. "Oh, no! Too slow, amigo!"

"Goddamn it."

Matty blew him a kiss. "I love you! Bye!"

Matty rushed through the kitchen, and in an instant decided not to grab the bagged lunch Rob had made for him the night before.

You were in a hurry. You forgot.

15

Matty heard Rob's groan of completion just as he shut the door, and the familiar, sensual sound hit him so hard that he almost headed back inside to lick up whatever mess Rob had made, and then mess him up again with his own jizz. But he girded himself against the temptation by taking another deep breath, in and out—slow and purposeful—and marched out into the already active, pre-dawn city, a gold medalist in his own mind ready for some rare alone time on the ice.

Chapter Two

Whistling, Rob took the stairs instead of the elevator up to the Sky Rink level at Chelsea Piers. The place smelled of coffee, sweat, funk, and ice. Until he'd met Matty, Rob hadn't realized ice had its own scent. Sure, there'd been plenty of snow in Montana, but it was always mixed with the scents of evergreen, cows, dung, and crisp, fresh air. It hadn't been until he'd started spending time in rinks that he'd come to identify the specific odor of ice. It was similar to the scent of air after a storm, all ozone and bite.

Red rectangular tables with rounded edges and attached red chairs took up the majority of the waiting area. Several of the tables were covered with purses, bags, and gear, as mothers—and one father—sat waiting for their young children to exit the locker rooms for early morning training. It never failed to boggle Rob's mind that kids, some as young as five or six, voluntarily woke up so early, even in the middle of summer vacation, to skate. But the proof was there in front of him. Ice was their brand of heroin.

Three tween girls stretched in a corner—none of them Matty's Sabrina. Across the room, two slightly older boys, nearly Ben's age, wore earbuds and worked on their leaps in socked feet. Rob thought he recognized one of them as the bronze medalist from Junior Worlds, but he wasn't sure. He'd stopped following the younger kids once Ben moved up to senior competitions.

On the other side of the concession stand, a scattering of teens of both genders chattered together. Snatches of conversation drifted over to him, the usual dishing about competitors, coaches, choreography, and diet tips.

Rob hitched his messenger bag up onto his shoulder and headed toward the west rink to see if Matty was still skating out his private ice time. Cold air hit him as he pushed open the door. Hair rose on his arms and a quick, hard shudder ran through his body. His short-sleeved blue-and-earth-tones plaid button-up shirt, picked at H&M under Matty's watchful and mostly approving eyes, felt far too thin in the chill near the ice. At least the chinos he wore to work were warm enough.

Matty's music hit his ears, and his pulse rose in anticipation. There was nothing like witnessing Matty's raw athleticism and artistic grace in its natural element to light up Rob inside with a combustible combination of pride, desire, and near-painful adoration. Well, nothing outside their bedroom.

Five small bodies crowded around the safety glass surrounding the rink, standing just high enough in their skates to see over the boards. Rob recognized several of them as the youngest students in Matty's early morning Free Skate group due to start practice in about twenty minutes. As Valentina's newest assistant coach, Matty had been relegated to coaching the youngest kids while she and the more experienced assistants spent time dealing with the 'big-time contenders'—her name for a select unit of elite teens and young twenty-somethings likely to bring home medals. It was a group Matty had been in himself, once upon a time.

Rob couldn't entirely blame Valentina for putting Matty with the children. He was in some respects uniquely suited to the job. Children, all of them, even the most butch of the young boys, craved Matty's attention like ice cream and chocolate bars, so they worked incredibly hard to earn it. When Matty's day was spent primarily with children he typically came home in a buoyant, joyous mood. The same couldn't be said of the days he worked with the senior skaters.

Matty didn't do things in half-measures. He was ambitious, driven, and, in Rob's opinion, hopelessly drawn to careers that were destined to break his heart. So, of course he wanted to work with the older kids and become a big-shot coach like Valentina or Chuck

Forenza one day. Matty's egotistical striving was charming, inspiring, and sexy even, but figure skating was and would always be emotional ground zero for Matty's worst trauma, and coaching hadn't proved to be much different so far.

The children by the boards whooped, fixing Rob's attention to Matty's figure flying over the ice. A hot pink tee over a black thermal shirt and black leggings screamed everything a casual viewer needed to know about Matty: transgressive, classic, amazing, and effeminate. Perfection in Rob's eyes.

Matty landed a fantastic double-Axel-triple-toe like it was as simple as breathing. His edge work fell in perfect rhythm and his arms lifted gracefully, fingers just so. His dark hair flew around his face, and his muscular ass was perfect in the tight leggings. Though he looked too thin, he was still strong. As the song moved into the bridge, Matty slowed into a bending, rolling move of such flexible, impressive agility that Rob swallowed hard, a curl of heat in his gut burning in answer to Matty's beauty and skill.

As Lady Gaga's "Applause" continued to pulse through the rink, Rob leaned against the boards watching Matty kill the routine he'd choreographed for himself the prior Christmas. It'd been for a charity show he'd done for his ex-agent, Joanna. But since firing Joanna due to lack of funds to pay her, he hadn't had any opportunities for shows anyway. Matty'd been nailed so firmly to the wall between assistant coaching for Valentina and his intense, new head-coach relationship with little Sabrina that he hadn't had the time to look for shows on his own.

Rob knew it lacked generosity to admit, but he wasn't sure Matty acting as Sabrina's head coach was actually a good thing. After all, what had her sudden blossoming brought them? A barely eked out bronze at Junior Worlds, even more tension between Matty and Valentina, and shit-tons of pressure from the Federation.

The beat throbbed on, and the kids added to the intensity of the building chorus by beating their hands against the tall safety glass along with the rapid drumbeat and recorded hand claps. Matty responded to their encouragement by throwing even more passion and expression into every movement. His hair swirled around flushed cheeks and his dark eyes stood out against his pale skin. His lips shone bright pink beside the pink and black of his training clothes and the white of the ice and boards. His hips swiveled and his back arched as he danced across the ice, and then he straightened, skated backwards to catch some speed, and went up for a triple Lutz, triple toe combination. He turned out on the landing, but no one cared; even Matty seemed too in the groove to focus on his mistake. The kids shouted encouragement.

As the song came to an end, he slid on his knees across the rink, his back arched and hair dragging along the ice, picking up snow. The last beat clipped off, and he stayed there, his chest heaving with exertion and eyes on the ceiling, his face flushed from the effort. The kids banged on the glass again in appreciation, and as Matty began to straighten, they all scampered off back through the doors to their parents and the final preparations they needed to make before the start of their lesson.

Matty didn't stand immediately, though. He kneeled in the center of the rink, his hair wet with melting ice that ran down his neck, as his eyes ran the length of the stands. Rob could see memories playing across his face: the cheers, screams, applause, and the potential of an Olympic medal not yet snatched away. His chest felt hollow for Matty as he heard the echo of long-past thunderous roars of approval. He knew Matty still ached for the sound as much as he ached for the missing gold that would have proved he was as good as he could possibly be. Better than the best. *Oh, sweetheart.*

Rob clapped his hands enthusiastically but didn't give in to the temptation to whistle, knowing Matty would take it as mockery instead of appreciation. Clapping was as good as he could give right now. Later when they were home alone, he could give something else to make Matty feel how very good he had been and always was. Something to interrupt the stream of negative thoughts he knew bombarded Matty at times like this. He'd give him something hard and difficult with a reward at the end to send Matty over the moon. That was Rob's specialty.

Matty swiveled to face him, clear brown eyes narrowed in suspicion until he spotted Rob. His face broke into the wonderful smile that had captured Rob's heart and soul on a snowy October day in Montana. Over the years, Rob had learned that Matty had many smiles — bitchy, tired, angry, faking-it, and media, to name just a few — but the real thing was pure and beautiful, like nothing had ever broken Matty's heart.

He met Matty by the opening in the boards as Matty skated off the ice and into his arms. Rob took a deep breath of Matty's scent — sweat, expensive cologne, and the ice that clung to him. He kissed the side of his head and whispered, "Good morning."

"Hey, you," Matty muttered against Rob's neck, his cold lips tickling and making Rob shudder. "What's up?"

"You looked amazing out there."

The huff of Matty's laugh heated the skin of Rob's throat. Rob held him even tighter, loving the way he fit perfectly against him. Taller in his skates, Matty didn't have to stand on his toes, and Rob could prolong the hug without effort.

"I looked sloppy. I popped one of my jumps. My height was bad. I under-rotated the — "

"You were gorgeous, Matty. Like always."

Matty pulled back, his thin but muscled shoulders shrugging under his tight shirts. He slipped on his purple blade guards as he said, "You'd think I was gorgeous taking a shit."

Rob's lips quirked up. "True. I do."

Matty's pale neck flushed, and he looked up at Rob and then away again as he straightened up. He swung his arms around and reached high into the air, stretching. "Your opinion is hopelessly biased and you know it. It doesn't matter, though. Sabrina's trip out to Colorado to participate in that *clinic*," he spit the word out like it meant something closer to 'prostitution,' "gives me extra room in my schedule to devote to improving myself. I've decided to keep her ice time booked and just step up my workouts. I need to get in shape."

"Just don't overdo things and aggravate old injuries."

"When do I ever overdo anything?"

Rob lifted his brows.

"Fine, but you have to admit, if nothing else, that what you just witnessed was not impressive. I've skated much better than I did today."

"You have, but I also thought you and Figure Skating were on the outs. Permanently."

Matty bit his lower lip, his gaze darting away from Rob's and settling on a place just over Rob's shoulder. "We are."

"Then you don't need to be at the peak of your abilities."

Matty stared off out the long, wide windows where the sun glinted off the Hudson and the buildings across the river in New Jersey. "Competition is over for me, Rob. You know that."

Rob stayed silent. Figure Skating wasn't just competition. It was so much more than that.

"I'm glad you're here, though, because I've got good news." He met Rob's eyes again and smiled enticingly. "You know how this morning you were saying we could use a financial break? Well, Julien texted. He's passing through on his way to do shows in Asia. And he said there's still time for me to book a few with him for early August. He said he'd be happy to pull some strings for me."

"It's still possible Sabrina will need you to be focused on her upcoming season by August."

Matty's expression shut down. "Well, that won't be a problem, okay? Not once her parents take her away from me."

"They aren't 'taking her away from you.' They're considering a move to Colorado Springs."

"It's the same thing and you know it."

"Maybe. But I also know that we aren't even certain that's going to happen."

Matty's eyes flashed. "Don't, Rob. Just—you have no idea how much this—how much *she* means to me. And you have absolutely no clue what kind of pressure she's under from the Federation right now. So, just don't."

Rob did have a very good idea, actually. He and Anja had experienced exactly what Sabrina's folks were facing when the Federation bore down on them like vicious dogs, demanding that for Ben's sake they send him to Colorado Springs to train with the very coach Sabrina's parents were being pressured to consider. He also knew how much Sabrina meant to Matty personally. Matty adored the girl, and if he'd transferred too much of his own failed ambitions onto her, well, Rob hadn't missed that either.

"I'm well aware of how stressed out everyone is, sweetheart. I'm not exactly a stranger to this sport or to you."

Matty's lashes lowered contritely, and he wrapped his arms around Rob's neck again, hugging and resting against him for a moment like he was pulling strength. "I'm sorry I snapped at you." Then he sighed and moved away to go stand by the windows, gazing out at the morning Hudson River traffic. "I'm sick of the Federation chewing my ass again. Like, didn't they get enough of me the first time around? They've gotta come back for more of my butt?"

"It's a pretty sweet butt."

Matty smirked, but his heart obviously wasn't in it. "Rob, there's nothing I can do. It's out of my control. She's not coming back to me."

His body tensed, and Rob could see the panic setting in. This conversation wasn't going the way he'd wanted when he arrived, but that was life with Matty, wasn't it?

Matty went on. "You haven't seen that training center, but I have. It's amazing. And what do I have to offer her as a coach? I'm just an assistant, really. As Valentina likes to remind me. 'Assistant have no say! *Nyet*, nyet, nyet! Bad coach. Give up or go home.'"

"Since when has Valentina ever told you to give up?"

Matty continued like Rob hadn't said anything with an unfortunately familiar litany of self-abuse. "I'm useless as a coach. I have no experience, basically no credentials aside from what I had to do to get accredited. Let's be honest. Compared to Chuck Forenza? I've got nothing."

Rob glanced over his shoulder and saw the kiddies pressing their faces against the glass doors to see if Matty was ready for them to come onto the ice. They still had twelve minutes before the clock gave them the permission they needed to barge on in, but he supposed Matty would normally have probably let them go on a bit early for some warm-ups or free skating.

"You've got me. And our home. And New York City," Rob reminded him. Matty's lips lifted in a sad smile, but his eyes stayed distant and dark. Rob went on. "Besides, if Sabrina couldn't survive Valentina as her coach, how is she going to deal with Forenza? From what I hear, he's just as tough but a hell of a lot scarier because he's got such a loud bark. She might get out there and choke completely."

"She won't. I've trained her too well."

The fact that Matty didn't see the juxtaposition between his confidence in Sabrina and the negative commentary on his coaching skills was a testament to the breakfast Matty hadn't eaten that morning. Rob was sure of it. He was a different person when he was hungry, a hollow man with an internal black hole inside that devoured positivity like a kid devoured candy.

Rob said, "Or she might decide she can't deal with him, or maybe her parents won't like him. Matty, there are too many variables in this for you to preemptively decide you've lost her."

"You don't even want me coaching at that level anyway."

"That's not true. I don't like how it draws you back into the sick parts of skating that make you anxious and unhappy, but I want you to be successful. I want Sabrina to be the best she can be, and I want you to be there with her. I just wish you could find a healthier way to cope with the stress. I know you don't like the idea of therapy, but..."

Matty shrugged, his lips drawn and his eyes dull with the persistent worry that had been there ever since the joy of success at Worlds had faded away. "Therapy's too expensive. It always has been. And I don't need it anyway. I'm fine."

Rob bit the inside of his lower lip. Matty wasn't fine, not really, and therapy would definitely help him if they could find a way to afford it, *and*, even more importantly, if Matty would consent to go.

Matty sighed. "They want to ruin me. The Federation won't let me succeed at anything. They still hate me too much."

Rob didn't say anything. Unfortunately, Matty wasn't being paranoid about the Federation being set on destroying his fledgling career as the head coach of a future contender. Rob had heard the rumors himself from Ben, who'd told him the word on the street was the Federation was all up in Sabrina's parents' grills demanding they get a "proven" coach for her who could give her the best chance at Olympic gold. Ben had been really pissed off about it—protective as always of Matty, but Rob and Anja told him to keep his mouth shut around his coaches or other people in the skating community. The last thing they needed was the Federation butting its nose in even more with Ben too.

Still, despite his mixed feelings about Matty attempting a move into head coaching, Rob wanted to believe that Sabrina's parents could see how Sabrina and Matty had bonded. He hoped they'd realize their daughter might be better off staying with the man who'd brought her out of her shell, rather than going with a new and untried relationship.

"We just have to wait and see," Rob reiterated.

Matty shook himself, and smiled with all-too-familiar faux brightness. "In the meantime, I'll work on a plan B. We need money anyway. If she bails, that's a third of my income gone. Poof! And we're barely making it as it is." Matty couldn't keep up the facade, though. He slid back into pensivity, chewing his lower lip. "Living in New York is so expensive. Maybe we should move to Jersey."

Rob's heart leapt, but he firmly pushed it back into place. He knew better than to get his hopes up that they might leave the city. "You love Park Slope."

"I know. But we can't afford it." He sighed as he studied the view out the windows. "Sometimes I wish we could move back to Whitefish. We were happy there."

"We're happy now." Rob wasn't in love with New York, sometimes feeling the weight of the city like a burden he could never shake, but he and Matty were happy together. He was sure of that.

"Yeah." Matty turned with a gleam of hope in his eye. "Actually, do you want to? Move back to Montana, I mean? Missoula, or

Billings, maybe. They're big enough I could probably round up a few students and teach some larger kiddie classes."

Rob touched Matty's smooth, freshly shaven cheek with the backs of his fingers. "Living in New York was always your dream. It's not anymore?" His heart beat hopefully against his ribs. He didn't want to allow himself to fantasize. There was no real possibility of going home.

"I don't know. It's hard to be happy or really enjoy it when the money isn't there." Matty was silent, and Rob could sense his anxiety bubbling under the surface. It was a familiar darkness and Rob shivered, wishing again for his coat.

"Remember how in Whitefish I was by far the absolute prettiest guy in town?"

Rob laughed softly. "Sure, sweetheart. I remember."

"Rob," Matty lowered his voice confidentially, like he wanted to make sure no one and nothing, maybe not even the ice, could hear. "I'm not the prettiest guy in New York City. Not even close. The other day, I saw Haley Gruff in the West Village, and the truth is I just can't compete."

"Who?"

Matty sighed and rolled his eyes gently. "Rob, how can you live with me and still not know Haley Gruff? The model?" Rob shrugged. Matty showed him all kinds of pictures from fashion magazines, and he mainly just nodded and agreed that whatever Matty was saying at that moment about whoever was in the picture was obviously right. Matty's voice arched up sharply as he went on. "The stunning one with long blond hair, fantastic, angular face, and a mouth like one of God's own angel's?"

"Oh, her." Rob thought he might remember which model Matty was talking about. Maybe.

"Yes, her."

"Well, she's very beautiful but she's not a guy. And even if she was, I think you're even prettier."

Matty batted away the comment with his hand like it was an annoying fly buzzing past. "Of course you'll say that, but no one else would agree. But she's not the only one. There are just too many people who are *much* better looking than me walking around in this city, Rob. Basically every single person Elliot even knows."

"Well, he *is* a fashion photographer's assistant." Matty swore Elliot's job was actually quite demanding, but as far as Rob could tell, Elliot's job description included going to clubs and partying with beautiful people, showing up to work hung over, fetching coffee, and making sure the lighting was 'good', whatever that meant. "Personally, I think *all* Elliot's pals look like they should eat some sandwiches."

Matty ignored him, focused on his lament. "Rob, everywhere I go there's someone who's so beautiful I want to puke. It's depressing."

Rob pressed his lips together to make sure laughter didn't slip out. "Okay," he finally said when he felt sure he could talk. "It's true that there are a lot of attractive people here, sweetheart, but what does that have to do with you going to Asia for shows, or training harder, or moving back to Whitefish?"

"I just want to be the best at *something*. Anything really. And let's be honest, I'm not the best in the city at anything, Rob. Not skating, or coaching, or being beautiful. No matter how hard I work, I'm just very average, actually, at everything I do."

"You were an Olympian. That's hardly average."

"Were. Was. Over. Done. Finito. Operative words there, Rob."

"Well, you're the best at being Matty Marcus. You've always been the best at that."

Matty paled and his eyes grew darker. "I don't want to be the best at being me. That's something you say to kindergartners to make them think they're special. Believe me, I know, I say that shit all the time to the kids and, mostly, I mean it, but that's not who I am. That's not what *I* want out of *my* life. I want to be the *best*. At something important. And being Matty Marcus is not important—not here in New York City, anyway. Period. The end."

"You're very good at very many things, Matty. But all that you just said? It isn't what life's about. It's about you doing you."

"You doing you?" Matty snarled, the darkness rising to the surface in a blink. "Have you been watching *Oprah* reruns with the other PTs over your lunch breaks again?"

Rob didn't take the bait. "Stick to the topic. Are you saying you want to move?"

Matty's eyes lost their caustic edge, but he didn't apologize. He crossed his arms over his chest. "And leave the city behind? Leave the vibrant, beautiful, constant ever-changing madness of it all? No. How could I ever leave that?"

"Okay then." Despite himself, disappointment settled on Rob like dust. He shook it off. "Let's go back to the beginning." Sometimes navigating Matty's thought processes was a kind of puzzle, sometimes it was a maze, and other times it was all about categorizing: this thought goes in this box, and that in the other to be dealt with later, and this one needs to be addressed now. "You said Julien's coming to visit and you're thinking of taking him up on the offer to help you get some shows."

Matty sat on the long bench beneath the even longer windows. Rob joined him.

"Yeah, if Sabrina leaves, I'll need to make up the lost income somehow. So a show or five in Shanghai or Moscow would provide a lovely, fluffy pillow for us to rest our pretty heads on."

Rob gazed over at the bleachers, thinking it over.

Matty lifted his finger. "Remember there was a time I paid for everything by doing shows, and I had enough left over to help Mom and Dad out too. The fans haven't forgotten me, Rob. I'm still popular in Asia. I get emails every day asking me when I'm going to do shows again. The girls in Japan will fly anywhere to see me."

"I know."

"But you don't want me to go."

"No, I'm fine with you going." He smiled gently at him, though he wondered who would make sure Matty ate properly. "I'd miss you, but you'll come home to me."

Matty looked up at him, eyelashes fluttering and his amber-brown eyes shining. "Always."

Rob took Matty's hand, winding their fingers together. He wasn't afraid of Matty leaving him for the road. His fears about Matty were based on something harder to cope with than that. He wasn't even sure if Matty knew about his insecurities. But it wasn't productive to dwell on them, so, aside from the few times he'd indulged in a sleepless hour or two watching Matty breathe and dream beside him in bed, he didn't spend too much time entertaining his own darkest fears.

"When's Julien arriving?"

"Tomorrow. He'll be here for a few days. He's staying in Midtown."

"Are there plans I need to know about?"

"Dinner and dancing. He wants to go to Club Cache for Salsa Thursday. I know you don't salsa, but I do. And Julien does. You can watch." Matty smiled sweetly and batted his eyes like this would distract Rob from how bad a plan that was.

"I see. So I'm going to sit alone at the table and watch you salsa with a guy you slept with?"

"Maybe? And, for the record, I didn't sleep with him. We fucked." Matty bit his lip and looked up, all wide-eyed innocence. "Besides, you know it meant nothing to either one of us. It was what it was and that was it."

"It's still something I might take a pass on."

"You'd rather I salsa with him alone?" Matty trailed a finger down Rob's arm suggestively. "With my body all up against his, while he grabs my ass and grinds against me? You'd rather that happened *without* you there?"

"Such a brat."

Matty widened his eyes and fluttered his hand to his chest.

Rob chuckled because Matty was right. He'd rather watch and then take Matty home to fuck him. "Fine. I'll go."

Matty jumped with restrained delight and hugged him tightly, another real smile creasing his face. He released Rob's neck and ran his hands down to squeeze his biceps. "Thank you. It'll be fun. You'll see."

"Ha. I'm sure. And, let me guess, the two of you want to go vegan for dinner?"

Matty smiled and licked his lips, a scary flash of hunger crossing his features. "Yeah. Blossom or Gobo. Probably Gobo. It's not fancy but it has Julien's favorite Vietnamese stir fry, apparently. I'd rather go to Blossom for the black-eyed pea cake, which is just so good." Matty shivered and his eyes rolled back a little at the prospect of one of the few desserts he would agree to even order. "And the place is a little fancier, but oh well. We'll bring the glam with our beautiful selves, right?"

"Absolutely, sweetheart. So, Gobo in the Village? Will Elliot be joining us?"

"No, Elliot has a date." Matty's eyebrows leapt up and down, and a dirty grin let Rob know just what Matty thought that meant. Rob could be expecting another highly descriptive story from the annals of Elliot's Anal Adventures by the end of the week.

"Anyone we know?"

"I don't think so. I hope not. I'm meeting up with Elliot tomorrow after my last class to get the four-one-one."

"Oh?"

"Yeah, we're making a date of it, so don't hold dinner for me."

"All right. I'll see if I can meet up with Ben tomorrow night."

There was a bang against the door, and Matty glanced toward it. A row of little faces waited for him to signal. "Oh, damn. Right. Well, I've got to be a pretty, pretty teacher now."

"A patient, patient teacher is probably a better thing to aim for."

"Pshaw, *anyone* can be patient. But not everyone can be pretty."

Rob kissed his cheek. "You're the most beautiful guy I know in all of New York City."

Matty smiled, pleased, but the smile disappeared suddenly and cautious curiosity flashed across his face. "But, wait, why are you even here? You said you got to sleep in this morning."

"Why do you think I'm here?"

Matty fluttered his eyelashes coyly. "Hmm. You wanted to stop by and thank me for your very special wake-up call?"

Rob smirked. "No, though it was very special. Thank you." Rob rummaged in his bag and brought out a sack lunch. He'd made it the night before as he always did because he didn't trust Matty's idea of a healthy midday meal for an athlete. When he'd opened the fridge to grab milk for his coffee, he'd noticed it hadn't been taken. "I'm here because you forgot something at home."

Matty's expression closed off just enough that Rob's suspicion was confirmed. He'd left it on purpose. Rob could see Matty's wheels turning, his mind tossing up excuses like a party boy throws up drinks. "Oh, right. I was going to get something here at the rink. Old Tony at the concession stand totally has a crush on me. He's always trying to get me to eat one of his corndogs."

Rob stayed silent. The idea of Matty eating a corndog didn't dignify a response.

Matty flapped his hand in annoyance and turned away. "What? Don't look at me like that."

Rob stayed where he was as Matty started toward the double doors where the kids waited. He didn't take the lunch bag.

"Seriously, Rob, it's fine. I'm fine. Just go on to work."

"Take your lunch, then."

Matty turned back, his face pale again with anger, his lips pinched. He still didn't take the bag. "Why? I'm a grown man and I can feed myself."

"I know you can. But you won't. I know you didn't eat breakfast either."

Matty gritted his teeth. He closed his eyes and took deep breaths. Then he opened them again and Rob waited to hear what excuse it was going to be this time. Since early spring they'd been mounting— *"I'll do better after Worlds!"* or *"That asshole Federation rep turned my stomach"* or *"I already ate."* Matty's eating disorder had its claws in, and the only thing that kept it from winning was a calm refusal to back down in the face of it. It was never easy. But Rob would win, and if he kept winning, maybe they could keep this thing at bay until they could afford to get professional help.

Matty went on, "I'm being very reasonable with my diet lately. I just need to lose a few more pounds to get back to a good training weight."

"You don't need to lose any weight and we both know it."

Matty stared at him, and his voice went down a notch as he lied, "Besides, maybe I wanted to get a salad at Blossom." It was the soft, challenging growl of a mama protecting her cub.

"Matty, don't."

Matty's eyes snapped with anger and he thrust out a hip, purposely misinterpreting Rob. "But why not? They serve the most delicious veg—"

"*Don't* lie."

Matty swallowed and held Rob's gaze. His dark irises shone with the morning light pouring in the windows. "Okay. I'm sorry."

Rob's throat went tight. He didn't know why the admission hurt so much. He'd known the truth, hadn't he? "Is skipping lunch something you're doing regularly now?"

He usually saw Matty eat at night and at breakfast, but lunch was something Matty could find ways to get around. Rob had hoped that the fact that Matty needed to set a good example for his students would have prevented him from skipping lunch altogether.

"Sometimes. I don't like eating in front of people. You know that."

"Because it makes you feel unsafe?"

"Right."

"And not eating makes you feel safer?"

Matty nodded.

It didn't make any sense. There were days when Rob wanted to drive to North Carolina and shake Matty's mother. He wanted ask her how she'd let this go on so long and just what she'd been thinking letting him eat—or not eat—that way for so many years. But he couldn't entirely blame Donna. It was like the diet tips he'd overheard in the lobby. In figure skating, all the kids did it. Even if skating moms tried to curb it, unless a kid was like Ben—headstrong and impervious—it was a given a champion would probably count calories at the very least.

"Are you cutting calories in other ways too?" Rob thought of all the times recently when Matty had run when he could walk, biked when he could take the subway, and scheduled extra workouts for himself—like this early morning session.

Matty's face flushed again, and a cold sensation trickled down Rob's back.

"I've been under a lot of pressure, but it's going to get better. Today's Sabrina's last lesson before her trip to Colorado Springs, and I swear—I *swear* Rob—I'm going to do a better job from now on. You don't have to worry about me." Matty took the lunch sack from Rob's hand, looked inside, and then held it up, a brittle, fake smile spreading over his lips. "Tuna salad, fruit, and cheese. Perfect. Thank you."

It was bullshit, but it was going to have to do. They didn't have much time left before Matty's class began. Matty swallowed hard. Rob clapped a hand around the back of Matty's neck. They held gazes as the double doors burst open and the kids clattered into the rink.

"It's time, Coach!" one of them called.

"Be right there. Warm-up laps, okay?"

The kids hit the ice, not caring what was going on with their coach, and much more interested in not wasting another moment of possible ice time.

"Rob?" Matty asked, his voice quiet, his eyes dark with insecurity.

"Trust is important, Matty. Can I trust you?"

"You know you can."

"Do I know that?"

"I swear, Rob."

"Okay." Rob wasn't sure that he could, actually. Not when it came to this. Matty was a genius at self-sabotage, and Rob wasn't going to let his ingrained and unhealthy coping mechanisms take over. He wouldn't let Matty hurt himself by screwing up *them*.

"Rob, I have to work now."

Rob nodded. He had errands he needed to run before heading out to Queens for the afternoon continuing education class. Matty stood by the boards as other coaches and skaters filtered onto the ice. The space set aside for his work was tight, and Rob watched Matty get to business. The children adored him, and responded to his commands instantly despite Matty's obvious distraction.

He waited until Matty glanced his way, then he smiled and waved goodbye. Matty smiled back, but it was Rob's least favorite smile of them all—the scared one—and he wished he had an easy way make Matty feel okay before he left. They had a word to call a halt to hard things. They needed a word that meant, "I love you, I forgive you, it's okay, and I'll never leave" all rolled up in one. He settled for calling out, "Give 'em hell, Yuliya."

Matty rolled his eyes, but his shoulders lost a little tension. It would have to do. Rob blew him a kiss, and Matty caught it, put it in his pocket, and covered his heart with his hand. Rob nodded and headed out. He'd done what he could.

CHAPTER THREE

"NYET!"

God, if Matty never heard that word again it would be too soon. It didn't matter that it was directed at eighteen year old Huxley Thorpe, Valentina's newest up-and-comer. It still sent an arrow of pain through his soul.

Valentina's dark hair was up in a very messy bun held by one of the rink's ballpoint pens, and her eyes were made up with heavy black liner. Matty wondered if a Federation rep was coming to visit. He couldn't think of any other reason for her to be wearing makeup. She wasn't wearing her usual pantsuit, though, which spoke against a Fed visit. She was instead bundled up in a new set of green and gray sports thermals and a fur-lined gray coat.

"Stupid child! You skate like rotten eggs."

Matty knew it didn't matter if her insults made sense or not. They still hurt to hear.

Huxley's amber-brown eyes filled with tears as Valentina continued to bark instructions and insult her in heavily accented English. The fact that Huxley had drastically improved since her last attempt at the triple Axel was completely ignored.

"Again! Go!"

Huxley's dark ponytail swished behind her as she headed back out to center ice. Then Valentina turned her critical eye on him.

"Why you frown at me?" Valentina asked, her whip-thin frame looming over him. Matty was disgusted as always to see that her coffee-stained teeth. "She is baby and need to grow up. Be strong. Commit to jump. Not be weak."

"She has to learn to keep going," Matty said, crossing his arms over his chest and shoving his gloved hands into his armpits. "If she messes up during a competition, she can't stop and start all over again. She needs to keep on all the way through the entire program. She's got to build stamina."

Valentina shot him a glare that could stop traffic. "She will move on when she do it perfect."

Matty rolled his eyes, and Valentina snapped her fingers at him.

"You think I have time for coach back talk?"

Matty pressed his lips together to keep from saying anything else. He fingered his necklace, touching the 6.0 tab that Ben had so painstakingly etched into the tin. It was worn nearly smooth now, the numbers just ghosts. He chewed on the inside of his cheek as he watched Huxley go through the first part of the program and, once again, pop the triple Axel.

"Take break!" Valentina yelled.

"She needs to keep going."

Valentina glared at him and then muttered under her breath as she turned away. Matty could make out words like "ungrateful" and "learns nothing,"

"Say it to my face, Valentina," Matty said, straightening up. "I won't grovel at your feet like I did when I was a student. That's not what you hired me to do."

She rolled her eyes and made a spitting gesture toward the floor. "Nyet. No more words from your mouth."

Matty's stomach flipped over, but he stood his ground. Valentina stomped away, turning her back on both him and Huxley.

He waited to see if Control had anything to say about his failure to get Valentina to listen to him. Unsurprisingly it did.

No lunch for you. You don't deserve it.

"But Rob..." Matty whispered.

He'll never know.

But Rob would ask, and Matty couldn't bring himself to outright lie to him again. He'd have to eat lunch and make it up to Control another way later. He'd bike over to Saks and not let himself buy anything. Or better yet, he'd buy everything he most wanted and then make himself return it tomorrow. That would hurt enough wouldn't it? That would make up for eating lunch, right?

Control was silent, so Matty thought it would probably be okay.

Before Huxley could even get off the ice, Valentina was back with a steaming mug of coffee and a renewed desire to punish.

"On ice!" she yelled, and Huxley's shoulders sagged as she made her way back to the center to begin again.

The rest of Huxley's practice continued with the same negative energy, and Matty could see her losing self-confidence as Valentina broke the flow of the program at every slight error. At one point, Huxley skated off the ice without permission to grab some water, and Matty saw tears in her eyes. He bent close while she put her water bottle back in her bag and whispered, "Hang in there, Hux. You're amazing. You're doing great."

"No play good cop!" Valentina yelled. "Huxley improve too slow, and you playing nicey-nice won't win her gold medal!"

When Matty had been in Huxley's shoes, he'd bowed to Valentina's whims; let her beat him down and, on rare occasion, raise him up in the hopes of achieving those promised medals. It had, for the most part, been good for him. But he wasn't her student now, and Huxley needed someone on her side.

"Hux, just do your best. If you want a private session with me to run through the whole program, we can do that without telling Valentina," he whispered. "We'll do it at City Ice if we have to."

Huxley smiled at him, her lips quirking up at the corners. Then she glanced toward Valentina, and darkness fell over her features again. "She hates me."

"She doesn't. She just...well...she has a harsh kind of love." He remembered the few times she'd held him, called him her good boy, and had loved him enough to get him past the toughest parts of failure.

Huxley rolled her eyes and pulled her bottle out again, covering her words with another sip. "She should save that kind of love for her husband."

Matty choked on a laugh. He found the image of Valentina, standing over balding, submissive Fredek while he licked her high heels utterly believable, yet horrifying.

Huxley threw her bottle back in the bag, smiled at Matty, and said, "Maybe I'll take you up on that extra practice."

He smiled back. "I hope you do."

"Matty! Huxley! This is work time not play!"

After Huxley's hour of torture was up, Valentina barreled toward Matty with a grim expression. He wanted to make off into the men's changing room to escape her, but he braced himself by the boards.

"You ruin her with nice," Valentina said, her sharp eyes and long nose hawk-like. "I never approve you giving instruction over me."

Matty tried to reason with her. "Not everyone can be treated like dirt, Valentina. Not every skater can be built back up once you tear them down."

"Like who? Who are you to say what a skater needs? Only medals matter. I get medals."

"No, the skaters get medals. You train skaters. Your training method isn't for everyone."

Her eyes narrowed. "You blame me then for your failures years ago?"

"No." Hell, Matty had done better under her harsh hand than he ever had with teachers who were more into loving kindness. He needed punishment and being hurt. He needed to earn everything the hard way, but not every talented skater responded well to being ripped to shreds by their coach. "You were a good coach for me."

"I was the best for you. And you almost flew, but meat stick judges shot you down. I remember. Don't you forget what I did for you. What I do now for you."

"I'd never forget. I owe you a lot."

"And for this job. You owe me for your job." Valentina pointed at him. "Sabrina was one bird in a dozen. You get big head and think you tell me how to run show? No. Be careful. My love for you is not without limit."

Matty swallowed. "Are you unhappy with me as an employee?"

"*Konechno!* Of course! You good with kiddies and puny girl like Sabrina, but with true champion, you too soft."

Matty blinked at her, a stone sinking in his stomach. "Are you going to fire me?"

"No," she scoffed like he'd insulted her by even asking. "You are my boy and I will train you as I see fit to be a good coach for children."

Matty stomach burbled uncomfortably, and his throat went tight. He kept silent, hard as it was, and let her go on.

"After Lauren returns from vacation, you work with kiddies only. Then we not have problem. No more switching schedules with Lauren until you be real man and tough up. Understand?"

Real man. Toughen up. He was tougher than any of her current students or assistant coaches. He knew that in his heart. "I'm a real man, Valentina. You know how much I've taken—and still take from the Federation."

"Pooh, pooh. Whiny boy. Always whiny. But you grow up and see you are best with kiddies. Leave big competitors to the strong coaches."

"Being strong isn't being mean." Matty thought of Rob, of his strength and tenderness. "It's being gentle when you're frustrated. It's being tender when you want to shake someone for being an idiot. It's being patient with a student when you can see how easily they could improve if they would just follow your instruction."

Valentina rolled her eyes.

Matty went on. "You need to see that people like Hux and Sabrina don't get better when you yell at them. They get hurt and they fail. You're making it harder for them to improve, not easier."

"Job is to get medals. Not make sweet loving feelings. Stop thinking you know my job, Matty." She brushed a gray-brown hair from her face and took a swallow of her steaming coffee. "You have your vacation coming soon, *da*?"

The generosity of the annual paid ten-day vacation was possibly the best thing about working for Valentina. "Yes. When Lauren is back from hers, I'll take mine."

"Good." She sighed and put her hand on his shoulder with some kindness. "Matty, when you come back, I want to hear no more of this, *da*? Learn place and love place. That is what you still have not put in your heart."

Learn to love his place? As what? As a failure at everything he wanted to excel at? Well, that was certainly something the world seemed determined to teach him.

The voice of Control was seductive.

Do what I say, and you'll be safe. Would I lie to you?

Control was definitely a liar. Matty knew that very well. So why did he still feel compelled to believe it?

CHAPTER FOUR

THE KITCHEN AND conference area of the clinic had a party-like atmosphere, with all the PTs and PTAs laughing, chatting, and milling around waiting for the start of the continuing education meeting. The conference room was already set up, and there were doughnuts, little sandwiches, coffee, sodas, and water laid out on the long table in the middle of the room. Chairs from all over the clinic had been moved into the space, adding to the cozy, crowded feeling and general sense of camaraderie.

Rob stood in a corner close to one of the entrances with his friends Susan and Arjun. He ate from a small plate he'd filled with doughnut holes and two sandwiches. Arjun was describing the exciting improvement one of his amputee patients had made the day before.

"It's like he suddenly just got it. Like he figured out how to make the mechanical knees do what he needs. He was practically running on them. The look on his face, man. That's why we do this job, isn't it? I could barely sleep last night I was so excited for him."

"It's an amazing feeling," Rob agreed.

"It's like when your stroke patient got her breakthrough," Susan said, her red curls bouncing with her nervous energy. "You were high as a kite over that."

"Yes," Arjun agreed. "I bet Matty got quite the greeting when you got home from work that night. Savita sure did yesterday."

Rob laughed. "He didn't complain."

"Neither did she!"

Susan, single and not happy about it, rolled her eyes.

41

Rob took a bite from his sandwich and asked, "When do you see him again? I bet he's pretty anxious to get back in here."

"Oh, yeah. He was upset when I reminded him I wouldn't be seeing him because of this meeting today. I think he was afraid he'd forget how to use them again by tomorrow, but I told him that rest and recovery is always part of advancement."

"I bet that went over like a lead balloon," Susan said.

Arjun laughed, his dark eyes twinkling happily. "You know it. He's a handful this guy, but he's worth it."

"Believe me, I understand." Rob patted Arjun's shoulder. Some patients were tough nuts to crack emotionally. In fact, many were. It was part of what Rob loved about the job—taking someone who was in a fragile place in their life and reminding them how strong they really were inside.

"How long do you think this meeting will last?" Arjun asked, running a hand through his black hair. "I told Savita I'd pick the kids up from Bharatiya Vidya Bhavan afterward."

"Probably at least two hours," Rob answered. "Hopefully not more than three." He didn't really know, since this was the first continuing education course organized for them by their boss. Normally they all had to fend for themselves and find conferences to attend or online courses to take to earn their CE credit. Rob made a mental note to tell Dr. Joiner how much he appreciated her creating this opportunity for them.

"Crap, I better let Savita know I won't be able to get them."

"You better," Susan agreed.

Arjun pulled his phone out of his pocket and scooted by Don and Angela making their way into the room as he exited. "Hey, my love. It looks like it's going to run long. Yes. Yes, I know, but…"

"She has him under her thumb," Susan said, laughing softly.

"She really does."

The sound of chimes alerted Rob to a text. He dug his phone out of his bag and couldn't help but laugh to himself.

"From Matty?"

"Yeah."

She rolled her eyes again, but good naturedly. "Speaking of being under people's thumb! Okay, well, I'm going to grab a seat at the table."

"Save me one."

"You betcha."

Matty had sent two pictures, one of his nearly finished lunch—a remaining bite of pickle, a half a cracker, part of the cheese, and a bit of sandwich—and another of him hamming it up with the last of the sandwich crust.

I promised and I delivered. Forgive me?

Rob hesitated a moment with his fingers over the screen while he thought of the right words. *Sweetheart, I'll always forgive you.*

It was true. Matty could rob, maim, or murder and he'd forgive him. And then go visit him in prison. But he refused to support Matty's self-destructive streak. So he began a second text: *That isn't an invitation to test me on it.*

But he deleted it without sending because he knew Matty well enough to recognize that such a statement *would* be considered an invitation to his subconscious, if not conscious, mind. He didn't need Matty's darkness giving either of them any more trouble than it already did.

He took another slow breath, closed his eyes, and pictured Matty in the mornings, sleep rumpled and grouchy, frowning into his coffee and acting like the world was a giant asshole to require him to wake so early for his ice fix.

God, he loved him like that.

But he loved him even *more* when he was laughing and breathless in his arms, flushed from lovemaking. And he loved him even more when he was plucking his eyebrows or fussing over which lip gloss was the best match for his outfit, or when he rolled his eyes at Rob for not being able to remember the name of or particularly care about the various skin care products and scents scattered over the small counter in their bathroom. And he loved him most when he gave it *all* over to Rob, body and soul, proving his bravery, his surrender, and his devotion.

He typed in a new text:

I want you healthy and happy. Show me how well you can do that.

He read it over again, poked at the edges of the comment, and decided that Matty's desire to prove himself to Rob would outweigh his urge to kick out against what might be perceived as an attempt to control. Though Matty would probably relish giving up control in a way that made him feel cared for and loved: in bed, where the cruelty of his self-doubt couldn't reach him because Rob drove it away. Wasn't that how Matty had described it last time, limp, starry-eyed, and naked on their dark green sheets?

He pressed send and watched his coworkers jostle for their favorite seats around the table while he waited for Matty's response.

His phone vibrated.

I'll do my best. I promise. I love you.

Dr. Joiner arrived looking pretty in a summer dress and sandals instead of her usual scrubs and sneakers. She escorted the guest speaker into the room, and Rob took the chair Susan had saved for him near the business end of the table. He grabbed one of the yellow legal pads from the center of the desk and a pen, ready to take notes on any particularly interesting or applicable parts of the lecture. As everyone else fell into their seats too, tingling anticipation rose inside of him. Fresh paper, a new pen, and the prospect of learning something: it was almost like being back at school.

"Here's your packet," the newest PT Amber said, passing a stapled stack of papers over his shoulder before moving to on to pass them to Jasmine and DeShawn. Rob looked over the inch-thick packet, examining the cover and the title page: *The PT Connection in the Triad of the Female Athlete.*

The explanation beneath the title said the course was worth six hours of CE credit under the sports medicine bracket. Most of Rob's past CE courses had focused on new developments in healing physical trauma, and only a few had looked at the sports medicine angle. As a generalist, Rob dealt with a lot of sports injuries on top of the usual strokes, car accidents, and developmental disorders, so the topic was applicable and useful. He popped another doughnut hole in his mouth while his coworkers shuffled and got settled as well.

"Okay, let's get started," Dr. Joiner said, clapping her slender hands together and motioning for everyone to quiet down. She frowned as Arjun scrambled into the last seat noisily, but Arjun smiled his pretty, white-toothed grin at her and she couldn't help but return it. No one was immune to the charm of his smile.

A bald man, Asian like Dr. Joiner but far shorter than her, stepped toward the front of the room, a gleam in his black eyes. Dr. Joiner put her hand on the man's shoulder. "Our guest speaker today is Dr. Hiraku Sato." She smiled at him fondly.

Rob stopped chewing on his doughnut for a moment, fully recognizing just who it was standing next to his boss. *Sato.* It had been a long time—a few years at least.

Dr. Joiner went on. "Dr. Sato is my cousin and a sports psychologist. He's been working in the field for twelve years, both as a practitioner and researcher."

Sato shook hands with Dr. Joiner and then turned to the room, taking control of it with a friendly glance. His stance and expression was relaxed but somehow held an authority that made everyone shift in their seats to sit up straighter.

"I'd like to thank Etsuko for inviting me to talk to you all today. As she said, I am Hiraku Sato. You may call me anything you like, of course, but most of my friends just call me Sato."

Rob barely held back his smirk. *Yes, except for the friends who call you Sir and the slave who calls you Master.*

The last time Rob had seen Sato was at a Brooklyn BDSM party about a month before Rob had stopped participating. He recalled that on that night, Sato had arrived wearing leather chaps and nothing else, escorting his slave, Josh, on a leash.

"Please call him Dr. Sato," Dr. Joiner interjected, her red lips spreading into a soft smile. "We'll give my cousin the respect he deserves."

"Etsuko has always enjoyed formality," Sato said, winking at her and then turning back to the group. "I'm less of a stickler among colleagues, however, and would prefer just Sato."

Dr. Joiner rolled her eyes and waved her hand to indicate that his preference should be honored.

Sato's eyes fell on Rob. One brow went up, followed by a brief nod and smile of recognition before he confidently returned his focus to his stack of papers. Rob was reminded of just why Sato was such a respected dom in the scene. He was never flustered, always in control, and everything about him exuded strength and calm, as well as a joyful sense of fun.

"As you can see, today's topic is about the female athlete. But let's be honest. There is no true divide between the things a female athlete does and what a male athlete might also do. But for therapists in your particular shoes, it's all about diagnostics and treatment and, thus, we must recognize that females do have different physical symptoms, as well as treatment outcomes, because their bodies are not the same as men's."

Sato took up the slim remote control on the podium and aimed it at the computer set up in the middle of the table. A slide flicked up on the wall opposite. It showed a photo of runners crossing the finish line at the Boston Marathon.

"I've always been curious about the extremes human beings will go to in order to reach a goal. Particularly a goal that is very dear to them for often inexplicable reasons. At least it's inexplicable to those who look in on them from the outside. Many people write it off to insanity or masochism, but I believe there's something more there. Sometimes working to achieve these goals comes at a great cost, both in terms of time and effort, and in actual cold, hard cash. Sometimes the cost is one's physical health. That's the psychological angle that I'm drawn to and what I focus on with my research."

The next slide showed a frail-looking, overly thin woman lying on the ground surrounded by emergency personnel only yards from the marathon finish line. Her joints and bones poked at her skin eerily, and her cheeks were dangerously sunken.

Sato sighed. "It's easy to look at this photo and make judgements, isn't it?"

A murmur rose around them.

"But I find that our instinctive judgements aren't always helpful in these cases. Over my years of studying the psychology of success, I became equally enamored with the psychology of defeat. Especially in terms of what humans will do to sabotage their chances of ever meeting their most important goals."

He indicated the picture on the wall. "In this woman's case, there was clearly too great a difference between her current weight and the reserves of fuel necessary for her to reach her goal. Unfortunately, this energy imbalance wasn't addressed before she had gone too far. She not only didn't complete the marathon, but she suffered from bone fractures, a weakened immune system, de-escalated healing, and, in the end, she required a hip replacement. This woman could easily be one of your patients. Understanding how she got here is important. So is understanding the effects such a massive energy imbalance might have on her chances of rehabilitation and healing. Let's start from the beginning. Please open your packets to the first page."

Rob settled into his seat, feeling the reassuring strength of the pencil in one hand and the slick paper under the fingers of his other. Afternoon light crept in the sides of the lowered blinds and illuminated the top half of Rob's packet. Clarity woke him up inside, and the sensation that something valuable was on its way flowed up over his skin.

Sato pulled a pair of wire-framed glasses out of his leather messenger bag and sat them on his face before pointing the remote at the computer and calling up the next slide.

"What is the Female Athlete Triad? It's a syndrome of three inter-related conditions: energy deficiency, menstrual disturbances, and bone loss."

Rob drew a triangle on his yellow notepad and listed the three conditions along the sides.

Sato clicked the remote three times, flipping through photos of a female gymnast, ballet dancer, and figure skater, pausing on the last. Rob recognized her as Trina Martin, the girl who'd taken the women's silver at Worlds.

"Let's look at energy deficiency first. It's the beginning of the cycle. Please turn to page two in your packet."

Bold letters lit up in the square of sunlight. *Disordered eating is **not** the same as an eating disorder.*

"Athletes like this one pictured exist within a culture of diets and intensely monitored scales. The number who meet the criteria of an eating disorder is quite slim, but the prevalence of disordered eating? That's another story altogether. In some athletic fields, one can assume that the majority of the athletes exhibit some sort of disordered eating—chronic restriction or compulsive dieting—with potentially dire health consequences and significant clinical implications."

Rob scribbled notes and jotted down follow-up questions, his thoughts occasionally straying to Matty and the teenagers he'd seen swapping diet tips that morning.

"This imbalance of energy, whether it be purposeful—in order to maintain or lose weight—or inadvertent due to schedule or training changes, can result in a wide variety of food-related pathologies."

Yes, I need this.

Boiling it all down to an energy imbalance seemed too simple and yet, when it came to the effects on the body, so real. Maybe there was something he could hook into here. Rob resolved to talk to Sato after the presentation if possible. A sports psychologist with a BDSM background had to be some kind of gift from the universe and he wasn't going to waste the chance to make a connection.

CHAPTER FIVE

A N HOUR AFTER his argument with Valentina, Matty tapped the beat of Sabrina's music against the safety glass. He smiled, watching his star pupil go through her routine. Fourteen, coltish, and positively tiny, Sabrina's long, black hair broke free from her loose bun to frame her fragile face, and her lively dark eyes shone with confidence as she glided across the rink. She reminded him of a young Yuna Kim, and not just because she was Korean. She had the magic that only true champions possessed.

Matty's heart rose at the sight of her sailing around the rink, and he nodded as she moved to center ice. Her baby-pink, short wrap skirt twirled around her and rippled wildly when she went into a sit spin. Then she rose to stretch toward the roof, her face bright in the sun that cascaded in from the windows.

After Rob had left that morning, it'd taken a while for Matty to stuff his mortification and shame into a manageable-sized box. He'd hurt and disappointed Rob, and the threat of drowning in the whispers of disgust that filled his mind had been serious. Luckily his misery had been no match for the children's good spirits. Being around them had forced him to act chipper and as he'd pretended to be, so he became. Not to mention, the adrenaline rush from the confrontation with Valentina cleared his mind the same way pushing himself on the ice or working hard during a "reset" in the bedroom always did.

Matty shivered as he remembered the last "reset" Rob had arranged two months before. It'd been a hard scene, and he'd done really well, earning Rob's praise and a fantastic orgasm, along with a lot of spectacular bruises that he'd admired surreptitiously for days after. The sparkling sense of clearness, like a bright light had exposed and expunged all the filth in his head, had lasted for a few weeks after that. But then it'd worn off. As it always did. And the voice Matty saw as the most miserable symptom of his failure as a person started hissing through his mind again.

Matty remembered the first time he'd heard the voice. It'd started after Nationals with Sabrina when bitch-extraordinaire Edna Johnson from the Federation had approached her outside the locker room. She'd greeted them with a bob of her short, gray hair and smiled at them both with perfect lipsticked lips. *You don't have what it takes, do you? Never have and never will.*

At first, Matty had thought Edna was the one who'd said the words, but then he realized they'd been in his own voice.

Edna had spoken cheerfully to Sabrina, saying, "You've come such a long way this year. No doubt your coach gets some credit for that, but you shouldn't get complacent now. You have to seek to better yourself always."

The voice came again, louder and more insistent. *You don't deserve her anyway. You haven't earned it. You'll never earn it.*

Matty shuddered and pushed away the memory. Control was silent now, washed away by the vision of his best girl doing her best work. He leaned against the boards, focusing on Sabrina while she skated out the end of a routine he'd helped put together as an exhibition piece.

The music was special to both of them. He'd chosen it because it was their song—his and Sabrina's—and it was infused with emotional power for both of them. It'd been playing when Sabrina, for the first time, pushed past her fears and into her talent.

Those early days as her coach had been the happiest days of his life. There'd been no voice then. Things had been so exciting, so good. He'd eaten without much thought—usually whatever Rob packed for him—and he'd been fatter, sure, but he hadn't cared. It was a different era: BC. Before Control.

Then everything had changed.

The song was a reminder of those good times. Matty clapped his hands to the rhythm for the footwork portion of the program. Sabrina's blades hit the ice with each strike of his palms together. His girl was shining today, like a spotlight was on her and every move she made was perfection. Pride flowed in him, and he wrestled the darkness that threatened to rise up and ruin it. He could do this. He could have this joy. Because it was almost over anyway.

He smiled when Sabrina shot him a giddy grin as she sped past for the final combinations. He glanced toward the stands where Mrs. Miller, Sabrina's pale mother, watched her daughter carefully. Her blond hair was in a low ponytail, and her unpainted nails tapped at her lips thoughtfully. Matty's fragile bubble of cheer deflated when he realized *she* wasn't smiling. He knew it wasn't because she was dissatisfied with Sabrina's performance; she often celebrated Sabrina's smallest achievements. It was, Matty suspected, because she felt guilty about the Colorado Springs clinic. No matter how it had been presented to him when Mrs. Miller told him about their plans, it *wasn't* just about attending a jump clinic to solidify Sabrina's new confidence. It was a full-on audition for a new coach, and they all knew it.

"I just want what's best for Sabrina." How many times had Matty heard that from Mrs. Miller over the last year and a half? They were in fact the exact words Mrs. Miller had used when she approached him about taking Sabrina on after Valentina had thrown her hands up in disgust over the timid girl.

Mrs. Miller had approached Matty, saying, "Sabrina says you're different. She says she likes you — that you actually help her."

Confident and with nothing to lose, Matty had put up his chin and calmly channeled Rob. "Competitive skating is about finding the guts to dig deep, Mrs. Miller, and sometimes it takes a gentle hand to help someone find their courage."

Smiling, Sabrina's mother had taken his hand earnestly, her blue eyes shining with hope. "Can you help her find the guts to dig deep, Coach Marcus? Please say you'll take her on. Skating is her dream and we believe you're the only one who can help her achieve it."

As a courtesy, Valentina had given leave for Matty to try his hand with the obstinately timid Sabrina. And eventually, with persistence from his alter ego, Yuliya Yasneyeva, he'd managed to undo the damage Valentina's harsh ways had done and start to build Sabrina up.

Eventually, he'd stopped teaching her as Yuliya Yasneyeva. He'd realized leaving Yuliya behind was an important step for Sabrina to take. She needed to know that Matty Marcus, Olympian, not just Yuliya Yasneyeva, joker and stress reliever, believed in her.

One day at the beginning of practice, he'd taken hold of Sabrina's hands before sending her out onto the ice, and said, just as the beginning of "Celebrate" by Mika blasted over the speakers, "Do you hear this music? Just like he says, remember, it *will* be okay. You've got this, beautiful girl. I believe in you. Go out there and believe in yourself."

She'd smiled at him, her eyes full of light, and she'd nodded. "I've got this Matty."

Then she'd skated out onto the ice, every muscle in her body committed and confident. He'd known as she went up for the double Axel that she was going to land it perfectly. He'd jumped up and down, screaming when she did, his heart pounding with joy as her face bloomed in a way Matty had never seen. Her next jump was stronger, and the one after that was sheer perfection. Matty had never been more proud of anyone—except maybe Ben—in all his life.

Once the breakthrough came, everything else followed fast. Quickly, Sabrina went from being afraid to try a double Axel to killing it. She'd even become marvelously consistent with the triple Lutz, triple toe combination. Suddenly, Valentina had expressed interest in coaching her again, but the Millers didn't want to break Sabrina's stride, and so she'd stayed with Matty through an entire year of competition, culminating in the achievement at Junior Worlds.

Now, after all they'd been through together, it looked like the Millers were caving to Federation pressure. They were going to take his beautiful girl away from him.

No wonder Mrs. Miller wouldn't look at him today. No wonder she wasn't smiling.

But Matty didn't want to think about that. He didn't want to encourage the voice to come back. He wanted to keep it boxed up inside, safe and quiet, safe as houses in Montana snow.

Focusing his attention on Sabrina, his throat tightened. Everything was temporarily perfect: the music, the lyrics, and the sweetness of his girl living up to her potential right there in front of his eyes. Sabrina moved across the ice to the final beats of Mika's song, joy enlivening her face as she executed each motion exactly. The piano and vocals built, and built, and finally crested. Matty's heart swelled along with it, and he wished he could capture this moment forever. It was better than hunger—better than winning. He could barely stand to let it pass.

Sabrina skated off the ice and into his arms, just the way he had with Rob that morning, and she hugged him tightly. "I'm going to miss you," she whispered against his shoulder. "You know, while I'm away. Will you miss me too?"

Matty wondered if Sabrina understood what this clinic was really about. Surely her parents hadn't kept that information from her? "Of course I'll miss you. You're my best girl, aren't you?"

Sabrina pulled back, a smile creasing her face and scrunching her eyes. Matty loved the white gleam of her teeth against her lovely, summer-darkened skin. "You're my best coach. No matter what else happens, Matty, I promise you'll always be the first and best for me."

Matty felt a lump rise in his throat. "But you're getting older and stronger, Beany-Baby."

He used his nickname for her to soften the blow of his words, because he knew they'd hurt her to hear, maybe as much as it hurt him to say. They'd grown up together as coach and skater over the last year. The emotions in that were complicated and tangled and, in a situation like this, incredibly raw. He wanted her to know he loved her.

"So it's okay if there's a better coach out there for you. It won't change how I feel about you if you need to go on to someone else now." He thought Rob would be so proud of him for saying that, because, fuck, it really hurt. "It's okay to outgrow me."

Sabrina's expression darkened and there was a hint of rising tears behind her doll-like lashes. Matty didn't want that, and he definitely didn't want Mrs. Miller to think he was guilt-tripping her daughter. He put his hands on her shoulders, smiled as brightly as he could muster, and said, "Come on now, you get, what? Three days off before you report to Forenza's jump clinic? What are you going to do with it? Sleep in? Eat decadent room service while lounging in your hotel room?"

She whispered, "I'm gonna skate every day and eat right, because when I go see this coach the Federation is pushing on me, I want to make you proud, and I want him to see what a good coach you are for me, Matty. For anyone who wants to learn."

Matty almost burst into tears. Her praise and confidence in him was so at odds with his fear, but he pushed it down. He squeezed her shoulders. "Make *yourself* proud, okay? Show him what a great skater *you* are and what an asset you'd be to his program. That's what's important. Don't worry about me."

Sabrina did start to cry then, and Mrs. Miller rushed down from the stands. Her expression was a mess of worry, exasperation, and a dash of anger. She put her arm around Sabrina's shoulders, and said stiffly to Matty, "We'll be in touch. We owe you a lot. You've been so good for her." She met Matty's eyes, and emotions warred there, guilt coming through on top. "We haven't forgotten that you gave her confidence when others had given up on her. It was a beautiful thing to see and be part of. We aren't ungrateful. I hope you know that."

"Of course. And I've learned a lot from being her coach. It was a mutually beneficial situation."

Matty heard the past-tense words falling between them like anvils.

"I'm glad." She cleared her throat, looking down at the top of Sabrina's head. "Come on, baby, it's time to go home and pack. You'll see Matty soon. I promise."

Sabrina nodded and let her mother pull her away, but she looked back at Matty and mouthed the words: *I love you.* He managed to blow her a kiss before turning away and starting to cry himself. He wasn't ready for Sabrina to outgrow him. But since when did what Matty want matter? Hadn't he learned that lesson by now?

He hadn't earned a student like her yet.

Chapter Six

"ROB." SATO GREETED him kindly, gripping his hand firmly as they shook. "It's been a long time."

"Over three years."

"Indeed." Sato waved at Dr. Joiner as she left the room to take a phone call. She had Arjun and Susan at her heels, both of them asking if it was possible to do another meeting like this one later in the year. Rob would definitely add his voice to that chorus later.

He and Sato exchanged pleasantries until the other PTs and PTAs filtered out of the room. It took a while, longer than Rob would have liked, because several stayed back to ask Sato some follow-up questions. When only the two of them remained in the conference room, Sato tilted his head, a bit of light from the window flashing against the shiny smoothness of his scalp, and asked, "And how are you really?"

"I'm doing okay. I was surprised to see you here."

"You thought I had nothing going on in my life but leathers and managing my slave, huh?"

Rob chuckled. "No. Obviously we all have lives outside the scene. I just didn't expect that yours would intersect with mine in exactly this way."

"Fair enough. And you—well, your life is entirely outside the scene now, isn't it? It's been years since I've seen you around."

"Well, my boyfriend, he's not—" Rob stopped short of putting it on Matty. "We don't play with other people. It's our preference to keep it private and at home."

"Sometimes that's the way it is," Sato agreed. "But keep in mind the community can provide a lot of support in ways that have nothing to do with play. I hope you know you're always welcome in any capacity."

"Thank you. I do know that."

"Excellent." Sato began to pack up some items like he assumed their conversation was finished.

"I'm glad we touched base about our common hobby..."

Sato snorted a kind little laugh.

"But that isn't what I really wanted to talk to you about."

"Oh? I'm sorry, did you have questions? About the content of my talk?"

"Yes. You see, my boyfriend's a figure skater. So, a lot of what you talked about today rang some bells for me. Big time."

"He competes?"

"Not anymore. He's a two-time Olympian, though. Matty Marcus is his name. You might rec—"

"Oh, yes." Sato's cheeks dimpled with his smile. "I remember him."

Rob grinned. "He's memorable."

"And quite a looker."

Rob felt a surge of pride and wished fleetingly that Sato could see Matty at his most submissive, working hard and beautifully for Rob's pleasure. Sato would appreciate what a gift Matty gave him every time he surrendered completely. But it wasn't a gift Rob was willing to share. "Speaking of lookers, how's Josh?"

"Long gone." Sato shrugged.

"I'm sorry." Rob didn't know if he was surprised or not. He hadn't known either man well enough to have an opinion on their relationship beyond the superficial.

"Don't be. He knew what he wanted and it wasn't me. Things work out the way they should, I think. I took on Todd Milner some time ago now and I'm quite happy with him."

"Todd... I don't remember anyone by that name in the group."

"Oh, no, you wouldn't. Todd came onto the scene after you left." Sato smiled so widely his eyes nearly shut. "But it only took a few weeks to know he's the man for me." Sato clapped his hands together and rubbed them, as though anticipating something delicious. "So, I take it you had some questions about eating disorders for me?"

"Or disordered eating. I'm not sure which."

"Some of the criteria is easier to determine in women. Amenorrhea, for example, is a good, clear marker."

"Right. The thing is, I've watched him go through phases over the years, especially back when he was competing, when he'd eat so little that I was certain he had a problem, and other times when he'd eat almost normally."

"But most of the time it's somewhere in the middle?"

Rob nodded.

"Yes, that's very typical of an athlete of his caliber in that kind of sport. Ballet, figure skating, gymnastics." Sato made a T with his fingers and then tilted his top hand one way and then another. "There's a fine balance in these sports between eating enough to put on muscle for the needed strength," he tilted his hand the other direct, "and weighing too much to get the needed height on jumps and whatnot. And of course there's the risk of joint damage at higher weights, but there is the opposite problem too: lower weight can lead to brittleness and a lack of joint resilience."

"Exactly. And Matty knows all that intellectually. But when things get tense, like when his best student started succeeding this season and the pressure started to mount, all of that understanding seems to go out the window in favor of restriction, restriction, restriction."

"Hmm. Well, I'd have to know more about Matty to give any indepth advice. But to ease your mind, there are a few key things to look out for."

"Hit me. I'm ready to learn."

Sato smiled and squeezed Rob's shoulder. "Good. I can see that you take good care of him."

Rob smiled. "When he lets me."

"Do you know if Matty, for lack of a better term, hears a voice in his head? Not like schizophrenia, but not all that dissimilar either. This voice would tell him not to eat or tells him how awful he is as a person, or athlete? Or the voice can attack in both ways."

"I don't know." Rob considered the question. "To be honest, I think he probably does. I'm basing that on some of the things that come out of his mouth when he's hungry. It's like it's not even him anymore. Matty's always hard on himself, but when he isn't eating he can't seem to see anything good in himself."

Sato nodded thoughtfully, stroking to fingers over his firm chin and narrowing his eyes. "Well, that's a little troublesome. In the psychology business, we call that the voice of anorexia. Most true anorexics, or those with a restrictive ED diagnosis, hear that voice."

Rob swallowed thickly. "Okay."

"But the real question comes back to the chicken or the egg? Does the abusive voice come when he's already hungry? Or does the voice instigate the failure to provide himself with enough energy?"

"I'm not sure."

"That's definitely something to try to discover. I take it he isn't seeing a counselor or psychologist?"

"No. Money is tight."

Sato nodded again. "Mmm. I see."

"Hiraku," Dr. Joiner called from the doorway. She was smiling, and had a "kid playing hooky" vibe in her summer dress, her red messenger bag slung over her shoulder, and car keys in hand. "I can drop you off on my way home if you want?"

"Thank you, Etsuko. I'll take you up on that." He smiled apologetically at Rob. "Sorry to cut this short, but heading out with Etsuko will spare me the cost of the taxi. Todd took the car to his grandmother's today."

"You live out in Rye, still?"

Dr. Joiner answered for Sako as he gathered the rest of his things. "Yes, our families have lived in that area for a long time." She smiled at Sako. "Rob's from Whitefish, Montana, originally. Can you imagine what a head-trip the city must have been for him at first?"

"Whitefish? Near Missoula?"

Rob nodded because the word "near" was such a relative thing and explaining the distance between Whitefish and Missoula in New York terms would make it seem far.

"I've never been, but I've heard it's very beautiful."

"It is."

"Do you miss it?" Dr. Joiner asked as she and Rob helped Sato unplug and pack up the computer and the last of the leftover packets.

"More than I ever expected."

He missed everything about Montana—the comfortable house, the sound of the cattle lowing, the crisp, clean air. He missed the open spaces the most. The city was claustrophobic, overly saturated with people and energy. He always felt covered in its grime, like a sticky film he could never fully wash off.

Dr. Joiner looked at him in surprise. "Really? You never talk about it."

Rob didn't talk about Whitefish because it made his heart hurt and his throat grow tight. Sometimes he felt like he couldn't breathe in the city when he remembered the wide, open plains and sky-scraping mountains. But most of all he didn't talk about Whitefish because he wasn't going back there anytime soon. "Matty's happy here, and that's what's important."

Sato's eyebrows quirked a little, but then he smiled again. "Ah, love. It does lead us down some unexpected paths, doesn't it?"

Dr. Joiner muttered, "I'll take your word on it. I wouldn't know. Love has only ever led me to divorce court."

Sato hitched his bags up on his shoulder and smiled ruefully at his cousin. "Maybe if you gave up on us wicked men and gave women a try you'd find yourself more satisfied."

Dr. Joiner's smirk was a little naughty. "How do you know that I haven't?" Sato squawked and seemed on the verge of following up on her jab when she turned to Rob and cut off any further discussion of her love life. "Rob, I'd offer you a lift too but—"

"No, no, I know. I'm the opposite way. Don't worry. I've got a loaded Metro card and I'm not afraid to use it."

She laughed and tucked her hair behind her ear again. "Tomorrow it's back to the grind. Let's all get out of here and enjoy the rest of the afternoon. It's a beautiful, sunshiney day."

As they followed Dr. Joiner from the room, Sato put his hand on Rob's arm to hold him back for a moment. "Here's my card," he said, slipping the rectangle of paper into Rob's hand. "Call anytime if you have more questions about Matty's situation or anything else we talked about."

"Thank you."

Rob followed them out of the building, turning the card over in his hand. As they headed down the street together, he listened with quiet amusement to their sibling-like teasing.

"Since when have you ever dated a woman?"

"Since when is that your business?"

There were times he wished he'd had a brother or sister. Someone to take the pressure off when his dad got too focused on Rob's many failings. And then when his parents had died so suddenly, he'd wished for someone to share the weight of his grief. Sometimes he wondered if he'd have made the same choices if he'd had a sibling to split the ranch with. Would he have even met Matty?

Rob tuned in again to hear Dr. Joiner razzing Sato about missing their grandmother's birthday party. "Yes, there's always next year," she chastised. "Because turning 101 wasn't a big enough deal. You're holding out for 102."

"There was an emergency at the office!" Sato exclaimed like he'd said it a dozen times already.

"A psychological emergency? What does that even mean? It's not as though you deal with people in the middle of psychotic breaks. Was a soccer player threatening to not imagine kicking winning goals while he fell off to sleep?"

"My job is a bit more complicated than that, Etsuko."

"Here's my turn," Rob said and they broke off their squabbling long enough to wave as he split away.

"Call with questions!" Sato offered again and then he took Dr. Joiner's arm, slipping it through his own as they headed toward a parking lot another block down. Rob heard their bickering voices for only a moment more before the sounds of traffic and the city swallowed them up.

CHAPTER SEVEN

MATTY STOOD IN front of the full-length mirror in their bedroom paralyzed by what he saw.

You shouldn't have eaten lunch. You could have avoided all this.

After work, he'd biked to Saks to burn off some of the calories from the lunch Rob had brought for him. Once there he'd grimly pursued the rest of his punishment. It played in his mind like a slow-motion movie, the way he'd systematically gone through the store buying whatever most made his heart hurt with longing. He'd ended up choosing mostly from the latest Adam Lippes stock: three blouses, silk track pants, and a pair of dress shorts. All full price. All crushingly expensive.

He'd let them bag the items up. He'd taken them home.

So now here he stood wearing a suede slip-on Louis Leeman on one foot and Giuseppe Zanotti gold metallic leather high top on the other. He was naked from the waist up, having been unable to decide which blouse he wanted to put on first. The clothes still had tags hanging from them because he had to take them all back. Tomorrow. First thing. So Rob wouldn't find out what he'd done.

He felt sick. Nauseous. Like he'd gorged on pizza and ice cream. Like he was going have to purge.

Return them tomorrow. We'll see how that feels. The humiliation might be enough.

"Oh God." Matty started to take off the silk shorts. His fingers shook and his stomach roiled.

The sound of Rob's keys jingling as he worked open the outside door sent icy-hot horror sweeping through Matty. "Fuck!"

He grabbed the shopping bags from the floor and tossed them into the bathroom. Then he looked around in a panic for something else to hide the evidence in. Snatching up his biggest duffel, he darted into the bathroom and locked the door behind him. He turned on the shower just as the bang of the apartment door let him know Rob was inside.

He tugged the shoes off and pulled the shorts down. He shook all over, panting in nothing but his underwear. A memory, like a thread that could pull him out of this time and into another, wove through his mind: thirteen years old, his brightly painted pet rock in his right hand, the satisfying smash of his mother's favorite lamp as the two connected, the endless questions of why, and his inability to cough up an explanation that could satisfy.

Bad kids grow up to be bad people.

But he hadn't been a bad kid. It'd been an impulse. A mistake. He'd been hungry and he'd thought—

It didn't matter what he'd thought. Not now. It was forever ago. What mattered was here and now. What was he going to say? Rob wasn't supposed to find out. He had to make sure Rob never knew he'd bought these things, no matter how temporarily. Rob didn't need to know about this self-punishment.

"Matty?"

"In the bathroom!"

The doorknob rattled and, before Rob could ask, Matty called out, "Just getting cleaned up. I'll be out in a little bit." His face in the bathroom mirror was both pale and flushed, gleaming with a sheen of fresh fear-sweat.

Rob's voice was infused with a seductive tease. "Planning to pick up where we left off this morning?"

"Yes." Matty quickly folded the blouses and shoved them along with the shorts into a bag, wincing at the crinkling noise. It sounded so loud in the small bathroom.

"Great. You get cleaned up and we'll have dinner first." Rob chuckled. "Then it's payback time."

"Sounds good." Matty put the shoes back in their boxes and

stuffed them into his backpack. God, how was he going to get the bags into the duffel, and then get it out of the bathroom without Rob wondering what was going on?

There was quiet from outside the door. "Everything okay?"

"Great! Just, you know, getting clean."

"All right."

Matty pulled his underwear off and got in the shower. His heart beat so hard he leaned against the tile wall, breathing in and out, trying to calm down. Minutes passed, and he still didn't know what to do about getting the bags into the duffel or getting the duffel out of the bathroom. This had been a terrible plan.

"Matty, there's no lemon for the salad dressing you like. I'm going to run out and get some."

Perfect.

"Okay! Um, can you get some Peychaud's bitters too? I'm almost out."

"If they carry it."

Matty climbed out of the still-running shower and waited until he heard both doors shut. He shoved the bags into the duffel, and then darted, wet and dripping into the bedroom, to kick the bag into the back of the closet. He'd grab it on his way out in the morning, return the stuff on his lunch break, and everything would be fine.

Using a towel to wipe up the water on the floor, he tried to calm his mind by mentally running through an old free skate program from eight years before. It was a task that took enough concentration to bring the whirl of panic down from a Category 5 to a Category 2.

Back in the shower, he attached the Cleanstream system and adjusted the water to the temperature he preferred for the awkward process of getting his ass ready for whatever they might want to do after dinner. He didn't really feel up to sex, though. His muscles ached from the morning workout, his hip hurt from his old injury, and he wanted to just sit down under the water and cry.

Instead he prepared the nozzle and worked it into his butt. He'd get clean for Rob and do whatever Rob wanted to do. Maybe Rob would see how much he needed it and give him a scene to help him stop feeling so dirty all over. It'd be hard to cope with his nerves so raw, but he could take it if Rob dished it out. He hoped he would. He couldn't stand feeling so mucked up and grounded. He hated being the bird that was always too fucked up to fly.

***

"HOW DID IT go with Sabrina?" Rob asked over dinner. Matty had been silent for far too long, and his spidey-senses were going off.

"She cried. I cried. We all cried."

"Did they give you any more information about what to expect?"

"Mrs. Miller used the past tense and thanked me for what I've done for her."

Rob put his fork down. "Oh, sweetheart." He reached out and touched Matty's hand. "She still has to perform out there. Her head could do her in."

"But I don't want it to. She's strong. She's better than she's ever been. A failure like that would set her back, and I want her moving forward. Even if it's without me."

"Of course you do."

They ate a bit more, the waning summer evening light pouring in from the front windows.

Rob looked around their tidy living room, trying to determine if there was something else amiss. Everything looked the same. His beige, IKEA pull-out couch was covered with the cream and gold throw pillows Matty had brought along when he moved in, and the low, sturdy, wooden coffee table he'd grabbed from off the street when he'd first come to Brooklyn was artfully decorated with Matty's fashion magazines, a scattering of shiny knick-knacks, and a cream colored vase which normally sported flowers, but stood full of decadent smelling incense sticks currently. Their coat rack was a mish-mash of Matty's colorful, sparkling coats, and Rob's dull, brown ones. Nothing seemed out of place, and yet there was something very off about the vibe in the room and it didn't feel like it was entirely about Sabrina.

"What else is going on?"

"Nothing. I have to put on my big boy panties and move on."

Rob took a bite of chicken and waited a few minutes. He was tempted to ask more about Matty's day, check in about how he'd gotten along with Valentina, and even ask after the lunch he'd delivered, but something told him it was best to let it go for a little while. Matty would tell him everything in his own time. He always did.

"I had an interesting day," Rob offered.

"Really? Somehow 'PT CE' and 'interesting day' seem mutually exclusive."

Rob chuckled. "It was hosted by a respected BDSM dom I knew from the scene back when I first came here from Whitefish."

Matty's eyes lit up for the first time that evening. "You had a PT CE meeting about BDSM? Like, about what? How to treat BDSM injuries?"

"No." Rob laughed, imagining Arjun's expression if Dr. Joiner had arranged that particular class. "No, it was about sports psychology and how that relates to sports injuries and PT."

Matty waved a hand, picking at his salad some more. "Oh. Well, that's a lot less exciting. I was expecting to hear about fisting gone wrong and groin exercises."

Rob laughed again. "Well, now that you've gone this direction with it, I feel like my day was a lot less interesting than it could have been."

"But you knew this guy from the scene?" Matty shifted a little uncomfortably, like he always did at any reminder of Rob's past in the local scene, short though it was. "Did he recognize you?"

Rob nodded. "Yes." He cast his thoughts back to those unhappy first months in New York City — missing Matty, desperately seeking the kind of connection they'd shared and never finding it. "He remembered me."

"What's his name?"

"Hiraku Sato."

Matty poked at his small wedge of smoked salmon and pressed

his lips together, his dark eyes focusing on the food on his plate as he asked with clearly pretended nonchalance, "What's he like?"

"Short. Bald. Japanese. Powerful. He's a cheerful guy, I guess, but I've seen him take command of a sub like it was as easy as breathing."

Matty pushed the salmon around on the plate. "Did he have a sub of his own?"

"Yeah. I liked his slave Josh a lot. He had a great sense of humor. I only knew Sato in passing because he was always busy. He liked working over other people's subs." Which might explain a lot about why Josh left now that Rob was thinking about it. "I remember Josh would wait patiently at the bar drinking whatever beverage Sato had approved for him and making some damn astute, wry, and smart-ass comments at the shenanigans around us. He cracked me up."

"Oh."

Rob took a sip of beer. "Apparently their arrangement ended, though. I'm not sure if he got tired of waiting around all the time or just moved on to greener pastures. Sato's with a guy named Todd now."

"So what did you say to each other? Was he afraid you'd expose his kink to the world?" Matty finally ate a bite of salmon.

Rob smiled remembering the flash of recognition in Sato's eyes and the assurance in his stance. "No. He knew neither of us would want that."

"Yeah, what would Susan think if she knew the things you do to me in bed? Or Arjun?"

"Arjun would be horrified and probably reluctantly titillated. Savita would probably endure some bondage play for a week or two, until she figured out that she should tie him up instead."

Matty laughed quietly.

"And, well, Susan could go one of two ways. Either she'd go off on some weird feminist rant about sex and power, or she'd take an extreme interest complete with requests for details."

Matty popped another piece of salmon into his mouth and chewed thoughtfully. "You think Arjun would get a hard-on if you described to him how you've gagged me, tied me up, wrapped string around my balls and dick, and shoved a dildo up my ass?"

"Do you like the idea of Arjun having a hard-on over the things I do to you?"

Matty shrugged, color coming up on his cheeks. "Maybe."

Rob chuckled.

"So what happened with the Sato guy?"

"We exchanged numbers. I think I'll meet him for coffee. There are some things, PT things mainly, that I want to talk to him about."

"But some not-PT things?" Matty didn't sound happy about that.

"Yeah. Just a few scene setup ideas I'd like to run past him — logistics and problem-solving. That sort of thing. It'll be good to have someone I can bounce things off sometimes. That is, if you're okay with that." Rob watched Matty push the final bite of salmon around on his plate, sliding it here and there, and feeling the other reason he wanted to meet with Sato like a phantom sitting at the table with them.

"Are you interested in doing a scene with him?" Matty's tone was apprehensive but challenging, like someone on the verge of accepting a dare. "Because I can handle it if you want me to handle it. I can do anything you need me to do."

Rob's stomach clenched. "I don't play that way with you."

"Because you don't think I can deal with it?" Matty's gaze bore into him.

There was no way Matty could deal with it. But Rob said, "Because I don't want it. Even if you want it, I don't. You're mine to love and hurt and punish. I don't need or want anyone else involved to do that." Matty seemed mollified, and Rob reached out and touched his chin, lifting his eyes from his plate until he met Rob's gaze. "I wouldn't want to even try."

Matty went back to eating, bites of salad following the salmon into his mouth, and Rob relished the way his throat moved when he swallowed. It turned him on to watch Matty consume food and always had. It was a weird kink, he knew, and he wondered if he'd still have it once any worry about just how many calories were getting swallowed was gone.

Matty didn't seem ready to let go of the topic of Sato yet. "But you want to keep in touch with this guy."

"Yeah. The scene can offer some good support. If you wanted, I could introduce you to—well, I could ask Sato if there is a sub you could befriend. He's a pretty relaxed guy. I'm sure he'd be willing to introduce you to his slave, Todd, but I can't really promise that."

The sun glowed against Matty's exposed white shoulder. The dark sleeveless T-shirt he'd put on after his shower over a pair of black briefs was a stark contrast to his pale skin. "You don't know any subs from the scene?"

Rob twisted pasta around his fork and cleared his throat. He knew a few. At least one or two of them had to be at the same number. They were all friendly and helpful enough. They'd be happy to talk to Matty.

But he'd fucked them all.

"So the only ones you know are the ones you dommed," Matty said, a tense edge to his tone.

"That's what I was doing back then, sweetheart. I wasn't taking subs out to lunch and talking over the Yankees' chances against the Orioles."

"Were any of them good?"

Rob's stomach tightened again. "They were good men, and I have nothing negative to say about any of them. But none of them were you."

Matty's mouth twisted into a smart-ass grin. "I know. An ass like this can't be found in every kink club in the world."

Rob smiled because he was supposed to, but made note of Matty's jealousy. It wasn't a good sign. When Matty was confident and sure of himself, his shoulders stayed straight and firm, and his eyes snapped with amusement, even if he was a little out of sorts about a topic. This was flat-eyed, slump-shouldered insecurity talking. It wasn't a good look on Matty, but more than that, it signaled the need for a hard reset coming on. It seemed like they'd just performed one. The idea of doing yet another was exhausting.

"So, that was my day," Rob said. "How was working with Valentina?"

Matty sighed and put his fork down, apparently finished. "Valentina and I got into it about Hux. She's doing so much better, but Valentina won't stop beating her down."

"I'm sorry." Rob tried to determine how many calories were still left in Matty's salad bowl. "Did you tell Huxley to buck up?"

"Better. I made secret plans to work with her one-on-one at City Ice."

"Is that a good idea?"

"She really needs the opportunity to get through her program without being screamed at. She needs that to build some confidence."

"Just don't let Valentina find out. She'll think you're poaching another student."

"Fuck her."

"Ah." Rob studied Matty's angry eyes. "If that's how you feel about it, let's have ice cream."

Matty shoved back his chair, a war of want and fear playing on his features. "We're out. You ate the last yesterday."

"Good thing I bought some while I was getting the bitters and lemons. I thought you might need some tonight after everything with Sabrina."

Matty's swallowed hard and met his eye. "What flavor?"

"Chocolate Fudge Brownie."

"My favorite." But his voice sounded like it was coming from far away.

"I know."

"It's been a bad day." Matty's gaze shifted to the freezer, and he stared at it like the ice cream might come bursting out with a machine gun. "Maybe I should just go to sleep instead."

Rob shook his head.

Matty's breathing visibly kicked up. He squirmed in his chair and sat on his hands. "You're going to make me eat it?"

"Do you need me to make you eat it?"

Matty nodded and then gasped, ducking his head like it hurt to

71

have admitted his need. Rob hoped to save another hard reset until after their anniversary trip. The city was just so wearing, and he might have more energy after a vacation. Still, Matty clearly needed something in the meantime.

"Stay here."

Rob strolled into the bedroom and over to the drawer that held the ties he had in mind. He flung it open and pulled out a soft rope he could use to bind Matty to the kitchen chair. He closed his eyes, getting a grip on the hot rush of arousal that image brought up in him. It fattened his dick and made his knees feel like liquid heat.

Yes, he'd tie Matty to the chair, work his briefs down, and give him a miserable-but-good blow job. Rob smiled. He was going to suck Matty's dick with ice cream in his mouth. He'd make him scream and squirm, he'd make him beg, and then when the ice cream had melted and mixed with Matty's pre-come, he'd pull off and kiss Matty, feeding the messy liquid to him.

As he passed the closet he saw a piece of paper sticking out from the top of his running shoe, and he bent to snatch it up for the recycling bin. He glanced down at it, and his brain slid in gravel, spitting it everywhere, as his thoughts screeched to a sudden stop.

***

MATTY WAITED AT the table for what seemed like a long time, his cock hard and eager, and Control busily telling him how he didn't deserve the ice cream or the sex, and he'd have to do something tomorrow to make up for it.

"Matty." Rob's voice was flat, but a fire in the tenor of it made the hair on Matty's neck stand up. "Come here."

Could Rob have changed his mind? Was he going to get something hard tonight? Something painful enough to shut out his evil, poisonous thoughts? He needed it so badly that the idea made his hands start to shake.

That hope only lasted until he walked in and saw Rob sitting on the bed, head down, and a long, slim slip of paper in his hands. The

Saks receipt.

"This morning I asked if I could trust you." Rob held up the receipt and shook his head, his jaw flexing. "You said I could." His lips twisted and his chin jutted out. "Another fucking lie."

Matty dropped to his knees by Rob's feet and tried to tug the receipt from his hands. Rob didn't let him. Matty couldn't find a voice to defend himself. What could he say anyway? It wouldn't make sense outside his own head. It wouldn't stand the scrutiny of Rob hearing the explanation spoken aloud.

"Almost seven thousand dollars," Rob said in a voice Matty barely recognized. "You know we don't have the money for this kind of bullshit, Matty."

Matty swallowed hard and tried to catch Rob's gaze, color rising hot in his cheeks. "I'm going to take everything back."

"Oh, that's fucking great. Are you lying again?" Rob's voice cracked and he rubbed his fingers over his eyes.

"No!"

Rob whispered, "We are down to less than a thousand in our savings account once the checks I've already written go through." He looked at Matty again, his expression like an open wound. Matty felt nauseous as Rob went on in a louder voice, the edges of it shaking in rage. "The checks I wrote for our rent, and our car payment, the payment I made toward our anniversary trip, and the automatic debits that come out of our account for other bills. Not to mention the check I gave Anja last night. How much is on your credit card?"

A stubborn anger rose in Matty. He wasn't a child even if he'd acted like one. "That's not your business."

"The hell it isn't!" Rob leapt up, and Matty fell onto his ass on the carpet, looking up at him. Rob had gone very pale now, his eyes strangely dark in his face, and his lips pressed into a tight line. "The hell it isn't. When we combined our money, we agreed that big purchases were something we'd discuss together. And big purchases were defined as anything more than two hundred dollars. Because that's how fucking tight things are, Matty. That's the difference between checks bouncing and bad credit."

"I know."

"How did you pay for this?"

Matty swallowed. It'd been a bad idea but when the saleswoman had offered it to him several months ago, he'd said yes. "On a Saks card."

"What?"

Matty nodded. "I have a Saks Fifth Avenue card."

"Fuck me."

Matty whispered, "I'll cut it up. I promise."

"Hell yeah, you'll cut it up. How much is on this card? Aside from this little fucked-up shopping adventure?"

"Eleven."

"Eleven hundred?"

"Thousand."

"Fuck."

Matty stood, his knees shaking, but his hands shook even more as he reached out to grab Rob. Rob pulled free and stormed out the door that led from their bedroom out to the back garden.

Matty followed as far as the doorway and waited there, watching as Rob stalked to the end and punched the tall back fence that separated their little yard from a neighbor's, yelling, "Fuck!" He threw back his head and gazed up to the sky, his shoulders heaving with his angry breaths.

Matty's stomach churned. He was going to vomit, sob, beg. He just didn't know which he was going to do first. Rob finally turned around, his eyes still dark, but he seemed a little calmer; more in control. Matty stepped aside when Rob approached the door, letting him back into the apartment without touching him. He whispered, "Everything else on it is old stuff and I was paying the bill myself. And this time I was going to take it all back, Rob. I was never going to keep it. I swear."

"When?" Rob unbuttoned his shirt and flung it aside. Then he sniffed his pits and started toward the bathroom. "When were you going to do that, Matty?"

Matty followed, watching him turn on the sink and splash his face with cold water. Rob leaned with his elbows against the counter, his muscled shoulders rounded, and his long fingers dangling into the bowl. Matty stood as close as he could, wanting to reach out and run his hand over Rob's long back, to feel the warm, familiar skin under his palm, but he didn't know how Rob might react. It'd been a long time since Matty had seen him this angry. Over a year at least. Maybe never.

"When?" Rob whispered, a water droplet hanging from his nose and splashing down on his wrist.

"Tomorrow or the day after."

Rob grabbed the hand towel and wiped his face. His hands still shook and his eyes were still a hard, but he sounded much calmer, almost like his usual self, when he reasoned, "Listen, we don't have any extra right now. Aside from our anniversary trip, I promised Anja I'd pay for Ben's new gear and two new costumes so she didn't have to ask her parents for even more cash. That's all of our extra savings gone. Just like that. And now you're telling me we have eleven thousand dollars of outstanding debt I didn't know about?"

"Why does my extra go to Ben's skating expenses?"

A fresh layer of cold anger settled over Rob's features. He didn't reply, letting the question hang there between them before turning his back on Matty and starting the shower. He shucked his work khakis and threw them at Matty.

Matty caught them, feeling the heat of the material, still warm from Rob's body, against his chest.

"I'm sorry. I didn't mean that." Matty's jaw felt tight, and he held the pants flush against his body. "I always want to help Ben. I love him. You know that."

Rob stepped into the shower and flung the curtain shut. "It'd be one thing if you spent this money on something you needed. Like therapy."

Matty threw the pants on the floor and jerked back the shower curtain, his jaw clenched hard. "I said I was going to take this stuff back to Saks, okay? What do you not understand about that?" He hated that he sounded like a petulant kid, but it was all getting too close, too dangerous. If Rob knew the whole truth...

Rob sighed, rinsed the shampoo out of his hair, and then skipped the conditioner, soaping up his pits, groin, and ass. "Okay, so you were going to take it back. But what I don't get is why you spent the money to begin with." He rinsed quickly and turned off the water, grabbing a towel from the rack and getting Matty's T-shirt wet as he stepped out, dripping, onto their green and gray shower mat. Rob met Matty's eyes in the mirror as he brushed his wet hair.

"I don't know either," Matty muttered. "It was stupid. I won't do it again."

Rob walked out of the bathroom like he hadn't even heard him. He opened the chest of drawers and pulled on his boxer briefs and a soft, old T-shirt he sometimes slept in. It wasn't until that moment that Matty realized he'd been half expecting Rob to get dressed again and walk out of the apartment, leaving Matty alone with his guilt and sin. But why would he think that? Rob had never done anything like that before. He'd always stayed. Always.

One day he won't.

Rob flopped on the bed, his knees drawing up as he leaned back against the headboard. Matty tentatively approached his side of the bed, aching to touch Rob again—to make up and be told he was loved anyway.

Like you deserve that?

Rob stared at Matty like he was looking at his insides— everything from his guts to his heart—and said, thoughtfully, "You're great at denying yourself. You think I don't know? That I don't see what you don't let yourself have? Or eat? Or be? I know Matty. I just want you to say it out loud. The truth."

The truth was terrifying. Better to start with a half-truth. Maybe he could keep the rest to himself.

Matty sat next to Rob on the bed and took his loose hand, holding onto his fingers and wishing they'd return his squeeze. "I just wanted something for myself, okay? I get sick of everything being so fucking hard. Not enough money, not enough experience as a coach, not good enough to keep Sabrina, not pretty enough, not strong enough, *nothing* enough."

The anger was extinguished in Rob's expression as he processed Matty's words. His eyes were still a wounded sea-green, but his expression was indecipherable. It made Matty's skin feel too tight and his heart pound. He wanted to make it go away, but he didn't know how, and he was afraid he'd already said too much.

"It breaks my heart, sweetheart, to think that's probably just the tip of the iceberg when it comes to cruel things you believe about yourself." Rob sounded so disheartened, so disappointed. It was like pins in Matty's heart.

"I just wanted to pretend for a little while that everything was the way I'd always wanted it to be, that I was wealthy and successful and it didn't matter how much money I spent. That I could buy whatever the fuck I wanted." He left out the part about how he punished himself by buying beautiful things he had to take back.

Matty breathed through the tightness in his chest, trying to let go of the fear clamping down on him. He squeezed Rob's fingers again, wanting to lean forward to press his face against Rob's still-damp neck.

You're going to lose him.

"You're holding something back. That scares the shit out of me." Rob stared at him, and Matty felt the words crawling up his throat. But before he could get them out, Rob pulled him down against his chest, kissing his head and whispering, "Pretend all you want, Matty, but don't let it translate into real spending. We can't take it. We're barely making it."

"I know. I already knew. I'm taking it all back after work tomorrow, I promise. You weren't supposed to even find out."

Rob rubbed his hand over Matty's back and mused, "How many other things are you keeping from me?"

Matty sat up slowly and met Rob's gaze evenly. "Nothing."

"This was unacceptable."

Matty put his chin up in challenge, and his guts seemed to tremble as he replied, "What are you going to do about it?" Oh God, the terror that roared through him as those words left his mouth. Control was going to have so much to say about that.

You think a reset will shut me up?

He knew it would. It always did. It just had to hurt enough.

"Ah. There it is." Rob let out a sharp breath and gripped Matty's chin, locking gazes again. "The real reason behind all this bullshit. It'd be so much easier if you'd just ask for a reset scene instead of trying to handle things on your own."

Matty wished he could just ask, but then it wasn't a punishment, was it? And if it wasn't a punishment, then it wouldn't be good enough to silence the nastiness in his head.

Matty nodded, keeping his focus on Rob's eyes. "I'm sorry."

"Dammit, Matty, this isn't even like you. Not anymore." But he didn't sound angry, just scared. It made Matty feel it too. A creeping coldness that he wanted to shut out but couldn't.

Rob turned his gaze up to the ceiling and took some long breaths. He pushed Matty back and then stood, putting the receipt on the nightstand. Matty watched as Rob bent to pick up the ties that had fallen off the bed at some point during their fight. He put them back in the toy drawer and then turned to Matty again. "Go scoop yourself some ice cream. Eat it all." He sighed. "And when you're done go get the credit card. I want to watch you cut it up."

Matty felt a wave of disappointment as he stood. Where was the reset he needed? Where was the pain, the punishment? The deeper humiliation? Where?

Rob grabbed Matty's hand as he headed into the kitchen and made him face him again. "Whatever else you do, don't lie to me."

"I won't."

"Trust is important."

It was the second time he'd said that in a day. Matty felt sick. He had no idea how he was going to eat ice cream. "I won't do anything like this again."

"Ask for resets when you need them, Matty."

A hot urge to scream, *I just did!* ripped up his throat.

But before it escaped, Rob turned away, adding quietly, "As for what I'm going to do about it? Nothing tonight. I can't touch you when I'm this angry. But don't worry. I'll think it over. It won't be an easy scene. I think you've definitely earned that much."

Relief made Matty totter like a weak-kneed kitten into the kitchen and lean against the counter before he scooped out a bowl of ice cream. Rob was going to take control. He was going to help him.

Thank God. Thank fucking God.

CHAPTER EIGHT

MATTY RETURNED THE CitiBike to the rack and started up 48th Street toward 5th Avenue. After a few blocks, his overstuffed duffel pulled at his chest as he approached the building, but he still paused to admire Saks' always-compelling window dressings. When he opened the door and stepped into his idea of heaven, the nervous rush drained away under the hot onset of humiliation. He avoided the eyes of salespeople and other customers as he dug into his duffel for his wallet.

Finding the receipt, he set off toward the elevator, smoothing the paper between his fingers, trying to make something perfect out of something ruined. But it was too crumpled from where he'd kept it tucked into the waistband of his underwear and leggings throughout his morning classes. It'd been itchy, uncomfortable, and a constant reminder of what an asshole he was. He figured he deserved that much and probably more. It was almost hilarious how pathetic he could be.

Stop, he thought. *Just shut up.*

"May I help you?" the woman behind the counter asked kindly.

Matty swallowed hard and pulled the first bag from his duffel. "I need to return this, please." He pulled the other bags out. "And a bunch of other things too."

The woman's expression shifted subtly to something more sour, and Matty sweated under her disapproval. He held himself ramrod straight, taking the tight lines of her face as his due. The deeper, horrible, cleansing humiliation began. His blood pumped faster, and the shame of what he'd done and why swam up to the surface of his skin to make him itch and burn all over. It was awful but perfect. It was why he'd done this after all.

He plastered a smile on his face and didn't allow himself the relief of rubbing his neck or shifting from foot to foot. Instead, he forced himself to behave as if he didn't feel the clawing horror of his bad behavior—his sickness.

"Do you have the card you made the purchases with?" the woman asked with an undercurrent of suspicion.

"No, I'm sorry. I cut it up last night."

She lifted her finely-plucked brow and called over a Customer Service Manager.

It hurt like a steel-wool scrub on raw skin, but when he finally left Saks divested of his inappropriate purchases, he felt exhausted and clean. More like himself.

After boarding the F at Rockefeller Center, Matty leaned his head back against the window, letting his eyes fall on the elderly Latina lady and her young grandson across from him. The small boy was scrunched up against her side, with his head resting on her ample breasts. She sang a lullaby as the boy drowsed.

Matty held very still to examine his emotional and physical state: he was hungry and he was ashamed of himself, but he was clean, yes. He'd managed to offload the suffocating weight of the voice of Control along with the shoes, blouses, and perfume, but even so, there was no corresponding lift to his spirits.

"Didn't I earn it?" he whispered, but he didn't want to hear the answer and was relieved when one didn't come.

Matty squeezed his eyes shut against the grandson leaning so trustingly against his grandmother, but he couldn't shut out the lullaby she sang. "And I will love you, *mijo*, with all that I have, and all that I own," she warbled. Unbidden, like a knife out of the blue, yesterday's expression of hurt and anger on Rob's face cut through him. Immediately, guilt settled over his skin, a new skim of filth. Matty rubbed his hands over his hair and bent forward, his throat tight. He wanted to get home and shower that shit off before it had time to settle, before he'd have to come up with another way to punish himself to get clean again.

The train emerged out of the tunnel and onto the elevated, above ground tracks, and his phone dinged with a message from Rob.

At home waiting for you, sweetheart.

Matty closed his eyes. He didn't deserve to be forgiven so easily.

Behind his lids waited Sabrina's tearful eyes and wobbling lower lip. He'd never been good enough to spare them both the pain of parting. He'd been doing what he always did—reaching for a reward he could never deserve.

You failed her.

Usually Matty loved riding the trains. He loved watching people get on and off, loved seeing their fashions, their shoes; he loved the bustle and the overheard conversations, but now he was tired and ached all over like he'd fallen too hard, too many times on the ice. He just wanted to get home.

Why? What waited for him there? What was left when his best wasn't enough? Had never been enough? Hadn't he learned that lesson before? So why was he still fighting it all so hard? What did he even have to fight for?

Rob.

Rob was always there. He'd never leave. He'd be there forever. Matty had earned Rob with the pain of those years apart.

You could still lose him.

There'd been a time in their relationship not so long ago when he'd known that nothing would tear them apart. But that had been before he'd started listening to the voice telling him not to eat, not to feel, not to let anyone truly see him because they'd see right through his skin to his too-visible bones and know that he wasn't special. Know that he was nothing.

Shut up. To Rob I'm special.

And you almost fucked it up over a sandwich and a shopping spree.

He needed to grovel. To apologize. To beg.

He needed to make a batch of brownies.

And not eat them.

Maybe that would be enough.

No. Not enough.

"Scoot, faggot," a voice to his right muttered, and Matty slid farther to the left, making room for the man's butt without even opening his eyes.

"Language," the old woman across from them reprimanded, but Matty didn't react at all to the slur, leaving his eyes shut, his face impassive. It was just another shitty moment to add to his already craptacular week. Feeling clean post-punishment had been more ephemeral than ever.

Two stops later the asshole was gone without another word, and the grandma was still singing her lullaby. Matty let the whole week roll through him like a movie — every shitty choice, every dumb decision — and felt tears sting his eyes. His nostrils burned as they approached 4th Ave in Brooklyn.

Gathering up his now-empty duffel, he stood to grip the pole. The metal felt cool under his hot palm. When his phone vibrated in his pocket, he glanced at the caller ID and took the call.

"Mama?" he answered, shuffling closer to the door.

"It's Mama today, huh?" Donna sounded like she was in a good mood. "Why's that? What's wrong?"

"Nothing. Maybe I just love you."

"Of course you love me. I'm the woman who funded your life's dream with the entire contents of her retirement account. You have to adore me."

The reminder of the money his parents sacrificed — and for what? — bit into him hard. He huffed a hurt laugh, and that got her earnest attention.

"Honey, what's happened?"

Matty wiped his fingers over his eyes, which betrayed him by spilling over. "Nothing, Donna. Nothing at all. Everything's fine." He hated to worry her, but he couldn't talk about Sabrina right now. Not in public. And he definitely didn't want his mother to know about his fight with Rob over his lack of eating and his little shopping punishment, because that was screwed up. And he could never, ever tell her about Control.

Shame was a rack, and he was on it again.

Donna tsked and softened her voice while somehow still sounding commanding. "Nothing? My cushy soft rear-end. Talk to me, Matty, or I'll have to call your better half to find out what's going on with you."

Matty supposed it was nice his mother and his boyfriend had such a good relationship, and that Rob didn't mind how open he usually was with his mother, since they talked about almost everything anyway. But Matty didn't talk to her about these things. He didn't want to worry her. He was supposed to have it all together now. He had the boyfriend, the place in the city, the job coaching, and the amazing student. He knew she'd love him no matter what, but he'd cost her so much over the years, both in money and pain, that he didn't want to let her know that he was losing his grip again—that the voice of Control was taking over his life, and it scared him a little. A lot.

"Hold on, Mama. I'm getting off the train."

Pushing his way onto the platform ahead of the other passengers, Matty hurried up the dark stairs that lead to 4th Ave. He emerged from the station door to the glare of afternoon sun and sounds of traffic. The scent and heat of the city pummeled him as he left the murky shadows of the bridge and turned to walk the few blocks home.

"So, what's the problem?" Donna asked when he still hadn't said anything.

Grasping at the first thought that came to mind, Matty said, "Joey hasn't asked me to be his best man yet. Joseph. Whatever."

Which reminded him that he really was kinda upset about that. Hadn't he been a good brother? Hadn't he embarrassed Joey enough by being a big, flaming homosexual on ice? Didn't he deserve the place of honor for being the reason Joey had to learn martial arts to defend himself during his teen years? He was even fairly sure that Joseph's fiancée Chelsea would be happy to credit Matty with Joey's vast patience in shopping malls. Didn't that deserve best-manhood?

"I'm sure he will, honey. You just have to give him time. He probably wants to do it in person."

"He lives in Atlanta. When's he going to see me in person, Donna? You know what I think? I think he doesn't want me up at the altar looking prettier than the bride."

She pffted and chuckled. "Chelsea's a beautiful young lady. She can hold her own."

"Oh my God, Mama, what if he asks that meathead ex-roommate of his? Rocket." Matty warmed to the distraction and chattered on, "Who the hell names a kid Rocket?"

"Matty, you know Jet has been like a brother to Joseph since they played little league together, and if your brother asks him to be best man, you'll just need to handle it with grace."

"I handle everything with grace."

Donna snorted. "Yes, yes, of course. I forgot."

"Name one thing I didn't handle gracefully."

"Oh, hmm, maybe those rough few months after the Olympics?"

Normally Matty would have laughed with her and agreed, but today it just didn't seem fucking funny. "What are you talking about? I handled the indignity of being cheated out of an Olympic medal with *shit tons* of grace, Donna."

"Honey, of course you did! I just meant—oh, never mind. I can see you're not in the mood for my jokes."

"I'm fine. I'm in a perfectly fine mood, Mama. Your jokes just aren't funny. But listen, you need to get Joey to ask me to be his best man or I'm going to start an honest to God 'I am the *best* best man' campaign. I'll start off sweetly by sending him links to very special sports videos."

"Please don't say what I think you're going to say."

"Joey always liked water skiing. It stands to reason he might enjoy watching hot, sweaty men engaging in other water sports, don't you agree?"

"Oh, Matty, what am I going to do with you?"

Matty's stomach twisted. "Love me?"

Donna sighed. "I do love you. It doesn't seem to fix anything."

It was a tease, just like the Olympics comment, but it stung anyway.

She shifted the conversation to some family gossip about a cousin who'd knocked up his much-younger girlfriend. Matty was relieved to have someone else's screwed-up life to talk about. It was so much more fun than thinking about his own.

"And so they're getting married a week after Joseph," she concluded as Matty unlocked the main door to the brownstone and then the door to their ground-floor apartment.

Rob stood by the kitchen counter. It stuck out to divide the living room and provided much needed preparation space. He looked up from cutting pan-fried tofu and portioning out spinach for salads and smiled at Matty. He didn't look like he was still angry. That was good. Undeserved, but good.

Donna went on. "I have to help Charlotte get everything ready in time. I told her some guests can stay at our house because there just isn't a lot of room at their place."

"That's great, Mama. Anyway, I'm home now and Rob's cooking."

"Well, tell him hello and that we love him."

"My parents love you more than me," Matty muttered after disconnecting the call, hanging up his now-empty duffel and toeing off his shoes.

"That's because I took you off their hands."

Matty made a face, snatched a piece of grilled tofu from Rob's cutting board, and popped it in his mouth. He didn't really feel like eating even though he was nearly faint with hunger, but he knew that acting eager for the food would make Rob happy and go a long way toward smoothing over their fight.

"Everything taken care of?" Rob asked nonchalantly, but Matty pulled the return receipt out of his pocket and put it on the counter. "Good. Thank you, sweetheart." He kissed Matty's cheek and handed him a larger piece of tofu. "Eat that. The salad will be ready soon."

Matty flopped into a chair at the table, watching Rob cook. "I had to sit next to a homophobic dick on the subway."

Rob's brows lowered and his eyes softened in concern. He abandoned the salads and stepped around the counter, his hands already reaching out to canvas Matty's body and his gaze running over him looking for hurt.

"It was fine. He was all bark and no bite. Apparently it was enough to call me a faggot and then sit there like he was a normal human after that."

Rob brushed the backs of his fingers over Matty's cheekbones, and then he bent and pressed a kiss to his mouth. "Did he see where you got off or follow you?"

"No. He got off the train before I did."

Rob kissed him again. "Good." He went back to the salads, cutting up some tomatoes and red peppers to add in. "Thanks for returning everything. I appreciate that."

"Not as much as you'd have appreciated me never buying it to begin with."

Rob shrugged. "I made a new kind of dressing with a cream base. You'll like it."

Forcing himself not to tabulate how many calories might be in such a dressing, Matty nodded and rolled his shoulders before standing up from the chair and throwing himself down on the sofa to wait for Rob to serve him dinner. He'd be absolutely obligated to eat every bite of it. In a way, it felt good to have the choice taken away from him.

"Sabrina called me crying today," Matty said a few minutes later, sitting up fully and taking the salad bowl and a glass of water from Rob, who sat next to him on the sofa with his own. "She's nervous about the jump clinic."

"She's always been sensitive."

"Yeah. I worry about that. I don't want her letting the sport destroy her self-confidence. It can be so brutal out there. Part of me gets why the Millers want to wrap her up in cellophane to keep her safe."

Rob's gaze lingered on him for a moment, and then he went back to eating. "Yeah. I get it too."

"But she's ready for this. If she can conquer her fear, she'll see that she's got this. She might be timid, but inside she has the soul of a lion."

Rob nodded with a sad smile. "So she called you up like the Wizard of Oz so you could give her some courage?"

Matty sighed. "I know, hilarious right? Don't look at the man behind the curtain, Sabrina."

"I don't know, he's a very good looking man. He deserves to be seen."

Matty smirked. "Cute." Then he messed around with his salad a little more before saying, "Yesterday, when she left with her mom, Mrs. Miller seemed to feel guilty."

"They love you."

Matty used his fork to wave that off. "You think everyone loves me."

Rob laughed and almost choked on a leaf. "Uh, no. I'm really very aware of the fact that a lot of people don't love you. I think they're idiots, of course. Because you are incredibly lovable."

Matty wanted to ask if Rob meant that, really and truly, even after yesterday, but he didn't want to fight again, and if Rob had forgiven him, well, he didn't want to stir up hurt feelings.

"I didn't know what to say, but I told her that I understood how afraid she was. And I reminded her that she was strong and amazing, and that it was totally okay for her to shine on her own, and that she was ready for that." His throat tightened again, and he put down his fork. He couldn't put a bite in his mouth right now. "I might have cried some too after I hung up."

Rob scooted over and put his arm around Matty, tugging him into the place next to his body, where he fit so perfectly. "She's special to you."

"We're a good team. I just don't get why her parents don't see that. Sure, she could do well with Forenza, but she and I clicked in a way that almost never happens. It was—well, I guess it just was. Because it's done now."

"They see it, Matty. They know."

"I just wish I could have proven myself."

Rob ate in silence for a while, his right hand lifting the salad to his mouth while his left played in Matty's hair. The lowering sun came in the living room window, heating the back of their heads, and the sweet smell of Rob's skin was comforting. Familiar. *Home.*

"I'm going to do better," Matty offered quietly.

"Then eat for me, sweetheart."

Matty swallowed thickly and grabbed the water, taking a sip to try to get his throat working again.

It took a while, and Rob was done long enough before Matty that he turned on a movie. It helped actually, giving Matty something to think about other than the food going into his body, making his cells plump up, making him just a little bit fatter.

"Shh," Rob said, kissing his ear at one point. "Don't think. Just eat."

It worked, and the voice stayed blessedly quiet, only grumbling once, but Matty squashed it with a reminder of the humiliation of Saks. He had earned a salad, goddamn it.

Eventually, the movie ended and Rob gathered Matty in his strong, warm arms. It was a perfect moment—the city block was quiet, there was no noise from upstairs, it was just the two of them alone in their living room. Together.

Rob kissed Matty's neck. "I'm not going anywhere. Ever. I'm going to be here, Matty, no matter what. You know that, right?"

"Yes." Right now he did. Right now he was sure of it. He was safe and they were beautiful, and Matty wanted to strip naked and kneel at Rob's feet to worship him for giving him that feeling.

Rob slid his hands toward Matty's waist and slipped beneath his training leggings to grip his ass. "Did you shower at the gym?"

Matty shook his head.

"Good. Then we'll shower together."

"Yeah?" Matty's pulse leapt and his dick fattened up in a rush. "Then what?"

"*Then* I'm going to show you our bank account and we can play a little game called 'Review the Family Budget.' We've played it a few times before but I think you forgot the rules."

Matty groaned, following Rob to the bathroom. Hopefully he'd get an orgasm before the tear-inducing boredom of a lecture about their precarious finances set in. And if not?

Well, Control hissed, *it's not like you deserve one.*

***

ROB OBSERVED MATTY from behind as he stood with his palms against the slick shower tiles, his skin flushed from hot water and his ass tilted up, begging. The shower poured down on the back of Matty's head, flattening his dark hair and rushing in thick rivulets over his cheeks and running off the end of his nose.

"Breathe out of your mouth," Rob said, like it was an order and not what Matty was already naturally doing to keep from choking on the stream. Water sluiced down the wiry muscles and sharp bone of his back and shoulders, making a pretty picture.

"Keep your hands on the wall."

Matty nodded, inhaling so his ribs expanded and contracted, a little too visible beneath his muscle and skin. Rob's heart squeezed in his chest. It was time for a reset at the very least but he had to find a way to get some money together for therapy. He didn't know if he could ask his old friend Bill for a loan—didn't know if his pride could handle it—but maybe it was time. That is, if Matty would agree to see someone and get some kind of help.

"Rob?" Matty sounded uncertain, and that wouldn't do.

"Just admiring you, sweetheart."

The lube was behind the shampoo as always, and it didn't take any time to get his dick slick enough. "Ready now?"

A nod was all he needed.

Pulling Matty's ass back onto his cock was so good, hot, delicious, and consuming. Matty groaned and lifted his head, water pouring into his mouth until he ducked down again and spit it out. Matty's skills as a bottom were evident immediately as Rob slid home, and Matty worked his muscles and hole to make the push in easy and ever more pleasurable as Rob went deeper.

"Good, sweetheart?"

Matty trembled and nodded again, his small pleasure sounds echoing off the tiles.

Rob squeezed his eyes shut against the sting of the shower raining down on them and gripped Matty's hip, the water making every stroke of his palm over Matty's skin halting and full of rough friction. He moved into the water stream to lean over Matty's back and hook his chin over his shoulder, and then set up the rhythm he was seeking.

"Touch me," Matty grunted, shoving his ass back and meeting Rob's thrusts eagerly.

"No. Show me how you do it."

Matty whined and shifted so his feet spread slightly wider, his asshole working on Rob's shaft and his breath coming sharper. "It's too hard."

Wrapping his arms around Matty's chest, Rob kissed his wet shoulder, tasting the tang of the metal pipes in the water and the salt of Matty's sweat. "You're getting so good at it, sweetheart. I know you can."

Matty moaned and shook his head, rolling it against Rob's collarbone, and then Rob fucked him faster until his noises rang in the bathroom, louder and louder, and undoubtedly traveling through the duct work up into the rest of the building.

As Matty dug his fingers at the wall, trying and failing to find good leverage, Rob pretended they were still in Montana. It was just them and their love. No one else for miles. He sighed, finding the place he needed in his mind: open skies, wide plains, and so much room to breathe.

As Rob slowed, enjoying his fantasy, Matty whimpered and took over. He jerked back and threw his hips into the fuck, seeking his own pleasure as hard and fast as possible.

"Yes, so good. Work for it."

Matty did just that, and the wet, jerky friction of the fuck was becoming hard to resist. Rob concentrated on Matty's flesh quivering around him, on Matty's gasps and moans, and forced his mind away from his own pleasure. It was a trick he used all the time to give

Matty what he needed. To put Matty first.

"Rob, I need —"

"You've got what you need, sweetheart. It's right there. Come on. Be a greedy boy and show me how you take what I give you."

Matty's hole gripped, and he groaned, throwing his head back against Rob's collarbone again. "So close. So fucking close."

"That's right. Show me how you do it," Rob said, shifting his stance to add his hands on top of Matty's against the wall to prevent him from giving in to the temptation to use them.

"Fuck, fuck," Matty whispered wetly as water poured around his face, and he fought for his climax, trying to get the angle he needed.

Finally, Rob took over again, thrusting hard, aiming his cock so it would stroke Matty's prostate.

"There," Matty said frantically, his hand pulling against Rob's grip. "There! There!"

Rob drove into him again and again as Matty went rigid and receptive beneath him, his hole flexing open, welcoming and easy, and then it happened. His favorite thing in the world. Matty shouted, his body clenching tight and his hole gripping hard.

"Rob!"

"Now. Give it to me now."

Matty cried out as the rhythmic, pumping, shaking pleasure of release ripped through him. His knees went weak, and Rob released Matty's hands to grab him around the chest and reach down with his other hand to jerk Matty's spurting dick.

"Fuck," Matty grunted, his body squeezing around Rob's cock.

Rob didn't let go of Matty's dick, prolonging the pleasure until it became pain, and Matty squirmed against him in protest. Then Rob thrust in hard and held, his own orgasm pumping out of him as he kissed Matty's neck and wet hair.

The shower water choked him a little as it got into his nose and throat, but the sweet pleasure of coming made up for the discomfort. He rode it all the way to the end before pulling out. Rob moved them both out from under the water's relentless stream and into the cooler air by the wall. Matty's chest was flushed deep pink and his eyes glowed as he looked almost shyly up at Rob. "I did it," he whispered. "Like you wanted."

"Good boy," Rob answered, pulling him into an embrace and kissing the top of his head. "Good work. Thank you."

"Rob?"

"Yeah, sweetheart?"

"I love you. I'm sorry about everything."

"I know you are." Their problems rose up around them like the steam in the shower, and Rob held Matty tighter. "I love you too."

Rob reached for the shampoo, washing Matty's hair and his own. The suds slid down their bodies, cleaning away the day's grime and the residue of the prior night's sadness and anger.

"We're going to be okay, Matty. We're going to figure this out. Together."

"No matter what?"

Rob heard the real question: no matter how hard I push you, push myself, and push the world?

"No matter what."

CHAPTER NINE

THE NEXT DAY, Matty showered in the locker room while Elliot stood outside the pulled curtain rattling on about his date the following night with someone he called Mr. Sykes.

"Seriously, Matty, how can I look that stunning bitch in the face and call him Ulysses?"

"Because it's his name," Matty called back, rinsing his hair and soaping his pits a second time, glad they were alone in the locker room. Not that an audience would curb Elliot's conversation much. "How did you meet him again?" He'd had his head under the water for that part and missed it.

"He handles my grandfather's investments. You know the old fart has always insisted on coming to New York for his financial advice? Well, his regular guy died and Mr. Sykes took over."

"Didn't you say he's black?"

"Oh, hell yes. And sexy as a panther. Rowr. I want to climb him and ride him until I can't remember my own name."

"Grandpa Dubs didn't freak out that a black man is in charge of his money?"

Back when they were kids in North Carolina, Elliot's grandfather wasn't exactly known for being racially tolerant. He was, however, known for being filthy rich and intermittently generous, so the entire family tended to pretend to be deaf, dumb, and blind whenever Grandpa Dubs made an inappropriate comment. Everyone except Elliot, who'd lost his place in the will due to not keeping his mouth shut. Well, and for being gay.

It hadn't mattered much, since Elliot had a ridiculous trust fund he'd come into when he turned twenty-four from his father's side of the family.

"He was remarkably sanguine about it. I asked Mama later if he was mellowing with age and she said he'd met a nice colored woman—her word!" Matty could almost hear Elliot flap his hands as he exclaimed, "Oh my God, Matty, *my family!*" He cleared his throat. "Anyway, he met her at church and decided that maybe *some* black people are all right after all. You should've seen how he took Mr. Sykes' measure, though. I think if Grandpa Dubs had known that his new black advisor asked for my number on our way out, he'd probably have pulled his money immediately. It would've been one bridge too far in his bigoted mind."

"Wait, so has Grandpa Dubs also met a gay man at church? Or has he decided to forgive you for your flaming ass?"

"Hell no, bitch. Mama insisted I help him get around the city. He decided to allow it because I guess I'm still good enough to catch him before he falls on the sidewalk and breaks a hip."

"Your Mom just wants you to work your way back into the will."

"Nailed it in one, baby doll! She thinks if he just spends some time with my fabulous self, he'll decide I'm a true delight and worthy of a few million. I told her I don't need it with Grandpa Ellis' trust, and besides it's a lost cause, but holy shit, I think he *did* actually soften to me a little."

"Well, you can be very charming."

"When has Grandpa Dubs ever cared about charm? No, but he legit patted my knee during the meeting because I asked Mr. Sykes why we didn't invest more heavily in Bitcoin. He declared that I'd inherited his money smarts."

"Then he hasn't seen your credit card bills."

"Har har, bitch." Elliot sighed. "True, though. But forget Grandpa Dubs. He's so beside the point. The point is, I'm telling you, baby, Mr. Sykes—or Ulysses, whatever—is *so* smoking hot. Like call nine-one-one because I'm on *fire* from his fucking gorgeous face."

"What's my emergency? My best friend went up in flames of lust." Matty splashed some water over his chest and thighs, washing

95

away the last of the suds.

"For real. I'm shameless and absolutely gagging for it." Elliot made a gagging noise for emphasis. "And he better live up to my past experience with black men, babe. Because stereotypes, Matty? They exist for a reason. The last black dude I was with? Huge. Like I thought I was gonna be wrecked forever."

Matty snorted and turned off the water. "Pass me a towel."

Elliot's pale hand with long fingers and nails buffed to a high shine stuck through, dangling a white towel. "Mr. Sykes has a fantastic body too. Like he has *got* to be all CrossFit and shit, because he's jacked. But it is so far beyond that. He's brilliant and emotionally strong."

"How would you know that?"

"The burden of that name alone is enough to give a man admirable character." He sighed dreamily as Matty toweled himself dry. "I wonder if he's one of those amazing success stories. You know the ones—raised by a single teenaged mother, six siblings in prison, and he's the sole one to get out of the ghetto and succeed."

Matty slid the curtain back and stepped out. Elliot was staring up at the ceiling, his skin looking a little shiny from the humidity of the shower. His blond hair, and wispy long, tall frame—always all corners and sharp places—seemed to shimmer in the foggy air, and that, along with his wide nut-brown eyes, gave off the impression of an angel.

Matty loved Elliot so much. Sometimes he wanted to grab him, kiss his mouth—close-lipped of course, because they'd been crayon-sharing babies together, so ew—and scream to the world, *"This slice of angelic assholery is my best friend. Admire him and his beauty, all you ugly, dumb, unshiny people!"*

But, he never did that. Instead, he just put up with Elliot's bullshit without question and held him when Elliot was dumped, yet again, by some stupid, idiot jerk who didn't deserve him. Sometimes, when they'd been drinking champagne or cocktails, Matty told him he was crazy beautiful and that he'd always love him. Because sometimes Elliot really needed to know. And Elliot, always, *always* did the same for him. And that's why Elliot was family. And family always got the brutal truth.

"Elliot, you're being a huge racist dick. Maybe you inherited that from Grandpa Dubs too."

Elliot snorted but his face went even paler and his freckles stood out, a sure sign he was worried. "Oh my God, what if I did? What if I'm a massive racist asshole?"

Matty dried his hair with another towel. "This Mr. Sykes is just as likely to be from a wealthy family. Maybe he went to Harvard. Maybe he has a fabulously successful dad in the business. Maybe he's where he is today because of, I don't know, nepotism. Or, gasp, because he *earned* it."

"Really, Matty? *Just* as likely? Because our society is absolutely set up for making it equally likely for a black man to be a Wall Street mogul as a white man?"

"Shut up and listen. You have no idea what his life has been like, so just watch what you say okay? Because if you're not careful you're going to cock-block yourself." Matty tossed the damp towel into the laundry hamper by the showers and walked toward the lockers.

Elliot, following behind, sighed and rubbed his hands over his cheeks, massaging color back into them. "You're totally right. I'm going to blow this thing and never blow *him*. I'm awful. I'm literally an awful person. Fix me and make me amazing like you, Matty."

"Sorry, I'm an awful person too."

"True." Elliot's eyes narrowed on him. "Why? Have you done something especially awful lately?"

Matty sighed. "Where to start?"

"Mmm, how about you start right at the beginning?" Elliot leaned against the locker beside Matty's and watched him dial in the combination on the lock and jerk the door open.

Don't tell him about anything. Don't tell him what a piece of shit you are. He'll think you're crazy.

"I was an asshole to Rob yesterday."

"Rob is perfect and amazing. How dare you be mean to him?"

Matty shot a glare over his shoulder at Elliot. "Uh, hello, who's your best friend here?"

"You are."

"Then shouldn't you be on my side?"

Elliot crossed his arms over his chest and regarded Matty as though he was seriously considering this question. "I don't know; *should* I be on your side?"

"No. I was an asshole." Matty huffed, jerking his duffel from his locker and unzipping it to pull out his clean clothes. He sorted through the items inside, making sure his skates and everything else he'd worn or taken out during the day were safely tucked inside.

Worse than an asshole.

"Exactly. Besides, by reminding you of his perfection, I am on your side. See how that works?"

Matty groaned. In addition to his endless well of Sabrina angst, he'd been beating himself up all day by thoughts of his nasty comment about Ben's skating expenses. He wished he could go back in time and unspeak it. Ben wasn't his son, and they'd never have that kind of relationship, but Matty loved him fiercely. He'd give his very last dime to help Ben's dreams come true if that's what it took.

Why had he said it? It'd been like some evil part of him rose up and lashed out.

And all of it had started over what? The pleasure of *not eating* a sandwich?

Sick. Fucked up. Wrong.

Elliot's right. Rob deserves someone healthy, loving, and strong. Not a pathetic, incompetent loser.

"Well?" Elliot asked. "What exactly did you do? Spit it out, babe. Confession is good for the soul. Great-Aunt Harriet says so, anyway, and she's the oldest and happiest person I know, so I figure her advice is sound."

Matty sat on the bench and chewed on his lip.

Don't mention the food. Don't mention Saks. Don't tell him anything.

"Come on. You can trust me." Elliot clucked his teeth at him and sat next to him, running his smooth, cold hand over Matty's chest and shoulders. "Jesus, babe. You're too skinny. You're headed back into skating-skeleton territory."

A sick thrill went through Matty at the description, a profound pleasure so wrong it was right. He tried to chase it away by breathing in and out slowly.

"Let me guess, you guys fought because you're not eating?" Elliot said.

A wild relief screamed over and around him. He hadn't betrayed himself. Elliot had just known. He could talk about it now. It was okay. "It feels so good to be in control of something. When I don't eat, I feel stronger than when I do. Safer."

"But you know that's just your brain playing tricks on you."

Bullshit. You're safe when you do what I say.

Matty froze. His stomach flipped over.

"Matty? Did you hear me? It's just your mind fucking with you, telling you lies. I see it with the models I work with all the time. Their brain makes them think eating a carrot will somehow magically make them fat."

Cautiously, hoping Control wouldn't barge in and disagree with him, Matty said, "Not fat. It's not about fat. Eating makes me feel unsafe. And bad."

Elliot's eyebrows lowered. "Oh, babe."

"Nevermind. It's fine. I'm okay."

Elliot tilted his head, obviously not believing him.

"Don't worry, Elliot. I've got it under control. Honestly. Like you said, I just need to find a way to trick my brain back to the right way of thinking."

"Sure. That's easy enough." Elliot's eyes narrowed, the sarcasm biting into Matty's fragile fake confidence. "What's Rob say?"

"He's sort of obsessed with what I eat. He's worried. He wants me to get therapy."

"You should! Therapy's great! I love my therapist."

"Yes, the wise, ever-patient Jill. But even if I agreed that I need therapy, which I don't, there's a little difference between you and me, Elliot. It's called a trust fund."

Elliot wrinkled his nose, obviously considering the situation. "I could help?"

"No. I'm not taking your money. I'm fine. I've got it under control."

"Okay," Elliot said doubtfully. "But if it gets worse, I'm going to help you whether you like it or not. Just like I helped you with your beauty fund."

"Fine." It wasn't going to come to that anyway. Rob wouldn't let it. No, *Matty* wouldn't let it. "But the worst thing about it all is I lied to Rob. What kind of person lies about why they didn't take their *lunch*?" He ignored the warning to shut up that hissed in his mind. It was Elliot he was talking to, and he'd say whatever he wanted. Fuck Control. Nothing bad had ever come of telling Elliot the truth. Matty swallowed a sour taste in his mouth. "And some sick part of me still wishes I'd gotten away with it. That I'd won."

*That **I'd** won.*

"Oh, babe. Who lies about lunch? I know the answer to that one. Maybe a person with an eating disorder?"

"It's fucked up. I'm fucked up."

"The whole world is fucked up. You're just trying to get by in it, Matty. So maybe this coping mechanism sucks, but you have it in place for a reason. Believe me. I grew up with you. I know."

Matty looked at him from the corner of his eye. "Yeah?"

"Skating, the Feds, your mom. I get it. I know where this comes from."

"What do you mean by that? My mother is amazing."

"Of course she is. She supported you through everything. But don't you ever wonder what would have happened if she'd ever sat you down at, oh, age fifteen and seriously said, 'You can quit, Matty. It's okay to quit.' Instead of doing everything in her power to keep you skating?"

"She knew how badly I wanted to compete, Elliot. It's all on me, okay. Not her."

"Okay," Elliot lifted his hands in surrender. "I'm just sayin.' It's a lot of pressure to put on a teenager."

"She never pressured me."

"Sure, she just mortgaged the house and emptied their retirement accounts for your dream. No pressure at all."

Matty bit down on the bitchy reply on the tip of his tongue. Aside from when they both agreed that his retirement from competitive skating was a good idea, he and Elliot hadn't seen his skating career through the same lens in a really long time. "You and Jill can talk all you want about my dysfunctional childhood at your next three hundred dollar therapy appointment, all right? But right now, I need help. Tell me, what do I do, Elliot? I *need* Rob to trust me. I *need it*. It's one of the most important things in my life."

"I know."

"So explain to me why I'd risk that over a tuna fish sandwich? I mean, Jesus, what if he *stops* trusting me? For good?" Matty's heart beat wildly against his ribs until he was dizzy and nauseous. "What if he leaves?"

Elliot scooted closer on the bench, bending so his blond hair brushed Matty's cheek. He took hold of Matty's chin and forced him to look into his big, brown eyes, so familiar and usually soothing.

"Have you met Rob Lovely?" Elliot let go of Matty's chin and started gesturing with his words, his hands skimming through the air. "Tall, blond, green-eyed, insanely, crazy, smitten-as-a-kitten, wildly, savagely, passionately in love with you? And has been for, oh, about five years now." He smirked and added, "He even waited while you and the U.S. Figure Skating Federation played out the end of your seedy, disastrous love affair."

Matty nodded, staring at Elliot's mouth, seeing his lips move and hearing the words, but not feeling them in his soul the way he needed, not the way he would if he could just go home to Rob right now, if he could crawl onto their bed while Rob wielded a paddle to take him some place harder than hunger. Then he'd probably be all right.

Matty was quiet for a moment to see if Control had anything to say, but there was nothing, just an absence Matty was grateful for.

"Five years," Matty murmured. "Our third real anniversary is coming up. He's taking me somewhere special on a weekend trip."

"Third real anniversary?"

He pulled on his underwear and stood to adjust himself, explaining the anniversary situation to Elliot. "We don't count Montana for anniversaries. It's too complicated."

"Right, but you're going away in July. You got together again in August."

Matty still felt a little swoony when he remembered that day. The anticipation of waiting for Rob outside the physical therapy center, the anxious ride with him to Park Slope, seeing his—now their—apartment for the first time, and not knowing until he was underneath Rob giving it all up for him, that yes, everything had paid off and he'd finally earned his happy ending.

Or whatever it was called when a person lived a stable, regular life without the devastating highs and lows of competition. That's how it had been before Sabrina's career had taken off. Coaching, as it turned out, was as emotionally demanding as skating but without any control over the outcome. He usually felt as nauseous before Sabrina's skates as he had before his own. That's why he'd stopped eating as much, and by embracing his friend hunger again, he'd left the door cracked for Control to come waltzing in.

Matty tried to shake off the anxiety that settled over him when he thought about Sabrina. He pulled his Rag & Bone sleeveless black silk shirt over his head. He wasn't going to give in to Control today. He was going to enjoy his time with Elliot, get a facial, and eat a nice dinner, no matter what the voice had to say about that. Then he'd go home to Rob, where he'd be safe to crawl into his arms and be held as long as he needed.

He'd earned Rob a long time ago, and he wasn't going to let Control convince him otherwise.

"Earth to Matty?"

"Um, yeah? I mean, yeah, so based on how we count it it's been three years."

"But you got back together in August." Elliot repeated, standing up to ruffle Matty's wet hair.

Matty smoothed his hands over it to prevent it drying funny.

"Yes, but think about it. August is a terrible time for me between the possibility of late summer shows and gearing up for Valentina's students' next competitive season."

Matty put on loose, silk wide-legged capri pants, feeling stronger and better just talking to Elliot. He needed to remember this: talking was good; talking helped.

"So I decided choosing a day in July to mark as our anniversary made the most sense. Rob went along with it, of course."

"Anything that makes it easier to celebrate makes sense to me, babe."

"Also, the sound of July sixteenth as an anniversary just sounds nice, doesn't it?"

"Totally. If I ever have an anniversary, that's the date I'd want." Elliot nodded and bumped Matty's shoulder. "It's perfect."

Matty smiled, a warm glow in his chest. So maybe Sabrina was gone. He still had Rob, didn't he? He didn't need anything else: not money, not food, not punishment. Just Rob. It would be okay.

"What are you getting him?"

The glow died.

"Shit."

"You haven't even thought about it, have you?"

Matty grabbed his makeup bag and headed over to the sinks. Rubbing in moisturizer, he fought the rising tide of darkness inside him, the one that wanted to swallow him up in hateful thoughts again. He smoothed his eyebrows and applied the Etude House BB Cream to even out his skin tone. "Rob's got something special planned, some sort of weekend trip, so whatever I get him needs to be kind of great. Something equally thoughtful."

"Well, you're getting a late start for that." Elliot leaned against the sink next to him, examining his own skin. He grabbed Matty's powder brush from his bag and ran it over his cheeks. "A weekend away sounds expensive. I thought money was super tight. He made you return those very reasonably priced Alexander McQueen heels you bought with me last month, right?"

Matty sighed. Those truly had been stunning shoes, and at four hundred dollars, they'd been nearly half off. "Yes, those shoes went back." Matty powdered his nose and chin and grabbed the brown eyeliner to give his eyes a little drama. "But he didn't make me. I have plenty of sexy shoes."

"You can't have too many sexy shoes, Matty. It's an impossibility."

"My life isn't like yours, Elliot. I don't go to clubs and fashionista parties every weekend, or any weekend, really. I don't have anywhere to *wear* shoes like that."

Matty did wear heels in the apartment, though, walking around in nothing but a jockstrap, his skater's ass lifted and on display. It usually only took a few turns around the place before Rob had him bent over the sofa, or the table, or the bed.

"Anyway, Rob told me he'd found a good deal for our trip, whatever that means." Matty grabbed Elliot's wrist. "Oh, my God, what if that translates from Rob-speak into 'we're staying at La Quinta Inn'?"

"Ridiculous, Rob's too perfect for a mistake like that. Besides, has the man ever taken you to a La Quinta Inn?" Elliot paused and thought it over. "Still, bring flip-flops for the shower just in case, babe." He brushed his hair back and grabbed Matty's lip gloss from the makeup bag. He opened it, sniffed it for scent, and applied some, smacking his lips. "So, what are you going to get him?"

Matty rubbed a hand over his face, and then smoothed his eyebrows where his fingers had ruffled them. "I don't know. Money's so tight. I haven't given it any thought. I've been so self-absorbed with Sabrina and Worlds and the fucking Feds and fighting with Valentina and…" His heart beat harder and a fine sweat broke out on his forehead. He closed his eyes, taking deep breaths. *Shhh. Leave me alone.*

"Welp. I guess we say screw the facials and go shopping instead?"

Matty rolled his eyes. "Money, Elliot?"

"It's not for you, though. It's for him. That's different, right?" Elliot nodded his head at Matty, urging him to agree.

True, but that didn't make money show up in Matty's bank account. He'd just have to be frugal. He'd find something. Surely. "All right. Let's do it."

Elliot's smile showed off his sharp eye teeth. "Perfect! I wanted to pick up something for my date tomorrow night anyway, and I know just the place for us to both get something for our respective special occasions." Elliot consulted his watch. "Chop, chop now, skinny bitch! There's very important shopping to do!"

Matty hugged Elliot close, kissing his forehead. "You're a dick and I love you."

"Matty, promise me you'll take care of yourself. You're my babe, right? What would I do if something happened to you?"

"Nothing's going to happen to me."

"I've seen it before, you know. There was a model Guyton photographed last year, and she died."

"I'm not going to die, Elliot. I'm not that sick." Matty gathered his stuff, shifting some of his priority self-care items from his training duffel to a kelly green Coach bag.

The door banged open, and some hockey players shoved by. One muttered something nasty under his breath.

"Well, I swan," Elliot hissed. "How many years have we heard shit like that from those clumsy clodhoppers?"

"Too many."

Elliot leaned against the lockers next to him and stared off into space, like he was looking through time. "Remember when we were kids and it was just you and me?"

Elliot always sounded dreamy when he reminisced about their years skating and being tormented together in North Carolina. Matty remembered it more as hell, but Elliot had given up completely on his failure of a figure skating career long before Matty had, and to him it was the good old days. "We always had each other's back."

"Always."

Elliot gazed at him softly. "Don't worry, Matty. I'll always have your back forever and ever. No matter what you do or how badly you mess up."

Matty laughed. "Thanks for your confidence in me."

"I do have confidence in you, you know. A lot of it. And I love you. So much."

"How much?"

Elliot batted his eyes and smirked. "Too much."

"Ugh. Don't make me cry, bitch."

"No time for tears and drama." Elliot held the door to the locker room for Matty as they headed out. "We have an anniversary present to find!"

CHAPTER TEN

SUNSHINE FILTERED THROUGH the leafy tree over the park bench where Rob polished off the last of his ham sandwich. Normally, he would have eaten with Susan or Arjun in the courtyard at the back of the Queen's Clinic. The receptionist was a garden enthusiast, and she'd taken it upon herself to make sure the small yard was blooming with roses, a variety of wildflowers, and delicious smelling mint plants. It was a pretty relaxing place to shoot the shit with his coworkers, but today he'd begged off for the public-privacy of the park.

Rob still felt shaky from the fights with Matty. He couldn't remember the last time he'd been so pissed off, and his hand still ached where he'd punched the fence. It'd been a constant reminder during massage the last few days as every flex of his hand sent a dull protest through his knuckles and tendons.

A hot summer wind, gritty with city grime, raced over his skin, and he yearned for the crisp, clean air of Montana. He'd done the right thing coming to New York City. He knew that. He was close to Ben, and he had Matty. It was just so loud and grating sometimes. Anonymous and busy, and too fucking hot in the summer. Montana was never this hot, even when the temperature was the same. He remembered when he'd been a kid, following his dad around on the ranch, playing with Anja in the fields, swimming in the lake, clambering up on his first horse, Lettie, and running with the numerous ranch dogs. He'd always had one that was special; one that was his pet and not just a work animal.

He missed Lila. She'd died not long after Matty had left him in

Montana in order to pursue his Olympic dream. It'd been a double whammy of grief.

Matty had mentioned getting a dog once when he'd seen Rob lingering over the picture of Lila in the hallway. But Rob had quickly put the kibosh on that. Sure, there were plenty of dogs in New York City. He saw them all the time, and it did stir a longing inside him for the sweetness of an animal to give and receive love so completely unconditionally, but the idea of cooping such a precious soul up in a Brooklyn-sized apartment was more than he could stand. No amount of walking or running with it on a leash would make Rob believe it was anything other than a horrible compromise to the full-tilt, unrestrained dash across horizon-wide fields all his other dogs had always enjoyed.

That he'd always enjoyed.

Even when he hadn't known what he wanted in life, he'd loved the land. He didn't love the city. Not the way Matty did.

Rob scrolled through his short list of Favorites on his phone—Matty, Ben, Anja, Donna, Arjun—and chose Bill's number. His oldest friend would be at his bar already, probably scrubbing the place within an inch, as always.

Two rings was all it took before Rob was smiling again.

"Well, if it isn't my asshole friend who abandoned me for the big city."

"I miss you too."

"Long time, no hear, though."

"You could have picked up the phone."

"Nah. I don't do that shit. Emotions. Reaching out. Expressing feelings or whatever. I leave that crap to Angus."

"I'm sure he beats some of those things out of you."

"Yeah. He's pretty good at that, I reckon." Bill's gritty voice was soft, sandpaper instead of gravel, when he talked about his husband. "He's all right. I got no complaints. Speaking of dudes we like, how's yours?"

"Matty's..." Rob trailed off, not sure what to say about Matty right now. "He's all right. I mean, everything's fine. I guess." He sighed. "I called for some advice, actually."

"Yeah? Hit me. I'm damn good with advice."

"It's Matty." Rob wished he was sitting across from Bill at his bar, the familiar Lysol-clean scent of the place wrapping him in memories and warmth. A car honked down the street, and Rob glared at it.

"What about him?"

"He's slipping back into old habits. Disordered eating. Acting out. I thought he could control it if he quit skating, but it's not like that."

"Nope. It's not."

"And the reset button doesn't work as well anymore."

"Reset button?"

"Yeah. Hard scenes. He pushes for them a lot more often now. We used to do one or two hard scenes a year. Now it's every month or so, which I don't mind so much..." Though they exhausted him emotionally and physically. "Especially when he asks for them with words, but lately he pushes with actions."

"Sounds like our princess."

"No. It's not like that. It's not cheeky or charming or cute. It's awful."

"Buddy, I don't know what to say."

"I know. It's hard. Because he wants — or maybe he needs, I don't know..." Rob sighed again, rubbing his forehead with his hand. "I think he wants whips. Hard whips."

Bill harrumphed, and Rob could hear the clanking of glasses in the background. "What's he want to be whipped for?"

"Coaching stuff. Everyone says he's not good enough to coach his star pupil, and he believes them. I think he wants a physical punishment for it.

"So give it to him. Whip the shit out of him and make it real damn clear just how good he is at taking it."

Rob squirmed on the bench, trying to find the words to explain why that wasn't the solution this time. "He wants me to hurt him more than I want to hurt him. It has to be really hard, man. Not our usual play. Not the way I enjoy it."

"Can you handle it, though? Can you go there for him?"

"Sure. A few times a year. But when it's not for my pleasure, or his pleasure, but it's mindfucks and control and pain that hurts me almost as much as it hurts him? I don't know. It may hurt me more, because I'm not a fucking masochist. And I'm not the world's best sadist, either."

"Well, speaking as the world's best painslut, I empathize with the kid. Sometimes you just need someone to beat the shit out of you so the world looks right."

Rob snorted, and he was pissed to feel frustration stinging his eyes. He wasn't going to cry over this. He could handle whatever Matty sent his way. He had to. No matter what. Just like he'd promised.

"All right," Bill said, his voice warm and concerned in his ear. "So he's in a bad place. Is there self-harm going on? Cutting or whatever the kids are into these days?"

"No. Just disordered eating. He's lost weight, but it's not a scary amount yet. He blew a huge wad of cash on new clothes, but he returned them. I think the overspending was a one-time deal. For the most part. I mean, he goes over budget a lot, but this was something else. And he's not a kid. He's a grown man, Bill."

"Okay, what fixed the self-harm last time?"

"It wasn't fixed. It just took a backseat for a while, but now it wants to drive again."

"Well, remind it just who drives Matty's car. Remind it good and hard. Make sure it doesn't forget."

Rob snorted. If only it was that easy. He'd tried that already. He was *tired*. He just needed someone to help him get his strength back. He needed Bill to say the right thing. "I think whatever is inside him, whatever it is that's eating away at him is stronger than me."

"Hell no it isn't. And don't ever let Matty hear you say that."

Rob shuddered as another hot wind brushed over him. The words *I'm scared* were on his tongue, but he swallowed them down.

Bill snorted. "Messy little shit, isn't he?"

Rob loved that mess, but he sometimes felt like Matty's mind worked to make his neuroses more and more complex, leveling up when one problem was defeated. Neither of them spoke, and Rob knew Bill was leaning against his bar thinking. If they were together, they'd both drink in silence for a while. Instead, Rob listened to the constant roar-honk-clatter of traffic and the shrieks of children on the playground.

Finally Rob spoke again. "Even if I can reach down deep and give him what he wants as often as he needs it, he's got public showers and locker rooms to consider."

"More control, less bruising?"

"Right."

"I'm into pain, so I don't know if I've got advice there."

Rob paused, watching pigeons fight over a half-eaten sandwich at the edge of the small park. Angus had been good for Bill. There'd been a time when Bill would hit on straight men just to get the fist he craved. Angus at least kept it all safe and sane.

Maybe that's what Matty was doing—trying to get his version of a fist from somewhere else because he couldn't count on Rob to give it to him as often as he needed it. His chest ached, and he felt the damn sting in his eyes again. Fuck, he needed to find a way to dig deep and give more. He had to be what Matty needed from him. He could be the fist. He could do it because he loved Matty so much. More than anything in the world.

"Okay, buddy, should I just sit here and listen to all those damn city sounds come over the line while you think it out?"

Rob laughed. "I was just thinking that Matty's a pro at self-sabotage."

"Damn straight. He's a big fan of ruining shit for himself."

"He hates getting something he doesn't feel like he's truly earned. But the issue is—he almost never feels like he's earned much of anything."

Bill didn't reply. Rob closed his eyes. He could shut out the city and pretend to be there with Bill, and he'd look into his brown eyes and remember that he was going to be okay. He'd leave feeling like himself and go home strong for Matty again.

"Yep," Bill said in his usual way of getting the verbal ball rolling when it had stalled.

Rob kept on the same thread. "Here's the thing, though, when I control his reward, and I decide if he gets it and when, then I can deal with the aftermath. I can hold him while he falls apart, and take him up again, and reward him for breaking. And, God, he breaks so hard. It's beautiful."

"You're making me a little jealous."

"Angus has you well in hand, I'm sure."

"Who says I don't have him licking *my* boots, huh?"

Rob rolled his eyes. "I'm sure you do." He went back to the topic that was consuming him. "But I can't control his whole life. I don't have the energy for it. Not with everything else on my plate."

Not with his job, his responsibilities to Ben's skating and being a father. Not when he wasn't sure if the goat investment was going to pay off. Not when they were broke, and he felt so damn closed in, and he couldn't find a breath of fresh air anywhere.

"Well, if you think there's a kink that will make the kid not a fucking self-sabotaging anorexic, then you've probably got another think coming."

Rob sat in silence. That was absurd, wasn't it? It was utterly and horribly absurd. "I know. No, what I really want is a way to just get there before he does. So he doesn't overspend or refuse to eat or attempt to control or self-sabotage, because he's safe and under my command already."

"All right. Hell, go all twenty-four-seven on his ass and really put him under your command."

"No. Denial and pain play on occasion is one thing, but twenty-four-sevening is another. Not my cuppa. Not even my tea store."

He could barely handle the stress of Matty's demands now. If he went to twenty-four-sevening, he'd break too, and then where would they be?

"Fine, fine, you're a coffee kind of guy. Plain and strong. I appreciate that myself. I don't know what to tell you. If you don't twenty-four-seven then how can he always be under your command when he starts on whatever his little brain gets up to?"

"That's just it. I don't know."

Bill sighed. "So, just deny him. I don't know if it'll be denying him the pain play, or refusing him a fucking trip to the beach, but deny that little bastard *something* until he can't figure out which way is up, and then deny him harder and again. If he's addicted to being denied, then *you* be in control of what he doesn't get access to—your cock, your mouth. I don't know what he likes best, but take it away from him. Even then, you're gonna have an anorexic on your hands. That shit doesn't just go away."

"I know." He did know. It was just that when Matty was challenged, truly challenged, at something he actually had a fighting chance to win at, he did so much better. But apparently pain play didn't do enough to dispel the stress of Sabrina's potential defection, the Federation's bullshit manipulations, and the ego-undermining difficulties of not being the best at anything in particular in New York City. "I'm pretty sure anorexia is kind of like an ax murderer. No matter what, she'll find a way to break down your door eventually if she's after you."

"Jesus, Rob, write a horror movie, why don't you? And get the kid some therapy."

"Therapy costs, and money is one thing we haven't got. My salary pays our main bills. Matty's mostly goes to Ben's skating and living expenses like food. My investment in the goats with Bing should bring in extra before long, but I'm not sure when. I told Bing I'd leave all of the business decisions up to him."

"Speaking of Bing, he's convinced me that investing in the goats is a good idea. Who knew there were all kinds of goat-eating holidays in the fall? If it all goes like Bing says, we should all bring in a pretty nice bundle in a year or so. So thanks for suggesting I talk to him about it."

"I'm glad. I hope he's right. Matty and I could use a break financially."

"Need me to help out in the short term?"

"No. Thanks, but no."

113

"So, we talked about Matty. What about you? You still missing home?"

Rob sighed, leaned back and looked up at the shifting leaves of the big-by-New-York-standards tree above him, and closed his eyes. It was relatively quiet where he sat, but it was still a din of constant noise compared to the miles of silence in Montana.

Sometimes he wished he'd never confessed his homesickness to Bill one night when Matty was out with Elliot, and he'd been sitting on the front stoop with a sixth beer, sick and tired of the hubbub of the city. He'd moved to New York to be near Ben and Anja. It'd been his secret hope to run into Matty there. Then, in what had felt like a Matty-designed miracle, he had, and Matty loved the city. In fact, earlier that week was the first time Matty had ever said anything about New York that wasn't pure ecstatic, unconditional love.

"Yeah, I miss the sky," Rob said. "The stars at night. Hell, I miss the mooing of the damn cows and the fucking rooster waking me up every morning. But Matty loves it here."

"Matty loves *you*. He'd go wherever you went. You know that."

Rob didn't know that actually. He liked to think it was true, but Matty was very ambitious. Whitefish, Montana would never give Matty the widespread recognition he craved. But, Rob had to admit, neither would New York City. It was a quandary.

"I want him to be happy. The city makes him happy." Rob rubbed his thumb over his eyebrow and watched as a woman with a toddler walked by, both with dripping ice cream cones.

"Does it really now?"

"I don't know. Who the hell knows? We're just in a tough place. We'll get out of it."

"Good luck, buddy. I wish I had something better to offer. If you need some money, the bar is doing okay and I could—"

"No. Like I said, we'll make it."

"Just promise me you'll come on home if things get too bad over there. I worry about you and the kid."

"I know you do."

After that, Rob talked to Bill about the bar and asked after Angus before he disconnected the call. He didn't know what he'd been hoping for. Some kind of comfort. Some kind of home.

Instead he wanted to close his eyes, sprout wings, and fly up out of the city until he couldn't see a single bit of it anymore and the land below was green, green, and more green. Matty had mentioned going back to Montana. Why had he steered him away from the idea so quickly? In the face of everything he'd learned in the last twenty-four hours, it seemed like getting Matty somewhere quiet and relatively peaceful—where he could truly shine—was the best idea either of them had ever had.

Immediately a text from Matty popped through. It was a photo of him and Elliot posing outside Big Gay Ice Cream, each with a giant triple-stacked cone. Someone else had taken the shot because they were posed together in their usual over-the-top way. A wide-eyed Matty held his open mouth over the top of the stack in simulated fellatio. Elliot, for his part, was holding his cone near Matty's skater's ass like he was going to ram it in.

Another text popped through: *I ate all of this ice cream bc I love you. And, fuck me, it tasted ammmmazing.*

Rob almost laughed, but his chest ached too much for it to escape. He enlarged the photo to get a better look at Matty's eyes. They were tired and, despite the faked enthusiasm, worry lurked in them.

He texted back: *Good for you. Have a decent meal with Elliot later and we'll call it square.*

Aye, aye, Cap'n. We good?

We're always good. Love you. <3

<3

Heart-sore, he pocketed his cell phone.

Something had to be done. But where would they get the money? And would Matty even consider a therapist? He should have had one ages ago. A sports psychologist might have changed the course of Matty's life entirely, but his parents had never been able to afford one.

But if Matty would concede to go, then it might be worth a few sessions. Even if it meant Rob couldn't contribute his fair share to

Ben's skating anymore. Matty's health had to come first. He'd have to do some research into his insurance situation, but it would be better to get help now before things spiraled more out of control.

Rob scrubbed a hand over his face, tired and edgy as the sounds of cars, trucks, children's laughter, and jackhammers bombarded him on his walk back to the clinic. He just wished there was an easy way to get and keep Matty's attention, some kind of a constant reminder of what was important: their life together, and their happiness.

They'd need to find a BDSM-friendly therapist too, or risk problems there. They weren't part of the larger scene, but the way they played together could easily be misunderstood by the wrong doctor. They couldn't see Sato. Matty's edginess about the scene would undermine that relationship, but maybe Sato would have a recommendation.

Just before he went back inside to meet his next patient, he pulled Sato's card out of his wallet and sent him a text.

Hi. This is Rob Lovely. Can we meet for coffee?

CHAPTER ELEVEN

"THIS PLACE ONLY has three and a half stars on Yelp," Matty said, poking at his phone as he followed Elliot across West 4th Street and turned right on their way toward Slap & Tickle. His mind felt clear and bright. The confession had done him good just as Great-Aunt Harriet had claimed it would. "I'm not sure this is really what I had in mind for an anniversary present, anyway."

"Reviews of sex shops can't be taken seriously, Matty," Elliot said. "They're basically performance art. Or comedic literature. Or something like that."

"This one *is* pretty hilarious. The customer's totally queening out about how the staff was rude. Apparently, they told her she wasn't taking her sex toy purchase seriously enough."

"Drama, drama," Elliot drawled, pushing through the barred glass doors. Matty followed him inside.

"Sex toys *are* serious business, Elliot." At least Matty's sex toys often were. They sometimes had quite the bite and left some impressive marks. "This other reviewer says that despite it looking like a shop for hookers, the staff is quite knowledgeable."

"Does this person think hookers don't need good information, too? Everyone has a right to information."

When it came to sex shops, Matty preferred a more refined place, like Shag in Williamsburg with all their chichi, vintage-inspired sex toys and lingerie. He only wished they carried ruffled panties to fit his skater's ass, but alas, they didn't the last time he'd checked. Regardless, Shag was absolutely a top-notch store, and Matty never felt gross going into it.

Elliot preferred the trashier sex stores of the West Village, like Pink Pussycat Boutique and this dive, which, Matty had to admit, did have a wonderful red-light district kind of charm to it.

"This place feels so…"

"Skank. I love it."

Matty ran his fingers over the cheap, hooker-looking lingerie dolling up the mannequins in the entryway. "Yeah."

A young salesgirl with a fresh face that looked far too innocent to be peddling the goods held deep within the bowels of the store approached. "Can I help you?"

"Yes, we want—" Elliot began.

"No, we're just looking."

She glanced between them and said, "Great! Are you looking for anything in particular? I'm happy to help you find it and answer any questions."

Elliot smiled and slipped an arm through Matty's. "I have a very important, hopefully very *big* date tomorrow night, and I need something to set the proper mood, if you know what I mean?"

Matty had no clue what Elliot thought they would find in this store to set the mood for a first date with his grandfather's investment advisor.

"As for our prima donna here, his anniversary is coming up and he wants to find something to please his boyfriend on their sexy weekend getaway."

"Oh, that sounds fun." She grinned and popped bubblegum. "I'm Clem, by the way."

"His boyfriend is a former rancher, so maybe something in that vein?" Elliot said, winking.

"Well, we've got some sexy cowboy and cowgirl outfits upstairs that might float his boat."

"You know, I think I just want to browse," Matty said, giving her his media smile. "I'm pretty sure it's an 'I'll know it when I see it' kind of thing, if you know what I mean."

"Sure, hon. What about you?" She turned her attention back to Elliot. "Is there anything specific I can help you find for your date?"

118

"I want a vibrating butt plug with a remote control," Elliot said. "But don't worry, darling, I know where to find them. Way in the back with all the other butt plugs, right?"

"Right," Clem agreed, smiling. "Okay, I'll let you browse. If it turns out you do need me, I'll be around. Just holler. Oh, that's Jaylyn behind the counter. She's great too, and always happy to help." Clem wandered away, straightening boxes of pocket pussies and red-lipped super suckers as she went.

"Why do you need a new one?" Matty asked. He picked a box from the shelf in front of him. It featured a naked lady and declared the contents as "My First Virgin Pussy and Ass Masturbator."

The lips of the fake vagina were disturbingly pink, and the asshole completely uncolored. He studied the fake clitoris. It was bigger than he imagined based on how many straight guys, including a very drunk Joey one night early on in his college career, had expressed difficulty finding it. Vaginas, even fake ones, *especially* fake ones, struck Matty as very weird. Not awful, just strange. He wondered what a real vagina would feel like and if he'd be willing to fuck Rob if he somehow magically and inexplicably grew one. He loved Rob a lot, and it might be interesting to try. But it was unlikely given they weren't living in fanfiction.

Elliot grabbed the box out of his hand, made a face, and put it back on the shelf. "Whatever you're thinking, just stop. As for my vibrating plug, the motor ran down. Completely ruined my last date, actually. I gave him the remote and nothing happened all night. I got super pissy and was a total cunt to him." Elliot rolled his eyes. "I thought I must have misjudged his Grindr profile, because clearly I'd inadvertently ended up on a date with a prudish, boring dickwad who was too chicken to turn the thing on. So there I was with a plug up my butt all night and just *nothing*. Nothing at all. Not even a quick on and then off again. So, like I said, I was a total bitch to him, and after he paid the check we went our separate ways. On the subway home, I flipped the switch thinking I'd at least pleasure myself if he was too uptight to do it, and I realized the fucking thing didn't work."

Matty laughed. "Only you."

"It was horrifying. Thank fuck New York City is vast in its way, and I'll never see the guy again. So embarrassing. Anyway, new batteries didn't fix it, so it's time for a new one. There's nothing quite like offering a guy the remote control to your plugged butt to say 'I expect you to plow my ass immediately following this pretense of a dinner.' You can tell a lot about what they'll be like in bed based on how they react to that gift."

Rob enjoyed that game too, though it wasn't usually Matty's idea, and dinner was never a pretense, but rather a requirement. If Matty didn't eat enough, the remote didn't get turned on and sex was not going to happen later either. Maybe it was part of the sickness, but he felt taken care of in a deep way whenever Rob set up and enforced eating rules. Even before Control made a home in his head, it was challenging sometimes, especially when it came to getting over his strong aversion to eating in public. But there was something so rewarding in the way Rob watched him put food in his mouth and swallow it. The vibrating plug game was just a bonus. One that Matty enjoyed but never suggested himself.

Matty didn't share all of that, though. "I live vicariously through you, you know. Never change."

"Well, one day I'm going to change. One day I'll find a guy who's worthy of holding on to my remote control forever, and when I do, I won't ever let him go." Elliot winked at Matty, whispering in his ear, "And I won't forget to get something for our haphazardly made-up anniversary either."

Matty rolled his eyes and turned his attention to the front-and-center dildo display. He contemplated the horse-sized one, wondering if his hole would ever return to normal after taking something like that. Then he decided he didn't want to ever, ever know.

Next to him, Elliot gasped and clutched his heart. "Oh my God, this is perfect. Tell me this isn't perfect!" He grabbed a box from the shelf he'd been perusing and shoved it at Matty. "Rob will love it."

"'Bessie the blow-up cow, for the ride 'em cowboy in you,'" Matty read aloud. "Classy."

"I bet Rob misses his cows. Didn't you say he had a special one, Matty? One he loved best?" Elliot stuck his tongue out playfully.

Matty laughed and threw the box back at Elliot. "Here, you've got..." Matty licked his thumb and went at Elliot's face like a mother hen, wiping a smudge of Elliot's mascara away. "There."

"Girl, you did *not* just put your spit on my face!"

"I did. And you suggested a blow-up cow fuck toy for my amazing, awesome boyfriend. For our *anniversary*, so I think we're even."

"Whore."

"You make fucking around sound so fun sometimes that I wish I *was* a whore. Why can't I be a whore, Elliot?" Matty sighed longingly, picking up a package of thick, purple anal beads to read the description on the back. *These classic beads are an essential sex toy.* He grinned at Elliot, his growing heart light as they played their usual verbal games.

"Because you're all uptight about who touches your body and who gets to put things in your mouth and ass. And you're monogamous. And loyal. And all those things I'm not and can only dream of being." Elliot pushed his way deeper into the small store.

Matty put the anal beads back and followed. When he caught up, Elliot had reached yet another shelf of dildos. Matty gasped at the size of the unpackaged, massive big black cock on display. That? Now, that, he might possibly be willing to try.

Elliot noted his interest and hefted up the big cock, shifting it from hand to hand. "Wouldn't really be for him, though, would it?" and put it back on the shelf. As he moved on, Matty followed him again.

"Look at this, babe."

Elliot held out a lacy, black nightie from a small rack of clothes, and Matty took it from his hands, turning toward one of the mirrors in the shop. His dark hair had grown a bit, and was wavier than usual in the city's humid summer heat. His clear, brown eyes popped with the black of the nightie against his pale skin, making his lashes seem darker too, like he'd put on mascara.

"Three years you've been Park Sloping it with him, so that makes it five years I've been living in the West Village? All this time with Zarah as a roommate has been maddening, but I suppose the location can't be beat, and I'd rather live here than end up in your world of babies and bicycles."

"Don't mock my neighborhood. It's heaven on earth." Matty held the nightie against his body and turned to the side, admiring himself.

"It's not the Village."

"Nowhere is the Village." Matty handed the nightie back to Elliot.

"What? Why not? He'd cream for that."

"Not really. Rob sometimes likes me in heels and frilly things, but it all just comes off in the end. I want something unique. Special. Perfect. Something super-amazing fantastic. Something that screams the two of us together. Something not found in this shop."

Elliot pursed his lips to think. "What did you give him last year?"

"Those amazing ODEMA driving moccasins with the to-die-for turquoise laces."

"Oh, yes, those are nice."

"And an hour-long massage that I gave him myself before giving him, well, myself."

"That sounds cheap. What did he give you?"

"A night at the Casablanca. He got it for almost-free because one of his patients is a manager there. Surely I described it to you in detail afterward? There were orgasms. Lots and lots and lots of them. Okay, three, but that's a lot for someone who needs his beauty sleep. How do you not remember that?"

"How do you not remember that I was in Milan this time last year? Doing that shoot with Guyton? I was out of touch the whole month."

Matty rolled his eyes. Guyton Romero was an award-winning fashion photographer and Elliot's boss, *and*, as far as Matty was concerned, an insufferable, conceited, arrogant, self-absorbed, and too-successful dick. "I don't get why you have to drop off the face of the earth when you travel with him."

Elliot rolled his eyes right back. "Who cares? I'm here now and not traveling any time soon."

"You missed out on hearing about a very important event in my life, so I care."

Elliot ran his fingers over Matty's forehead, smoothing back his hair. "You don't have to be jealous of Guyton."

"I'm not."

"I'm not saying you are."

Matty narrowed his eyes at him.

"I'm just saying I'll always love you best. Now back to the Casablanca and dirty-hot orgasms all night." Elliot grinned. "Bitch, if I didn't love you, I'd be jealous of you and what you've got with Rob. But I have to say, your gift of moccasins and a massage sort of pale next to his night at a theme hotel."

"I know. I think I might be awful at presents, Elliot. Imagine that, me being a complete failure at yet another thing in my life."

"Drama queen." They rounded into an area of the shop featuring adult DVDs, and Elliot gasped again. "I've got an idea."

"I'm not making some crass porn vid for him for our anniversary, if that's what you're thinking." Matty cocked his head at a DVD cover featuring a Buffy the Vampire Slayer look-a-like and wondered if there was a *Downton Abbey* porn spoof, because he'd be on board for that. "Let me tell you now, if I ever do make a porn video, it will be absolutely high class. I'll hire Jake Jaxson to direct, and it will co-star Rob, of course." He spread his hands, illustrating the scene. "It'll be intimate and filmed under low, flattering lighting. Or maybe in gentle morning sunshine." Matty mused on that picture a moment before bringing his finger up to punctuate the next point. "But, most importantly, it will have an automatic self-destruct built into the file. You know, lest the Japanese fans somehow get hold of it. Or my mother."

"Wow, you've really given that some thought. For what it's worth, I approve of your vision. But no, that's not my brilliant idea." Elliot pulled out his cell phone and started typing away. "Give me a minute. This is why Guyton hired me. I'm great at this kind of thing. Hold on."

123

Matty moved past the penis lollipops and the penis confetti to examine some special Ben Wa balls, held together with a thick retrieval string, and intended for anal or vaginal use. He'd convinced Rob to buy some a year back, and once they were in, they didn't really *do* anything interesting. The only good part was taking them back out, but that didn't last very long. So, all in all, they'd been a disappointing buy. "These are boring," he said to Elliot, gesturing at the balls. "Don't buy them."

"Too late. I made the same dull mistake a few years ago. Thick, beaded anal wands are so much better."

Matty had to agree.

"Okay, it says here, the traditional gift for a third year anniversary—"

"We aren't married."

"—is leather. Fuck being married, Matty. It still applies, so come on, let's see what they have in leather goods."

Elliot moved toward the back of the store and started up the stairs to explore the large assortment of costumes and black leather goods. Matty followed him as far as the bottom of the steps, where he was arrested by a peg wall full of chastity devices. He stared at the pictures on the packages—metal, plastic, and silicone devices all designed with one thing in mind—the prevention of an erect penis, and, ultimately, orgasm.

Matty shivered, reaching out to take down a package featuring a clear, nearly enclosed cock cage. He licked his lips, staring at it. What would it be like to be locked up without access to his own dick? What would it feel like to lose control over his own ability to come? Rob would be in true command of his orgasm.

He swallowed hard and took a slow breath, putting the package back. His head buzzed with his pulse, and he waited for the ominous voice to pipe up with an opinion, to tell him he hadn't earned that kind of game, but it was silent. Wonderfully silent.

He took up another one. This device featured a metal contraption that went into the urethra, like a sound. Blue spots appeared in his line of vision, and he felt his cock thicken in his cigarette slim silk-crepe pants. Matty shoved the box back onto the peg, his heart thudding wildly and the back of his neck going cold with a fine, sudden sweat.

He greedily scanned the other designs. Some were more open than others, which would probably allow for some touching and rubbing of the caged penis, and some seemed to allow for "growing room", so to speak, allowing for partial hard-ons. No matter the design, they were all exciting, and his dick fattened even more.

"Control. Real control," he murmured to himself, lifting yet another package to examine more closely. This one was made of polycarbonate and promised a comfortable fit with enough weight that a man wouldn't forget it was there. He considered the meaning of that, and a vague, familiar feeling settled over him—a sense of surrender, like when Rob burritoed him up in a blanket until he couldn't move, and then took control of his cock and ass.

He looked around for Clem, because he suddenly had a lot of questions.

Elliot's voice called from up above, "Yes! Perfect! Matty, come up here!"

Matty looked up the stairs and saw Elliot standing at the top, scrambling at a selection of leather sale items. "In a minute!"

"Why? What did you find?"

"Nothing. I just have some questions about something down here."

"Nothing, something, whatever. Just get up here when you're done."

Clem appeared at his side like she'd been waiting for him to need her. She popped her gum as she took in the chastity device in Matty's hand. "Oh, that's a quality one. Keeps a guy nice and tight. Would this be for you or for your boyfriend?"

"For me."

"I figured."

"Why?"

"Well, you sort of scream bitch-boy, don't you?" She winked. "Don't worry, that's a compliment." Her smile was all apple-pie sweetness. "Anyway, this one would be a wonderful place to start and a great anniversary present for a man who likes to take control. There are, of course, some issues to consider in choosing which device would be right for you." She ticked them off on her fingers. "Activity level, and how long you intend to wear it. Personally, I like my man to wear his twenty-four-seven for two or three weeks at a time, so I like to have an open end to keep the piss spray to a minimum. But honestly that can be solved just by sitting on the toilet."

"You've put your boyfriend in one?"

"Not my boyfriend. My slave." She popped her gum again and grinned cheerfully. Matty blinked at her, trying to picture someone so young and fresh having a sex slave.

"Oh. Does he like it?"

"Loves it. Keeps him horny as hell and eager to serve. I seriously never get better oral than when he's locked up. Otherwise it's all about *his* cock and *his* orgasm and *his* needs, but cage that thing up? And I've got myself a desperate pussy-eating champion. I'd put money on my caged-up slave bringing the most frigid woman alive to a screaming orgasm."

"So, do cock cages make most guys really horny?"

I bet you couldn't earn an orgasm. I bet he'd never let you come.

Matty kept back the growl that creeped up this throat as the whisper of Control in his head made him almost gasp with sharp arousal.

"Short-term, yeah. It's like a few days or a week of going out of your mind for your dick. Because you can't have it. Suddenly everything in the world seems super-sexual. Sucking on a pen makes you want to suck a dick—if you're into sucking dick. My guy wants to suck my cunt, but you know what I mean. A clit, a dick, whatever can go in the mouth. Which is why I think this could be a great gift for your boyfriend. I mean, who doesn't want their pleasure, and only their pleasure, to be their partner's complete focus at least some of the time?"

Matty swallowed and stared at the box in his hand. He had to admit, for the most part, his pleasure was Rob's sole focus. There were times when they played hard that Rob never came at all, because once Matty got off, he needed to be held and comforted to make sure he came down safely. Sometimes, by that point, Rob's orgasm seemed extraneous to the entire scene, and he just let it go in favor of holding Matty longer. Wouldn't Rob appreciate the same kind of focus given to him for a change?

Nothing for you. Nothing by mouth, nothing by dick. Nothing at all for you.

"Anyway, for the snuggest fit, with the least amount of chafing, it's best to get one with multiple base ring options, so you can make sure you're comfy. Especially if you work out a lot, which I can see you do." She nodded at his arms, which, Matty had to admit, looked amazing—all toned, cut, and pale in his sleeveless silk crepe shirt.

No way you'll do it. You're not brave enough.

"I'd ask your top before you buy, though. Some of them get testy about it, especially if the sub is pressuring them for something they don't want. Chastity probably shouldn't be a surprise gift. I don't know a lot of tops who'd like that. Most of them want to be in control of how it happens and when. So, you know *you're* interested. That's the first step. I'd suggest going home and telling him you want to give this gift, and see what he says."

Matty nodded. Rob would say yes. Well, he thought he would. Maybe he wouldn't. "Why would he say no?"

"Oh, you know, he might think it doesn't fit your lifestyle in some way. Or he might not understand what it means to you, or how it would please him. He might not give a fuck about his own orgasms and just really like watching you have yours. Hard to say. But as a dominatrix, I'd get pretty pissed if my slave bought a device like this without asking and expected me to use it on him." She smiled and popped her gum again.

"Well, I'm not his slave. We're not like that."

Clem smirked. "Whatever you're like? You should still ask first."

"Matty!" Elliot called. "Come look at all this glorious, cheap leather!"

Matty reluctantly left the chastity devices and Clem behind to head up the stairs, where Elliot greeted him by shaking a pair of leather chaps in his face.

"Now, it's always worth going to Leatherman for quality, of course, but these could provide a night of fun at half the price."

Matty took the hanger out of Elliot's hand and immediately put it back on the rack. "No. My anniversary is not about indulging your leather daddy fantasies."

"But come on, Matty. Admit it. Rob would look smokin' hot in those." Elliot pulled them off the rack again. "So would I for that matter."

"As it happens, I like Rob in his natural state of Rob-ness." Rob's handiness with an everyday brown leather belt came to mind. "He doesn't need a costume to boss me around."

Elliot faked another gag.

"I don't think there's anything here I want," Matty said, his mind going immediately to the snug, thrilling chastity devices below. *Except for one of those.* "I'll figure something else out for him. Maybe a leather bowtie to keep to the theme of the year, like you suggested."

"Because Rob wears bowties?"

"Or a leather whip."

"That sounds more your speed," Elliot smiled, knowingly.

Rob had plenty of whips, and Matty wasn't going to get him a leather bowtie either. He definitely didn't want to tell Elliot about the chastity device if Rob might say no. Then he'd have to explain why he didn't get to put his dick in a cage as a present. He rubbed his fingers over his eyes, trying to take in this new, intense turn of his thoughts.

You won't do it. You won't be able to handle it because you can't have us both. It's me or it — me or him.

"It's still early in the day," Elliot said. "We can go somewhere else."

Matty shook off the voice of Control, determined all the more to convince Rob about the cock cage. "No, let's not. If we hurry, we can still make it to Pretty Please for the facials. So get your butt plug and let's go."

"All right, all right. And then we're having dinner. You promised Mr. Lovely to eat a good meal, did you not? And I, for one, like to do what your perfect boyfriend says."

Matty steered Elliot toward the stairs down to the first floor. "Great, and you should lick his balls while you're on your knees for him."

"Oh, babe, I so would. I so, so, *so* would." Elliot patted his cheek. "Oh! I know! We'll eat at Rockin' Raw. They have a to-die-for vegan cold-pressed Peruvian coffee mousse pie. You'll love! I promise!"

"I thought you once said vegan is just a cover for anorexia."

"Oh, it is. When it's *you*, bitch. When it's me? It's healthful."

After surprisingly little deliberation, Elliot chose the exact same design and model of vibrating butt plug he'd had before. He bought it along with the leather chaps. As they exited, Clem called to Matty, "Hope to see you back here! I know your boyfriend will say yes. It's a great present."

"What's she talking about?" Elliot asked.

Matty shrugged. "A toy I saw. I don't know if Rob would like it."

"Rob will like any toy that means you're going to come for him. Even I know that."

Matty's neck prickled. But that was just it, wasn't it? He diverted Elliot's attention away from further discussion by saying, "Weren't you going to tell me something awful about Zarah?"

"Oh my God, yes!"

Elliot babbled the entire walk to the subway about Zarah's latest boyfriend-slash-horror-story. By all rights, Matty should have been fascinated by his raunchy tale of walking in on Zarah pegging the Neanderthal on their shared sofa, but as they boarded the F train toward 23rd Street, Matty had to admit to himself he'd barely heard anything Elliot had said. His mind was entirely occupied with the chastity devices he'd seen and his conversation with Clem. How long could he stand to wear one? What would it feel like? Would Rob want that kind of power over him? Would it truly be a perfect, one-of-a-kind present, or was he kidding himself?

"And so I said, 'That is *not* sanitary!' and she just looked at me like — hey, are you even listening to me?"

"Yeah. Of course. It's not sanitary. What did she say?"

Elliot narrowed his eyes, and Matty knew he wasn't fooled, but he went on, grabbing Matty's hand to pull him up as the train drew to a halt, leading him to the exit.

"She said she was sorry, but, girlfriend, I'm making her pay to have that thing steam-cleaned before I'm going to sit on it. I'm not a big whiner when it comes to shit, and by that I mean literal shit, but when it comes out of that barbarian's asshole? I won't stand for it."

Matty let Elliot drag him up the steps and out into the summer brightness on 6th Ave.

Rob deserved something amazing this year, something he couldn't get from just anyone. After all he did to keep Matty sane and functioning, he deserved the kind of thank you he'd never had before. Something to prove the devotion Matty truly felt for him.

"Come on, Matty, snap out of it. Just let it go," Elliot said. "It's summer and we're going to spend ungodly amounts of my money on facials, so stop brooding over things you can't control." Then his smile twisted and he whispered, "Let it go," again in a way that Matty knew what was coming next.

"Don't start singing. I mean, it Elliot. Don't."

Elliot's lips twitched, and he broke into song. The words and melody of the Disney film hit were too much for Matty to resist. As they fell into step beside each other, swinging their hands between them and singing loudly, they garnered smiles, but mostly glares, not caring even a little as they strolled to get their facials at Pretty Please.

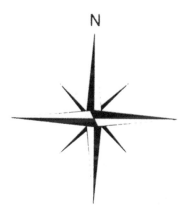

PART TWO:

STRIKING DEALS AGAINST DESPAIR

CHAPTER TWELVE

A FTER HIS PHONE call with Bill and his decision to contact Sato, Rob spent a suitable amount of time trying to concentrate on work, shuffling through his downtime paperwork and getting nowhere.

Eventually, he put his patient files away and headed into Dr. Joiner's office.

"Rob, how can I help you?" she pushed her dark hair behind her ear and smiled. Now that Rob knew her relationship to Sato he swore he could see the resemblance.

He shut the door behind him and returned her smile, hoping to sound breezy as he asked for something he'd never even considered requesting before. "Dr. Joiner, I need to take off the rest of the afternoon for a mental health break." He paused. "If that's okay."

Dr. Joiner tilted her head, her thin eyebrows lowering, and the edges of her dark eyes creasing with concern. "Is there anything I can help with?"

"Thank you, but I just need some time to meditate. Get a breath. Life's been..." How could he sum up his feelings recently? "Overwhelming."

Dr. Joiner nodded kindly. "It happens to everyone. I know it's been a long time since your last vacation, but aren't you taking a day off next week?"

Rob nodded, gripping the back of the plush seat Dr. Joiner kept directly in front of her desk for the PTs to plop into when they came in to bitch about patients or whatever else. "I know it's not the best timing to ask for additional time off, but —"

"I wasn't complaining, Rob. Just clarifying. Of course you can have the afternoon. You work hard and, more to the point, I know you wouldn't ask if you didn't truly need it." She stood up and crossed to him, gripping his elbow. "I just want you to come to me if this problem can't be resolved with some meditation. Okay? You're a valuable employee and you do good work. I don't want you to burn out."

After agreeing to spend the afternoon in self-care, Rob gathered his things and headed out into the blistering heat, the noise of the traffic and other people on the street feeling like small fingers tearing at scabs on his skin. He couldn't wait to get home.

He'd taken the car in that morning, mainly because he'd gone out to move it to the opposite curb for the street cleaners, and after forty minutes of circling, he'd given up on finding another spot and had driven on to Queens. He was relieved when he hit Park Slope around two in the afternoon and found a parking spot right in front of their apartment.

"Keep your trash can in your corner over there," Mr. Wegman, the upstairs neighbor, barked between his cigarette-stained teeth from where he sat smoking, curled into a seventy-something year old question mark, on the front stoop.

"Good afternoon, Mr. Wegman. Working tonight?" Rob asked as he moved the trash can over a half a foot into the corner Mr. Wegman had designated "theirs." He didn't know why it mattered so much to the old man, but it wasn't worth fighting about.

Rob resisted the urge to wave the drifting smoke out of his face. He could feel it adding a slick, sticky layer to his already dirty-feeling skin. He'd run and then take a shower. But first, he needed to know if there'd been a change to Mr. Wegman's schedule.

"Bar's open, isn't it?" Mr. Wegman barked. "Bar's open, then I work."

It wasn't exactly the truth, unless the bar Mr. Wegman owned had some really fucking weird hours, but Rob had never argued with Mr. Wegman before and he wasn't going to start now. "Well, have a nice night, Mr. Wegman," Rob said, brushing by him to slide the key into the outside door.

"Tell your boyfriend..." Mr. Wegman's voice sounded somewhat nasty, and Rob braced himself to hear some comment about Matty's sex noises, a cold dread and hot rage flashing through him at once. In Montana, he'd never needed to consider things like neighbors or how loud Matty got while they fucked. "My waitress Gloria put on some figure skating documentary in the bar yesterday. Saw him in it. Guess he was pretty good?"

"Yeah. He was — is — amazing."

Rob glanced down at the bald spot at the crown of Mr. Wegman's gray head and waited to see if there was any more to be said, but Mr. Wegman just stubbed out his cigarette, dropped the butt into an empty decorative flower pot he emptied fairly regularly, and stood, shuffling off down the street toward his bar. Rob realized he didn't even know the name of it. Neighbors were different in New York. Or at least his were.

He headed into the apartment, changing from his work clothes into running shorts. It was hot enough that he eschewed a shirt entirely. As he took off upslope toward Prospect Park, he ran hard, feeling the burn in his calves, thighs, and ass.

Each pounding beat of his foot against the pavement rattled him to his bones, and he tried to free his mind of the traffic and crosswalks, the pedestrians and strollers, the blinking white and red men that told him he could move forward or had to run in place. He reached into his mind, seeking the soft dirt paths of his running route on the ranch in Montana. The give of the rich earth beneath his shoes, the joyful dash of Lila and any number of work dogs beside him, and the endless, wide open sky that stretched over to the mountains — his guardians and beacons, his inspiration to stand tall, his ambition to weather any storm and stand stronger for it.

Here, it was all brittle buildings and sharp edges, gray and glittering, and red brick with splashes of distracting color. The only swaths of green were curated and designed, a bit of wilderness to keep everyone in the city from going completely crazy without it.

Finally, he jogged into the park itself, the relief of open space

135

rolling through him like thunder, momentous and promising a break in the status quo. He cut across the grass of the Long Meadow, slowing a little to prevent his ankle from twisting on any patch of uneven earth. He worked to ignore the people in the park, pretending they weren't there at all. He was alone for miles around. The green rose around him as the blue sky stretched away to the city behind him. Sweat ran down his back and dripped from his nose, and his breath and movement was solid and steady. Capable. Strong.

As he approached Dog Beach, he slowed even more. Five dogs played in the water, and their owners grouped together talking. One of the dogs was a gray and white Australian Shepherd mix, and Rob's heart clenched as she splashed in the water. The dog tossed a small green Frisbee for herself and then swam out to get it. He missed Lila a lot lately. He missed her happy dog smile, her understanding eyes, and he missed what she meant: *home.*

Rob kept going, but at a much slower rate, cooling down and looking for a good spot to meditate.

A quiet place in a cove of shady trees seemed just right, and he stretched before lowering himself down and working to clear his mind. When he first came to New York City, he'd taken up meditation. It'd helped him cope with the culture shock, and now he returned to it, seeking the peace it used to bring. He'd tried to teach it to Matty, but he hadn't had much success. Matty always grew bored far before Rob was ready to be done, and so he'd stopped asking Matty to practice it with him at all.

As he sat in the quiet shade of the park, he worked hard to dismiss every thought, every noise of passerby, every bark, every worry that skittered over his mind, and focused only on his breath. In and out. In and out. Peace descended slowly on him, calm and certain. He let visions of mountains and the old ranch play behind his eyes, but didn't allow himself to attach any particular thought or dwell on any feelings the images brought up. He just let it all slide through, as though his brain was a sky and the memories and images were clouds sliding across it until they were out of view.

Rob wasn't sure how long he sat there, but when he opened his eyes it was to a new world. The grass was greener and the air shimmered. He knew it wouldn't last, but for now he was grateful for it. He'd need this sense of peace to get through the reset scene he'd planned for Mr. Wegman's absence tonight.

He stood and did some more stretches. He was ready to turn his thoughts to the business at hand. Matty needed a reset, something emotionally hard, physically painful, and maybe a little terrifying. And Rob knew he needed to deliver before too much time had passed, before Matty thought he couldn't trust Rob to take care of his needs and started looking to punish himself again.

As he walked out of the park and back downslope toward home, he made the plans. With his clear mind, he realized that the perfect instrument to bring Matty's walls crashing down was already in their apartment. It wasn't going to be an easy night for either of them, and if he hadn't meditated then he wouldn't even have the strength to do it. But for Matty, he could do anything.

Back in the apartment, Rob showered and changed into the black jeans and button-up shirt that Matty would recognize. It was his preferred costume to signal the beginning of an interaction between them in which he'd take on the role of dominant and Matty the role of submissive.

Unless Matty used his safeword, he'd need some serious aftercare tonight—they both would. Rob decided he'd make his mother's soup, the same one that he'd made for Matty years ago before they'd fallen to the Pages' kitchen floor and gotten each other off for the first of perhaps a thousand times. He regretted that he'd never kept track. It would be amusing to know.

He checked the cupboards and refrigerator and made a list. Before heading back out to the store, he left cheese and crackers on the counter with a note: *I'll be back soon. Eat these. Dinner will be late.*

With a straight back and a refusal to acknowledge just how temporary a fix this was going to be, he focused on the priorities at hand. Shopping. Scene. Aftercare. He could do this. He could be cruel and unrelenting and make it hurt like hell. He could do that. For Matty.

CHAPTER THIRTEEN

MATTY WRAPPED A towel around his waist and paused to check his reflection in the mirror. He'd eaten the crackers and cheese Rob had left because if he had any chance of convincing Rob to consider his idea about the chastity device, he couldn't start off on the wrong foot by not eating. Though between the snack and the meal and ice cream earlier, he was so far over his daily calorie preference he was sure he could feel his fat cells growing. Still, if Elliot was right, maybe that was okay. A skating skeleton was probably not something he should aim for, even if it made his blood sing a little to hear himself described that way.

He dried his hair with the blow dryer. He'd heard Rob come back while he was still using the Cleanstream. Part of his plan was to demonstrate just how exciting he found the idea of the cock cage and he wasn't above using sex to get what he wanted. He'd been surprised when Rob didn't come in to say hello, but he supposed Rob was busy making dinner. He'd heard him clattering in the kitchen, and when the wonderful, comforting odor of Rob's mother's soup seeped in from under the door, his stomach did a happy squirmy dance, even though he was full.

Matty stepped out of the misty bathroom, busy calculating how many calories were in the soup and how long it took to make it, and wondering if Rob would go for a walk around Park Slope while it stewed, maybe after some calorie burning sex, and —

Matty stopped in his tracks.

Rob sat on the end of the bed, dressed in the nice black jeans Matty had chosen for him a couple of years before, his black button-up shirt with the collar open to the second button revealing chest hair, and his sleeves rolled up to three-quarters length. It was his "I mean business" outfit and, in case Matty wasn't already sure about the sudden turn of his evening, resting across Rob's knees was a black riding crop.

Matty swallowed hard, his cock rushing with blood and rising eagerly to press against his towel. "What's that for?"

Rob looked up at him, his face impassive. "I think you know. We have a little issue to clear up. A reset to perform." Rob held his gaze, and his eyes were calm if a little tired looking. "When you confessed about the eating, the spending, and the lying, you asked what I planned to do about it. Remember?"

Matty's blood rushed in his ears and he felt lightheaded. "Oh."

"This is what I plan to do about it. So, unless you have something else to say, like your safeword, go to the closet and bring me the humbler."

Matty's knees went weak and his breath hitched on a gasp. "No. Please, Rob. Something else."

"The humbler."

"Please, anything else? Just give me the crop alone. I don't need any restraints to keep still for it. I promise. Let me show you how good I can be. Please."

"I know how good you can be, sweetheart. I've seen it before and I love watching you work hard for me. You're amazing. But that's not what this is about. Today I want the humbler. So go get it."

Tears pricked Matty's eyes, and he stared at Rob. His towel hung loosely around his waist as a drop of cold wetness slid down his back. He gritted his teeth, trying to hold back the first swell of tears. *Fuck*, this was going to be tough if he was going to start crying before it even truly began.

"I can't. It's too hard, Rob. Please."

Rob held his gaze.

"I'll cry. You *know* I'll cry. And I don't want to cry."

That was a lie. A giant lie. He just needed Rob to *make him* cry. Just like he'd needed Rob to make him eat the ice cream the other night. Being forced was the only way it would work.

Rob waited calmly, fingering the black leather at the end of the crop. Matty's heart thundered, and small black dots swam in his vision. He took a slow breath to calm himself.

"You've got a word. Do you want to use it?"

Matty squirmed.

Rob tilted his head, taking in Matty's hesitation. "You pushed really hard to earn this, which makes me think you want it pretty badly. I think you need a reminder of just who's in charge." Rob clicked his tongue against his teeth. "Still, it's your choice." He slid the crop through his hand, stroking the length of it, and then slapped it hard on the bed. Matty's feet were rooted to the floor, and his entire body flinched at the sound.

Breathing shakily, he somehow forced himself to move. In a buzzing haze of cold, rushing fear, he walked to the closet, slid back the door, and moved aside the obscuring row of clothes to reveal the wall of implements. His dick tented his towel.

"Let me see your body," Rob said from where he sat on the bed.

Matty took off the towel, his hands trembling, and hung it on a hook to dry. His cock slapped against his stomach and his balls drew up close to the base of his dick already.

"Show me."

Matty did a slow turn so Rob could examine him from head to toe. In the mirror by the closet, he saw himself—dark hair on pale skin, burning cheeks and neck, and his cock straining up in defiance of his trepidation.

"Now bring it to me."

Matty shuddered as he reached in the closet and touched the wooden device. It was a beautiful piece Rob had given him during their second year together in New York. They'd been fighting about the way Matty was training for a series of shows he'd agreed to perform.

On a particularly sweltering summer evening, Rob had come home with a wrapped box and Matty had torn into it, excited as hell. He'd been confused about what it did when he first saw it, but Rob had pointed out the details of the device: the smooth hole that would go around Matty's scrotum, the perfect placement of the screws that would clamp the two pieces of wood together to capture his balls tightly, and the curve to cup the back of his thighs when it was pulled between his legs. It also sported O-rings on the side of it for easily restraining Matty's hands so that he'd be truly face-down-ass-up without any way to protect his vulnerable and exposed balls and hole.

Matty had been excited to try it out immediately, but when he'd found himself with the device pushed between his legs and hooked behind his thighs, forcing him forward and dragging his balls back to an uncomfortable, completely exposed position, his excitement had dissolved into terror.

Over the years with Rob, he'd been tied, he'd been whipped, and he'd been restrained in any number of ways, but the humbler never failed to trigger a deep, lizard-brain fear. Despite reassurances, he felt like his balls, stretched back between his legs, were captured in such a way that a quick, uncontrolled jerking movement, like in reaction to pain, might rip them off. He liked whips and restraints, he liked leather belts, and even having his cock tied up and balls tortured, but the humbler was too much.

Because of Matty's fear, Rob rarely used it. In fact, Matty had almost forgotten they owned it. When he'd measured out the risk/reward of his flailing protest against reality at Saks, he'd bet on whips or a hard cropping, or maybe the cane, but never the humbler.

Yet, as he took the smooth, wooden implement from the wall, and held its curved weight in his hand, he had to admit it would be effective. It would be a very quick trip through terror and pain to transcendence, and he wanted *that* so much, even if it was a very hard, scary road getting there.

He shut the closet, buying a few seconds, and then turned back to Rob, who still sat exactly as he had before, his eyes dark with lust and smooth control. Matty crossed to him and held out the device, waiting for Rob to take it.

"Tell me," Rob said.

"Tell you what?" Matty's voice shook, and he knew he was just stalling for a few more seconds.

"You know what, Matty."

Matty clenched his jaw and looked down at the humbler, a sick feeling of *no, no, no* in his stomach. This was so much easier when it was *anything* else. Any other toy or device or restraint, any other promise of pain. He swallowed down the queasy resistance. "Please, can we skip this part?"

"No."

Matty didn't know why he was balking now. Either he gave his safeword and it was over, or he stepped through the process. He gripped the humbler more tightly, feeling its cool, smooth wood against his hot palms. "Please, put it on me."

No, no, no.

"And then?"

"Hurt me. Punish me."

Rob placed the crop on the bed next to his thigh and took the humbler from Matty's hands, his dry, soft fingers sliding against Matty's damp ones. He spent a long minute or two examining the device closely, checking the screws that held the pieces together and running his fingers inside the hole that would hold Matty's sac. He nodded his satisfaction and set it down beside the crop.

"You hate this. Tell me why you want it."

Matty closed his eyes and took a slow breath, trying to find the center of peace in his core, the surrender to Rob's control and the freedom that brought.

"Look at me when you answer."

Matty opened his eyes to take in Rob's face, and he relaxed a little under the calm, affectionate expression he found there. "Because I hate it. I want it because I hate it."

"Good enough."

Matty flinched, and Rob ran a hand over Matty's hip and flank, gentling and tender. "Do you want to add anything to that?"

"I *need* it because I hate it."

"And?"

Matty reached out, needing reassurance to confess more. Rob took his hand, kissing his fingertips before turning it over to nuzzle his palm with soft, wet lips. Rubbing his other hand up and down Matty's side and hip, he leaned in and kissed Matty's hip bone, avoiding his cock pressed up tight to his stomach. Rob smoothed the wet spot away with his thumb and then met Matty's eyes again as he whispered, "Out with it."

Matty whispered, "I need this so I won't punish myself."

"Like?"

"Not eating, compulsive exercising, giving into the horrible things in my head." *There*, he'd said it aloud again.

Rob's face crumpled for a moment like Matty's words hurt him and then smoothed again. He mouthed: *Good boy.*

"Fighting with Valentina, the Federation, pushing away Sabrina's parents, spending money we don't have."

"Anything else?"

"Not right now, but I'm sure I could think of something. So you should punish me for whatever I might be forgetting too."

Rob laughed softly and kissed Matty's other hipbone before trailing kisses down his hip and thigh, sweet and gentle. Matty quivered, knowing gentle wouldn't last. Not with the humbler sitting so ominously by Rob's leg.

"One more try, sweetheart."

Matty swallowed and dug down deep. He hated saying the words, hated it so fucking much. "For not being good enough. As a coach. As anything."

"Mmm, that sounds like the truth in your eyes. The truth in my eyes is that you *can* do this for me because you are more than good enough. At everything." Rob slapped Matty's ass and said, "Crawl up here on the bed. Kneel beside me and we'll put it on."

Matty's stomach knotted as he took the position. When Rob reached out to take hold of his balls, working them down as low as he could to make room for the cuff of the humbler, it was all Matty could do not to push his hands away. Instead, to reduce the temptation he crossed his arms behind his back without having been told.

Rob acknowledged his struggle by saying, "That's good. Giving this up to me is hard, I know, but you do it so well, Matty."

The praise was nice, but Matty's aversion to the humbler overwhelmed the brief swell of pride. He knew the scene would be rough and ugly. The last time they'd used the device had been awful, but there'd been at least an hour of play beforehand, so he'd been deep in surrender—what Rob called subspace—when the humbler had been put on.

Tonight was going to be raw and fast, though. He could tell. His muscles jumped under his skin as he struggled to hold still while Rob fastened the device around his balls and tightened the screws. The weight of the wood pulled at his scrotum uncomfortably, and Matty cleared his throat to keep from complaining. He knew it was going to get much worse, so when Rob tapped the side of his thigh and said, "Spread," Matty stayed frozen for a long moment until he finally made himself shift his knees apart on the mattress.

"Obedient. I like that. Thank you." Rob rested his hand on Matty's stomach and then moved around to the back of him, dragging his palm soothingly along Matty's side as he went. He reached between Matty's thighs, turned the wooden humbler ninety degrees, and brought it and Matty's scrotum back between Matty's legs. The pain forced Matty forward onto his elbows, and he broke into a hard, cold sweat as the humbler hooked behind his thighs, effectively trapping him in a crawling position.

Matty didn't know if it was because of all the hours and hours he'd spent in a frigid ice rink, but his balls had always ridden high and tight. Rob had told him in the past that the humbler wasn't as difficult for guys with loose balls that hung low. But for Matty, until his body adjusted and his sac stretched enough to allow some movement, it truly felt as though his balls were on the verge of being ripped off. Even his breathing, which shifted his body up and down, made the stretch hurt a little more.

But more than that, having the tenderest bits of his body forced into such a vulnerable position left him queasy with adrenaline. The psychological effect was an immediate drop into absolute compliance. There wasn't much Matty wouldn't do to keep his balls from being pulled harder, or touched cruelly—even though he knew that was exactly what was coming.

"Please, this is enough," Matty whimpered, a sob in his throat. "I'm sorry. I'll be good if you take it off, just please, Rob, please, please. Please."

Rob soothed him, kneeling by the bed to lean in close. His expression was tender and loving as he ran his hand through Matty's hair. "You're all right, sweetheart. I've got you. I'll only give you as much as you can handle."

"I can't handle *this*."

Rob waited a moment and murmured, "You remember your safeword."

It wasn't really a question. They shared the same word and had for years. "Yes."

"Do you want to use it?"

Matty shook his head.

"Because this is what we're going to do, Matty. I'm not changing my mind. So, if you want it to stop, you have to say the word."

Matty squeezed his eyes shut as some tears leaked out. "Shit, shit, shit," he whispered, trying to quell his panic.

"You can do this, Matty. Just breathe. Close your eyes, relax. Let yourself accept where you are. Remember the key to *everything* in life is this: when you resist, you're fucked. So don't resist."

Matty swallowed down a mouthful of pooled saliva and took some shuddering, deep breaths as Rob ran his fingers in his hair. He wished he dared to look at Rob's face right now, but he was afraid of the mask he'd see. The one Rob wore when Matty pushed him this far, because these punishments were for Matty's sake and not Rob's pleasure. Matty knew that.

"It's just I had plans..." Matty said brokenly. "Plans for tonight."

"Let them go. This is what we're doing. This is what you're going to feel."

"Oh God!"

"Shh, that's it. Just accept it," Rob whispered and stood again.

"Accept how much this is going to hurt." His grip on Matty's hair was rough as he jerked Matty's head up to meet his warm, gentle gaze. "Because it will hurt a lot, Matty."

Fuck. His body convulsed, painfully and involuntarily pulling at his sac as he fought his flight and fight impulses. He forced himself not to reach between his legs, unhook and remove the device, and—in an instinct that frightened him deeply—hit Rob with it.

"Breathe now. Just let where you are right now sink in." Rob rubbed his hand up and down Matty's back, speaking slowly like he was still adjusting to the truth in the words too. "I'm not going to be easy on you. You're going to scream. You're going to cry. You're going to hurt."

"I'm so sorry."

"But you're also going to come. And I'll be there with you through it." Rob smiled lovingly at him. "And when it's over, I'll take care of you."

"Please."

"Just let that all sink in, Matty, and accept it now. It'll make it easier."

Rob released his hold on Matty's hair, and Matty let his head flop, squeezing his eyes tightly shut again for a long second, straining uselessly for the calm surrender he needed. Rob trailed a hand down Matty's back and over his ass, running one finger into the crevice and slowly circling his asshole, eliciting a tingling feeling that didn't come close to overriding his still escalating panic.

God, he hated this fucking toy. He'd burn it when this scene was over. He'd put it on the hibachi on the back patio and watch it turn to ash. He'd never be put into it again. His breath came in short sharp sobs and he felt tears welling. *Fuck*, he was going to look like so much swollen shit tomorrow if he couldn't get it together and calm the fuck down.

"Hands," Rob said, pressing softly on Matty's back so that he went chest down to the mattress. Soft rope tied his hands behind his back, and Matty was grateful Rob hadn't used the O-rings on the humbler itself. At least if he jerked his arms he wouldn't be pulling on his balls at the same time. He really only had to concentrate on keeping his legs and torso as still as possible during whatever Rob had planned for him. He could probably manage that.

Rob's fingers canvassed him again, skimming over his ribs and shoulder blades, ruffling in his hair, sliding down to trace his hip bones, his ass, and then rubbing in tender circles over his captured balls.

"So beautiful," Rob whispered. "It's okay to cry, sweetheart. Don't hold it back."

Matty gritted his teeth. He wasn't going to cry this soon. He *wasn't*.

Then he screamed, jerked, and screamed again as pain slammed into his gut and exited through his mouth. He choked and sputtered, realizing the permission to cry had been his warning. Rob had flicked his nuts, one after the other, with his fingers.

"Don't fight it, Matty. Let it take you or this is going to be a very hard hour."

Matty shook his head, the mattress against his cheek making it a half-aborted gesture. Rob kissed his shoulder blades, the knob at the base of his spine, and breathed hotly against his asshole and then his sac.

"You look amazing," he murmured. "I'd love to lick you and suck you. Taste your hole."

Matty breathed, wanting to curl up on himself, but that would only stretch his balls in a different way. He held very, very still instead.

One of their cell phones chirped, and Rob moved to the nightstand to deal with it. Matty concentrated on relaxing his muscles, barely registering the sound of Rob setting the phone back down on the stand. But then Rob stood beside him again, and Matty tensed up in anticipation.

Rob ran soothing hands over Matty's shoulders and down his back, stroked over his lean muscles, and hummed his approval. Matty's dick trembled, and his pelvic muscles clenched. A sharp shot of pure arousal pierced the messy, hurting, scared miasma of his emotions.

"You're so hard," Rob observed, reaching beneath his body to touch his cock. "There's pre-come on the duvet already."

Matty moaned.

Rob grabbed hold of his hair, lifting him up off the mattress again, and bent low to examine Matty's face. Rob's pupils were dark, with tense lines around his eyes—the effort, the mask that meant he was working almost as hard as Matty. "You are so fucking amazing, Matty. Did you know? Have I told you often enough?"

Matty whispered, "Yes."

"Good. Let's do this."

Matty let out an involuntary cry when Rob picked up the crop from the bed and showed it to him. Then Rob kissed his mouth hard and let his head fall back to the mattress.

"There will be no warm up. Twenty. Count it."

Matty counted as commanded, struggling to recall the numbers after nine as he fought the urge to straighten his legs against the light smacks on his sac. Rob brought the leather tongue of the crop down on one ball, then the other, not hard enough to make him vomit or damage him, but it was devastating all the same.

The steady whaps built and built until Matty couldn't help but yell, tears running freely until he rubbed his face into the duvet and bit the material to try to keep quiet. The serious sobs started around seventeen when he failed to hold himself still. He scrambled at the bed with his knees, instinctively trying to crawl away. He cried out at the wrenching pull, freezing in place as Rob gripped his shoulder hard and set him back in place.

"Easy now," Rob murmured. "Take a deep breath. We're close." He lightly slapped Matty's sac again. "Eighteen."

Matty tensed all over to keep from screaming.

"Okay, sweetheart?"

Matty nodded, tears smearing on his cheek. "Two more," he gritted out. "Please Rob. I can do it."

"Nineteen," Rob said quietly as he brought the crop down against Matty's aching balls. "Breathe through it. You okay?"

"Get it over with! Fuck!"

"Twenty."

Matty panted against the bedspread, his mouth drooling and his nose snotty. *Fuck, fuck,* he wasn't coping well at all. He tried to force himself to go to that space where he just gave up and gave in, but his body was not having it. He fought against the instinct to struggle and pull against the humbler, knowing if he did it would yank his balls painfully, but his inability to fight his muscles' twitching attempts was terrifying.

The crop landed on the bed next to him.

"So beautiful, sweetheart. You took that better than I thought you would." Matty didn't agree, but he couldn't speak as he panted against the blanket. Rob kissed his shoulders and the top of his head. He took up the crop again. Matty squeezed his eyes shut. "Sweet, sweet Matty. I trust you to safeword if you need to. Promise me."

"Promise," Matty rasped, though he had no idea what "need to" looked like, not when he wanted to hurt like this, not when he needed it so badly. "I trust you to take care of me," he whispered.

"Always. I've always got you. I know it hurts, but each strike is pretty gentle." He demonstrated on Matty's flank, and Matty barely felt it. "It builds up when it it's on your nuts. But you're fine. I've got you."

Rob kissed the top of Matty's head, and a few seconds later, he felt the bed dip. Turning his head the other direction and opening his eyes, Matty saw that Rob had situated himself at the head of the bed, reclining against the headboard and spreading his legs.

He watched as Rob unbuttoned and unzipped, pulling out his half-hard cock. Matty whimpered as Rob jerked it twice, getting it fully hard so it stood up out of his open jeans like the flag pole signaling his goal.

"Crawl up here and suck me, Matty."

Matty's hands twisted behind his back. "I can't."

"Sure you can. You can do all kinds of incredibly difficult things when you put your mind to it. This is no different."

Matty took some long breaths, his eyes on Rob's dick. He desperately wanted to get his mouth on it, to bring Rob pleasure for taking up the gauntlet Matty had thrown down, for giving Matty what he needed instead of the less intense, mutually enjoyable kink Rob preferred.

Matty grunted, tensed his stomach muscles, and hefted his torso up from the bed. It wasn't simple with his hands tied behind his back, but he was strong and limber, and did much more complex moves on the ice all the time. It wouldn't be a physical effort to rise up onto his knees at all without the humbler. Matty groaned as the change in position yanked against his balls.

"Good job, sweetheart." Rob took his cock in hand again, lazily jerking it as he kept focused on Matty. "It seems like a long way right now. But I'm right here. I could catch you before you even hit the mattress. You're safe."

"I can do it."

Rob smiled as Matty nudged one knee forward, tightening his core muscles to keep from toppling over. "I know you can. Not everyone could. Your body is so trained."

Matty paused, sweat trickling down the side of his face, and he took a few steadying breaths, his eyes on Rob's dick—his prize for making it across the bed, which seemed to be acres wide now. He wanted to feel it grow heavy against his tongue. He wanted to press the spongy head to his lips and suck until he swallowed all the hot jizz from Rob's balls.

"Fuck, your abs and the way your thighs flex. Christ, you're amazing." Rob's cock flexed in his hand and a drop of pre-come welled at the slit as he watched Matty move. "Seeing you work for me like this is so hot."

"I want you in my mouth," Matty gritted out.

"Come on then, sweetheart. I'm waiting."

Even though he'd only gone a few inches and he wanted to move faster, Matty had to pause. His balls were aching so badly it radiated into his gut, chest, and up to his teeth. He had to take a breather.

"That's good. Know your limits," Rob murmured as Matty trembled in place for a few moments before moving forward again. "So strong. So brave for me."

Matty worked harder, his balls stretching with each flex of his muscles, each inch earned with the pushing forward of his knees against the mattress.

His hair was stuck to his forehead, and sweat slid down his chest and back, gathering in his groin and the small of his back, making him shiver. He was a live-wire of sensation from nipple to cock, head to toe.

Rob's voice broke through his concentration. "If you can't find another reason to feed yourself, then do it for me. So your body is healthy enough to work for *my* enjoyment. You'll eat so I can have you healthy and alive for a very long time."

Matty whimpered as he inched toward Rob, his stomach muscles burning with the long-held crunch. Rob spread his legs farther apart so Matty could move up between them. He put his hands on Matty's hips, guiding him in, and when he was close enough, Rob smiled tenderly, whispering, "Good work, sweetheart. Good boy."

Matty panted, his abs on fire and balls hurting. He almost fell face forward, but Rob put one hand on his shoulder and steadied him where he was. Rob's other hand dropped back between Matty's legs to rub his taut balls. "You haven't shaved in a while."

Matty nodded. He'd let his pubes grow out after the last time Rob had fun with waxing.

Rob didn't seem to care, though. He smiled and ran his fingers over and over Matty's scrotum. Matty squirmed and gasped, the movement tugging his balls against the humbler and making tears well up again.

"Mmm, don't struggle, sweetheart."

Matty shuddered and forced himself still, his legs quivering with the effort not to move away from Rob's tickling hand.

Rob frowned, a flicker of worry in his eyes. "Your skin is hot against my fingers. Are you doing okay? Any unusual feelings I should know about?"

"No."

Rob's expression didn't relax. He looked so determined and dedicated Matty could fall hard into him and land safely in Rob's net. "Tell me if that changes." Then his hand twined in Matty's hair, and his voice was a command when he said, "Suck me, sweetheart."

In relief, Matty collapsed down into Rob's lap, the pull on his balls lessening as he rubbed his cheek against Rob's velvety cock, rough jeans, and soft silk shirt. He lifted to take Rob's dick into his eager mouth and realized the blow job was going to be exhausting work without his hands to steady him. But Rob grabbed handfuls of Matty's hair to lift his head and guide Matty's open mouth down onto his cock. Matty unhinged his jaw as far as possible and let Rob slide in as deeply as he wanted, his cock slipping into Matty's throat.

"Mmm, yes, just like that," Rob murmured, holding Matty's head in place and fucking up. "You take it so well. Open wider. Oh, fuck, sweetheart, just keep open for me."

He pumped into Matty's throat, and Matty's eyes rolled up as he worked to breathe around Rob's plunging dick, sucking air past it as best he could even when Rob lodged it deep and held it there. He gagged a few times, but not too hard, and Rob praised him constantly.

"Such a good little cocksucker. Such a sweet, hot mouth."

Rob groaned, shoving Matty down onto his cock, and Matty's nose smashed into Rob's pubic hair, the scent of soap and arousal tingling in Matty's nostrils. "Swallow," Rob grunted.

Matty obeyed, working his throat around Rob's cockhead.

"Fuck, sweetheart. Again."

Rob's quivering breath and straining hips were his hard-earned reward for being an excellently taught cocksucker, so he fought all instinct and did it again.

"*God!*"

Matty twisted his hands against the ropes, his own cock jerking with desire as Rob's shaft swelled in his mouth and spurted thick ropes of come down Matty's throat. He swallowed fast and nearly choked as Rob's come overwhelmed him, pungent and familiar. He swallowed as much as he could, only a little sliding back out of his mouth to soak Rob's curly blond pubic hair. Rob shuddered and hunched up one last time before pulling Matty off his cock and collapsing back against the headboard, panting and stroking his fingers through Matty's hair.

His face landed on Rob's hip by his still-quivering dick, and Matty licked his pubic hair clean before kissing his softening shaft. When he'd stopped twitching, Rob pulled Matty up into a kiss that made him cry out into Rob's mouth as his balls stretched back tight.

Rob released him and checked in on him again. "All right?"

Matty nodded. He was great, amazing even, now that he'd given Rob some pleasure too. He didn't want this to be only good for him. Rob's orgasm was as important to him as his own pain.

Rob kissed Matty again, their lips sticking together and tongues touching. "Love how I taste in your mouth," he muttered, pressing his cheek to Matty's and panting there. He reached down to stroke Matty's aching cock.

The tight hotness of Rob's palm was a wonderful distraction from the discomfort of his balls, and Matty hunched into the strokes. His shaft grew quickly slick from his own leaking pre-come, making Rob's hand that much better.

Rob targeted Matty's nipples with his free fingers, pinching one hard enough that the burn extended deep into Matty's pec muscle. He groaned into Rob's mouth straining into it, wanting it more, harder, until it was consuming.

"You love pain so much, don't you, sweetheart?"

Matty felt tears rise up again, the words touching some ashamed place inside. He wished he didn't still had a place like that. He wished Rob had whipped, spanked, and fucked those places clean.

"You're beautiful," Rob said, twisting Matty's nipple. "Strong. Stubborn. Closer than you know to breaking." Rob kissed his lips again. "Do you want to break for me?"

Matty shivered, his arms ached, and his whole body felt the strain of the position he'd held during the blow job. "Yes."

"Okay. We'll do that." Rob rubbed his hands up Matty's arms and down to where they were tied behind his back. "First, we'll undo these."

Matty almost shook his head because if his hands were free, he might give in to temptation, reach down, and undo the humbler. He didn't want to have that choice. He *needed* to not have it. But Rob had already worked the knot undone, and he rubbed Matty's wrists and arms. "Feel okay?"

"Yeah."

Rob tucked his soft cock away and slid out from under Matty to stand by the side of the bed. "Headboard."

Matty swallowed and reached out to grab the wood frame he'd first come to love in Montana. He was kneeling now, and the position pulled on his balls a lot more than when he was face down on the bed, but he concentrated on breathing through the pain while Rob tied his wrists to the O-rings on the back of the headboard.

Directly in front of him was a blank wall, painted sage green, a color he'd chosen because he'd read in a magazine it was restful. He found it calming now as he waited for whatever might come next. He turned his head enough to watch Rob, to see if he could anticipate what that might be. Probably the crop again, or maybe Rob's fingers. The crop had been hard, but the sharp pain of the finger flick had been nauseating.

"Now," Rob said, straightening his clothes. He rubbed a hand through his own hair and took a slow breath in, exhaling through pursed lips. His cheeks were flushed and his eyes glossy, but he seemed entirely in control if maybe a little softer now that he'd orgasmed. Matty felt a weird sinking in his gut at that. He didn't want to have come this far only to have Rob go easy on him now.

He *needed* this.

"Let's see," Rob said, checking Matty's hands again and then bending over to look at his balls. "They feel okay?"

"They fucking hurt."

"Aside from that, they feel okay?"

Matty almost huffed a laugh, but just that much movement made his balls throb. Rob *did* laugh, sounding somehow tender and empathetic, despite what he'd done to make Matty ache. "All right, sweetheart." He picked up the crop from where it still rested on the mattress, and with a calm, brave, loving smile still creasing his face he said, "Fun times are over. Let's hear how loud you can be."

The crop fell hard and solid on his ass. "Fuck," Matty yelled. He jerked when the crop came down again and the sharp tug on his balls hurt so much he saw flashes of blue dots. A fresh wash of sweat broke over his skin.

Rob smoothed his cool palms over the places he'd hit and murmured praise. Then he paused and cursed softly under his breath. Matty almost asked what was wrong but then he heard the bang of the door upstairs and heavy footsteps from the apartment above.

"He's home early," Rob snarled. "Fuck."

Matty's head spun. Was it going to be over now? He'd just had his concern that Rob was going to take it easy on him dispelled, but if Mr. Wegman was home early what were they going to do?

"Gag," Rob said. "I'll get a gag."

But then the heavy footsteps overhead seemed to reverse their path, and the sound of the door slamming again rattled down to them.

Rob kept his hand on Matty's back and hip, gentling him. Now that they were both still and listening hard, Matty could hear their harsh, aroused breaths as well as the chirp of birds outside.

Their neighbor stomped down the interior stairs of the brownstone. Both of them relaxed as the front door slammed and keys rattled in the lock.

Matty let his head fall forward to rest against the side of his arm. His balls hummed with pain, worsening when he shifted his weight from one knee to the other. He shook all over, and the ache gripped him hard, making him moan.

"How are we doing, sweetheart?"

"Please, Rob. I need this now. *Now*."

Rob kneeled beside him on the bed, grabbed Matty's hair, and lifted his head back. The move pulled his balls, making Matty groan again, a hot line of stretch and pain tugging from his sternum to the root of his cock, deep into his pelvis, and then screaming through his nuts.

Rob kissed him before releasing his hold on Matty's hair to wrap his arm around Matty's throat. Rob's hot green eyes raked over Matty's face. "I love you," he gritted out and pressed his lips to Matty's mouth, putting pressure against his Adam's apple with his forearm as they kissed.

Gasping, the kiss ended, and Matty yelled as the stick of the crop fell hard on his haunch. Blinding pain drove through him, leaving him breathless and buzzing as red washes of pain lapped up from the strike point until it cascaded over his whole body.

"I love you," Rob said again as the crop fell, and Matty screamed, his mouth opening to Rob's again. Their tongues slid together, breath mingling, and Matty's body vibrated with the need to fight, to struggle against the pain he knew was coming, while his brain scrambled to make a valiant attempt to stay very, very still.

Rob pressed kisses to the side of Matty's mouth. "Here we go. Another."

Matty heard his wail from far away. There was so much buzzing in his ears he couldn't hear much beyond his heart pounding and blood rushing.

"I love you so much, Matty," Rob whispered.

And then Matty was truly incoherent, a mess of reaction and nerves, shouting and struggling, because the crop was unforgiving against the sore flesh of his ass. His balls were yanked miserably with each jerk of his muscles, but Rob wasn't taking it easy at all, not even a little. He kissed Matty's wailing mouth and whispered his love, but hit him with enough force that Matty couldn't even breathe through the pain of several strikes.

"That's my good boy," Rob murmured when Matty begged him to stop, to let him catch a breath. Rob released him and helped rest his head against his arm again. Matty shuddered and shook, sweat dripping from the end of his nose, along with snot and tears. Rob kissed the top of his head, his shoulders, and the nape of his neck, whispering how well he'd done.

When Matty wasn't shaking quite so badly, Rob murmured in his ear, "Do you need to tell me a word, sweetheart?"

"No." His voice was completely ragged.

"You sure? Okay, go on, breathe a minute more, because the next part is where things get really bad."

Matty shivered and took hitching breaths, trying to prepare himself, but he knew there was no way. And that was why it was exactly what he wanted, what he needed, what he'd hoped Rob would give him: no escape, no charming his way out of it, nothing to do but surrender to the pain completely. Or safeword.

"This is how it will work. We'll start with ten. And then move to twenty. Then thirty if you haven't finished it yet. You have two options—come or safeword. Either one ends this scene. Otherwise, we stop when I think you've had enough."

Matty tried not to react to the words and focused on breathing because it might be his last chance before the tears started up again. "I understand," he offered up, his voice wrecked from crying so much already.

Rob moved behind him, kissed his shoulders and ran his hand down his back. He kissed the crop marks that still burned and ached into the muscle of Matty's ass, and then spread him open, cursing softly.

"Your hole is so perfect. Pink. Tight. Fucking love it," he whispered and Matty groaned as he felt the scratch of Rob's stubble against the welts from the crop, and then Rob's wet, hot tongue on his asshole.

He held still and breathed as his hole clenched, ticklish at first, and then so fucking *good, great, yes.* Being rimmed was the perfect distraction from the aching of his balls, the heat from his ass cheeks, and whatever was coming next. Matty's arms ached where they were tied above him to the headboard, his nipples tingled, his thighs trembled, and his hole was the nexus between pleasure and pain.

Rob pulled back and kissed his ass cheeks. "I love you, Matty."

"I love you too," Matty whispered, shaking all over, and his asshole spasming wetly. "*Now*, please, Rob. I need it. Please."

Rob sighed against his hip and rose from the bed. "Hold still, sweetheart."

Matty gripped the headboard and lifted his head. It was time.

The count started out manageable like the first time, but by the time he reached ten, Matty was grunting and half-shouting with each light whap of the crop on his nuts. After a short reprieve during which Rob kissed his mouth, checked the restraints on his hands, and inspected his balls for problems, the count to twenty started up. By the time it was over, Matty was incoherent and sobbing against his arm, tears running off his nose and snot clogging his throat.

Rob wiped Matty's nose with a tissue and kissed his hair and neck, whispering to him that he was being so incredibly good. "You either come or safeword, sweetheart. Search for the pleasure in this, or its going to go on for a very long time."

For the next count of twenty, Matty felt caught in an undertow. He knew he had to let go and go with the pull or he'd drown, but his body wouldn't stop fighting.

"How about a little predicament play?" Rob murmured, setting the crop aside. He checked Matty's shaking body all over again, helped him rest his head against his opposite arm, and wiped his nose. "Breathe for me, sweetheart. I'll be right back."

Matty was exhausted. Skating was going to be tough between the bruising on his ass, his physical exhaustion, and the ache he knew would stay in his balls until tomorrow morning.

It would be perfect.

"Here," Rob murmured, sliding an altered fleshjack between Matty and the headboard. It was a lubed tube that felt great to fuck into and had a suction cup on the bottom Rob had added months before to facilitate a fantasy about Matty had of fucking someone while getting fucked. (It'd been pretty hot.) Now Rob positioned the toy in such a way that, with a little painful effort and further straightening of his legs, Matty could fuck into it.

"That will help you get off. But it'll pull down here when you thrust." Rob stroked his fingers over Matty's tender balls, and Matty hissed. "Predicament: hurt more intensely for the short term, or hurt less for a longer time? Up to you, Matty."

The pain from his balls echoed in his nipples, his fingertips, his toes, and vibrated somehow at the very apex of his head, like it was going to burst open and bright pain would scream into the stratosphere.

"You've made a big spot on the pillow case where you're dripping." Rob took hold of Matty's aching dick and it was enough, almost, for Matty to come—or it would have been if his balls hadn't been held so far back, making his orgasm something he was going to have to really strive for. "Let me help you, sweetheart," Rob said, guiding his dick toward the fleshjack. "Tilt your hips, and there."

Matty groaned, his head going back and his eyelids fluttering. The stretch hurt so badly, but the lubed fake-asshole of the fleshjack felt so fucking good.

"Now," Rob whispered. "Thirty."

Matty shook his head. "No. No, no! Give me just a—*fuck!* Fuck!"

Rob did the counting. Matty was lost to pain, and he fucked his cock into the fleshjack frantically trying to end it. His balls ached and burned, and the gentle but agony-inducing thwap of the crop went all the way up into his gut and rattled his breath. Each thrust into the sweet slick of the fleshjack took the edge from the pain just slightly, and he focused as hard as he could on the pleasure of half his cock sinking into it.

"Twenty-seven," Rob counted, gently slapping the flat of the crop against Matty's right nut. "Twenty-eight. Breathe, sweetheart. In and out. There you go. You're doing great." His fingers massaged Matty's balls gently.

"Finish!"

"Twenty-nine. Thirty."

Matty convulsed, and the movement jerked at his balls as the fleshjack sucked at the head of his dick. He heard the inhuman sounds tearing from this throat, and he didn't want them to stop. There was a poison he needed out of his body and pain-laced screams were the only way to drain it.

"Fuck!" Matty jerked when Rob thwacked his balls with the flat of his hand, and the bed dipped as Rob moved to a better position beside him.

"You're so sweaty, sweetheart. You're doing such hard work. I'm proud of you." He reached for Matty's cock and pulled him free from the grip of the fleshjack. "Don't worry, you'll get it back when you're ready for forty."

Forty. Matty shuddered and shook his head. "Please, no twenty is enough. Thirty was too much. I can't. Please."

"Come then. Or safeword." Rob gripped his chin and whispered, "I love you, Matty. I'll love you just as much if you use your safeword."

"I can't! I can't!"

"Why not?"

"Because I need you to hurt me!"

"Oh, sweetheart."

Rob didn't need to be told twice. He fed Matty's cock into the fleshjack. Matty fucked into it, a jolt of sickness rushed through him, and on its heels, a shock of pleasure and heat. His skin prickled all over, nipples tingling and balls burning, stinging, up into his gut and he moaned, working harder, waiting for Rob to take him to the point where he couldn't hide or lie or pretend, where he was pain and pleasure, where he was broken open and all the poison spilled out for good.

Rob whispered, "Here's forty."

Matty fucked the fleshjack frantically, jerking his own balls hard with each forward thrust and then enduring the unbearable thwap of the crop on the pull back. By nine he was shaking and screaming again, sobbing, choking on his own tears, and by ten Rob was calling out encouragement.

"Do it! Come for me, sweetheart!"

"Oh, *fuck*!"

Matty bit down on his arm hard, and his body shattered with sensation, agony and ecstasy as he came, aware of nothing but convulsing pleasure-pain until he was in Rob's arms, the humbler still attached but no longer between his legs, and his arms freed.

"You're all right, sweetheart. You're okay," Rob soothed him, held him, and kissed him as he cried. "I've got you. I love you."

Matty shuddered and burrowed against Rob's body, grateful for Rob's arms around him, the scent of his skin and the hard pounding of his heart, vibrating his soft shirt against Matty's ear and cheek. "Thank you," Matty whispered. "Thank you so much."

He was limp and wrung out. Floating in silence and echoes of sensation.

Long moments passed. Finally Rob murmured, "Was this what you needed?"

"Yes," Matty whispered, his throat sore from screams and being used. "Thank you. I needed it so bad, Rob."

"All I want is to give you what you need, Matty."

"You do. You really do."

"I'm glad, sweetheart. Now you drink, then eat, then nap."

"Mmm-hmm."

"Good." Rob sighed and unhooked the humbler. Matty whimpered as his balls released. "You're so amazing, sweetheart."

Matty would have laughed, but he was still far down in his body, high on pain and orgasm, feeling loved but so quiet inside he didn't have even the smallest thought left.

CHAPTER FOURTEEN

ROB CURLED ON his side, watching Matty's eyelashes blink while he watched the mindless television program he'd chosen. It was a streaming Netflix show about fashion, and Rob couldn't care less, but Matty was *absorbed*. Every once in a while Matty muttered something under his breath about the clothing or the designer, usually something scathing, and then he'd drop back down into the quiet stillness he'd been in ever since Rob had untied him.

They were in their tiny living room area with the noise of street outside creeping in from the windows behind the couch. Rob had pulled out the sofa bed so they'd have room to lie down together, and so Matty could spread his legs with a towel-wrapped bag of peas on his scrotum, just in case there was any swelling—though everything had looked fine the last time Rob had examined it. Matty had slipped on his red silk dressing gown, and Rob idly stroked the soft material of his sleeve.

Matty was never more settled into his skin than he was after a reset, and Rob wondered what it would take *(therapy, loads of it)* to get him this settled all the time. He wondered how he'd feel about that. Would he miss Matty's fidgeting, or the striving dissatisfaction that drove him? Probably. He'd miss the way his heartbeat quickened when Matty reacted instead of absorbed. Still, Matty was beautiful like this: pale, peaceful, satisfied.

A car honked outside and voices raised in shouted greetings, threatening their peacefulness. Tired from the scene, Rob had to work harder than usual to push the intrusion out of his mind. In Montana, he'd open the windows and let fresh air pour in. He'd have a dog to curl up with them both, and he'd —

No, he needed to stop these thoughts. He wasn't in Montana. He was here. And Matty loved the city.

"Feel okay?" Rob asked when Matty paused the program and turned to him.

"You're obsessed with me."

Rob lifted his brows. "Huh?"

"You're staring at me." He gestured at the TV. "When you could be watching that."

"You're more interesting than, uh," Rob peered at the screen, "some fashion show about buying the perfect purse. I don't carry purses."

"But I do, and how many times have you been grateful for that fact?"

Rob wasn't sure where this was going. He shrugged and waited.

"So many times, Rob. Like every time we're out and I've given you lip balm or a tissue or the little airplane bottles of vodka that got you through that horrific dinner with your ex-in-laws."

"Sweetheart, I adore your purses." He thought that might be the right answer. He also thought the effect of the scene might already be wearing off. Jesus. He really didn't have it in him to do another one like that for a long, long, long time. The shouts from outside died away and a siren blared past. His chest was tight, like there wasn't enough air in the room — in the entire city.

"And are you grateful?"

"For your purses? Sure, Matty. Thank you for carrying them."

Matty blinked at him, long lashes lowering over those clear brown eyes that Rob had tried for a long time to find a way to describe. He'd finally settled on honey, because that sounded sweeter than amber, and in Rob's opinion, few things were as sweet as Matty's eyes.

Matty laughed softly and shook his head, gazing at Rob with quiet amusement. "You love me so much. So, so much." He touched Rob's cheek with his fingertips, dragging them over Rob's stubble and making him tingle. "You are so whipped."

"Huh. If I remember correctly, you were the one taking a crop earlier."

Matty shivered, and Rob put his arm around him, drawing him against his body, seeking reassurance in Matty's strong muscles and sweet scent.

"Yeah, that was me, wasn't it?" His voice was full of wonder. Rob felt that same wonder all the time when he thought of what Matty could and would do. "Hurting so much and coming for you. Begging."

Rob's dick pulsed and thickened. "Beautiful and strong. Taking more than you thought you could. Surrendering to me." There was a click in Rob's throat as he swallowed. If they were in Montana, he might have the strength to jerk off on Matty right now, but he could feel the clock ticking toward the moment Mr. Wegman would return home for the night. Not to mention there must be something going on a few streets over because three more police cars screamed by. His brief flame of arousal guttered out.

Matty snuggled closer. "Yes. God, it was amazing. Thank you." He nuzzled Rob's neck.

"So it was what you wanted?" Rob asked again, needing to feel sure. The scene had almost taken him apart too. He was as worn as an old pair of jeans and ready to rip open. He had to know he'd done what Matty needed from him, that he'd been good enough and strong enough for him.

"Oh, yeah, I promise. Exactly what I needed." Matty slid his fingers into Rob's hair, kissing the side of his chin. "Did it scare you?" he whispered.

"No. But it was big. It felt big." Rob didn't know how else to describe the responsibility that came with a scene like that. Holding the space, keeping the calm, letting Matty lose control—it wasn't an easy thing for him to do. He couldn't shut off for even a second of it, and letting that much emotion flow into and through him, opening himself up to the feelings that provoked, was beyond words. And tonight it had left him raw as hamburger meat, red, tender, and limp. He wanted to sleep for hours, but he needed to see Matty all the way down first.

"You handled it so well," Matty said softly. "I love that I can trust you to hurt me like that."

Matty's words helped filled him with a measure of strength. "I love that you trust me to handle it."

"I feel like I can think and breathe for the first time in months." Matty pushed up enough to wrap his arms around Rob's neck. "Thank you, thank you." His lips were soft and slick, and Rob wallowed in the tenderness of their connection.

After long minutes of tasting each other and nuzzling noses, Matty broke the kiss to rest his head on Rob's shoulder. "I just want this feeling to never, ever go away."

"Endorphins are powerful, but they only last so long."

"It's not just endorphins. It's you." Matty's expression softened, and he looked so vulnerable that Rob wanted to rub his face against his neck and just breathe in his sweetness. "I know you'll always give me what I need."

Rob swallowed hard and nodded. He would and he could, but it didn't mean it was easy for him. He didn't know if Matty even understood how fragile the night had left him feeling. He needed to guide Matty all the way down, and then maybe... No, he couldn't let Matty know. He'd feel guilty. It'd ruin everything he'd worked so hard to achieve with the humbler.

"Let me see the bruise on your arm again," Rob murmured, sitting up so that he could unwrap Matty from the dressing gown. Matty let Rob maneuver his arm free and then lay back on the white sofa bed sheets, one hand on his forehead in a feigned swoon, as Rob poked at the bite mark.

The skin wasn't broken, but the bruise was pretty nasty. He'd applied arnica earlier when he gave Matty some ibuprofen. Rob kissed the bite again and murmured, "You just had to add that extra kick of pain, huh?"

"No. You got me there with what you were doing. I was just trying to dig deep and hold on, but then I remembered I had to let go. Soar up into it and fly. Be your blackbird with his heart on his sleeve." Matty smiled, his eyes crinkling at the edges. He trailed his soft fingers over Rob's arm, tracing the line where his T-shirt met his bicep. "I want to pay you back for everything you do for me." He looked up, his eyes wide and almost shy.

"Sweetheart, being what you need is the only thing I want to do."

Matty rolled his eyes. "You're ridiculous and way too in love with me." He was pleased with Rob's response, though. Rob could tell by the way Matty's cheeks flushed and his eyes glowed beneath his lowered lashes.

"How can I be too in love with you?"

"I don't know. It's just, well, I forget sometimes how much you love me. But then we do something like this, and I can barely deal with knowing it." Matty squeezed Rob's arm urgently, his fingers digging in and his brown eyes seeking Rob's with a fevered desperation. "Between how much I love you, and knowing how much you love me, I sometimes feel like I might actually die."

Rob knew exactly what he meant. He felt that way sometimes, and it took his breath away and shook him to the core. It was why he was with Matty at all—because despite everything, no one had ever made him feel as wanted, needed, and *adored* as Matty did. He ran his hand over the soft silk of Matty's dressing gown. "Love shouldn't kill a person."

"It feels so good. Better than I can stand. Knowing how you love me." He grabbed Rob's hand and threaded their fingers together. "Right now, I feel amazing."

"I'd think you'd feel sore."

Matty laughed softly. "*Fuck*, my balls do ache," he conceded. "Because you love me enough to do this for me. You love me so fucking much."

Rob chuckled and kissed Matty's hair, his heart aching and full, so full it made him feel like he might cry.

Matty rambled on, "I'm drunk on it, aren't I? I'm babbling and being a mushball. But do you know how lucky we are, Rob? What if I'd never gone to Montana? What if I'd never met you? We are so lucky. So, so lucky. Do you know that?"

"Every day."

Matty shook his head, a damp, dark curl sliding down over his forehead. "No, not every day. Not on the days when you're annoyed because I didn't take out the trash and I bought four hundred dollar shoes."

"Even then."

"No, not then."

"Even then, Matty."

Matty searched his face. "This is a ridiculous conversation."

"Maybe. But that's okay."

Matty snuggled back, and looked toward the television again, taking up the remote control. "It's because I'm flying so high right now. I'll be a bitch again tomorrow. I promise."

"All right."

"I'm serious."

"Okay, then."

Matty clicked play, and as someone on screen started explaining the various pockets in a blue and green leather handbag, he sighed happily. "I swear on my purses, I'm going to pay you back."

"If you eat and take care of yourself, I'll consider it all worth it. Beyond worth it. Just making you happy is worth it."

"See? Obsessed with me. You should seek therapy. It's probably not healthy."

"I'll get therapy when you do."

Matty laughed and shrugged. "Who needs therapy when I've got this?"

You. But Rob just snuggled Matty closer, breathing in his fresh-from-the-shower scent, and wishing he could climb right into Matty's skin.

CHAPTER FIFTEEN

"I HATE SHAVING," Matty declared.

Rob's head ached around his jaw and temples, and he'd already swallowed two pain relievers that morning before sitting down at the table with a big glass of water and a bowl of comforting Cookie Crisp cereal. He was crammed into the corner between a joist in the wall and the edge of the table. There was just barely enough room for him to crook his arm to lift his spoon without hitting the wall with his elbow, and the table was just wide enough for the bowl and the iPad he was reading, scrolling through Ben's Facebook page.

Sacrifices are made when you love someone; when you support them. He'd thought he was better than a ranch. He'd wanted to stick it to his father more than he'd wanted to admit who he really was. He did love physical therapy, but maybe he could have sold Bing only half of the ranch so that he could have had both.

But if he'd stayed in Montana, he'd have missed Ben growing up. He'd have never found Matty again.

He'd have come looking for me.

It was probably true. But what if he hadn't?

Then Rob wouldn't be sitting there dazed and suffering some pretty severe top drop for one. And he wouldn't be on the verge of losing his mind with worry over his difficult, demanding sweetheart. He'd be solid, quiet, and alone. He'd be without the thing that made his heart feel like effervescent blood was beating through it. He'd be bored.

Matty was probably right. How he felt about him—what he would give—probably wasn't healthy.

"It's tedious and it just grows back." Matty slipped past him in the cramped space of their kitchen, his cheeks bright from the fresh shave, and happily slammed open a cabinet to pull out a blender.

Rob winced, braced himself for the inevitable roar, and turned back to the iPad and his perusal of Facebook. "Well, then stop shaving. Beards are hip these days."

Matty pffted. "*I'm* a pretty, pretty princess."

"So is Conchita Wurst, but she has a very handsome beard."

"If anyone in this relationship should grow a beard, it should be you."

The Cookie Crisps were almost gone, and he didn't feel that comforted. He should eat some protein. "I don't feel the need to prove my virility with a bunch of fur hanging off my face."

"A beard could be hot. I wouldn't object." Matty jerked open the refrigerator and pulled out fresh strawberries, kale, celery, and some creepy vegan yogurt that Rob was not only skeptical of, but as a former cow and goat farmer, actually offended by. "You've almost got one now, anyway."

Rob rubbed his fingertips over the thick blond stubble. It wasn't quite a beard, but if Matty pushed for it he might be persuaded to let it turn into one.

Matty threw his strange collection of mismatched foods into the blender and leaned against the counter, one hip out and one bare foot stacked prettily on top of the other, each toenail sparkling with glittery nail polish. He was still talking about something to do with beards, but Rob wasn't paying much attention. It was like his brain just couldn't process it today.

Trailing his gaze upward, Rob took in the rest of Matty. He enjoyed the rare view of him with his eyes and lips still adorably devoid of any trace of mascara or lip gloss, and his dark hair still damp from the shower. He appreciated the show of Matty's wiry muscles and slight line of chest hair beneath his strappy, lightweight, gold-shimmery top. Matty's muscular, tight skater's ass was wrapped up in white feminine-cut shorts that showed off his strong legs and would probably be paired with the equally gold and strappy sandals Rob had seen sitting out beside the bed that morning.

Rob loved Matty's summer clothes for a lot of reasons, but mostly for all the skin they exposed. Even if Matty could stand to put on eight to ten pounds, the mix of feminine and masculine all at once did things to Rob that he still didn't entirely understand. It aroused desire and affection, amusement and adoration, and made him want to kiss, touch, fuck, and show Matty off because he was just that amazing in every way.

Leaving the ranch was worth it for this. For this morning in the kitchen with Matty smiling at him, radiant and relaxed. Every other thing that he loved or hated about the city be damned. This should be all that mattered.

"You look nice this morning, sweetheart," Rob said, shoveling in a final, hearty spoonful of Cookie Crisps. "Are you feeling okay?"

"Yeah. I feel great." Matty flashed a bright smile. His shoulders were relaxed, and his eyes twinkling. "My ass is bruised from the crop. It's beautiful. My balls feel fine. And the rest of me feels fucking fantastic. It was amazing last night. Thank you again." He popped over and kissed Rob's cheek and then gripped his chin to kiss his lips, whispering urgently, "I mean it. You know me so well. Thank you."

Rob kissed him lightly and smacked his ass. But Matty's wince didn't fill him with amusement or pride like it usually did. Instead he felt even more exhausted than before, and a little nauseous. The emotional equivalent of having his cock touched after he'd already gotten off.

He cleared his throat and hoped Matty didn't notice. Protein would make him feel better. "Can you get me a boiled egg? They're in the butter box in the fridge."

Matty fairly danced over to the refrigerator, humming to himself. He grabbed the egg and tossed it to Rob instead of crossing the few steps to hand it over, and then flipped the switches on his blender until it roared aggressively.

Rob felt the sound everywhere in his body, but especially in his temples. He wanted to crawl back into bed. He would have called in sick, but he had that vacation time coming up and yesterday's mental health break was more than he'd ever asked for before. There was no way he'd push it.

He sat through the seemingly endless blending of Matty's breakfast shake with Facebook open, ostensibly watching a video from Ben's latest practice session, but really trying to figure out how he was going to make it through the day. He felt ill and a little disturbed by the way he'd pushed Matty so hard and so far the night before. Worse, his chest felt heavy and his throat tight. It took him a minute to realize he actually felt like crying. Nothing about how he felt was good.

But Matty was happy. He'd done a good job for him. He should be happy too.

Somehow that realization made him feel even worse.

Rob had never felt this way after a scene before. He couldn't remember ever dropping out of top space this hard. He didn't even know what he needed, or how to ask for it. He just wanted to go back to bed.

"Rob, I need to tell you something."

A feeling like a crack began at the base of his skull, and he had a brief terror that he was going to put his head down on the table and sob. But he took a slow, calming breath as he pushed aside his iPad and gave Matty his full attention, hoping he had enough of whatever Matty needed now, because he couldn't break down. There wasn't time. There wasn't space. There wasn't even room to breathe if he did. He had to stay together. For Matty.

"Yesterday, Elliot and I went to a sex shop," Matty said, his body tensing slightly and then shuddering hard.

Rob cracked into the boiled egg and peeled the shell and skin away. "What kind of sex shop?"

"A kind of prostitute-y one. Totally not my usual style, but Elliot likes it so we went."

"Prostitute-y?"

"Oh, not like there were prostitutes *there*, but like there *could* be."

Rob took a bite of the egg, the chalky yolk sticking to this tongue and the top of his mouth. He rested his elbow on the table and tilted his head onto his fist. "A fine but notable line."

"Here's the thing." Matty released a quavering breath. "Rob, I saw something there I can't stop thinking about." Matty rushed on, "It's really hard and challenging, and, honestly, kind of scary." He quivered from head to toe. "And I really want it. A lot."

Rob had to take a big drink of water, washing egg down. His heart pounded and he felt the world pressing in on him from all sides. He'd pushed himself so hard to give Matty what he'd needed, but it hadn't been enough? Matty needed more?

Matty sat down across from him, his shoulders squared and eyes bright. His breath came quicker than usual, and his pupils went dark and dilated. Rob felt his own heart rate quicken in response, and he rubbed his forehead, his temples throbbing.

"Whatever you say will be all right," Rob murmured. He willed strength to come in like a tide. He needed it. Because he couldn't not be enough for Matty.

Matty trembled as he smiled with a wicked edge. "We were looking for an anniversary present. Well, Elliot was looking for a vibrating butt-plug and ended up getting some leather chaps too, but I was trying to find something special for our anniversary."

"In a prostitute-y sex shop. I'm honored, sweetheart."

Matty's lips broke into a shaky, excited smile. "Shh. I know, all right? It was dodgy. But, here's the thing." He licked his lips nervously. "I think I found the perfect gift for you."

Rob's muscles twitched. He reached out to touch Matty's cheek with the back of his fingers, then turned his hand and brushed back into his soft hair. Matty's eyes seemed darker than before and his face paler, though a redness creeped up his neck.

"Why don't you spell it out for me?"

Matty swallowed hard before kneeling on the floor in front of him, so beautiful with his eyes wide and pleading. He ran his hands up Rob's thighs. "Please don't just say no when I tell you okay? Let me explain why I want it first."

He took hold of Matty's hands and squeezed. "All right. I'm waiting."

"Well, first of all, even though I really want to do it, this would be a gift for you." His eyes sparked, and the red washed up his neck and into his cheeks. "A fantastic, amazing, special, one-of-a-kind, only-Matty-can-give-it-to-you gift for our anniversary."

Now Rob could add skepticism to his unspooling reactions to the conversation so far. If this so-called present needed to be sold so heavily, and needed Rob's okay to even proceed, then he doubted it was truly just for him. But he could work with that.

"Just tell me what it is, Matty, and we'll go from there."

Matty looked down at the floor, made a few aborted moves to rise, but then stayed put, turning his big, beautiful eyes back up at Rob with a near-patented expression Rob found so arousing and annoying and sexy and heart-tuggingly perfect that he fell in love again every time he saw it.

Matty licked his lips and spoke. "It's a chastity device."

"Ha!"

Now that Matty had dropped his little bomb, Rob was relieved enough to laugh. He could handle this. There was so much he didn't think he could handle right now, but this? This he could do.

"No, listen, really. It would be for me, of course."

"I thought you said the gift was for me."

"It is! I want to give you control of my orgasms for our anniversary. For as long as you want, really."

It was nothing he ever would have planned himself, but that was exactly what made Matty so maddeningly sexy, wasn't it? All the ways he took Rob by surprise.

But he really *should* have expected it. Matty craved being denied: food, control, gold medals. It only made sense that orgasm, a reward Matty always pursued eagerly, and had suffered terribly for just the night before, would be the next thing Matty targeted when he felt out of control and undeserving.

"I already have control of your orgasms. You come when I tell you to come and that's that."

"I know, but you *always* tell me to come. Even last night, when I had earned a terrible punishment, the scene ended when I came." Matty's nervous fingers rose to twist into his own dark hair. He forced a humidity-determined curl around his finger, tugged it, and then fixed Rob with those eyes again. "I *want* you to tell me I can't come."

"I don't need a device to do that."

Matty swallowed and his breath hitched. "It's about so much more than that. I want you to own my orgasms, Rob. I want you to have them locked up with a key. I need that. I mean, I want you to have it. Because of Control."

Rob's stomach clenched. "Explain."

Matty hesitated, his gaze on his hands. "It's no big deal."

"Okay. Then tell me." When Matty was silent, part of Rob wanted to shake the explanation from him, but he stayed calm. "You know you can tell me anything."

After a painfully long moment, Matty nodded.

Rob listened, heart breaking, as Matty explained that for months a voice in his head had mocked him, instructed him not to eat, told him he was a bad person who hadn't earned the good things in his life, berated him, hurt him, and pushed him to starve and punish himself. Matty didn't meet his eye for the most brutal parts of his confession.

It was just as Sato had warned him.

"Sweetheart," Rob started and then his voice gave out. He didn't know what to say. He wanted to fall at Matty's feet and grovel, beg him for forgiveness for failing him so terribly, but he knew that reaction would just mean he'd failed Matty even more.

Matty's eyes met his again. "When I saw the chastity device, Rob, I just knew this was something that would help me."

"Why?" Rob said, brushing his fingers in Matty's hair, wanting to hold him and reassure him, but determined to listen to everything first.

"Because I know the resets are hard for you." Matty swallowed, and his eyes went dark and his cheeks redder. "I know it takes a lot out of you. Last night, you slept like the dead and I was up half the night rushing on endorphins. And this morning you're so tired and I'm still so wired. I see the difference between us, Rob."

"It's nothing I can't handle."

"I know." Matty smiled and pulled Rob down to rub their noses together. "I know you can take care of me. But I think this chastity thing could be a way for my brain to always know..." his voice dropped to a shy but eager whisper, "you're in charge of me."

"I wish you'd told me about Control before now."

Matty looked down, his shoulders hitching a little. "I wanted to handle it myself. I wanted to prove that I'm strong."

"You're the strongest man I know. That's what resets are about."

Matty buried his face in Rob's lap and wrapped his arms around his stomach. "But I couldn't do it. That Saks thing, the rest. I need you to take care of me. Please."

Rob's heart ached so painfully that he nearly couldn't breathe. "Oh, sweetheart. I'll take care of you. We'll deal with this together. I promise."

Matty nodded and held on while Rob rubbed his back, feeling the muscle and knots of bone. He had to help Matty get what he needed until the goat money came in and they could afford therapy. And if that didn't happen soon, he'd have to admit to failure. His portion of Ben's skating money would have to go to therapy for Matty. It wasn't ideal or fair, it wasn't even what Matty would want, but it was the only way.

Matty gazed up at Rob, his voice breathy and his eyes dilated. "And, here's the best part. The part that's totally and completely, one hundred percent for you. I vow to devote my ass and mouth to your service for as long as I'm wearing the device. As a gift."

"A gift."

"Yes. I want to give you a whole month where my orgasms don't matter. Only your pleasure will be important."

"A month? I don't think we'll start there, sweetheart. Try a few days at first."

"Fine, three weeks then."

Rob chuckled, leaving that discussion for later to move on to more immediate practicalities. "Can you even skate in it?"

"People work out in them. I did some research on my phone last night while you were sleeping. One guy on a message board I was reading does marathons in one. Another guy is on a university rowing team."

"But do these athletes twist and jump, and do splits in the air? Do they fall on their ass?"

Matty's chin jutted out slightly, his eyes sharpening. "No, but I can make it work."

Rob made another mental note to come back to these issues later too. "I'm sure you can, sweetheart. But did it occur to you that I get a great deal of pleasure from making you come and watching you shoot for me?" And Matty had just gotten really good at hands-free, which Rob found shockingly arousing. He didn't want to give that up.

Matty's tongue darted out to lick his lips, and his neck flushed again. "I know you like it."

"I love it."

"I love it too, but I'll be so much more attentive to your pleasure this way. Less greedy. I promise. If you just let me try it, you won't regret it."

Less greedy? Rob didn't believe that for a minute. He ran his hand through Matty's soft hair, feeling the waves slip through his fingers. He liked it best slightly longer like this and hoped Matty didn't cut it soon. Then he cupped his cheek and studied him closely. Matty looked down and away, but Rob kept hold of his chin and leaned in to kiss him—fast, but passionate and reassuring. He pulled back and said, "If we do this, then we do it my way."

Matty's eyes glowed and his smile was the beautiful real one that stopped Rob's heart. "Of course, because it's mostly all for you anyway." Matty sounded both certain and insecure, and more than a little scared.

"You're going to do great with it. I know you will." And because Rob didn't want Matty to think he didn't want the gift he added, "It's a generous gift, sweetheart. And you're right, it's something only you can give me."

Matty shifted where he knelt on the floor at Rob's feet, still staring up at him. Rob could see his erection tenting his shorts. A coil of heat twisted through Rob too, and his dick pressed against his chinos.

"You think you'll really like it?"

"You giving your cock to me? I'll fucking love it." Rob leaned forward and pressed his lips to Matty's sweet mouth, the heat between them rising fast. Their teeth clashed as Rob deepened the kiss, and Matty moaned, rising up and grabbing hold of Rob's shirt in both hands and hauling him forward. Rob broke away and pulled Matty onto his lap, nuzzling and kissing Matty's neck.

"Can I go buy it today?" Matty asked.

Rob shook his head, and then said hoarsely, "No, don't buy anything yet. I'll choose the device after I've done some research into it."

Matty's body trembled as he whispered in Rob's ear. "I did a ton of research last night on my phone, like I said."

"I'm sure you did. You can show me what you learned later."

"I'm so horny just thinking about it. Do we have time? Please?" He groaned, and Rob kissed his collar bone and closest shoulder. He unbuttoned Matty's shorts and slipped his hand inside, gripping his hard cock.

"Tell me what turned you on so much."

"There are these blogs...oh, God, fuck that feels good...and, uh, they're written by these guys *living* in chastity, liked weeks and weeks of never being allowed to come. Oh, please touch right there, harder, and, um, I don't think I could go that long, but I really want to try it."

"Sounds hot." Rob meant Matty's moans and breathy attempt to talk while getting jerked off as much as he meant the chastity information.

"Yeah, they said it was amazing and liberating. Some say they don't come at all, and it makes their heads completely clear so they can think. And other guys can still come from the prostate stimulation, but it's totally different without their dick involved at all."

Rob shoved his other hand under Matty's shirt to tug and pinch his nipples. Matty squirmed against him, pushing his ass into Rob's hard, yearning cock. He wished they had time to fuck, but there was no way. "Not everyone can do that."

Rob remembered the first time Matty had completely let go and given over to the intense pleasure of his prostate. It'd been in Montana, and it was an amazing and very loud night. Lila had howled along with Matty as he'd gone over the edge again and again. Recently, they'd been practicing it and Matty was getting good. Good enough to almost do it on command, which was ridiculously, stupidly hot.

"These guys claim they experience pleasure entirely through their ass now."

"Sounds like their fantasy more than reality. Though you do have a very responsive prostate and the anal fixation to go with it."

"Oh, *fuck*," Matty's hips snapped forward.

Rob removed his hand, keeping Matty from getting off. He sucked kisses into Matty's neck, rubbed his hands down his thighs, and calmed him. He didn't really have time to make this last, but he couldn't seem to help drawing it out. "I'll research it all and make a plan."

Matty shuddered, and his eyes rolled up a little. "I love when you make plans for my body."

Rob laughed and put his hand over Matty's crotch, giving him something to grind against. "I love making plans for you."

"I want you so much." The hitch in Matty's breathing and his dilated eyes were more than enough for Rob.

"Get back down on your knees," he murmured, turning sideways in his chair and unbuttoning his pants to pull out his cock. Matty moaned and licked his lips, sliding to the floor and eagerly taking Rob in. Heat and wetness engulfed him, and Matty sucked up and down, using his tongue and then opening his throat to go all the way, his breaths coming muffled and damp against Rob's bunched-up pants.

"That's it. You're so good at this." Rob rubbed Matty's back with one hand and held his head down with a fistful of hair in the other. Matty relaxed around him, his body going slack, and Rob recognized it as him fighting down his gag reflex. "Mmm, that's perfect." He lifted Matty up and off, and Rob's cock slapped up against his green polo shirt. Rob released Matty's hair.

"Now get yourself off."

Matty eagerly let his shorts pool at his knees and took his long, curved cock in hand. Rob admired the bright head and his dark pubes, and he took another handful of Matty's hair and guided him back to his dick. "Suck me."

Matty's hand moved fast as he sucked Rob greedily until Rob stood up, shoving the chair away with the back of his thighs, and thrust deep into Matty's throat. Matty gagged but then relaxed, stopping his own jerking off. When he was steady again, Rob thrust harder, Matty's pink lips tight around his dick, his throat expanding as Rob pushed into it, and his tongue sticking out to touch Rob's balls with every sweet thrust in.

"Fuck," Rob moaned as Matty started stroking his own dick again.

"Mmnnmf," Matty vocalized, and Rob realized Matty was going to come. He pulled out of Matty's throat, fell to his knees, and covered Matty's mouth with one hand and pinched off his nose with the other. Matty's eyes flew wide and his irises were barely discernible from his blown pupils as he reached for his orgasm. "Come on, sweetheart."

Matty shuddered, and Rob could feel him trying to pull air under his palm.

"Give it to me. Do it."

Matty convulsed, and his cry vibrated on Rob's palm as bursts of hot come landed on Rob's pants and shirt. He didn't care—so what if he was late to work? He had the most important thing in the world right in front of him. Fuck it, he'd be late. He held Matty's breath for another heartbeat, prolonging the intensity of the orgasm, and then released. Matty collapsed against him and Rob held him close, his own cock still hard and aching. But his own orgasm always felt so much less urgent than meeting Matty's needs. He whispered, "You're beautiful like this. So good. So perfect, sweetheart."

"I love you."

"I love you too. So much." Rob kissed Matty's head before standing slowly. Matty's eyes were glazed, but he tipped his head back and opened his mouth.

Rob pressed inside, the head of his cock so sensitive and his body so close to the edge after the gorgeousness of Matty's surrender that he only had to stroke himself twice and slide his cock between Matty's beautiful lips before he was coming, grunting and knees quaking, as Matty eagerly swallowed with an expression of deep gratitude.

CHAPTER SIXTEEN

HEALING BLENDS WAS a new herbal tea shop a few blocks from the Queens clinic. Rob walked in from the blinding summer light and stood in the shadowed entry for a few moments waiting for his eyes to adjust. As the room sharpened, he noted the dark wood floors and even darker wood booths running along one side of the room. Large pots of tea leaves lined the wall behind the mahogany counter, and a couple of guys with afros worked there, while a woman with dreads talked on a phone and made notes on what looked like a ledger.

"Rob!" A hand waved to him in the gloom of a booth near the back of the room.

As Rob approached, he saw that Sato was wearing glasses. They made him look slightly nerdy in a handsome sort of way. Sato rose and stood on his toes to embrace Rob, patting his back heartily.

"Good to see you." Sato pulled away and slid into the booth. "Let me call Edie over and she can get your order. I already placed mine."

Rob sat across from him and rubbed a hand over his hair. "I'm good right now. I want to take a minute to look over the menu."

"Maybe this isn't the way to greet an old friend, or acquaintance, but you're looking awfully tired," Sato said, his brow creased with concern.

"I am?"

Sato nodded. "Are you feeling well?"

Rob shrugged and plucked one of the menus from the holder at end of the table. "I had a long night, and I'm having a hard time coping today." There was a crashing noise from the back room, and a

181

police car's siren blared in the open door. Rob winced and closed his eyes.

Sato didn't say anything, and when Rob opened his eyes again, he flushed to see Sato observing him with a concerned, knowing expression.

"Are you having trouble sleeping lately?"

"A little. The city is so loud sometimes, don't you think?" He scanned the contents of the menu, but in the low light he couldn't quite make out the words. He tossed it aside, deciding that water would be the best thing to order anyway. He was probably dehydrated.

"Sometimes," Sato conceded. "Your long night last night, did it involve a heavy scene by any chance?" Sato took a sip of his tea and pushed his glasses up his nose. "Don't look so surprised. I've been around this stuff for almost twenty-five years now and I recognize top drop from experience both personal and professional."

Rob let out a short, tired laugh. "Yeah, I suppose that makes sense." He cleared his throat and confessed, "I've never dropped out this hard before."

"It happens."

Rob fiddled with the edges of the menu, embarrassed to look at Sato's face for some reason. He hadn't been this much of a raw nerve since just after his parents' death. He swallowed against tightness in his throat, suddenly afraid he might cry.

"So, you have experienced some kind of top drop before? Just never to this extent?"

"Yeah. Never with Matty, though. This is the first time ever with Matty."

"Ah, that makes sense then. You're used to feeling extremely connected with him after a scene. That's a testament to your relationship and fit, so of course it's even more disconcerting to experience a hard drop like this when the scene was with someone you care so much about."

Rob couldn't look at Sato. He felt like his skin was transparent and Sato could read the fears and secrets deep in his heart. "Yeah. I feel like I'm coming down with the flu or something. My muscles ache, and I'm not the one that got worked over." He laughed, trying to lighten the moment.

"Emotionally you got worked over, though. It was a hard scene for you too, I'm guessing. Harder than you expected?"

Rob shook his head. "No. I knew going in that I'd struggle with it."

Sato raised his brows in a question, and Rob didn't wait for him to voice it. He lowered his voice to a near whisper. "I did it because he needed it. And I didn't know what else to do."

"A good scene is mutually satisfying, and even then top drop is a natural consequence if our reserves are running low. It takes a lot out of us to be there for our subs and to take them where they need to go. Did you find any pleasure in the scene?"

Rob closed his eyes and let his head rest on the high back of the booth. "A little. I let myself come early on, because I knew I wouldn't be able to otherwise. I was hoping if I got off, then the rest would be easier." He opened his eyes but kept them averted from Sato. "It wasn't."

"Ah. That kind of scene."

"Yeah."

"Was there aftercare?"

"Of course. I'd never let him down on that. He was soaring and seems to be exactly where I wanted him to be this morning: happy, relaxed, and not under the command of his anxiety. The scene worked."

"I meant aftercare for you."

Rob rubbed his temples. "Matty's version of it, I guess. He told me how happy he was with the scene, how much he loves me..." Rob's voice broke. Fuck what was wrong with him that he was falling apart talking about this? "We cuddled. Ate nutrient-dense food I'd prepared. Drank plenty of water." He cleared his throat. "Well, Matty drank plenty of water. Maybe I didn't drink enough."

Sato lifted his hand and nodded at someone from the counter. One of the guys with an afro came over and said, "Edie's still on her break, but I can help you, Dr. Sato."

"Wonderful, Dion. A tall glass of cool water for my friend, please."

"Of course."

Rob watched the handsome man walk away. "You come here often?"

"When I meet Etsuko for lunch we usually come here. She likes the chicken salad sandwich with her orange spice tea. I prefer the egg salad, or the salmon burger if I'm feeling especially hungry."

"The lobster pie looks good."

Sato sipped his tea and let Rob look over the menu more closely while they waited for Dion to return with the water. When he did, Sato said, "He'd like to order some food."

Rob started to object, but Sato raised his hand. "I insist. You need to increase your energy input to match your output. A good meal will go a long way toward that."

Rob asked for the lobster pie, and Sato smiled winningly at him.

"Good. You'll feel better after you eat."

Rob chuckled softly. "You're doing the dom thing on me."

"I am. Someone needs to. Obviously you're no one's sub, but sometimes everyone needs someone else to take the weight from their shoulders and tell them what they need to do. In this case, I'm telling you that you need to take care of yourself. Not later, not once Matty is well, or whatever it is you're hoping for from him. But right now. This second. And I'm happy to help you do that."

Rob snorted softly but didn't protest. It would be nice to have someone deliver nutritious, delicious food to him that he didn't have a hand in preparing. The bill for the lobster pie was going to suck, but right now he didn't care about that. He just wanted to eat it and not worry for a change. He wondered if Matty had felt similarly when he'd bought the clothes at Saks. A release from the tyranny of money.

"So who takes care of you when you need it?" Rob asked.

Sato smiled. "Usually, it's Todd. He's very good at sensing when I'm low on reserves, and he steps up his servitude to include a level of pampering that is truly embarrassing at times. If something is happening with Todd that he doesn't notice, or it can't be him, Etsuko's been known to give me the what-for and make me slow down."

"Does Dr. Joiner…"

"Know about the BDSM? To a degree. She knows Todd and I 'play a slave game' as she puts it, but she sticks her fingers in her ears and sings Japanese pop songs whenever I go into any detail." Sato tilted his head. "What about your family? Do they know about what you and Matty do together?"

"No. My best friend, Anja, she's very supportive of my relationship with Matty but she and I have never actually discussed my sex life with him."

"That's understandable."

"I used to talk to her about guys I was involved with when I was younger, and she knew about my BDSM activities in Missoula. I didn't mind talking to her about those scenes because, well, they didn't work for me, really."

"I'm surprised you tried it again in the city."

"I was hoping to find a connection like what I have with Matty."

"But you didn't."

"No. Everyone was very kind, but what I found here in New York wasn't compelling enough for me to keep coming back even before Matty returned to my life."

"You were together and then you broke up for a time?"

"Yeah. We have a complicated story. Let's just say he had to go for his Olympic dream before he could commit to me."

"How did you feel about that choice at the time?"

"You really are a psychologist, aren't you?" Rob said wryly.

Sato shrugged. "Sorry. I try to hold it back with friends, but it's just part of who I am. Does it bother you?"

"No. I don't usually talk about that kind of thing much. Matty's the feelings person in our relationship. I'm the solid one who keeps him anchored while he rides the waves of his emotions." Rob smiled fondly. "They're big waves."

"Sounds like you've got yourself a handful."

"And then some." Rob's chest warmed and his stomach squirmed as he thought of Matty and his proposition that morning. "He's got the best and worst ideas. Sometimes at the same time." He smiled involuntarily. "He's amazing."

"I can see that. Your entire face changed when you were thinking about him just now. Whatever's going on, it's clear your feelings for him are deep."

"He's the reason I wanted to meet with you, actually. I told you before that he was struggling with food."

"Ah, yes. Did you ask him about the voice?"

"No, but he volunteered to me just today that something he calls Control fills his head with awful thoughts. I'm guessing that counts."

"Hmm. That's worrisome. Did he say when it started or what triggers it?"

"Yeah. It started about a year ago, and he says it gets worse when he fails in some way, or if he doesn't do what Control tells him. If he eats something I make for him and Control says he shouldn't, then there's hell to pay in his head. Sometimes another punishment is concocted—additional restriction or something more elaborate. There was a shopping spree so he'd suffer the humiliation of returning the items. He's not well. In fact, I'm not sure I've ever seen him this way." He swallowed. "When I met him, he restricted his food to a degree that worried me, but when he quit competitive skating, I thought we were done with all of that. And we were. Until his student started to succeed, and he started arguing with his boss and money got tighter."

Sato was a freakishly good listener. His face was interested, but he never interrupted and Rob found himself saying more than he ever had to anyone else besides Bill.

"That's where last night came in. He wanted a punishment. He'd acted out in ways that were designed specifically to get me to give him something he'd hate. He was doing everything but getting on his knees and begging me for it. Which I wish he would just do instead of all the other shit he pulls."

"You feel like the eating is part of that?"

"I don't know. It's all such a mess that I'm having a hard time sorting it out anymore. I know he told me this morning that when I do a reset scene—a hard scene where I don't give him any way out except a safeword—he feels better for a while and Control goes away. He said it helps."

"And how was he this morning? You said he was feeling good?"

"He was happy. And full of ideas. He wants to try a chastity device for a while, which I really should have seen coming." Rob glanced up, a little surprised that he'd told Sato about Matty's suggestion. "I told him we could try it. He thinks it'll silence the Control voice and I'm willing to attempt anything to help him with that."

"Ah, yes. Is he into service or is he a painslut? Or both?"

Rob laughed. "He's not into service. I'm not sure if painslut is the right term for him either. He's hard to categorize."

"Okay, I know the type." Sato smiled and waved toward Rob's water glass until he took another sip. "I may have been wrong about you not being anyone's sub."

"Excuse me?"

"It sounds like your Matty is that special bossy sub who runs the show, and you're the dom who reacts to his bad behavior instead of anticipating it."

Rob stared at Sato, a denial on his tongue, but then he remembered Montana and how he'd known somehow whenever Matty was going off the rails, and he'd pushed him back on track before things got out of hand. It'd been like that when they first got back together too, but somehow, somewhere along the way things had changed. And Sato was right. Matty was waiting for Rob to step in and guide him. But Rob simply wasn't doing the job.

"I used to be better at that."

"What changed?"

Rob closed his eyes and thought about his life the last few years, especially after Sabrina had come along. "I've realized..." He trailed off. He hadn't told anyone this. Not Matty. Not Anja. Not Bill or Ben.

"You've realized?"

"I'm not happy in the city. I'm a country guy, and I thought I wasn't. I thought I wanted to be anywhere but on that ranch I grew up on, but…" Rob laughed under his breath. "I was wrong." He winced as another blare of a horn reached into the tea shop through the open door. "I feel like I'm constantly fighting just to stay sane here. Like I'm in over my head and there's too much stimulation all the time. I miss the spaces and the silence. I miss being alone."

"Alone?"

"Not without Matty. That's not what I mean. But alone where it was just the two of us for acres and acres. I miss the sky. And the stars at night."

"So you're burdened constantly with this living situation, and it's left you tired and vulnerable. Does your sub not see this?"

"Matty's a little self-absorbed sometimes. Most of the time. All the time lately." Rob chuckled. "He actually thinks that's something the chastity device will change."

"It could. I've seen it happen with some boys. They get their minds off their dicks and suddenly they're all about providing service to their dom, and doing community work, and saving orphans in Russia. And other boys go out of their mind with lust and basically finger-fuck themselves into a stupor. It could go either way."

"I'm betting on a finger-fucking stupor." Rob sighed. He could handle this. He would handle it. He had to. "He thinks it will help him feel under my command. He thinks it will help him deal with the voice of Control."

"It might, but it sounds like he could use some professional intervention at this point. I can't in good conscience not suggest that."

"Listen, Sato, we can't afford the kind of psychological help for him that we both know he probably needs."

Sato nodded, a thoughtful crease appearing between his brows.

Rob cleared his throat. "Do you think it's actually worse for him, what we're doing? These reset scenes or to do the chastity device? Am I making the wrong choices for him here? Should I refuse to keep going with it?"

"I think in your gut, you know if it's giving him something or taking something important away."

"I do. He's better after a reset. Stronger." Rob let out a slow breath, his emotions getting the better of him again, rising up in his chest and threatening to turn to something messy. "I'm sorry. I know you probably have some ethical restrictions here and I'm asking a lot but—"

"Don't be silly. I'm happy to talk this out with you." Sato took off his glasses and set them aside, pausing while a redheaded female waitress delivered the lobster pie to Rob and refilled his water glass to the brim. "Thanks, Edie," he said to her with a secret smile.

She blushed and went on her way.

Sato went on as Rob took a bite of his meal. "At this point, you're talking about stop-gap measures, not a solution. But yes, from what you're saying, the BDSM sessions are probably providing him with the interruption he needs to put a stop to the thought cycles." Sato took a sip of his coffee, the steam fogging up his wire-rimmed glasses. "I don't think the chastity device is a terrible idea. But have you considered a twenty-four-seven relationship? It might reframe things for him in such a way that he can stay on track more easily."

"That's not something I'm interested in."

Sato cocked his head. "Why's that?"

"I don't want it to be my way or the highway all the time. I don't want that kind of responsibility."

"Even if your sub would thrive on it?"

Rob laughed." You haven't met Matty. Believe me, twenty-four-seven is not what he'd thrive on. He'd take it as a daily challenge to see how far he could push it; what sorts of punishments he could earn. Like I said, he's not into servitude." He rubbed his forehead, a slight headache starting behind his eyes. "Honestly, it'd be too exhausting. I couldn't hold up my end of the deal."

Sato motioned for Edie again and asked for a feverfew infusion to be delivered to the table. As she walked off, he said, "That's fair. You're already struggling to cope with your life here."

Rob rubbed his napkin over his mouth and pushed the lobster aside. He wasn't very hungry after all. Sato looked sad but didn't say anything.

"I don't think I have it in me. Even if it's what Matty needs, I can't deal with it." Rob's throat went tight and his heart beat panic-fast. This, *this* was his worst fear. That he couldn't be what Matty wanted. That he wasn't the person Matty needed in his life. His head swam, and he felt a little nauseous.

Sato touched his hand gently. "It's okay, Rob. You don't have to be the sole provider for Matty. He's a grown up. He can and should be able to stand on his own. Your role as his partner, as his dom, would be to help him do that. Not take full responsibility for it."

Rob shook his head.

"Oh dear." Sato sighed and squeezed Rob's fingers before pulling away. He took a sip of his tea again. "You're going to end up needing your own counseling. A good dom takes care of his own needs first. Maybe staying in the city isn't a good thing for you. If you and Matty are going to work out, it seems like a move to the country, or even back home to…Montana was it?"

"Whitefish."

"Well, you might want to give that some thought. If you're coming apart at the seams, you can't hold him together. I know you don't want to let him down, Rob. But you're going to if you don't take care of yourself first."

"I understand." He did, intellectually, but the idea of going home to Matty and telling him they'd have to leave the city because he couldn't cope was impossible. He had to be Matty's rock, his strength, so he had somewhere firm to land when he flew. Rob couldn't be shaky all of a sudden. Matty deserved more than that.

"I hope you really do understand. Your mental health is every bit as important as his. In fact, if you let yours slip too far, you're endangering both of you. To be honest, he seems like the kind of sub who wants to be more service oriented but can't get out of his head enough to manage it."

"Maybe, but I don't know if I'm the guy who can do that for

him."

Rob thought about a docile Matty, the kind of slave-sub he'd seen before. He'd heard some of the doms he met describe their happy homemaker who had dinner on the table and gave massages every night before offering him or herself up for use, and then allowing the dom to drift off to sleep while he or she cleaned the kitchen and bathroom and polished silverware. Rob didn't want that. He loved taking care of Matty. He loved making dinner for him and watching him eat it. He loved that Matty was flighty and headstrong and made bad choices because at least he was thinking for himself.

Oh, God. What if he loved Matty sick? What did that say about him?

"Take another sip of water. You're thinking too much."

Rob chuckled and did as he was told. "I never did before. I used to have a really quiet head."

"I bet you did. In Montana."

Rob smiled wryly.

"Matty loves it here, I'm guessing? New York? It's a dream of his to be here?"

Rob nodded.

"I see." Sato sighed again. "Well, it's clear you like to please him." He smiled. "Which is sweet of you. Loving."

"But not very dominating."

"It's okay. We all have our own dynamic. But I'm asking you to consider whether or not your pampering of your sub is helping either of you be healthy and happy."

Rob swallowed hard.

"You don't have to make any choices right now. There's time. But, as it is, it does seem like a good idea to have a twenty-four-seven reminder that you *can* take charge of him at any moment. It would keep him calm, to remind him that you can handle him if he needs you to. I think he might respond well to that."

"A ring? A necklace?" Rob smirked. "A collar?"

"All of that is up to you. But I was referring to the chastity device he's requested."

The waitress arrived with the feverfew infusion. She fumbled it as she put it on the table with a clatter, her cheeks red and her fingers shaking.

"That was fast," Sato said as she sat the pot and cup down on the table.

"We had some steeping already, sir, for the lady by the window."

Sato nodded and smiled up at her, making her neck flush. "Thank you for your service, Edie."

"Thank you, sir," she murmured and she blushed so hard Rob was certain even her thighs were red. "See you Friday?"

"Of course."

"You're taking on women now?" Rob asked as Sato poured the herbal infusion into the cup.

"No. She's Mario's. She's just new and easily embarrassed by memories of what she's seen."

"Ah."

"Here, it's good for headaches," Sato said, pushing the cup and pot toward Rob.

Rob took a sip of the bitter tea and felt gratified by Sato's satisfied smile. Damn, the man was good.

"I'll be frank. If things escalate, you'll have to seek therapy. In fact, if you're comfortable with it and he is too, I'd be happy to take him on a pro-bono basis for a time. Especially if he develops excessive fatigue, lanugo, tingling in his hands or feet, or thinning hair."

"Oh God," Rob whispered, taking another sip of the tea.

"If you're not seeing any of those things, then it's possible that it's disordered eating and not an eating disorder. Which, I know, is a cold comfort, but it truly is preferable, believe me."

Rob nodded. "Okay. I'll keep an eye out and consider what you said about me spoiling him." He took a deep breath and summoned strength from within. "Do you have any advice about the product itself?"

He could do this. He could be what Matty needed. For Matty he could do anything.

"I do. But my advice is to start making decisions that will allow you to leave the city, Rob. That's what you really need."

***

SABRINA'S VOICE WAS quiet over the line. "Matty, I miss you."

"I miss you too, Beany-Baby. How are you doing out there?" Cars honked on Seventh Avenue in Brooklyn, and Matty veered off into the quiet of St. John's Church garden so he could hear her better. "Is everything okay?"

"It's fine. Everything is fine." There was the sound of a door shutting and then a muffled sob. "But Matty, he's not you."

"Of course not. I'm one of a kind." Even though she couldn't see him, he tried to smile, but failed. "Is he being too hard on you, Beany?"

"No." She sniffled. "He says I'm good. He yells, but not at me much. He's scary anyway, though."

"Why?"

"I don't like his chest hair," she whispered.

Matty sat down on the closest white bench, the scent of flowers drifting to him. "His chest hair?"

"It tufts out at his collar."

Matty tried not to laugh. "Oh. Okay. Wow."

Sabrina's voice wavered. "It's upsetting."

Matty sat with that for a minute, his mind spinning at the implications. "Is he handsome at all?"

Silence squirmed down through the phone, her discomfort clear. "He's a grown up. I don't know."

"Oh." Matty remembered being Sabrina's age. Weird hormonal surges that made boners appear without warning, and his budding attraction to grown men that felt scarier than it was exciting. "Is that something you can deal with?"

"I guess. I just wish he'd shave it."

Matty snorted.

Sabrina sighed. "He thinks we'd make a good team."

Matty swallowed hard. He could do this. He could let her go.

"What do you think?"

"Well, my parents think my jumps have improved at the clinic."

"Yes, but what do *you* think?"

"I think that I'm getting better. He has some good advice, and I like the facilities. He makes me nervous but not too nervous. He doesn't call me names like Valentina did. No meat sticks or lazy pigs."

"That's good."

"But Matty, he doesn't make me laugh and never tells me I'm pretty. Not that I want him to! If he did, I think I'd freak out and cry or puke or have a panic attack!" Sabrina sounded like she was having one just at the thought alone. "I miss you. We have something special, don't we? You just get me."

Matty wanted to tell her that they did, that she should come home to him and be his girl forever. Instead, he said, "I'll always be here for you, Sabrina. But you have to be brave now and step up your game. I don't want to hold you back. I never want to be the reason you don't achieve your dreams."

Sabrina was quiet for a few moments. "The facilities are unreal. Figure skating isn't an afterthought here. It's surreal. They even have a whole team of physical therapists that work with us to prevent injuries. And a sports psych team. I've already seen a therapist once and...she said the same thing you did. That I have something great with you, but it's okay to step out on my own."

"She's right. And it sounds great." Matty felt a small stab of envy. He'd never had support like that in his home rink or any others he'd trained at in his career. They didn't have that kind of support here in New York for their students either. All of those extras were left up to individual parents. What would it be like to be involved in a program like that? "I'm happy for you, Sweet Bean."

There was a knocking noise in the background, and she called, "Hold on." Then her breath was a little hectic in his ear. "I have to go. I'm supposed to be at the rink in thirty-five minutes and I still need to practice piano."

"At the hotel?"

"Yeah. I do it in the lobby. I love you, Matty."

"I love you too."

The call disconnected, and Matty dropped his phone back into his purse. The sunlight smacked him in the face, and he stood, walking into the heat of the morning. He lived in the most amazing city on earth, he had a job, and a man who loved him enough to hurt him until he felt clean. There was no need to be envious of a little girl who had her whole career ahead of her and more support than he'd ever dreamed of. He was just lucky to have been part of her journey for a few minutes. He'd always get to have that.

A small buzz began at the base of his skull, in the very back of his head. Bees in a bonnet. The precursor to a visit from Control. He closed his eyes and remembered the humbler, the roaring pain in his nuts as the gentle strikes built and built, and the promise of a chastity device to remind him, always, that Rob was the boss of him. Not some asshole in his head who wouldn't cut him a break or shut the fuck up.

Rob could handle him. That was all he needed.

CHAPTER SEVENTEEN

"THE SILICONE IS more comfortable for long-term use," Rob read aloud, pointing at the iPad screen.

Matty's stomach leapt with excitement. It'd been almost a week since they first talked about the chastity device. Matty's vacation started the next day, and he was so happy Rob had decided to move ahead before it started. He'd already spent his evenings doing everything in his power not to harass Rob about making a choice, and he'd worn himself out. He'd tried to keep himself busy by purging kitchen cabinets and organizing his shoes by designer. He'd also spent some time sorting Rob's clothes by color, and playing with makeup possibilities for their night out with Julien, and basically trying to keep Control at bay. Finally, the day he'd been waiting for had come.

Matty was curled into the corner of the sofa, cradling his mug of hot water and bitters, and stroking fingers in Rob's hair. Rob lay lengthwise on the couch with his head against Matty's leg so they could cuddle and both still see the screen easily.

"But I don't want it to be comfortable. I want to know I'm wearing it all the time," Matty reminded him.

"Where does what you want come into this? I thought it was my present?"

Matty chewed on his bottom lip. "I don't want to forget even for a few minutes that you're in charge of me. *You*, not Control."

Rob made a soft, contemplative noise, looking back at the store's online page to read a few reviews. "Chafing isn't something I want to happen. It needs to be easy to clean, comfortable, and simple to get off in an emergency."

"The polycarbonate ones just need a wire cutter," Matty said, pointing at the description of the safety features.

"But the silicone can be cut off with a pair of sharp scissors."

Matty's entire body flushed at the idea of a pair of scissors near his junk, and he wasn't sure if it was so-fucking-hot-he-might-die or holy-shit-no-way-in-hell, because sometimes they went hand in hand. "But what if I decided to cut it off myself? Just because I could?"

Rob's eyes flashed hot and he lifted a brow. "Seems like there would be consequences for that."

"You know how much I love consequences."

Rob smirked and flipped back to the page featuring the polycarbonate chastity device Matty most wanted. "The device you like best is less expensive," he said. "It makes sense for the trial run not to spend too much money."

"We're on a budget," Matty agreed, mostly because it worked to his advantage.

"Let's see. It only comes in clear," Rob flicked to the page with the silicone device again. "This one comes in hot pink."

"Clear is fine. I like clear." Matty cast his eyes up to the ceiling, contemplating the star-spatter pattern a moment. "Metal is prettiest, though. But I guess it should be whatever color or design you think will look hottest. You'll be the one who has to like how it looks."

Rob leaned closer to the iPad screen and read over the description again, then flipped between the two pictures of a model sporting the cock cage. "And you're sure they have this exact polycarbonate one in stock at Slap & Tickle?"

"Yes, Absolutely sure. This is the one I was looking at."

"They probably have something similar at Babeland and it's closer. We could head over tonight before we go out with Julien, and —"

"But I know they have it at Slap & Tickle and the salesgirl Clem was really helpful." Matty's skin seemed to itch with his antsiness to get the cock cage and get it on his body. He hadn't had much interference from Control since the reset scene, but he didn't want it creeping back in without him noticing. It seemed possible when he had to work with Valentina and squash his coaching instincts. "I've got the time to go over there before work."

Rob frowned. "Who's teaching the kids?"

"Phuntsok."

"He's pretty gruff with them, isn't he?"

Matty shrugged. "It's good for them. They'll love me more when I get back."

"So, you're working with Valentina again today." Rob's tone expressed his reservations.

"Just until Lauren comes back from Honduras. But don't worry. After my vacation, it'll be nothing but the little angels for me from now on she says." Matty gave a tight smile. "So you and Valentina can both be happy."

"Hey. Don't think for a minute I don't support you in your career goals, Matty. I just don't like when you work with Valentina."

"You loved her back when she was my coach."

"That was a different power dynamic. I don't like how she treats you now. There's not enough respect. At least when you were her student she seemed to respect your work for her."

"A little anyway." Matty smiled and took a sip of his hot water and bitters.

"So long as she doesn't open up space for Control in your head."

Rob was protective, and Matty appreciated that. But if Sabrina was leaving him, then he had to step up his game and prove himself to Valentina as a coach, just like he had as a skater. With the memory of Rob's crop close at hand, his mind was calmer than it had been in a long time, and he thought he'd done better at submitting to her will, taking her orders and backing her up since the reset. And what choice did he have, anyway? Despite their problems, Valentina was his best opportunity at career advancement.

"I just want Valentina to see that I bring something to the table. I want to prove that I can learn to handle tougher personalities. Besides, letting Phuntsok take the kids this morning frees me up to get ready for our anniversary trip. I need peace and quiet for that."

Rob's expression shifted from concern to confusion. "Sweetheart, there's plenty of time for packing."

"Sure, but I need to go buy this chastity device today, and I have most of my free time booked this week. I need to get waxed and have my nails done, and I have to see Deegan for my hair too, of course."

Rob sat up and turned so that his bare feet hit the floor with a soft slap. "Money, Matty."

"It's on Elliot. He gave me a year's worth of beauty care for Christmas, remember?"

"Right. How could I forget?"

"It was very generous."

"It was."

"The perks of having a trust fund kid as a best friend." Matty took another sip of hot water before giving Rob his most winning smile. "You should try it."

"Then we'd be set."

"Totally." Matty shrugged. "You know how long it takes me to pack. I have to choose my outfits, which takes forever, and then I need to pick out a few for you too, in case we go out somewhere nice." He tilted his head and looked at Rob through narrowed eyes. "We will be going somewhere nice at least once, right?"

"Maybe. Maybe not. Either way, I know how to pack for somewhere nice, Matty."

"I know. It's just this way we'll complement each other and not look too matchy-matchy."

Rob rubbed a thumb over one eyebrow, his eyes looking sleepy and resigned. "All right. But I don't want a repeat of our trip to Vegas."

"What are you talking about?"

"I just mean I don't want to come home to find you buried under the entire contents of the closet, tears and snot streaming down your face, wailing about not being able to choose between a black knit top and a gray silk blouse."

"I wasn't crying. I was just feeling overwhelmed."

"Okay. Sure, sweetheart."

Matty rolled his eyes and pointed at the picture of the chastity device they'd chosen. "But back to the important thing: my very special, very amazing gift to you. I can get it today at Slap & Tickle. It's not a big deal. I'll just take the F to the Village and then walk to work. It's only thirty minutes and I could use the exer—" He caught himself. "Well, I'll eat dessert at dinner tonight to make up for it."

"All right. I don't really care where you buy it. But this model is the one we agreed on, and this is the one I want you to get. If this Clem, or any other sales person, suggests you get a different one, we'll talk about it first, all right?"

"Yes."

"And if they tell you something negative that we haven't found online about this particular model, then don't buy it until we can discuss it."

"Okay, control freak." Matty kissed Rob's cheek. "Got it. You might want to consider therapy for your need to have the final say."

"Sweetheart, if we're putting something on your dick, a piece of you I happen to value very highly, then I want to make sure we know everything about it." Rob picked up the iPad again, considering the device they'd chosen. "I feel good about this one, though. I talked to Sato over coffee yesterday and he suggested we buy from Holy Trainer. I consider his advice sound, but this is the same product he mentioned. So I think it's fine to buy it from Slap & Tickle."

Matty cleared his throat and shifted on the sofa. A tickle of irritation beginning at the base of his spine. Every time Rob mentioned Sato's name the tickle got stronger and Matty was reminded of the years he'd missed out on, the years Rob had sucked and fucked other guys, and Matty didn't even know who or how many times. For all he knew, he could be buying his organic produce from someone who'd had Rob's cock in his mouth. It shouldn't bother him, and most days it didn't, but when Sato's name came up, for some reason it really did.

"Sato said it's heavy enough to keep your attention, like you wanted, but you should be able to skate in it." Rob rubbed his hand up and down Matty's back, musing, "You'll probably have to wear something over your leggings unless you want everyone to see your new bulge."

"I can do that."

Rob stood and stretched, his T-shirt riding up and showing a strip of skin above the waistband of his sweats. "He said his boy-friend Todd likes the one with the spikes inside. Apparently, the pain helps get rid of stubborn half-chubs."

Matty chewed on the side of his cheek. He had to know. "So, did you meet Todd? What's he like?"

"No, I didn't meet him." He looked up at the ceiling, frowning as Mr. Wegman stomped around.

"Oh." Matty picked up the iPad and clicked over to a page of chastity devices featuring spikes designed to push painfully against a swelling penis. Rob loomed over him to see what he was looking at and snorted softly.

"Of course you'd be interested." He laughed. "I tell you what, if this first cage works the way you want it to and you want to step it up, we could try the model with the spikes. Especially if half-chubs are a problem for you. Though knowing how much you like pain, that might backfire."

Matty didn't look away from the screen as he asked, "Did you ever...do a scene with Sato or one of his, uh, slaves?"

Rob reached out and tilted Matty's chin up, forcing him to meet his tender eyes. Matty leaned into his palm when he brought his hand up to cup Matty's cheek, enjoying Rob's gentle fingers that had grown so much less calloused since he'd left Montana. "No, sweet-heart. Sato doesn't share his slaves. But more importantly, in case you've forgotten, I was never going to get what I wanted from that scene. Because no one I met was Matty Marcus."

"Oh." He'd heard that before, but he'd needed to hear it again. "I'm a rarity, it's true."

"Definitely one of a kind." Rob kissed Matty's mouth, and a flut-ter in his stomach made Matty lean into it. Rob pulled him to his feet, pressing their bodies together, his hands sliding down to squeeze

Matty's ass.

"Mmm. Sadly, I've got to get to work. You buy the chastity device, okay? We can try it on tonight when we get back from going out with Julien. We'll make sure it fits the way we want." Rob opened the fridge and pulled out a bag. "I've set aside a lunch for you. The last of the leftovers."

Matty's stomach rumbled, and Rob chuckled. The night of the reset, Rob had made enough of his mother's Southwestern Chili Burger and Bean Soup to last a few days. The scent and taste of the soup was a warm blanket of memories: Rob's farmhouse, mountains, and big Montana skies.

"Zap it in the microwave. Eat it all."

"You're the best boyfriend in the whole world."

Rob kissed Matty again and grabbed his messenger bag, heading toward the door. "Love you."

Matty waited until he heard the lock click before heading into the bathroom. He dropped his dressing gown on the floor and examined his ass in the mirror. The bruises from the reset were already gone, and he wished they'd lasted longer. Years of falling on the ice had primed Matty's butt for bruise-resistance. It was depressing that the evidence of his strength had already disappeared.

Sighing, Matty climbed into the shower, carefully adjusting the temperature of the water. He wanted something permanent. A tattoo. A scar. Something he could turn to again and again as a reminder that he was Rob's. He needed a serenity prayer on his body.

CHAPTER EIGHTEEN

CLEM'S HAIR WAS dyed a fresh pinkish-red, which somehow only made her look even younger. Her eyes lit up when she saw Matty walking toward the counter. She came around the other side, calling over her shoulder, "Jaylyn, can you take over the register? I need to help this customer."

She wore a yellow crop top over a daisy-print high-waisted skirt, and was chewing gum again. Sliding her arm through Matty's like they were old pals, she guided him back toward the wall display of cock cages. "So, your guy liked the idea of your dick all locked up just for him?"

Matty leaned close and whispered, "It was harder to convince him than I originally thought, but I have my ways."

"Aw, that's sweet. He must enjoy your pleasure. That's always a good quality in a dom."

Matty handed her the slip of paper on which Rob had written down the brand and model they'd both agreed on. "This is the one."

"Oh, that's a nice one. Keeps a guy weighted a little, but also high and tight." She pulled the box down and checked it over. "So, let's talk for a minute. I'm sure you've both done your homework, but let me warn you now that this whole locking-your-dick-up experience is a pretty intense mind-fuck for a lot of guys. Don't be surprised if it's a helluva lot harder than you're expecting."

"I've got a safeword."

"Of course you do. With a responsible, giving dom, I wouldn't expect anything less." She winked at him, the apples of her cheeks a charming pink. "Seriously, don't feel like a failure if you struggle more than you're expecting to now."

Matty didn't know what kinds of subs Clem dommed, but he was sure none of them had been Olympic athletes. *He* was accustomed to deprivation and hard work. *He* had made a career out of suffering. He'd be the exception to the rule, and he'd excel at this. He would easily deal with being denied, and Rob was going to be so pleased with his performance. He'd be the very best at chastity in New York City.

***

ROB WAS HAPPY Matty had talked Julien into Blossom instead of Gobo, citing its closer proximity to Cafe Cache as his most compelling reason. The restaurant was fancy enough that Matty and Julien didn't look out of place. Though Matty, wearing a pair of black dressy shorts (Rob wasn't quite sure of the material, but it was soft and very light weight), and a sheer white shirt with a fake black lacy bra design over the chest definitely stood out from the crowd. Even in the dark, cozy corner table the hostess had pressed them into, Matty's pale skin appeared opalescent in the low light, and his hair, which had grown slightly so it curled at his nape and on his forehead, was almost as black as the risqué accent on his shirt. He was eye catching, and lifted his chin arrogantly whenever he caught someone looking at him.

For his part, Julien wore an expensive-looking blue linen dress coat with three-quarter sleeves covered in a gold coins pattern over a white, form-fitting shirt with a pert collar, and navy blue pants that fit so beautifully Rob swallowed hard when he'd first glimpsed the sweet curve of his ass. His blond curls were shorter than the last time they'd met, and he looked almost butch next to Matty, but not quite. His eyes were a wide, innocent blue that, when paired with his French accent, would make any top worth his own dick a little weak in the knees.

He knew Matty and Julien had fucked at least once before, and he'd jerked off a few times imagining it. He knew they'd done it raw because Matty had admitted that much. He felt squirmy inside about that, probably because of what fucking bareback meant to him. Three years into his permanent relationship with Matty, he still wasn't over how intense it was to leave a part of himself inside Matty's body. So he didn't really relish the thought of Julien having done the same.

But the rest of what Matty and Julien had done together was an arousing mystery. He hoped it'd been in a hotel room, on a big white bed that framed their beautiful bodies nicely. He imagined Julien had been rough with Matty, giving him what he needed. In his imagination, he envisioned Julien's muscles bunching as he held Matty down and made him take it hard, flexing his sexy ass with each thrust until Matty had begged to come. Rob hoped it'd been as good as he knew it could be for them; as good as he could have made it if he'd been there to tell them what he wanted them to do to each other, and how hard.

Matty sat across the narrow table from Rob next to Julien. An unusual choice, but the restaurant was so crowded that only three chairs remained at the table, the fourth having been pulled over to another group of diners. The restaurant was also quite loud, making it hard to hear each other talk. Since Rob generally had less to say, he'd encouraged Matty and Julien to sit beside each other so they could hear more easily.

It was a beautiful view too. Julien and Matty pressed their heads together and exchanged skater gossip while they ate. Rob listened to what he could hear and watched them closely. As they discussed the finer points of the prior skating season, a topic that had been well exhausted by Matty and Ben already in Rob's opinion, he let his imagination take flight.

Between mouthfuls of fake meatballs and escarole, Rob spun a fantasy of grabbing them both by an elbow and hustling them several blocks over to a nice hotel. First, he'd order them to take those beautiful clothes off each other. Then he'd ask them to kiss. Rob desperately polished off his glass of wine as the fantasy advanced to Matty kneeling in front of a naked Julien, pushing back his foreskin and —

205

God.

How was he going to deal with his erection if it didn't subside before it was time to get up from the table? No matter how sexy Julien and Matty were together, a threesome was not in their future. First of all, he knew Matty would never be able to handle any situation where he felt someone else was competing for Rob's attention, and any expression of physical pleasure at the hands of another person would be seen as just that. And to be fair, despite the group sex he'd had in the past, Rob wasn't sure he could handle something like that either. When it came to Matty, Rob wasn't always rational. He'd never loved anyone else as completely and possessively.

He motioned to the waitress for a second glass and groaned softly as Julien caressed Matty's cheek in a demonstration of a pairs choreography in a performance he was critiquing. This, *this* was the real reason Rob didn't always enjoy hanging out with Julien. Though tonight, he had to admit, he was enjoying the pleasant distraction of fantasy. After the last several weeks of stress, seeing Matty shine with his beautiful friend was delicious, and imagining the various sexy, arousing things they might have done together was good, hot, harmless fun.

Julien's pink lips spread and puckered in a lovely way as they formed words. "In my heart, I know you still fly with the best, Matty. The fans in Asia love your beautiful soul. Haven't you missed the applause? Don't you miss all those people loving you so loudly?"

Matty shrugged and glanced toward Rob, his dark eyes cutting into Rob's arousal and making him harder. Christ, if it was this hot just watching them talk, the dancing later was going to make him come in his pants.

"Of course I miss it. But I've got responsibilities here."

"Yes, tell me of your Sabrina. There is much gossip. What's the truth?"

"Your wine," the waitress said, delivering the much-needed glass. Rob smiled at her and took a sip as Matty started talking about Sabrina.

"I know you've probably heard that she's a spoiled brat who thought she was too good to have to march to Valentina's orders."

Rob was surprised to hear that was the skating world's take on sweet Sabrina.

"I believed that was untrue if you took her under your wing," Julien said, pushing a bouncing curl off his forehead.

Matty smiled and brushed his shoulder against Julien's. Rob took another sip of wine and wished the table was larger so he could stretch his legs out. He was cramped and aroused and buzzing on wine. He grinned to himself.

"The truth is she's shy and timid, and that's her parents' fault, really."

"How do you mean?"

"She was adopted as a baby from Korea after her parents had two stillbirths. Do you know that word?"

"Babies that are born dead, yes? How sad."

"Yes, it's very sad. It's terrible actually, and I feel so awful for them that they went through that. They're wonderful people. No one deserves that kind of pain, but especially not them."

"Yes, it's awful."

Rob nodded. He already knew this about Sabrina and preferred to focus on the arch of Matty's neck as he tilted his head toward Julien.

"It may sound strange, but it's been hard on Sabrina too. Her parents want to give her the world, but they're terrified of her getting hurt. The harder jumps scare them. They used to freak out about them. Especially her mom. She'd gasp and clutch her chest, and that scared Sabrina, of course. But it's this huge mixed message, you know? She's trying to be perfect for them, to make up for everything they lost with their own babies. She is trying to be daring, and brave and wonderful, just the way they want her to be, and yet she has to also be safe, and careful, and make no mistakes, and never get hurt, and definitely never die."

Julien shook his head sadly. "So much pressure on such a small girl!"

"She's doing better, though. I like to think I helped with that." Matty smiled and puffed his chest up.

"You definitely did," Rob said.

Matty went on, "She's actually out in Colorado right now looking at Chuck Forenza's program. She wouldn't have been asked out there a year ago."

Rob took a sip of wine, mentally toasting the work Matty had done to free Sabrina from her fears and the generous view he was taking tonight of Forenza's clinic.

As Matty talked more about Sabrina, Rob settled into the night. The city had a way of casting an elegant spell once the sun went down, with certain company, and under the influence of wine. Something tight inside unwound, and Rob reached out to touch Matty's hand where it rested on the table. He touched his knuckles, and Matty took hold of his fingers, squeezing as they shared a small smile.

"Oh, but you had everything to do with her success," Julien said, earnestly. "Your Federation is fuming. Pissed. Shaking their fist, drinking vodka, and vomiting in their toilets pissed."

Matty released Rob's hand to take another bite of his food. "That's the British pissed, babe. Here it's angry, not drunk."

Julien grinned. "They are so angry they are drunk and sick with it! Here is Matty Marcus sticking his pretty gay nose in figure skating again, *and* breaking the rules! Thinking he can be a head coach for a contender? Oh, my! The daring! The Federation is furious. Valentina must have told you what she's heard? She never held back when I was her student, but maybe she is less forward, no, *forthright*, with her assistant coaches? Meat sticks and other nonsensical madness be damned, she always reported the truth."

"I haven't had to hear the news from Valentina. Representatives from the Federation have been happy to passively aggressively scold me personally." Matty rolled his eyes.

"And Sabrina's parents? They hear about it too?"

"Of course. That's why they're in Colorado right now. They're caving to the Federation's demands and taking her away from me."

Matty shrugged like it was no big deal. Rob caught his eye to smile tenderly at him before taking another sip of his drink.

"Oh, Matty. It's a pickle."

Matty laughed softly, a sweet sound Rob loved. "Where did you pick up that one, Jules?"

"Oh, I pick up many things." Julien met Rob's eye deliberately and lifted his lips in a sly smile full of innuendo. "But many things don't pick up me."

Rob laughed and shook his head, taking another large swallow of wine and motioning to the waitress for a third glass.

Matty looked at him in surprise. "Are you drinking enough to salsa, Rob?"

"Just trying to ease into the night, sweetheart."

"More like swim in," Matty said, and then plucked up his own wine glass and took a sip. He caught Rob watching, smiled, and took another sip before winking. "You look handsome all flushed like that. Doesn't he, Julien?"

Julien smirked, his eyes full of knowing. "I believe in your country you call him, what is the word? Oh yes, engorged."

Matty broke up laughing. "You mean *gorgeous*."

"Do I?" Julien laughed.

Rob smiled and cleared his throat. "Thank you."

"So, tell me about the rest of your summer," Matty said to Julien, eyes shining with interest. "Are you looking forward to traveling?"

"I can't wait to get back out on the street," Julien said.

Rob chuckled and Matty laughed, putting his hand on Julien's shoulder. "Out on the road, Jules. Being out on the street means something completely different."

"It does? But road and street are interchangeable, yes? When I say cross the road it is the same as saying I cross the street. People understand."

Matty said, still laughing, "Well, yes, but not in this case. To go out on the street implies that you're a prostitute, or homeless, or a homeless prostitute."

"It does?"

"Yes."

Julien threw back his head and laughed. "Now I see why the man I said this to earlier seemed *very* interested in my travels and asked me what corner I worked. I told him all corners of the world, but Asia was my personal favorite because of the dumplings. He was very confused, and so I tried to tell him about all the different dumplings—har gow, sheng jian, momo—and he just walked away like I was a crazy person!"

Matty laughed harder and put his head on Julien's shoulder. "English is a tricky language."

"For the record, going out on the road means you're traveling," Rob explained. "It's always okay to say that."

Julien rested his head against Matty's. "This mix up is quite funny and a little embarrassing. I do many things for money, but never sex."

Rob grinned and took a sip of his fresh glass of wine. Now he was imagining *paying* Julien to fuck Matty while he watched, and that was a hot fantasy in a completely different way. After tonight, he was probably set for jerk-off material for a few months at least.

"Speaking of sex and mistakes, is it true," Matty asked, leaning close and shout-whispering to be heard over the background of chatter in the room, "that Vance and Cory broke up because Vance was on Grindr picking up guys when he was out on the road doing shows?"

"Vance was very flaunting about it, yes."

"Flaunting?"

"Careless, perhaps? Yes. He posted pictures even."

"No way! Of his face?" Julien indicated no and Matty gasped. "Of his dick?"

"Yes. And then he met up with strangers for sex." Julien shook his head and shrugged. "Alas, people make bad choices in this world. They hurt each other and love ends. It is tragic, but common enough."

"So Cory's leaving him?"

"Yes, rumor says Vance is heartbroken. But, to me, he is better off this way. Humans aren't meant to be tethered. They are meant to fly free. Vance will see that and be happier to explore the world without obstacle."

Matty's lashes lowered and his brow creased. "But poor Cory."

"You loved Cory once, yes?"

Matty nodded and glanced at Rob, as though he might be jealous of whatever puppy-love Matty had felt for Cory-the-bottom. He smiled reassuringly and Matty went on. "I did. A long time ago now."

"Yes, I remember how he hurt you, Matty. Karma is a good friend to you in this case, no?"

"I don't know. He broke my heart but I never wanted this to happen. Well, not *exactly* this. Not in *public* anyway. He must feel so humiliated."

"Yes, it is sad for him." But Julien didn't seem particularly sad. He rolled his eyes and huffed softly. "I never liked Cory. He's a star fucker and a bad lay." He glanced toward Matty. "Yes, yes, he is no angel, now is he? I had him once before you dated and I never told you because I didn't want to hurt you. You're a good friend."

Matty blinked at Julien. "You and Cory?"

"He was boring. Like a floppy fish. The quickie you and I had in the locker room was much more exciting and we both know how — what is that new word Ellie taught me? Perfunctory. Yes, you know how perfunctory that was."

"Yeah," Matty agreed but he looked like he was still trying to process that Julien and Cory had slept together. Rob, however, was trying to process the rest of it.

"Your 'quickie in the locker room'?" he asked.

His elaborate fantasies of the two of them in hotel rooms performing long, drawn out sixty-nines followed by headboard-banging rough sex crashed down at his feet. He tried to convince himself that a locker room scenario could be hot enough, especially if it was rough, but Julien had said perfunctory. Did he really know what that word meant?

"Forgive me, the wine has gone to my head. He did know, yes?"

Julien murmured to Matty who was looking at Rob with a pink, open mouth and wide-eyes, his expression tumbling through multiple emotions.

Matty reached out and took hold of Rob's hand. "He knew. It was nothing. Right, Julien?"

"It was nice but nothing important to either of us."

"Perfunctory?" Rob said, his buzz from the wine combined with the sharp absurdity of disappointment making him want to laugh. He hoped that maybe Julien meant something more like 'hours upon hours of our beauty all tangled up together in locker room showers, over the benches, and in toilet stalls.'

"Fast, quick, pleasurable but not intimate," Julien said. "Isn't that right, Matty?"

"Exactly. Not intimate. Just friendly." Matty sounded breathless and his voice quavered as he squeezed Rob's hand. "Perfunctory is the perfect word for it."

Rob swallowed hard and took a gulp of wine, feeling alcohol swirling in his head, muddying his thoughts a little. *Goddamn it.* Now they'd never know how good they could have been together—how sexy, how hot. *Fucking hell.* He smiled tightly. "That's fine. It's fine."

Matty slid his chair around the table to sit next to Rob, resting his hand on Rob's knee and pressing his torso against his side. "I love you," he whispered in his ear.

Rob kissed him and nuzzled his cheek. "I'm okay. It's fine."

"Lovebirds. You are the, how do we say it? The exception to the rule. Your love sets you free. Always fly together, you lovely, beautiful birds," Julien said, holding up his glass in a toast.

Matty clinked, and Rob did too. They moved on from the awkward moment when the waitress arrived with their desserts. Rob dug into a lemon fake-cheesecake and tried to get a grip on his bizarre disappointment that his boyfriend hadn't had better sex with the beautiful Frenchman sitting across from them.

***

Matty stayed close to Rob as they walked down Columbus, turning left on West 81st by the leafy green trees of Theodore Roosevelt Park. Julien walked at a faster clip slightly ahead of them, singing something about moonlit nights and love in melodious French. Matty could speak enough of the language to get by when traveling in France, but something about singing always confused the enunciation enough that he could never follow all the words of songs.

Passerby ignored Julien's lovely baritone cutting through the breeze that thankfully poured down the street. Normally, Matty would have found it delicious to be walking with Rob and his dear friend on such a beautiful summer night, the air full of the city smells and sounds, his stomach full from a wonderful dinner, and his head buzzing with wine. But Rob hadn't quite seemed himself, and perhaps it was because of Julien.

"Hey," Matty said, pitching his voice low enough he knew Julien wouldn't hear. "Maybe I shouldn't dance tonight. I'm still a little tired from the reset."

Rob slowed as Julien moved on ahead. Matty realized he'd miscalculated when Rob looked down at him, eyes full of worry. "You were feeling fine earlier. It's been days, sweetheart."

"Maybe delayed sub drop? But really, if you want to go home—"

Rob stopped walking entirely. He put a hand on Matty's cheek, trailing his thumb over Matty's lower lip as he gazed into his eyes. Then his lips lifted at the sides and his eyes danced. "Oh, I see. Listen, you don't need to worry about me being jealous of Julien. I've told you a dozen times—I'm not. Okay? Besides, you've been looking forward to salsaing. You never get the opportunity. So stop. I'm fine. You're fine. We're fine. Got it?"

"You're not jealous?"

Rob laughed softly. "Is Julien a threat to our relationship?"

"No, of course not."

"Is Julien going to make you submit to him? Does he make you come so hard you forget your name?"

"No," Matty gasped, his knees going weak and his nipples hard-

213

ening against the soft fabric of his blouse.

"Is Julien going to take you home and put a cage on your cock and hold the key to your dick until he decides he wants you to have access to it again?"

Matty's throat clicked as he swallowed. "No."

Rob's smile was hot and slow, taking in Matty's reaction to his words. And God, the reminder of the cock cage back at the apartment, still in the bag from Slap & Tickle, made Matty want to tell Julien he was suddenly feeling terribly ill so they could go home immediately.

"Then why would I be jealous? I don't like that you didn't use a condom with him, but it's years ago now. Over and done. Obviously when I was younger I didn't use condoms a few times myself when I probably should have. Luckily, instead of a disease, I got a cool son out of it." His smile crinkled his eyes. "No sweetheart, I'm not jealous of Julien. Not like that."

Matty stared into his eyes, trying to read his mind. Rob's reaction in the restaurant had been so strong. He'd gone tight and tense all over, and his smile had frozen into something crisp and polite, not at all the usual sweetness that Matty loved so much. Worse, his green eyes had gone dark like an ocean after a storm, like they did when they fought.

"You're sure?"

"Never more sure."

The mention of the cock cage at home reminded Matty of the invite Clem had given him as he'd left the sex shop that afternoon. He hadn't mentioned it to Rob, but something about this situation made him want to poke at the edges of their relationship to make sure they had the same boundaries.

"The girl who sold me the cock cage invited us to a party at her house."

"Weird."

Matty cleared his throat. "I think it's a scene party. She's a dominatrix. She said we could come and I could show off."

"No."

214

Matty swallowed hard, relief flowing over him with the breeze down the corridor of the street. "You don't want to?"

"No. I don't share you."

Matty's eyes narrowed. "Because you're jealous?"

"Because that's not how we work together."

Matty glanced down the street to where Julien was strolling pretty far ahead, likely not wanting to intrude on their conversation. "What if I wanted to go to the party?"

"You don't."

"How do you know that?"

Rob chuckled. "I make it my business to know you, Matty. To figure out how your brain works. And I don't think you want to go."

For some reason, Matty wanted to deny it, but the reality of going to something like that, of having men see him not as Matty the athlete, but as a prospective casual sex partner, of seeing Rob looking at other men with lust in his eyes, or worse, touching them... No. There was no way he was going to be a dick and insist he wanted something he didn't just to prove a point.

"Yeah. You're right."

"Let's catch up to your friend."

Matty's mind slid back to the package waiting at the apartment, and a shiver of excitement went up his spine. He pulled against Rob's arm. "Let's just go home. Don't you want to see what it looks like on me?" He batted his lashes dramatically. "I do. I want to know if you like it."

"Oh, I'll like it," Rob murmured. "But you're going to go dancing with your friend, and *then* we'll go home and play."

"But I want to play now."

"Uh-uh. Your friend's waiting."

Matty's pulse rushed with anticipation of the evening after salsa, and he wished he could dance in fast-forward to get to the part of the night where Rob locked him up tight and kept the key.

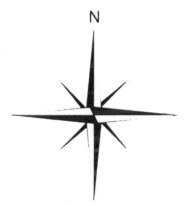

PART THREE:

INTO THE ARMS OF CHAOS

CHAPTER NINETEEN

"OH, GOD," MATTY moaned again, holding his legs behind the knees to keep himself spread wide open for Rob's hands and mouth. His toes curled and uncurled, his hips twitching up and down to meet the thrusts of Rob's three fingers fucking into him and the swallowing grip of Rob's throat on the head of his cock. Matty rested his heels on Rob's shoulders, drumming them when the sensations became overwhelming and he needed an outlet for the so-good-it-hurt tension growing from the root of his cock and gripping his whole body.

"Rob, fuck, I'm gonna come."

Rob increased the tempo of his finger-fucking and sucking, and Matty gripped the back of his own thighs so hard his nails dug in sharp little marks of pain mixed in the pleasure. Just as his balls drew up hard and sweat broke over his body, Rob pulled off and out of him, leaving him cursing and humping the air.

"Fucking hot," Rob grunted, his eyes raking over Matty's straining body. Rob was hard, and his thick cock leaked a sliding drop of pre-come down the side of his veiny girth. "Sweetheart, you're so beautiful like this. The most beautiful man I've ever seen."

Matty scoffed and tugged his knees up so his asshole beckoned for Rob's attention.

"Mmm, look at that. So tight and sweet. Want me inside you?"

Matty nodded and swallowed a sudden mouthful of saliva, a desperate hunger for Rob's big cock making him shake.

"I bet you do," Rob murmured. "I bet you want me to fuck you until you come squeezing around my dick."

"Fuck, yes!"

"Hmm, well, maybe that's not what I want tonight."

Matty moaned, shaking his head. "Please. I want you. I want you so much."

"I can tell. Too bad." Rob slid over to the nightstand and threw open the drawer. "Maybe I've got other plans."

"Oh God, yes! Whatever you want. Just let me come soon. Please, Rob."

"Maybe. Or maybe I'll get you so close and make you wait. Put the cage on you and just keep you miserable and aching for it."

Oh fuck. Matty's entire body convulsed as a jet of come leaked from his betraying dick, and Rob laughed, grabbing it around the base and squeezing hard to stop him from losing any more of his load.

"Uh-uh, you don't get to do that. In fact, that probably gets a punishment. What should it be?"

So long as it wasn't making it so that he didn't get to come at all (as hot as it sounded in theory), Matty didn't really care how Rob punished him. He just wanted him to bring it on, whatever it was, so they could get to the part where he could end the aching in his balls and cock and finally crest over to orgasm.

"How about this?" Rob held up his fist, and Matty shuddered.

"Oh my God," Matty whispered.

"We've only done it once."

He'd had a rough time taking the whole of Rob's hand, and he'd almost used his safeword. Matty quivered and said nothing, knowing it wasn't up to him anyway.

"No, I've got a better idea." Rob went to their closet, his cock bobbing as he walked, and the dim light glinting on the sparse blond hairs on his ass. He pulled out the nipple clamps that hurt the most. Amusingly, they were actually little table cloth holders with sharp, biting teeth, and red cherry-shaped weights on the end.

Matty squirmed and let his heels fall to the mattress, pinching his nipples in preparation for the clamps. Rob chuckled, his cock bouncing as he approached and then walked on his knees across the mattress.

"Such a whore for me." Rob squeezed open the clamp and examined the tines carefully before he was satisfied.

"Fuck!" Matty cried as soon as the first clamp bit in, and he arched his back, trying to find space for the sharp hurt, only to cry out again as the second clamp pinched his other nipple. "Goddammit," he muttered. The pain seemed to dart across his pecs and finally pulse down into the muscle, making his entire chest burn.

"Now," Rob said, his smile growing looser with arousal. "Let's see about these." He grabbed Matty's hands and pulled them back to the headboard, using ties that had been left there to bind his wrists quickly. "Oh, sweetheart, you're so fucking *mine*."

Matty whimpered. "That goes both ways."

"Yeah, you know it." Rob bent and kissed him hard, taking his breath with his urgency. The pain from the clamps dulled into an ache but grew in size until Matty's awareness swung between the clamps and Rob's lips and tongue, his breath, and his taste.

When Rob shifted and took hold of Matty's dick with a slick hand, it was sensation overload and Matty almost came at once. Rob broke the kiss and ducked his head to bite one of the clamps, adding unbearable pressure that crawled out of Matty's throat as a scream. Then Rob's hand was over his mouth, his breath hot in his ear as he straddled Matty and pushed down against Matty's straining dick, holding it still with his other hand. Matty flexed his hips up when he realized what was happening. *Yes.*

With his arms stretched back, he had to press his heels into the mattress to gain purchase to fuck up into Rob's tight hole, both of them groaning when Matty's cockhead popped past the tight ring of muscle and into the hot grip of his body.

"You feel so good," Matty whimpered. "I won't last." Sweet pleasure/pain ricocheted between his aching nipples and the exquisite, thrumming heat of Rob's hole as Rob bore down to take him in.

"I always forget how big you feel inside me, sweetheart," Rob said, sweat sliding down his forehead and his green eyes shuttered.

221

"Perfect. Thick."

Matty knew he wasn't as impressively sized as Rob, but he loved that Rob felt him so keenly. "I can't hold it," Matty warned as he thrust up, going deep into Rob and setting a fast, desperate rhythm until Rob leaned back, pushing down to hold Matty's hips in place and using his weight to ground them both.

"Fuck, Rob! Just let me!"

Rob laughed and shook his head, plucking off one nipple clamp and then the other, the rush of blood back into the area making Matty wail. Rob covered his mouth again and pinched his nose, one of their favorite, most dangerous ways to play, and rode Matty hard for several seconds.

It didn't take more than that—Matty's cock plunging in and out of Rob's tight, grasping heat, the screaming pain throbbing in his nipples, compounded with the heady rush of no air. It left him with no place to go but straight into ecstasy. He came inside Rob— thrumming, convulsing, hard, pumping pleasure that chewed him up and consumed him entirely. He gasped in air as Rob pulled his hand away and used it to jerk himself off against Matty's quivering stomach. Throwing his head back and calling out to the ceiling, Rob came in hot, white spurts, rhythmically gripping the base of Matty's cock still lodged deep inside him. Matty watched him blearily, his hands still bound, his heart racing, and his balls aching with the suddenness of release.

"Okay," Rob panted, his legs quaking a little as he lifted off and Matty's cock slid out. "Okay, so, yeah. Fuck." He fell over to his side and curled up to Matty, kissing his chest, licking his sore nipples, and breathing hard.

Matty tugged at his restraints. "Want to hold you now."

Rob trembled as he pulled the string, untying the bows that held him. They weren't scary or tight like knots, but Matty hardly ever fought being bound anyway, and it made the release so much faster. They clung to each other, kissing and tasting each other, their bodies slick with come and sweat that chilled in the breeze from the standing fan.

"Good?" Matty asked.

"I'm supposed to ask you that."

"Another thing that goes both ways."

Rob huffed a laugh against Matty's neck then leaned up on his elbow. "Good. Are you ready to lose access to this?" He took hold of Matty's soft dick. "For...however long I decide?"

They'd agreed Matty's first trial run would be four days, and if he liked it, they'd try it for a full week. Matty would be on vacation during that time, so it wouldn't interfere with his work and they could see how he coped emotionally. But Matty appreciated Rob's attempt to add a thrill to the whole thing by pretending they hadn't agreed to that part already.

"Yeah."

"Okay. Let me catch my breath and then I'll let you give me your very special, only-Matty-can-give-it-to-me present." He grinned.

Matty squirmed, digging his heels into the mattress as his spent cock laid soft and slick against his stomach. The reality of the clear polycarbonate device sitting in pieces on their bedside table, along with a tiny metal lock, took Matty's breath away in anticipation.

Rob sat next to him naked, his back against the headboard and long legs stretched out in front. Matty ran his eyes over Rob's body, loving the way it glistened, still damp from their shared shower after dancing. Rob had only watched Matty and Julien salsa, but had been eager to join Matty under the water. Matty was still damp, and newly shaven and trimmed in all of his tender, exhausted private areas to accommodate the cage. He brushed against Rob's bush of pubes, taking hold of Rob's cock and enjoying the way it flexed and filled a little against his palm, even as Rob continued to read the instructions for chastity device.

"It looks a little complicated, but I'm sure we can figure it out." Rob put the paper on the nightstand next to the parts and turned on his side to face Matty. They kissed and breathed each other in, tenderness and desire passing between them, too soon after their last encounter to escalate into full-on need.

"I love you so much," Matty whispered, his heart clenching with affection. "You're so good to me."

"You deserve it."

"But it's your present. I want to show you how devoted I am to you, Rob. I want you to understand what you mean to me."

"Sweetheart, I know that already."

"Just hold me a minute."

Rob pulled him close, and Matty whispered his love and devotion again. "No one, Rob, no one on earth is as amazing as you. I want to be so good for you."

It took a little while to determine which base ring was the best fit, but after that, it didn't take long to fasten on the device. Matty kneeled with his hands behind his back as Rob worked his testicles through the base ring one at a time. Rob slipped the small, dick-shaped, confining cage over his soft cock, and then screwed it to the base ring. Its design left an opening at the end for urination, but the rest of his cock was covered completely and there was very little room for an erection. There was no doubt that even a half-chub would be painful. The device itself felt a little heavy on his dick. Matty swallowed hard as Rob inspected the fit, feeling all around and examined it closely to make sure it wasn't too tight or too loose. Then he put the little lock through the attaching hoop, met Matty's eye, and clicked it closed.

"Happy anniversary," Matty whispered, his tongue thick and his legs shaking with post-sex exhaustion. Sometimes he marveled at how he could do two Pilates classes and skate for hours without the same kind of bone-deep tremors he got after sex with Rob. It had to be something chemical that triggered such an intense physiological reaction to their lovemaking.

Rob tweaked a sore nipple, making Matty squeak, and kissed him gently. "Thank you. I'm curious to see what it does."

"I think it just does this," Matty said, waving at his limp dick wrapped up in the polycarbonate.

"Oh, I was promised a lot more than that. I'm sure we'll see how it works tomorrow."

Matty huffed a laugh and curled up as Rob's little spoon after they turned out the bedside lamps. He lay in the dark, warm and happy, his back pressed up against Rob's stomach and chest, and his ass cupped by Rob's pelvis. He closed his eyes and waited for sleep to come.

But it didn't.

Instead, he couldn't stop thinking about his dick—how it felt in the cage, how the material had warmed so that only the weight of it was really noticeable, how if he had to pee, he'd need to sit down to do it, how his balls felt fuller already, like the spunk they held knew it wasn't going to be released anytime soon. He shifted onto his back once he heard Rob's even breaths pulling in and out.

Matty tried to copy his breathing pattern, hoping he'd follow him down into sleep. But his mind couldn't let go of his dick being locked up. He reached down to cup the cage, adjusting it a little, and his cock thickened inside. Not a full erection, which would be impossible, not even a half-chub, but a rush of blood under flesh that made him shift anxiously, wondering what would happen if his body did try to get fully hard. How would it feel? Would he like it? Or hate it? Or—?

Now he knew. His cock pushed against the cage, and he had to pinch his sore nipples to get it to deflate a little. Groaning, he turned over onto his stomach, but then rolled back to his side again when that proved an uncomfortable position.

Matty lay in the dark with Rob sleeping next to him, and wondered what the hell he'd gotten himself into.

CHAPTER TWENTY

"OH, BITCH, WHAT have you done to yourself?" Elliot sat on Matty and Rob's bed staring wide-eyed at Matty's cock and balls, on display because Matty held down the top of his sweatpants to prove that, no, he wasn't fucking kidding about putting his dick in a chastity device.

Elliot shook his head and murmured, "You've lost your mind. This was your idea?"

"It seemed like a great one at the time," Matty said, pouting down at his bound penis. He jerked up his sweatpants—which he'd borrowed from Rob since they were nice and loose against his groin—and sighed. "But now I'm horny all the time and I feel like if I don't get a dick in me *right now* I might die. I'm not feeling especially choosy, either." He eyed Elliot. "Even you're looking good."

"Oh, hell no." Elliot shook his head firmly. "You know I only top for true love. Besides, it'd be like fucking my brother." He grimaced. "Gross."

"Don't mention your brother," Matty whimpered, flopping back onto the bed and covering his eyes. "Last time I saw him, he was all grown up with loads of manly hair on his legs and chest. His face wasn't too bad either. Fuck, I bet he's hung."

"Shut up. He's straight and I don't want you thinking about his penis. Besides, you should be ashamed of yourself; he's still younger than your brother."

"Ugh. My brother." Matty stilled. "Oh, hey that worked. Joey. Joey. Joseph." He pictured his brother in his head—his stupid little smile, his football jersey and blue-jeans casual wear, his pretty little

226

fiancée, and his horrible baseball cap collection. "Yes. Perfect!" He thought more about his brother. Cute little Joseph and his cute new job as an assistant to an incredibly hot ad exec. "Oh, no! No, no, no!"

"You're getting aroused thinking about your own brother?" Elliot sounded disgusted.

"No! He's working for this super-hot silver fox. So unbelievably hot." Matty rolled his head around on the bed, trying to shake the images free. "Annnnd now I can't stop thinking about role-playing some hot office sex over a desk with neck ties used as restraints and that silver fox working me over." He grabbed hold of Elliot's arm. "I'm doomed. I'm so damned doomed. My horniness knows no bounds. I had to cancel my hair appointment with Deegan because I can't see him like this. Elliot, I might literally fuck myself with a cucumber or something if Rob doesn't come home soon."

"What's wrong with a dildo?"

"Rob locked up the sex toys." Rob looked a bit grim as he'd done it, and now Matty was sure he had regrets about that given the texts Matty had already sent that morning before inviting Elliot over as a distraction.

"Wow. Well, honey, hate to break it to you, but you've got a long day ahead of you."

Matty shuddered and scrubbed at his face. "Next time I have a brilliant idea that involves my sex life, stop me."

"Uh, I don't think I have the authority to do that. You should talk to Rob about how he gives in to you too much. What kind of dom does that, anyway? He should deny you everything you ask for and make you suck him off while calling you his dirty little slut." Elliot was clearly warming to his topic, because his eyes glowed as he went on. "And he should force you to do his bidding with no hope of any reward, and —"

"Shut up. Oh my God, *shut up*. That was the whole idea, don't you see?" Matty squeezed his eyes shut and willed his cock to stop pressing so relentlessly against the cock cage. It was painful and awkward enough. Elliot was not helping.

"Uh-huh, so what's the problem?"

"The problem is now it's working and it's awful. I haven't been able to stop thinking about sex for more than three seconds since he put it on, unless you count the two hours of sleep I got after he finally fucked me senseless this morning before work and I passed out."

"Can you come with that thing on?"

"Um, kinda. It's different. It's not as strong, but it can go on a long time, and there's no real refractory period, I guess. But it's not like coming with your dick. It's doesn't *satisfy*. It just makes me want more."

Elliot tutted at him and rolled onto his side, propping himself on his elbow to look down at Matty. "Have you tried talking to your mom?"

"About my dick being locked up? Uh, no."

"No, stupid, just *talking* to her. If thinking about Joey helped, I'm sure talking to your mom, or better yet, your dad, would be water on the flames."

"They're on a cruise for her birthday," Matty moaned.

"What crap timing. For you, I mean. I hope Mama and Papa Marcus have a great time, but they would've been the perfect cure." Elliot pondered. "Have you tried going skating? Getting out on the ice might help." He tilted his head. "Can you even skate in that thing?"

"I can, but not today. I'm too tender down there from being half-hard all the time. I can't put on any pants tighter than these sweats. If I can get calmed down, maybe I could head over there to burn off some of this excess energy. Although it's the first day of my vacation and I'd rather not visit work."

"Such a mess you're in." Elliot sounded like he might laugh. "How about just getting out of the apartment? Maybe you should take a walk? I'll go with you. We can get fro-yo."

Matty shook his head. "Oh my God, no. No."

"Why?"

"My balls hurt too much to walk. I just want to find a way to come."

"Well, I can't help you with that."

Matty flung an arm over his eyes, blocking out Elliot's amused expression. "You're an awful best friend."

"The worst."

"Call Rob for me. Tell him it's an emergency. He's got to come home. Because I need him. Now."

Elliot laughed. "I'm totally sure that'll work, babe. That sounds just like Rob to drop his patients and his responsibilities to come service your butt."

Matty lifted his arm to glare at him. "I'm supposed to be servicing him, asshole."

"Mmm-hmm, well, I hope you've learned your lesson." Elliot rolled away from Matty, stood and yawned, and ran his hand through his blond hair and over his now somewhat wrinkled jacket. "You know what? I'm regretting agreeing to spend my day off with you."

"Please don't leave me."

Elliot shook his head. "I can't just sit here and watch you be horny all afternoon. That's weird. I mean, sure, we already have a weird friendship. And that's great. I like that about us. But hanging out while you squirm around in some horndog stupor is just...no."

"Would you at least run upslope to the store and buy a cucumber for me?"

Elliot gaped at him. "Are you serious right now?"

"Yeah. Like a really thick one, okay?"

Elliot threw his hands up. "No. And on that note, I'm going home."

"Why? What are you going to do at home that you can't do here?"

Elliot put his hands on his hips. "I'll tell you what I can do there. I'm going to take a nice long, preparatory shower, douche my butt, and hit someone up on Grindr for sex that will end in a fantastic orgasm. With my dick."

"No!" Matty groaned. "It's not fair!"

"You know what's not fair? Getting vicariously worked up by all this sex mojo you've got going and knowing that *you're* going to get thoroughly banged later by the man of everyone's dreams." Elliot flipped him off. "You suck. Meanwhile, all I've got is a couple hundred utterly not-dreamy strangers to choose from. *That's* not fair, Matty."

Matty saw an opportunity to prolong Elliot's stay, and besides, he was really curious. "What happened with that Ulysses guy?"

"Oh. Him." Elliot's face twisted like he'd sucked a lemon. "Not going to work out."

"Why?"

Elliot collapsed back down on the bed next to Matty. "Because I fucked up."

"Oh, babe."

"I know." Elliot chewed on his bottom lip, his big brown eyes looking hurt and angry at once. "It's my own fucking fault."

"What happened?"

"He didn't turn the vibrator on."

"Prude?"

Elliot shrugged. "I don't know. He says he isn't. He handed me the remote at the end of dinner and said, 'Listen, I'm not afraid to turn this thing on. It's just that I like you, and if I turn it on we both know what happens next. Let's not rush things.'"

"That doesn't sound bad."

"I guess. But I sort of didn't react well."

Matty rolled up onto his elbow to gaze down at Elliot's face. "What did you say?"

"It's more like what I did. I kind of got fucked in a little, teeny-tiny, not that big of a deal orgy right afterward? Like an hour later?"

"What? Why?" Matty blinked at him. "I mean, wait, an orgy? With who? How do these things even happen to you? Wait, no, answer my first question. Why?"

"Because I was so fucking embarrassed." His cheeks flushed. "I mean, I gave him a remote control to a vibrating butt plug in my ass, Matty."

"I know."

"And he didn't use it."

"Because he liked you too much to use it. That's kind of sweet."

Elliot chewed on his lip some more and then shook his head. "Oh well. Fuck it. I ruined it anyway."

"Does he know you went to an orgy?"

"No, but I know what I did and why I did it. Isn't that enough?"

Matty's stomach clenched. He got that, he did, he just hated that Elliot felt that way.

"Anyway, I didn't answer his texts after that. He stopped when I didn't reply to the fifth one."

"Well, here's what you need to do. Text him back. Apologize. Tell him you were embarrassed and ask to try again."

"Am I allowed to do that?"

"Yes!"

Elliot considered this and then bounded up from the bed again. "Maybe I will. Maybe I'll do that instead of some miserable Grindr hook-up. But I probably won't." He kissed Matty's cheek. "Thanks, babe. You're the best. Good luck with your dick problem."

Matty sat up on the bed and called after Elliot as he headed into the living room and grabbed his keys from the counter. "You can do that later, Elliot! Please stay. You have to distract me. I will literally lose my mind if you leave me here alone."

Elliot shook his head. "Oh, no. You made your bed. Lie in it."

Matty moaned. "That's what Rob said when I texted him."

"Ha! Good for him."

"I tried to pretend he meant it literally." Matty ran his hand over the rumpled duvet. "At least lying here for a while imagining I was following his orders was kind of hot." Matty whimpered and fell back against the bed again. "Maybe I could get him to give me a few more orders. That might help."

"Annnnnd, I'm out," Elliot called from the doorway. "Don't bother getting up. I'll lock up with my key. Enjoy yourself, idiot. Love you."

Matty waved him off and rolled over onto his stomach, humping helplessly at the mattress as he heard the door shut and lock. No real friction reached his cock through the polycarbonate, so he flipped back over and stared up at the ceiling.

Only eight hours until Rob got home.

That morning Rob had laid out his expectations for the first few days of using the device: he wanted it to remind Matty at all times that he was under Rob's command and not under Control's, and he wanted to see how Matty coped with not being able to touch his cock. So far, the first thing was working out just fine, but the second? Not so much.

He pushed down his sweat pants and looked at the cock cage again. His dick looked small and his balls seemed somehow larger. He wasn't sure if it was an optical illusion or if they truly were swollen from the unreleased jizz from the backed-up orgasms he wasn't having.

He just needed *something*.

Twenty minutes later, he was writhing on the bed, three fingers shoved up his ass and his arm trembling from the effort. Matty missed the depth and thickness of a dildo, but his fingers were taking the edge off at least.

He knew they didn't have a cucumber in the house. He'd looked earlier, but maybe they had a banana? Or a carrot?

He rolled out of bed, hitching up his sweat pants, to go in the kitchen to see. It wasn't like Rob had said he couldn't put *anything* at all up there. Though the lock on their toy drawer full of dildos was obviously a command of its own kind. Still, he hadn't actually *said*.

But fuck, there were no bananas. Or fruit or vegetables of any phallic nature. There *was* a hunk of ginger, and Matty briefly considered it, but figging was a punishment best enjoyed with a partner. Matty looked down at his barely hanging-on sweatpants and considered going out to the corner store after all to buy a fat plantain or cucumber, but he couldn't be seen in public wearing Rob's sweatpants. Maybe if he dressed up with a glitter-bomb T-shirt it might seem like he was starting a new fashion? A super-horny insane person's fashion.

Back to fingers.

He flung himself face down on the sofa and reached around to rub the pads of his fingertips over his asshole, but it didn't feel as good as when someone else did it. He moaned and slid his hand to the front and gripped his caged cock, cradling it sweetly in his hand like a long lost lover.

Matty held very still on the sofa, breathing in and out slowly like the calming meditation he'd watched on YouTube had encouraged. After a few long, intense minutes, he finally felt like he was calm enough to talk to someone without bursting into hysterical horny tears. He picked up his phone and chose a name from his Favorites list. The call went straight to voicemail.

A few seconds later, Matty's phone binged, alerting him to a text.

Why are you calling me?

Because I need to talk with you.

Is everything okay?

I just really need to hear your voice.

The phone vibrated and trilled in his palm. Matty answered gratefully, "Oh, thank God."

"What's wrong?" Joey asked. "Are you okay?"

"Yeah. I'm just missing you."

"You miss me." Joey sounded skeptical.

"Uh-huh."

"Okay? Um, I guess I miss you too? Maybe?"

"Good. You should. I'm the best brother in the world."

"Yeah. You've said that before. I'm still not buying it." Joey sounded even more skeptical. "I'm at work so...what's up?"

"Um, hey, how are the Cardinals doing?"

"Good."

"Who'd they play last week? I don't remember."

Joey was unable to resist someone actually asking to talk about the team of his heart, and Matty got comfortable on the sofa, stretching out and settling in. He listened eagerly as Joey gave a rundown on the Cardinals entire season thus far. He barely listened to the actual words, but the sound of Joey's voice was a complete and total turn-off. It was perfect. He just had to keep him on the phone for—he glanced at the clock—seven hours. Unfortunately, Joey stopped babbling after only four precious minutes.

"Tell me more."

"About The Cardinals?"

"Sure. Or I don't know. Some other team."

"What's going on with you? You don't give a damn about sports."

Matty gasped. "Excuse me? I'm an athlete!"

"You don't care about sports with balls, I mean. Do *not* make a gay sex joke out that."

"I wasn't going to."

Joey scoffed.

"You know I can only take so much of Rob's Yankees obsession." Matty always tuned Rob out when he started in on the baseball talk and sometimes even picked up his phone, dialed Joey, and handed the phone over to Rob, saying: *Here's someone who cares.*

"Uh-huh."

"Sometimes I need some Cardinal love sung so sweetly in my ear. Tweet-a-leet-a-leet, Joey."

"What's this really about?"

Matty opened the curtains behind the couch and looked out front, watching a neighbor girl bounce by on a pogo stick. "Can't I have a nice, long, loving conversation with my brother?"

"No."

"Why not?"

Joey's sigh was fantastic. No arousal could get to Matty while his brother was on the line. "I'm at work, asshole."

"Oh! Perfect!" Matty sat up eagerly. "Tell me about work. Are you liking it? Are you learning to be Don Draper?"

"You're creeping me out."

Matty frowned. Why did Joey have to be so skeptical? "Fine. Tell me about the wedding."

"Is that what this is about? Mom told me, you know."

"Told you what?"

"That you're upset I haven't asked you yet."

234

Matty groaned. "I'm not upset! Actually, you know what? I am upset!" He got up and started pacing the apartment—couch to garden door to couch again. "Haven't I always supported you? Haven't I always been there for you?"

"Not really. You've been all over the world a dozen times but you never came to a single one of my football games or swim meets."

Matty gasped. "I was training!"

Joey sounded like he was shrugging. "I'm not blaming you. I'm just pointing out that you haven't always been there for me. Sometimes you were really busy trying to go to the Olympics. And that's okay."

Matty stopped in the kitchen. His brain shocked into silence. "Are you pissed about that?"

Joey made a thoughtful sound. "I guess. Well, no, I'm not now. I used to be, though. Mom went everywhere with you and I was sort of the second-thought kid, you know?" He shuffled papers on his end of the line. "But in the end, that's okay. I had a normal life at least."

Matty leaned against the counter in silence, his head whirring, and he braced himself for the voice of Control. But it didn't come. He closed his eyes. "I'm so sorry."

"No. Don't be sorry."

Quietly, Matty offered, "It's okay if you want to ask Jet. He was there for you when I wasn't."

"Jet's not my brother, dude. Anyway, I've got to go. Some of us have work to do." Joey was quiet for a moment. "Wait, why aren't *you* at work? Did you get fired or something?"

"Not yet!" Matty said as cheerfully as he could. "My vacation started."

"Good. It would totally stress Mom out if you lost your job. And then she'd call me wanting to talk about you, asking me if I think you're okay and if you're eating enough and all the other shit she worries about when it comes to you. Those phone calls get old, dude. I can't imagine what all Dad has to listen to before he gets annoyed and she resorts to calling me. You should stop doing things that worry her. Be, I don't know, as normal and sane as it's possible for you to be."

"I'm working on that, actually."

"Huh. I don't think you are, actually." He chuckled. "This phone call isn't normal, for example."

"I'll try harder."

Joey shuffled papers around in the background. "You do that. Okay, talk to you later. In person soon, maybe."

"Okay, Joey. But, hey, I love you, and I'm sorry I wasn't a better big brother."

Joey was quiet for a second but then he said, "You were a pretty good big brother. I especially liked the makeup in our bathroom growing up. That was always a blast to explain to friends."

Matty snorted. "Your friends got involuntary diversity training at our house."

"They're all better for it. It's all good." There was a pause. "No, that's not the right form—hold on, Matty—yeah, I'm sure Mr. Ponticello said he needed the—hey listen, I have to go."

"Sure. Sorry to bother you at work."

"Okay, bye. And, wait! Matty, of course you're gonna be my best man."

CHAPTER TWENTY-ONE

R OB APPROACHED THE row of brownstones that led to their own with more hesitation than he cared to admit. The texts and phone calls from Matty throughout the day had left no doubt as to what he'd find when he got inside.

Part of him was excited by it, but most of him was already raw from a rough day at work — an angry paraplegic and a crying twenty-year-old recovering from meningitis had been a difficult combination. Then there'd been Matty's needy texts and calls, and he'd missed the train home because he got stuck behind some slow-walking tourists he couldn't bring himself to push past.

A busker in the subway station had almost made his head explode by playing the "Careless Whisper" saxophone solo over and over, and he'd been accosted by an angry street person as he'd exited the subway station near home. The heat had left a layer of grime over his skin that he couldn't stand, and he swore if he heard another car horn, he was going to lose his mind.

He hesitated on their stoop. Vaguely, beneath his soul-saturated exhaustion, he was amused by Matty's surprise at the reality of chastity. He'd clearly believed his own sales pitch about just how great this "gift" was going to be for Rob. Matty had honestly seemed to think that having his cock locked away was going to be a cinch, and make him less greedy and much more giving during sex.

But Rob wasn't surprised at all. As he'd said to Sato, he expected Matty to finger-fuck himself into a stupor. Because Matty, when it came to sex, was the very definition of greedy — more, more, more, and me, me, me was pretty much his chant.

In Montana, he'd loved Matty's greed, and he would have been eager to return from a day of dealing with a stray cow entering federal lands to find an aroused, needy Matty begging for his cock. He'd have been delirious with lust himself and eager to find out how Matty would cope with pain without the distraction of imminent orgasm to mitigate it. He'd have probably paid money to see what Matty would be willing to do to satisfy his greed when gratifying his cock wasn't on the menu.

But he wasn't in Montana. And as he stuck his key in the door, he didn't know if he could deal with what he was going to find inside.

What he found left him swaying on his feet. Matty was on the floor, face down, ass up, knees spread enough that Rob could see his hole, and already flushed with desperate lust and sweating with need. Lube sat out on the coffee table, and Matty's asshole was slightly red from what must have been aggressive and prolonged fingering.

Christ.

Rob's heart pounded. His cock responded. But he was so fucking tired.

He took a deep breath and gathered himself. He could handle this. He could deal with Matty. He just needed to summon the strength. "It's a good thing I didn't invite Arjun back to the apartment for a few drinks like I planned," he said. "What a surprise this would have been."

Matty didn't move, though his rib cage expanded and released with quickened breaths, and his asshole opened and squeezed in an involuntary spasm.

Rob squatted behind him, taking in the way his balls and cock hung clumsily in the device, and the slight tremble in his thighs. "Or would you have liked Arjun seeing you like this? On your elbows and knees waiting for me. Hungry for what I give you."

Matty's hole flexed again, and he shivered all over.

"Good to know."

He'd never let anyone see Matty like this, but it was an interesting thing to threaten.

"So," Rob said, reaching out to slide his index finger down Matty's crack and over his hole. Matty's body quivered in anticipation. "What did you do today?"

Matty gasped and made a sound of struggle before thrusting his ass back at Rob with a small sob.

"Huh. Sounds like a busy day." Rob stood and hung up his coat, kicked off his shoes, and stripped down to his boxer briefs and T-shirt. He folded his clothes carefully and sat them on the coffee table beside the lube.

Stooping low enough to stroke down Matty's back as he walked past him toward the kitchen, Rob spoke calmly. "I don't know about you, but I'm exhausted. Walking around all day in this heat takes it out of me."

Matty half-sobbed.

"You just rest there a few more minutes. You look good like that."

He pulled out a beer from the fridge and pried the lid free with Matty's rhinestone ice-skate-shaped bottle opener. "Wait there. I'm going to shower."

He took a leak in the bathroom. After washing his hands, he splashed his face with cold water and grabbed a clean towel from the linen closet. Then he showered quickly, getting the worst of the city off him. After he dried himself, he put on a clean pair of boxers and headed back into the living room.

Passing by Matty again, he stroked a hand over his hair, soft and product-free, flopping over where his forehead rested on his crossed arms. Matty's shoulders trembled, and his ass lifted up again in desperation, but Rob continued to the sofa, where he threw down the towel. He collapsed into a comfortable seated position and spread his legs.

"Please," Matty whimpered.

Rob let his head fall back and took a few deep breaths. His dick was hard, but he was just so fucking worn out. After a few moments of listening to Matty's breathing, he picked up the remote control, clicked on the television, and pulled his cock out of his underwear.

He jerked it casually a few times. "When you're ready, you can come over here and suck me off."

He flicked through the Netflix selection, trying to choose something that would be nice to watch while getting head. He went with *Mad Men*. Matty enjoyed the tortured Don Draper character, but Rob had a not-so-secret hard-on for Pete.

Rob glanced over to where Matty's ribs were still expanding and releasing, too thin, but not scary-thin, thank God, and he asked, "You ate lunch?"

Matty clenched his hands into fists and sat up, leaning back on his heels, his cheeks burning red against the paleness of the rest of his face. His cock pressed grotesquely against the cage. "Cottage cheese. A salad. Almond milk shake with kale and honey."

"Good. Tell me what else you did today."

Matty licked his lips, his eyes dark and pupils blown wide. "I double checked the outfits I packed for our trip. Elliot came over. I talked to Joey. Took a nap. I read more of those chastity blogs. I prepared for tonight, cleaned up, and then I waited for you."

Rob rubbed his thumb around the head of his cock. "Did the sub guys in those chastity blogs talk about ignoring a clear invitation to suck their boyfriend's dick? Because I thought you said something about being less greedy and giving all your attention to my orgasms?"

Matty's neck flushed as red as his cheeks, and Rob had to hold back his laughter. He wasn't going to get tired of flinging that in Matty's face—at least not for a while. It was far too amusing. Matty's fists tightened and relaxed, and then he set his jaw stubbornly, walking on his knees toward where Rob sat on the couch.

Rob chucked his chin up. "I don't want a grudge-suck."

Matty stopped between Rob's legs, his hands on Rob's knees, and looked up at him with big, dark liquid eyes as he licked his lips. "I want to do it. I love sucking your dick. I'm just kind of keyed up." He shifted, obviously uncomfortable with his cock pressing against the cage. "But you're right. The cage is your anniversary gift."

"It's a great gift, sweetheart."

Matty smiled, and it was a cross between his fake smile and his anxious one that meant he was in over his head. He took hold of Rob's cock and set about giving him a thorough, wet, sloppy-good blow job that Rob dragged out a lot longer than he normally would have, watching three-quarters of an entire episode of *Mad Men* and then flipping over to the cable to pretend to watch ESPN analysis of the Yankees' chances against the A's.

It was self-indulgent and delicious. He couldn't remember the last time he'd let himself sit back and enjoy sensations this way. He kept Matty's pace slow enough that he didn't come, but fast enough that his groin flooded with heat again and again. His cock ached and his balls throbbed, and he didn't come, and he didn't come.

Matty grew frantic as he worked. His fingers straying back to his own ass several times before Rob took his hands and placed them on his balls and shaft. "This is about me. Your hands, your mouth, your body — it's all for my pleasure right now."

When Rob's cock was almost too tender to come, and Matty's lips had grown red and swollen from his efforts, he finally closed his eyes and gave in to the next escalation of pleasure. "Swallow."

Matty reacted to that word by redoubling his efforts, and Rob grunted, his balls jerking up tight as he came into Matty's eagerly sucking mouth. "Fuck, sweetheart. Fucking hell."

When he could open his eyes again, Matty's expression was hopeful as he licked his lips and gazed adoringly up at Rob. His body trembled from the work he'd put into Rob's orgasm, and probably from the adrenaline still stringing him along after a day of obsessive fixation and fantasies.

"Climb up here beside me. Elbows on the armrest, ass up."

Matty didn't hesitate, and Rob tucked his own cock away. He reached for the remote control, turning the volume up so he could hear what the sports analysts were saying a little better. Then he picked up the lube, coated his fingers, and slid two into Matty's ass without any other preparation. Matty arched and moaned in gratitude.

Rob hammered Matty's prostate with the pads of his fingers.

Within minutes he was admiring the string of fluid that drained from Matty's caged cock to the towel on the sofa. Matty was so worked up that if his cock had been free, Rob knew he'd have come almost immediately.

Instead, he panted and writhed, his entire body flushing and tensing. "Oh my God, I need it," Matty cried, seeking and seeking, but not finding release. His asshole gripped Rob's working fingers. "Please, please!"

Rob knew Matty had come from having his prostate massaged before, but the cage seemed to be containing even that release tonight. "Just relax into it, sweetheart."

Matty moaned and squirmed on his fingers, and Rob shifted so he could get better access, pressing a third finger in. He loved the sight of Matty's asshole stretching and finally accepting the additional intrusion, and the sexy little gasp that went with it. He vigorously finger-fucked Matty until he was shaking and keening, crying out to God and begging for more.

"I need it. I need it," he moaned mindlessly. Rob wasn't even sure what Matty was referring to—Rob's cock, orgasm, or his own dick.

"Okay, sweetheart. Change position for me." Matty was too out of it to move, so Rob helped him let go of his death grip on the armrest of the sofa and turn around. His eyes were glazed and his face flushed; he didn't even seem to see Rob he was so lost in need. Rob pulled Matty over his lap, feeling the warm, hard cock cage flop against the skin of his leg before Matty curled up into a ball with his face in Rob's crotch and his ass in the air.

Rob grabbed the lube, added a lot more, and worked a fourth finger in while Matty groaned and gripped Rob's thighs, his short nails digging in sharply. He sobbed hot gusts of breath against Rob's half-hard dick.

He'd gotten his whole fist in only once before, and Rob doubted they'd go that far tonight. But Matty was so out of it, so far gone, focused completely on his hole, loose and lost to the world, that it was the perfect time to practice. He folded his thumb in and worked the narrow end of the resulting "duck head" into Matty's gaping, star-shaped asshole.

"Open up, sweetheart. Take my hand."

Matty reached back to spread his cheeks, his body flushed and shaking hard as Rob plunged five fingers into his gripping, sucking heat. Soon Matty started to convulse, his body spasming as he shouted and groaned, muffling his sounds poorly against Rob's hip and thigh. A gush of hot, wet fluid poured from Matty's cock onto Rob's leg.

"Beautiful, Matty. Good work."

Rob wasn't sure Matty had even heard him. Jizz flowed from his cock cage like a river, and his breathing came as hard and fast as it did after an entire routine on the ice.

"Relax. Open up for me."

The thickest part of Rob's hand squeezed against Matty's dilated anus, and didn't go in. He reached for more lube and drizzled it over his five fingers and the knuckles of his hand. It was good lube, but not good enough to allow for full-on fisting.

Matty's asshole quivered, open and greedy. Rob fucked five fingers in again and again. He watched Matty come apart. Matty's thighs shook, and his body trembled as he rode Rob's hand. Rob glanced toward the clock. It wasn't even eight o'clock yet. They'd been at it for less time than he'd thought. There were hours yet before Matty would be ready to sleep.

Matty was a sweaty, crying, sobbing mess. He scrambled at the sofa and Rob's thighs, scratching him with his short nails, wailing as he reached ecstasy again. Come gushed from his squashed cock, falling hot and sloppy onto Rob's thigh, and Matty's body shook so hard that Rob had to hold him to keep him from falling off the sofa.

"Are you okay?" Rob murmured.

"What happened?" Matty moaned. "What did you do?"

Clearly, Matty had reached orgasm, or whatever height of pleasure he could attain without his cock being involved. Rob's high was wearing off, and his arm was getting tired. But Matty was insatiable. He was already pressing his ass up for more, his breath quavering as he begged. "I need it. Again. Please. I need it so much."

Rob let his head fall back as he pushed his fingers back inside Matty's clenching hole.

It was going to be a long, long night.

CHAPTER TWENTY-TWO

M ATTY WAS FAILING at chastity.

On a scale of one-to-his-first-Olympics, he had to privately admit to himself that he was verging on Olympic levels of failure. If the idea was that he wasn't going to think about his own pleasure but focus only on Rob's, well, that wasn't happening at all. He'd had the cage on for nearly seventy-two hours and he'd spent a good number of those with Rob's fingers or dick in his ass because *he* needed it, not necessarily because Rob wanted it. Worse, he was too incredibly horny to even really *care* about how much he was failing at the execution of his gift.

His steady state of constant arousal confused him because there'd been plenty of times over the course of his life that he'd gone as many as three or four days without getting off. There'd even been that time at the height of his Olympic training with Valentina when he'd been so physically exhausted that he'd gone three weeks without masturbating. Eventually, he'd woken with his hand on his cock and he'd just let it finish. After that, he'd gone back to his regularly scheduled masturbation program.

But the constant weight of the cage, as well as the other little things, like having to sit to urinate, asking Rob to help him wash the device in the morning with a Q-tip so that he stayed fresh and clean, all served to remind him of his penis and of sex and of how good it would feel to come. And then he'd start to think about his ass, since it was still available. And then he'd beg for more and more and more.

The second day of chastity, Rob had fucked him with a dildo

until finally, at some point past midnight, he'd said, "Sweetheart, I'm exhausted. I have to stop. I need some rest."

Yes, he was failing *completely* at his very fucking special only-Matty-can-give-it chastity gift.

Dinner with Ben and Anja to celebrate his and Rob's anniversary was also turning into a disaster. All he could think about was leaving so he could get Rob's dick up his ass. He was so horny his hands shook, his skin hummed, and fluid leaked from the end of his dick. He could feel it pooling in the cage and soaking his underwear, all while he tried to smile cheerfully and act completely normal in front of Rob's son and best friend. The only thing that could be worse and make him feel even more disgusting would be if his mother and father were sitting across from him instead.

Matty took a deep breath and brought his attention back to the table. Ben had finished telling them about some summer school courses he was taking to catch up after a tough year of intensive skating training that had paid off with a gold medal at Nationals. Now Rob was telling Anja about his last phone call with Bing about the old ranch in Montana.

"It looks like the profits are going to be great when they come. It's like I always knew—plenty of money in that line of production between the goat milk and the meat—but Bing's being smart and reinvesting to grow the venture." Rob chuckled. "He suggested I get a place upstate to start a second branch."

"Would you actually do that?" Ben asked, shoving a hank of blond hair off his forehead and leaning forward with an earnest shine to his blue eyes. He was almost eighteen now, a senior in high school, and had grown nearly as tall as Rob, with broad shoulders and a narrow waist over his skater's butt. He was a handsome kid and had a warmth about him that drew friends easily.

"I don't know."

"C'mon Dad, I know being a cattle rancher wasn't your thing, but you're not exactly New York City material."

Matty lifted his head from where he was moving the salad around his plate. "Rob looks lovely against a city backdrop," he said.

Ben snorted. "You'd think he looked good anywhere."

"The beach, the farm, the desert," Matty agreed. He flushed. Thinking about how Rob looked in different settings was *not* a good line of thought. His arousal began to peak again.

"I don't know," Rob mused. "I wouldn't hate having some land. Maybe a ranch wasn't for me, but a truly small-time operation might be something I'd like to do again one day." He looked Matty's way. "When we're older and the city isn't such a draw."

Matty wasn't sure the city could ever be less of a draw, but he smiled rather than reply because his mind was stuck on a memory of Rob astride a horse with Montana mountains rising up behind him. Handsome, strong, in control. Sexy. Hot.

"There are places where you could keep your day job and still have a small farm," Anja said thoughtfully. Her blond hair was up in a ponytail, and she wore a green dress that made her pale skin shine. "I know you love physical therapy." She said it smugly, blue eyes sparkling. It'd been her idea, after all, for Rob to sell the farm and go back to school to become a PT. "But you do seem out of place in the city."

"Physical therapy work is very satisfying," Rob agreed. "But it's not my passion." He glanced toward Matty, and everyone clearly saw it: the devotion and adoration pouring off him. It made Matty's dick thud painfully against the polycarbonate.

Anja chuckled. "Yes, well, we all know where your passion lies."

Ben rolled his eyes, but smiled. "You guys are stupid in love. We all know nothing else compares to your love for Matty."

"Except my love for you," Rob said to Ben.

"Whatever, Dad." Ben rolled his eyes again but seemed pleased. "Anyway, I like goats. They're a lot more fun than cattle. You should move somewhere you can have goats. Don't you think, Matty?"

"Sure," Matty said, his mind still stuck on Rob's passion and its focus on him. He really needed to stop thinking about sex, because he might agree to move upstate if it meant getting out of here and getting Rob's fingers in his ass again.

"Baby goats are really cute," Ben said.

"They make terrible accessories, though," Matty babbled, keeping his mind on goats because now that he was picturing them, they weren't a big turn-on. "I'm not a big fan of goat hair. But goat milk soap is great for skin. I'll give the critters that much."

He felt Rob's hand on his knee, and the weight of it and the weight of the cock cage combined made his head spin. He was owned, claimed, secure. He wanted their experiment to be over so he could concentrate again, and he wanted to descend into it even further—giving up his life to do nothing but roll around in bed wanting Rob.

Danger, danger. His cock cage felt tighter, making him squirm with discomfort.

Rob squeezed his knee and murmured, "Eat a little more, sweetheart."

Matty resented needing the reminder. If he wasn't so aroused that he couldn't stand being in his own skin, he'd be a lot better able to please Rob by eating without being prompted. He took a small bite of his salad and sipped his wine, trying to focus on what Ben was saying now. Something about skating, which should really be up his alley, but it was like everyone's words just slid through his brain and poured out his ears.

Blinking, he refocused on Ben and Anja. They were both quite good looking—blond, blue-eyed, with peaches-and-cream complexions—but also completely not-sexy. Maybe if he kept his focus on the two of them, his arousal might fade to a manageable level. If not, he was going to cry. And that would be hard to explain.

"Matty, are you really so happy coaching that you're not going to do shows at all anymore? Not even for Christmas?" Ben asked.

"Well," his voice squeaked, and he pushed some hair off his sweating forehead. Rob rubbed his thigh maddeningly. "Um, well, Julien is trying to get something for me at the end of summer." Matty flushed, remembering what had happened after he'd gone dancing with Julien, and *all of this madness* had started.

Fuck.

"Matty? You feeling okay?" Ben asked.

Anja added, "You're all flushed."

"I'm fine." Matty took another gulp of wine and half-choked on it. "It's spicy. The salad, I mean. Lots of peppers and—hot. It's very hot."

"Shows?" Rob prompted, obviously trying to get his mind back on track.

Matty cleared his throat. "Right. So, I'll probably do those shows with Julien and maybe I'll do some this holiday season too. It would be a nice way to pay for Christmas expenses if nothing else. And I might try to book with a small Asian tour next summer."

"Really? That would be awesome." Ben pursed his lips mournfully and looked down at his plate. "I wish tours weren't so hard to come by these days. It's not like the olden days anymore."

"Oh, yes, the olden days of Matty's long ago youth," Rob said, laughing.

"Well, seriously, Dad. It used to be if you were National Champion," and Ben puffed up at that. "You could count on spending your summer on tour with one of the tours like Champions or Stars, but now you have to pray someone with some strings to pull, like Julien, wants to do you a solid."

"How does Julien have strings to pull anyway?" Anja asked. "He never performed that well at the international level and while he's handsome enough to have fans, he's not that strong of a skater."

"He's screwing the showrunner, Mom. Everyone knows that."

"Oh."

Matty wasn't surprised that everyone knew of Julien's dalliance. It wasn't true love, but it was a regular bit of fun that paid off in shows and power, and Julien always seemed to have fun with the man. Matty didn't judge. But, God, he really needed to not be thinking about sex right now.

"You have other things to do this summer. You have summer school and you've got to get ready for next season," Anja said, pertly, taking a bite of her spaghetti.

"Yeah. I gotta get the quads down. I know, Mom." He brightened a little then and added, "And Cardew and I are working on a partners thing together just for fun."

Matty almost asked who Cardew was, but he didn't think he could manage even another minute at the table. His taint was tingling and he thought he'd lose his mind from the crazy, itching, coming out of his skin horniness that just would not stop.

"That's your blond friend from the rink?" Rob said.

"Yeah. We've been couples skating during down time and it's making my coaches insane. They're terrified I'll look gay if I do a pairs program for our rink's holiday show with Cardew."

Matty couldn't respond. He could somehow smell Rob's sweat and spunk—as visceral and real as if he'd just sucked him off. It seemed to layer over his tongue and fill his nostrils. He gripped the edge of the table, wondering if he was going to scream, or burst into tears, or maybe somehow, impossibly *come* right there in front of everyone in the whole restaurant.

"Sorry, I'll be right back," Matty said breathlessly as he stood up on shaking legs. He hoped his cock hadn't leaked enough that there was a spot on his leggings. He looked down and adjusted the fall of his Rag & Bone black-and-green striped blouse to make sure his crotch was covered. As he pushed his chair in and moved to leave the table, his cock pushing angrily against the cage, he touched Rob's shoulder and whispered, "I'm fine. Just have to use the bathroom."

Rob nodded and squeezed his hand before letting him go.

Matty overheard Anja saying something about the Federation as he walked away, but he didn't pay attention, too absorbed by his pulse pounding in his cock and rushing in his ears, and wondering just what he was going to do in the bathroom to get his mind off his need. Because he was nothing *but* need, and fuck, he was *not* winning at this chastity thing. *At all.*

***

ROB TURNED TO watch Matty go into the men's room. Ben was right. He had seemed flushed, but it was probably the salad, or maybe the chastity device. Once he used the restroom and splashed some water on his face, he'd probably be fine.

"Is he okay?" Anja asked.

"Sure. He's just..." Rob shrugged.

Anja gave him a strange look, but she turned her attention back to Ben. "Honey, you don't want to push the Federation that way. Look how that affected Matty." Anja shoved a strand of her blond hair behind her ear.

Ben, unsurprisingly to Rob, stuck up for Matty. "You know what? Matty might not have won the medals he deserved but people will remember him *forever*. Unlike Hank Babikov or Ian Schwartz. No one will care about them before long. Why? Because they're good but they're boring. Matty was never boring. Cardew is never boring. I don't want to medal by being boring."

"Cardew isn't half the skater you are," Anja said.

"Cardew is amazing."

Anja sighed. "He's a mess. His sister can't keep him under control."

"His sister?" Rob asked, confused as to why the boy's sister would be held responsible for his behavior.

"Don't you know about it, Rob?" Anja asked.

"No."

Why would he? When he saw Ben they didn't gossip about his skating friends. They had father-son time spent talking about the Yankees or playing football in Prospect Park, unless Matty stole Ben's attention away by taking him to the rink or spending the entirety of dinner discussing costumes and choreography and, somehow, shoes. Women's shoes, men's shoes, any kind of shoes. It was boggling how much patience Ben had for Matty's endless discussions of shoes.

"Their father died of cancer when Cardew was twelve, right, Ben?"

"Yeah."

"And their mother died in a car wreck two years later," Anja added.

"How awful," Rob murmured around a bit of food.

Ben's eyes were bright, though, when he said, "Ebru is amazing. She was only eighteen when it happened and she stepped up to take care of Cardew." He shot his mother a look and finished with, "And still does."

Rob's brow went up. "This girl's name is Ebru, did you say?"

"Yeah, it's Turkish."

"Is Cardew a Turkish name too?"

Ben laughed. "No, of course not." He seemed think that was hilarious and laughed through a few bites of his food. Rob tried to catch Anja's eye but she was busy frowning at her spaghetti.

"Why is that funny?" Rob asked.

"Oh, it's just...well, Ebru is adopted from Turkey. Cardew's not."

"I see."

Ben went on unprompted. "Anyway, she's like five years older than Cardew, and three older than me."

"You're almost eighteen, so twenty? Or twenty-one?"

"Twenty. She's beautiful. She's got this glossy black hair, and these amazing eyes that aren't green, but aren't brown. I guess they're hazel. They're just..." He seemed breathless. "Amazing."

"Interesting." Rob caught Anja's eye, and she finally smiled a little, dimples appearing in her cheeks.

Anja said, "I guess this must be father-son stuff, because he's never shared *these* particular thoughts with me before."

"Oh, come on, Mom. You *know* Ebru."

"I wouldn't say that."

"But you've talked with her before about your 'concerns' about Cardew. Which, by the way, went over terribly, and just pissed Ebru off."

Rob noted that Ebru being upset seemed pretty important to Ben. He wondered if Anja realized that her son was in love.

"She's so young. I thought she might appreciate getting some input from someone a little older."

"Yeah, well, she's older than you when you had me."

Anja sighed. "Having a baby and having a teenager isn't quite the same thing."

Ben glared at her. "Well, she felt like you were saying she wasn't doing a good job with Cardew."

"She's not! Anyone can see that Cardew needs taken more firmly in hand. He's a disaster in the making if someone doesn't help keep that boy steady."

Ben's eyes narrowed, and his usually lush mouth folded in on itself. Rob cleared his throat, but Anja and Ben didn't break eye contact.

"I saw some pictures of Cardew on your Facebook. He doesn't look Turkish," Rob said a little loudly, taking a bite of his spaghetti and hoping to at least put off the all-out argument that was about to start between Ben and Anja. "I take it he's not adopted. Or is he adopted from somewhere else?"

Ben turned to Rob and squared his shoulders to exclude his mother from the conversation. "He's not adopted. Cardew's parents thought they couldn't have kids, but then when Ebru was five, voila, he showed up after all." He glanced angrily at Anja as he added "From what I hear, he was gay as glitter from the get-go, and that's not going to change any time soon."

"Ben, I have no problem with glitter or gayness," Anja said archly. "As you damn well know. It's the parties and rumors that worry me."

"He's fine. He tells me everything, and he's not doing anything wrong. He's just having a good time."

Anja raised her hands in surrender and shook her blond head slightly. "All right, all right. You win. Let's drop the subject and I'll apologize to Ebru the next time I see her."

Ben didn't seem to know what to do with that, so he turned his attention to his food and took another big bite of his burger.

They ate in silence for a few awkward moments, and Rob wished Matty would return from the bathroom to lighten the mood or introduce a new line of conversation. Anything would do.

Anja broke the silence by saying, "Excuse me. I need to call my parents before they go to bed."

"Oh, right. It's your dad's birthday. Tell him hi from me," Rob said.

She lifted her brows.

He chuckled. "Or not."

"Tell Grandpa I love him," Ben said as Anja walked away.

Rob glanced toward the men's room, wondering what was taking Matty so long. He decided to give it a few more minutes, and then he'd go check.

"So, what does this Ebru girl think of you?" Rob asked after Anja stepped outside the restaurant.

"Oh. Well, she hates me. I don't know why." Ben frowned, but then his face softened into the same dreamy expression he'd fallen into when she first came up. "But she plays hockey. Like really well. She's in our rink's mixed amateur team. And she doesn't shave her legs. Or her armpits. Because she's too confident to be oppressed by beauty standards like that."

Rob had to fight to keep the bubble of laughter down. He covered by taking a bite of his food before saying, "She told you that? Or you just somehow intuited her motivations?"

"I know because I made the mistake of asking about it." He flushed and rolled his eyes at himself. "I swam with them at their apartment complex last month. Cardew is a lot like Matty, so you can just imagine what he thinks of his sister not shaving. He started giving her crap about her legs being hairy." Ben's eyes lit up. "She was so not having it, though. She went on and on about the way shaving is a tool to force women into a box designed by men and for men and focused only on men's pleasure." Ben's voice was full of awe, and he didn't sound like he thought Ebru's lecture had been at all boring.

"Are you sure she's not a lesbian?"

"Dad, that's stereotyping."

Rob shrugged. "Stereotypes exist for a reason. Look at Matty."

Ben laughed. "No, she likes guys. Well, Cardew says she likes guys. She doesn't like me, though." A note of glumness crept into his otherwise dreamy tone.

"And you don't have any idea why she doesn't like you?"

"No. I don't get it. I'm always nice to her but she just hates me. Cardew doesn't get it either. But he and Ebru have a parent-kid relationship, so, he's not really much use there. Besides, I think he doesn't want me to…you know…like her."

"Because *he* has a crush on you?"

"What? Ew!"

"What's ew about a guy having a crush on you? Would you say ew if Cardew was a girl?"

"No, Dad, you don't get it. It's not that." Ben dismissed the thought by brushing some hair out of his eyes. "Guys crush on me all the time and I don't care." He flushed, clearly embarrassed by his assertion. "Well, I mean I get a lot of fan mail from gay guys."

"I'm sure you do."

"What I'm saying is, Cardew's my best friend, and he *doesn't* have a crush on me."

"Are you sure about that? You guys are together a lot from what I see on Facebook, and you're handsome and kind."

"He'd say ew too, I promise. He likes big, beefy guys anyway. Like, um, bears or whatever you call them. But, you know, our age. He's crazy about guys who look like they drink beer and burp and fart for fun. Isn't that right, Mom?"

Anja had returned in the middle of Ben's last description of the guys Cardew liked. Again, she looked less than thrilled at the topic of conversation.

"Grandpa sends his love," she said. The she sighed. "And, yes, Cardew has very questionable taste in boys. I wish he'd at least stop throwing himself at the college-age hockey players at the rink. They carry big sticks for God's sake, and you can't protect him from fifteen of them." She rolled her eyes at Ben's guffaw. "That was not a euphemism."

"None of them seem to care about Cardew," Ben said, warily, clearly realizing his mistake in soliciting his mother's input on this particular topic. "They aren't all assholes. Most of them are okay with him. I've never heard any of them harass him, anyway. Besides, Ebru would kick their butts."

255

"All it takes is one jerk who gets offended."

Ben huffed incredulously, like he couldn't believe what Anja was suggesting, and neither could Rob. "He can't live in hiding, Mom. He is who he is, and he's not going to change for anyone, and why should he?"

"Well, the Federation has no love for him, that's for sure, and you being his best friend can't possibly help your reputation with them either."

Ben clenched his fists on the table. "Who cares? My skating is enough, and if it's not, then screw it. I'm not going to throw Cardew under the bus because the Federation is still a homophobic organization of shit bags."

Anja lifted her fingers to her temple and rubbed. "Let's not talk about Cardew. We always argue when we talk about him."

Rob made a note to speak to both Anja and Ben separately about just what it was about Cardew that brought strife between the two of them. Surely it wasn't just about the Federation. Anja had mentioned parties and rumors. Rob had some ideas about what a horny, young, and far-too-pretty gay kid without strong parental supervision might get up to in his spare hours. He doubted it was anything Ben would get dragged into, though. Ben was serious, studious, and devoted to skating. Still, Rob would investigate later, when the likelihood of a fight was lower.

He sighed to himself. Another thing to add to his responsibilities. More stuff to take care of. Sometimes he wished he could just walk out of the city and keep going until he found a field where he could lay down and just fucking rest.

Anja glanced toward Matty's empty seat. "Speaking of people the Federation doesn't love, Matty's been gone a long time."

"I'll go check," Rob said, his stomach tensing.

***

MATTY SAT ON the toilet and shook the cock cage, rattling it to the best of his ability. The vibration of the lock on the polycarbonate resonated against his straining flesh, but it gave him no relief. "Fuck, fuck," he whispered, needing more stimulation, needing anything that would take his mind off his desperate need to come.

He'd never, ever felt so horny in his life. He knew this was true because while every single hour since putting on the cock cage had consisted of escalating horniness, rising unbearably moment to moment, the fact that he'd been so overwhelmed at a dinner with Anja and Ben was a first. That he'd had to leave the table and frantically, uselessly masturbate in the toilet stall said it all. Hands down, it was both the most horny and most mortified he'd ever been. Well, maybe failing at the Olympics was worse. Or that time with Rob and the toilet in Montana, but that had ended up being weirdly intimate. Oh, God, he didn't need to think about anything *intimate*.

"Matty?" Rob's voice preceded the fall of his footsteps and the sound of the bathroom door swinging shut. "You okay in here?"

"I'm fine."

"What's taking so long?"

Matty looked down at his dick, pressed hard and miserably against the polycarbonate cock cage, and at his swollen, aching balls, already so full of unreleased spunk. Fuck, he *needed* to come.

"Are you alone?" Matty asked.

"Yes."

"No one else is in here?"

"No."

Matty unlocked the stall door and pushed it open a little. Rob appeared in the opening and he held the door open wider, staring down to where Matty sat on the toilet, his leggings around his ankles, his shirt held up, and his poor cock smashed against the clear sides of the device.

"Well, I guess I see the problem," Rob said, quietly. Tired lines appeared around his eyes. "I admit I'm not sure where it came from, though. Dinner conversation was pretty unsexy, I thought."

"It was you," Matty whispered. "I could smell you."

Rob's eyebrows went up, and his lips twisted into a small, fatigued smirk. "Smell me?"

"I swear I could smell your dick and I started salivating every time I inhaled."

"Sweetheart, there's no way you could smell my dick."

"No, I could smell it. I could almost taste it," Matty gasped, rattling his cock cage again, trying to get some good friction. "*Let* me taste it. I just need to suck you and I'll be okay." He reached out to grab hold of Rob's hips, but Rob moved out of his grasp.

"Wait, no, hold on." Rob left the stall, and Matty heard him curse softly. Water ran and then he returned with a wet paper towel and handed it Matty. "Here, wipe your face down and clean up. Then fix your clothes."

Matty did as he was told and handed Rob the towels. Rob steered him toward the sink. "Splash your face with water. Cool down."

The water was refreshing, and Matty stared at himself in the mirror—wild-eyed and red-cheeked. He dried his face with the paper towels Rob handed him. His cock throbbed painfully in the cage, and his asshole ached for touch. It was miserable. "Oh, God, Rob, fuck. I can't do this. Help me."

Rob's expression was grim. "All right. Listen to me, okay?"

Matty turned away from his reflection, sickness in his gut. "I'm sorry. I'm messing everything up."

Rob took hold of his shoulders. "Meet me out front. I'm going to go tell Anja and Ben that you're sick."

Matty wiped his mouth with shaking fingers. "Thank you. I'm sorry, I'm sorry, thank you."

"Shh." Rob kissed his temple and closed his eyes, holding Matty close.

"Rob?"

"Yes?"

"This is counterproductive." He pulled himself free.

Rob ran hands over his hair and shook his head with his eyes closed. With a quick puff of breath, he nodded firmly. "Ready?"

"I think? Maybe. I'm losing my fucking mind."

Rob's jaw clenched. "Okay, go out front and hail a taxi. I'll say you're not feeling well and we'll go home. But we're going to have to

258

talk about this." He waved his hand toward Matty's crotch. "Under-stand?"

Matty nodded. He kept his eyes on the tile floor, counting the black dots, as Rob washed his own hands. "Rob, are you angry?"

"No. It's okay. I can handle it."

Matty wasn't sure if he was talking to him or to the mirror.

CHAPTER TWENTY-THREE

Rob HAD NO idea what excuse he'd made to Anja and Ben before he'd hustled Matty into a cab and paid an exorbitant amount to get them away from the overly loud restaurant and the bustle of the street. But even the back of a cab was chaos between the radio and the dispatch, the honking horns outside, and the jerking maneuvers that send them careening across the slick seat.

"I need it off," Matty murmured. "Just for a few minutes. I don't want to come, Rob. Okay? Don't make me come."

Rob caught the driver's eye in the rearview mirror and pulled Matty close, kissing the top of his head, but said nothing.

The apartment was dark, but Mr. Wegman's lights were on upstairs. The bar must be closed, or else Mr. Wegman was full of shit about his claim to work whenever the bar was open. Rob was betting on the latter.

Inside, Rob kneeled by Matty's feet, working his leggings down slowly. He touched Matty's balls tenderly. The hair was growing back, and he stroked the stubble lightly. If they kept on with this game, they'd need to shave him again soon, so the hairs didn't pull in the device.

The key slid easily into the lock, and the device came off smoothly. Matty moaned and dug his hands into Rob's hair as though willing himself not to touch his cock as it filled and grew hard. It rose determinedly, brushing Rob's chin and cheek in its ascent, and Matty let out a breathy gasp full of lust and wonder.

"Take your shirt off," Rob murmured, tugging off Matty's shoes and getting him naked.

"Don't make me come," Matty whispered, tossing his shirt aside carelessly, his eyes wild and dark, and his dick trembling with his heartbeat.

Rob's cock was hard too, and he adjusted it, squeezing the head as he took in Matty's quivering body in the low bedroom light. He pulled Matty closer, hands on his hip bones, holding his smaller body steady. He rubbed his face along Matty's thighs, kissed his balls, and took in the scent of his skin and the lingering leaked pre-come. He shifted forward and took Matty's cock into his mouth, cleaning the tender skin with his tongue.

"Fuck!" Matty pressed the back of his hand to his lips, soft sounds escaping. His hips stuttered, and Rob held them still, going down on Matty slowly at first, and then increasing speed until he was fucking his own mouth with Matty's cock.

"Don't want to come," Matty gritted out as Rob slid spit-slick fingers into his ass and deep-throated him viciously. "Please make it last. Don't let me—oh, fuck!" His thighs shook and his eyes rolled back.

Rob pulled off, a string of saliva between Matty's dick and his lips.

"Get on the bed."

He did as he was told. Matty's cock was brutally hard, veins rising up and the head nearly purple. Rob admired it as he bound Matty's hands to the headboard and his feet to the O-rings under the end of the bed, leaving Matty spread eagled on his back for Rob to tease and torture.

The vibrator wasn't one of Matty's favorite toys, but it would do the job. Rob plugged it into the wall and then pressed the end to Matty's taint, turning it on the middle setting and watching Matty writhe against the restraints. Kneeling over Matty on the bed, he pushed the vibrator against his skin hard and sucked him in again, using his hand and mouth until Matty was keening and thrashing. Then he pulled off, wiped the back of his mouth with his hand, and kissed the head of Matty's pulsing dick.

"Sweetheart, that looks painful."

"Don't want to come," Matty insisted, his eyes squeezed shut and sweat sliding down his face. "I just need a little time. I'm okay. This is okay."

He sounded like he was trying to convince himself.

Rob grabbed a small throw pillow from the desk chair to prop the vibrator against Matty's taint and then picked up the cock cage from where he'd left it on the floor. He went into the bathroom and washed it thoroughly, leaving it to dry on the counter.

Matty was shaking on the bed when Rob returned, his eyes rolled up, and his cock dribbling pre-come onto his stomach. Rob sat down on the edge of the bed, adjusted his cock, and dragged his eyes up Matty's body. Nipples hard, stomach jumping, his balls tight and poised to shoot. He thought Matty might orgasm if Rob even breathed on his cock; he was that much of a live wire.

"Rob?" Matty's voice sounded breathy and wild. "I don't want to come yet. I can do this. I can. I'll be the best at it. Please."

Rob's lips twisted on the edges as he fought a too-revealing smile. "I'm not sure we can stop you from coming at this point, sweetheart. You're so worked up."

"You can. Turn off the vibrator. Get the humbler if you have to. Just...I don't want to give up yet." Matty's cock quivered like just speaking was going to make him come. "I'm going to be good at this present for you. I swear to God, Rob."

Rob slid one hand into Matty's sweaty hair, and even that gesture made Matty's balls draw up higher and his cock pulse out a wet glob of pre-come. "Matty, you *are* good," Rob whispered, his voice thick with emotion. "You're such a good, good boy."

Matty's eyes went wide, he grimaced and squirmed. "No!" His body flushed all over and his legs pulled against the ropes as he twisted and *came*. Hard.

Come exploded from his pulsing cock as he cried out, eyes scrunched closed as tearful whimpers tore from his throat and his body convulsed, jerking as aftershocks rattled through him.

Rob stared in shock. *Jesus Christ.* He recovered himself quickly, stroking his hand in Matty's hair again and saying, "That's a good boy. Come for me. Good Matty. So good."

Matty trembled and whimpered, his nipples hard and chest flushed, his muscles still twitching and his cock helplessly pumping spurts across his stomach and chest.

"You're so beautiful when you come."

Rob loved the way Matty collapsed when he orgasmed. The vulnerability, the unguarded expressions, and the dazed heat in his eyes. Matty moaned and turned his head toward Rob, his eyes a glowing brown, his lips rosy and wet. Rob leaned down to kiss him, tasting his tongue and breath, feeling the shuddery gusts of Matty's breath against his lips and the roof of his mouth.

"You're amazing," Rob murmured as he ended the kiss, touching Matty's cheek and seeing his eyes flutter open at last.

"I messed up," Matty muttered, relief, satiated bliss, and frustration warring on his face. "I didn't want to come. Can we try again? I just want to be good at it."

Rob stood and removed his clothes, putting them neatly on the chair near the bed. He didn't know. The experiment didn't seem to be going the way Matty had hoped, and he didn't see any reason to think it would go more smoothly if they tried again. "I don't know, Matty. It's been a long three days. Why don't we sleep on it?"

Matty nodded, his eyes blinking heavily, all the near-manic energy that had been pulsing through him for the last two days gone now. "I'm not a quitter."

"Of course you're not." Rob slid onto the mattress next to Matty and murmured, "You're a fighter, sweetheart. A champion." Then Rob took hold of his own cock—hard since he'd undressed Matty and aching ever since Matty had come—and stroked it as he watched Matty's eyelashes drift down and his breathing speed up.

"Let me help you," Matty whispered.

"Mmm-mmm, you just lay there and watch."

Matty squirmed a little, but it only took a few strokes before Rob grunted and his come joined Matty's, smearing over Matty's firm abs and pecs.

Rob took a few slow breaths, rubbing his face against Matty's side, making him laugh and whisper, "Tickles." Rob kissed his ribs and the edges of muscle and bone before pulling himself together enough to stand.

He freed Matty's arms and legs, rubbing them gently, and then whispered, "Be right back."

In the bathroom, he stared down at the cock cage drying there. "Practice makes perfect," he murmured. If Matty wanted to try again, he could always put a stop to it if it wasn't working out. That was his right.

Rob wet a washcloth and scooped up the parts of the chastity device. He returned to Matty and rubbed the warm cloth over Matty's stomach. He kissed Matty's lips and smiled down at him. "How do you feel?"

"Tired. Drained. Like I shot a week's worth instead of just a few days."

"Do you really want to try again? Can you be in charge of it this time, instead of letting it rule you?"

Matty shivered. "I can do it. I know I can. Try me."

"Show me how you can master this," Rob murmured.

"Thank you," Matty whispered with all the enthusiasm his exhaustion could apparently muster. The sexual tension that had accumulated in him and exploded so unexpectedly seemed to have left him almost entirely drained. He lay passively as Rob put the cage on him again, and was drifting off to sleep when Rob returned from the bathroom and climbed into bed beside him.

"I need you to be calmer this time," Rob whispered to him. He wanted to give Matty what he needed, but he couldn't deal with another day of Matty's out of control descent into sexual mania. Things had to even out now. They had to.

"I've got you for that," Matty murmured and rolled over to sleep with his head on Rob's chest. Rob stared at the ceiling, sleep somehow just out of his exhausted grasp.

***

MATTY, IF YOU don't stop texting me inappropriate things at work, there will be a punishment when I get home.

Perfect. I'll have the whips waiting.

Matty had all the whips lined up for Rob on the coffee table from smallest to biggest, and he waited with an intense, needy urgency that had him nearly vibrating out of his skin. He didn't know what it was about the chastity device, but he'd never felt so manic and out of control. It was terrifying, and he hated it almost as much as he loved it. Horniness had obliterated Control, and stress, and hunger, and everything else in his life. It was as close to religious ecstasy as he'd ever experienced outside of skating and actual orgasm.

The only other thing that compared to the constant rush in his body, the simultaneous fear and arousal, was being tied up and gagged, with Rob's hand pinching his nose closed so he couldn't breathe. That surrender was so dangerously complete, in a way that he could never replicate, that he didn't think anything could match it.

But the surrender of the cock cage was intense. It left Matty with nowhere to go but into blinding sexual pleasure or complete submission. Being whipped while locked up sounded so impossible to cope with. He wanted to prove he could do it. In fact, he didn't know which outcome he wanted more: whips with orgasm or whips without. If Rob would just whip him without mercy, he'd take whatever outcome came his way. He was woozy with hunger and lust, but he *needed* pain so damn badly. He was sure the pain would clear his head for a few days. It always did.

The sound of the key in the lock was such a relief and thrill that his knees went weak and his asshole spasmed in anticipation. He wondered which implement Rob would use first and where. Would he want him on the bed, or against the wall, or over the kitchen counter? Would he want him upright over the back of the couch, facing the windows, just a curtain away from the outside world seeing him being whipped and fucked and whatever else Rob wanted to do to him? His nuts were swollen, and his cock ached as it pressed against the cage. He felt faint as the knob turned, and he nearly collapsed to his knees as the door opened and Rob walked in.

"You look good in my jeans," Rob said by way of greeting. "They're big on you, but sexy." He flicked a glance toward the whips on the coffee table and frowned. "I brought takeout from Rachel's."

"I can't eat it now," Matty said, shaking and breathless. "I need you to—"

"*You* need?"

"Yes, first I need you to—"

Rob tossed the bags in his hand on the kitchen counter and rubbed his forehead. "Stop."

Matty's heartbeat thundered at the command in his tone.

Rob went on, his voice quiet and laced with anger. "I thought this gift wasn't about focusing on your needs, Matty. It was, according to you, all about you focusing on what I need." He met Matty's eyes, his gaze cool. "And I need you to stop. I need you to eat your damn food. I need to rest. Got it?"

Matty swallowed hard, resentment raring up inside him. He'd been waiting all day for this. The last three hours of horny anticipation had been almost more than he could take. And now he was going to have to eat first? But Rob wouldn't whip him on a full stomach. He'd want it to digest. And if he waited for it to digest, then it would be late, and then Rob probably wouldn't whip him at all.

Matty glared at him and turned his back, pulling off his shirt and Rob's jeans and tossing them aside.

"Don't push me, Matty."

He ignored the warning and climbed up on the sofa. He rested his arms across the back and thrust out his ass. "You said you'd whip me."

Rob's voice was a whisper. "I said there would be a punishment."

Matty gritted his teeth together. Rob never lied, and he was right. He'd never specifically mentioned whips. "Use your hand. Just hit me. I fucking need it."

There was silence in the apartment. A dog barked outside, and a child's bike bell rang six feet away on the sidewalk beyond the curtain window. He almost begged for pain again, but pride kept him silent. He pushed out his ass again and waited.

Matty heard the rustle of Rob unpacking the bags he'd brought in, and the smell of food hit him in the solar plexus, making him dizzier than he already was.

"You're really pissing me off," Rob said. "I'm this-close to saying the word to end this Matty. Because I've got a safeword too, remember?"

Matty jerked and gasped. Rob hadn't used their safeword in years. Not since Matty had held him down and breathed in his ear until he gave up. That'd been in Montana. Slowly, Matty turned around on the sofa. The hot fury in Rob's eyes pierced him, and he swallowed hard. Had he ever seen Rob so angry? Even after the Saks shopping mess, he'd looked less enraged.

Matty sat gingerly on the couch. His cock deflated in the cage, no longer pressing eagerly against the polycarbonate. He didn't know what to do. Part of him wanted to throw himself on the floor and have a full-on tantrum, but most of him knew he'd come close enough to that already. That was why Rob was so pissed.

God.

He was failing at this. He was failing so very hard.

"Rob?"

Rob turned away from him, rummaging in the cabinets for plates and silverware. He brought out glasses and filled them with the filtered water in the fridge. When he spoke again, it was even and measured. "I want you to eat the food I brought you."

"All of it?"

Rob's eyes went soft, and he looked Matty over carefully, taking in his nudity, and canvassing every muscle and bone he could see from where he stood. "Half is fine."

"But you never whip me on a full stomach." Matty couldn't let it go yet.

Rob's jaw clenched. "I'm not whipping you tonight. I'm not fucking you. I'm not fingering you. I'm going to eat dinner and go the fuck to sleep."

Matty felt the blood drain from his face, and his heart sink to a stone in his stomach. "Okay." It was a whisper. He wasn't sure Rob even heard.

Rob opened the fridge and took out a beer. He popped the lid off, but before he even took a swallow, he sat it down on the counter and headed into the bedroom.

Matty stayed where he was, uncertain if Rob wanted him to follow or not. The back door opened and shut, and Matty knew Rob had gone out to the garden.

Minutes passed and Rob didn't return. Matty picked up the whips and put them in the closet where they kept them, and then pulled on his silk robe. A glance out the window showed Rob pacing the back end of the garden talking on the phone.

Matty realized that the little vegetable garden Rob usually tended wasn't weeded or even planted this year. How hadn't he noticed that? And who was Rob talking to right now? Was he talking to them about Matty? About this?

He's saying he hates you.

Matty squeezed his eyes shut and hit his head with his hands. "SHUT UP," he whispered urgently. He hadn't eaten anything all day. What more did the stupid fucking voice want? It couldn't be back. It couldn't. He hated it so fucking much. It was killing him. It was going to ruin everything. He was ruining everything.

Exactly. I didn't have to. You already did.

"What do you want from me?"

Everything. Because I'm greedy. Like you.

Matty looked out the window again. Rob nodded and closed his eyes, his head tilted back and his free hand clenched at his side. Then he disconnected the call, rubbed his hands over his face, and shook his head. As he mounted the few stairs that led up to the back door, Matty sat down on the bed, his chin trembling and his stomach roiling. He didn't know what was about to happen.

"Stand up," Rob said as soon as he came in.

Matty did, though his knees felt weak.

Rob dug in his pocket and brought something out. Then he lifted Matty's chin with two fingers and looked down at him, his eyes wild and his lips trembling. "Are you listening to me?"

"Yes."

"Cowbell. Cowbell, Matty." He took Matty's hand and pressed a key into his palm. "Unlock yourself. Do whatever you want. I can't do this anymore."

He turned, and before Matty could register what he'd said or what had happened, the apartment door shut behind him and Rob was gone.

CHAPTER TWENTY-FOUR

ROB SIPPED SOME sort of licorice tea concoction the dreadlocked woman at Herbal Blends had served him. Her name was Skye, and she'd patted him on the shoulder when she delivered it.

"Sato said to give you this tea when you arrived and to apologize that he's keeping you waiting."

"It's no problem."

"You look beat, honey." She'd smiled warmly and indicated the cup. "That should help your nerves."

Rob felt his phone vibrate again in his pants. He knew it was Matty. He knew he should answer or at least text a reply. He took a sip of the tea, letting it burn his tongue a little before swallowing.

The darkness of the back corner booth, the same one he and Sato had sat in before, was almost gentle enough for him to relax. Herbal Blends had their door shut, and the only sound to reach his ears was soft, tinkling music that must have been louder than it seemed because all the other patrons' conversations were blocked out.

He pulled out his phone. Five missed calls from Matty. And a text.

I'm sorry. I love you. Please come home.

Rob took another sip of tea and a second text came through.

I'll be better. I swear I'll do better. Don't shut me out.

He rubbed his face and thought over the day. He'd had an important parenting conversation with Anja and then faced some hard hours with his most difficult patients. All day long Matty had sent him pictures of his ass and multiple messages that were entirely inappropriate for the workplace. He'd called and begged Rob to come home early. He'd kept him up half the night before wanting more, needing more, crying when he couldn't come from ass play, and then trembling and asking for it again when he finally did.

I can't do this anymore, Matty. Cowbell.

I get it. Cowbell. I'm good with Cowbell. I respect Cowbell.

Eat your dinner.

The bubbles appeared and disappeared a few times before he replied.

If I eat dinner, will you come home?

This isn't a negotiation. Eat your dinner. When you're done, jerk off. If I'm not back by then, go to bed.

The bubbles came and went and then:

Now I say Cowbell. I need you here.

Rob groaned and rubbed his forehead before responding.

I need you to understand that I can't deal with this right now.

Matty's reply sounded desperate. *I'll eat. I'll be a better person. I'll do whatever you want.*

I just told you what I want.

The door dinged, and Rob turned to see if it was Sato. A young, tall redheaded man in blue jeans and a short-sleeve plaid shirt came in and caught his eye. Sato was right behind him, his hand on the young man's back and dressed in a similar outfit. They both looked relaxed and happy. Rob's stomach twisted.

I'm meeting with a friend. I'll be home later.

He turned off his phone.

Sato motioned for his companion to sit at the tea bar and then smiled at Rob, heading toward him alone. As he slid into the booth opposite Rob, he said, "I'm sorry I had to keep you waiting."

"Is that Todd? He's welcome to sit with us."

"No. You're in a crisis and you asked me, not Todd, to meet you. He's fine over there. He likes Skye. They'll talk about the latest Dragon Age update and we can talk about you."

Rob glanced toward Todd, who was already laughing with Skye. "Okay. Thanks."

"You sounded like you'd reached the end of your rope on the phone." Sato tilted his head. "I was worried."

271

"I'm...I'm..." Rob squeezed his eyes shut. He felt like if he kept talking he was going to say too much, and he didn't even know if he was ready to hear what would come out. "I don't know what to do. I feel out of control."

Sato nodded but said nothing.

"I don't do well when I feel out of control."

"Most of us don't."

"I don't have a lot of practice at it. When my parents died, that was out of my control, and it fucked me up for a while. Then when Matty left. That was bad too. Now, it's like the control has been gradually slipping out of my hands and tonight I just lost it completely."

"Unraveling, huh?"

Rob's throat ached. "Yeah. I got a call today from Anja, my son's mother." Rob caught Sato's eye and saw surprise there. "Yeah, I have a son with my best friend. It's long story."

Sato shrugged. "There are a lot of long stories in our community that end with a child or two. It's not a big deal."

"Yeah. That's true." Rob rubbed his face, feeling shaky inside and out. "She called today. She caught our son skipping summer school."

Sato's eyebrows went up. "Ah, youth. Always getting into trouble."

"Apparently, my son wanted to escort his friend Cardew to meet up with some college guy he'd been chatting with online. But my ex is pretty pissed. Apparently it's not the first time, and she's worried how this friendship is affecting him. She wants to pull our son from the rink where he practices." Rob cleared his throat. "My son's a figure skater."

Sato nodded.

"Anyway, she wants to move him to another skating program, away from 'bad influences.'" Rob rubbed his temples. "All the usual mama bear stuff."

"What do you think?"

Rob shook his head and laughed a little bitterly, taking another sip of the licorice tea. "I think I can't fucking deal with this right now.

I've got two new patients this week who are taxing my patience at every turn. I've got money problems that I can't solve no matter how hard I try. I have a boyfriend with a fucking eating disorder — or disordered eating or whatever the hell. And now our BDSM play has spun away from me somehow. I'm not in control anymore and I feel fucking afraid of our kink play for the first time in our relationship."

Sato made a soft sound.

Rob went on before had a chance to regret what he'd confessed. "I don't know if I can do what he wants, and I don't think I have it in me to give him what he needs."

"Rob —"

He wasn't done, though. "And all the time the city wears on me. I wake up every day and tell myself that it's all in my head. I just need to fix my outlook and the city will become magic to me like it is to Matty. But it doesn't happen. Every day it's like someone's slowly peeling off my skin."

Sato's expression was soft. "You're a sensitive person." He murmured, "You haven't told your boyfriend any of this, have you?"

"Not really. Not before tonight."

"I see."

Rob looked over Sato's head, studying the grain of the tall wooden booth. "I don't like to burden him with my problems."

"Because you think it's up to you to fix his."

Rob shrugged.

"Well, you can't. Only he can fix his problems. All you can do is support him along the way."

Rob covered his face with his hands, tears pushing at his eyelids. He was *not* going to cry. Sato gave him a moment and then asked, kindly, "Tell me, what brought you to New York to begin with?"

Rob cleared his throat and rubbed his hands on his pants. "It's complicated."

"Hey, we've got time."

So Rob told Sato how he'd ended up in New York, and Sato listened patiently. Rob finished his story as he finished his tea. "I'd spent a lot of years resenting my life in Montana, so it was easy enough for me to choose to go with Ben and Anja when they came to Jersey for Ben's training."

Sato cocked his head. "Why did you resent your life there?"

"Daddy issues, Anja would say. Before he died, my father managed to suck all the love I had for the land out of me. It took a while for me to get it back. But I still don't think being a cattle rancher was ever the right thing for me. I love physical therapy. I enjoy working with clients. I wouldn't want to walk away from that." Rob sighed. "This is hard." He smiled self-consciously. "I don't like talking about myself."

"You're doing fine."

"Matty's good at talking about himself."

"Is he any good at listening?"

Rob bit his lip and looked down at the table. He didn't know what to say. He didn't give Matty the opportunity to listen, did he? He rubbed his finger against the grain of the wood and avoided the question. "I'd like to work with goats again, though. I kind of like the furry little shits."

"Goats?"

"Yeah. I had goats back on the ranch. My buddy Bing, who bought me out the property, is still raising some. I've got money wrapped up in that and hopefully it will pay off this fall. We still have to wait and see."

"That's very interesting. I know nothing about goats."

Rob smiled, remembering the way the goats used to follow Matty in Montana, chewing at his pants and sleeves. "Matty even likes them."

"All the better." Sato motioned over Rob's shoulder for something. Tea showed up for him shortly. Sato took a sip and said, "So your son moved to New Jersey, and you followed him there?"

"No, I didn't go to Jersey. I got my place in Park Slope."

"Why's that? The romance of the Big Apple? Proximity to BDSM connections?"

Rob shook his head. "I chose it because I knew Matty was training in the city. I actually had a better job offer in New Jersey, but I knew I'd never run into him there."

Sato leaned back in his seat as Skye put an iced scone in front of him. "Thank you," he murmured. She smiled and walked back to Todd at the bar. "So you sought him out."

"No. I..." Rob trailed off. "It's hard to explain."

"It's always hard to admit weaknesses, but we all have them."

Rob refilled his cup with tea and watched as Sato ripped the scone in two, indicating he should have half. Rob hadn't eaten his dinner, so he accepted. The icing was sweet, and he licked it off his thumb. "When I met him, I thought he was possibly the best thing that had ever happened in my life and the most annoying human being I'd ever met all at once. It was a pretty irresistible combination."

"It happens like that."

Rob smiled. "Yeah. But it had pretty much killed me when he left the first time. Bing and Bill, my best friends out there, were worried about me. Anja practically camped out in my living room with Ben because she thought I needed the constant reminder that they need me." Rob huffed and rolled his eyes. "But I won't lie. I was a mess after he left for a long time."

"It sounds painful."

"Yeah. And I don't like pain. So, when I got to New York, I didn't have the guts to look for him."

"It's a big town."

"No, that had nothing to do with it. He would have been easy enough to find. There are only so many skating rinks, after all. And it was common knowledge in the skating world where he was training." Rob swallowed. "I was afraid to find him. And I was afraid to not find him. I was scared shitless."

"So how did you end up back together?"

"He found me." Rob remembered the shock of seeing Matty in his old PT therapy room. "He hunted me down, refused to go away, and convinced me to give him another chance."

Sato smiled warmly. "I'd love to meet him."

Rob sighed.

"It's not over with him?" Sato asked, his brows lowering.

"No. I need him." He felt sick as he said it. He'd never told anyone. "I need him. Probably more than he needs me."

Sato's expression was so tender that Rob was ashamed. He must seem so weak; so overwhelmed.

"Of course you do," Sato said. "I understand completely."

Rob pressed his lips together and looked away. He hadn't expected that, and his throat was tight again.

"But you're not happy, Rob. Because he's sick, and you're exhausted."

Rob nodded.

"What did Matty say when you told him how you're feeling?"

"I didn't." Rob rubbed his hand over his face. "He's distracted right now. You know, the chastity device."

"Ah." Sato looked toward Todd and gave a fond smile. Rob glanced over his shoulder and saw that Todd was gazing at Sato with a besotted expression. Seeing Rob, though, he turned away, striking up a new topic with Skye, who was busy washing tea cups.

Sato said, "Too greedy, huh?"

"Yeah. You could say that." Rob shook his head. "I had no idea. I couldn't cope with it. I safeworded tonight," Rob said, his ears burning. "Gave him the key. Told him I couldn't do it anymore."

Sato smiled. "Good for you."

"No. I mean, yes, it was the right thing to do, but no, I wasn't good about it." Rob shook his head. "I left. I walked out and left him there. Alone."

Sato's eyebrows went up and his bald head crinkled. "Have you let him know you're okay?"

"Yeah. We texted. He wants me to come home."

Sato nodded. "Are you going to?"

Rob squeezed his eyes closed, a tight panic clenching his throat and chest. "I don't know. I don't want to go back there. Ever. Fuck, I almost didn't come here to meet you either."

Sato sipped his tea. "Where did you want to go?"

"To the airport. I wanted to get on a plane and fly home." Rob laughed and rolled his eyes. "Like a child."

"Why didn't you?"

"God, so many reasons."

"Like?"

"Well, say I did fly to Montana. Where would I go? The ranch isn't mine anymore. Bing's family lives there now. I'd have to crash at Bill's, and he'd ask questions. Besides, I don't want to hurt Matty." He shook his head. "More immediately, I'd agreed to meet you here. I always keep my word. And I have a job. I have patients who rely on me. I've got my son living here. I've got Matty to deal with. I've got rent and bills and a whole life I chose for myself." Rob felt his eyes stinging. "Fuck. I fucking chose this for myself. God."

"Drink your tea."

Rob did, letting the anise flavor roll around on this tongue. A silence descended between them that the tinkling music was eager to fill. Laughter cut into it, but it was a warm sound that didn't grate on his nerves. Finally, when Rob had drained his cup again and poured more from his small teapot, Sato reached out and touched the back of his hand with cool fingertips.

"You have two options. You can let your relationship self-destruct or you can truly take control of it. I haven't met your Matty, but I'm betting that he'd be grateful for you to take the decisions out of his hands." Sato sat back and stroked the handle of his tea cup. "You love him. You want him to be happy, and you've crafted your life around what he says he wants and what he claims he needs. But does Matty really know what he wants or needs, Rob? Do you truly think catering to his wishes first and foremost has put you both on the right track?"

Rob sighed and rolled the back of his head against the high wooden booth, letting it massage his scalp.

"This situation with your son, could it be a good reason for you to assert yourself? For you to make the choice to move away from the city?"

Rob stared at the ceiling. Was it? Could he use Ben as an excuse to uproot them all and head home? "I don't know. I wasn't in a good place to listen to Anja earlier, and I'd need to find out Ben's point of view on it all. He's a solid kid. I believe him. But I understand what she's worried about."

"You're a really just and fair person. I can see that you want to accommodate everyone and make everybody happy. But Rob, you can *never* make everyone happy. Right now, you've got to find a way to save yourself. You're spiraling and that's not safe for you or your possibly anorexic sub. It's probably not safe for your kid or your employer or your patients either. The truly responsible thing for you to do is to admit your unhappiness to Matty and assert your dominance. He'll fall in line about where you choose to live. I promise. He'll be relieved that you're taking the burden off his shoulders."

"Even if that's true, and I'm not sure it is, because Matty is a complex creature to say the least—but if it is true? I don't know if I can handle the burden on mine."

"I'm going to be blunt. Get out of New York. It's not a good fit for you. Some fresh air. Some sunshine. Roosters waking you up in the morning. That's what you need. Within a week, you'll be right as rain and ready to deal with whatever life or your boyfriend throws at you. Because Rob, the food issue isn't going away until it's seriously addressed, and you don't have it in you right now to fight that battle and win."

Rob swallowed and nodded. "I know."

"Good. I'm glad you're admitting it."

He thought about Sato's words. "What do I need to do for him when it comes to eating?"

Sato sighed. "There's an approach that I've seen be fairly successful with the athletes I've studied and worked with. It focuses on refeeding and works mainly to correct behaviors around food. There's no deep delving into what caused the anorexic behaviors to begin with, because, honestly, that doesn't matter." Sato shrugged. "Causation will always be around. There are always going to be stressors in any life. So, the goal is to refeed, teach the body and mind to move out of the cycle of starvation, and on to a healthier way to cope."

"Where do I start?"

Sato motioned at Todd, who came over with a book in hand. He handed it to Sato. "Thank you," Sato said. "Please order cake and tea for yourself."

"Yes, sir," Todd replied, smiling. He nodded at Rob before sitting down at the counter again.

"He's a handsome boy."

"Isn't he?" Sato practically glowed. "That boy has my heart. He could break me in two if he wanted. Luckily, he doesn't seem to want anything other than my approval."

Rob gave a close-lipped smile, his chest aching. He wasn't sure he'd want Matty to ever be that docile, but happy? He'd like him to be happy, satisfied, and growing as a person, instead of stagnated and obsessed.

Sato slid the book across the table. It had an apple on the front and the name of several doctors including Sato's across the bottom. "This is a good place to start."

"Thank you. How much do I owe you for it?"

Sato waved his hand. "I have a stack of them in my office. It's not a problem."

"So you think I've got a shot at helping him get well?"

"I'd say that you're his best bet, actually. We recommend full-on family involvement, and I think you care enough about him to see it through." Sato smiled kindly. "But like I said, you need to take care of yourself first. You'll burn out before you help either of you if you don't."

"You keep saying I should leave the city." Rob chuckled. "Which brings up the question: how do I afford to do that? It takes money to move and that's something we don't have."

"You're a creative, determined guy partnered with another creative, determined guy. The two of you will find a way. The first step, though, is admitting that leaving New York is what you want." Sato leaned back. "The second step is admitting it to Matty and not just to me."

Rob nodded. "I feel like I should pay for your time."

Sato made a face. "Absolutely not. I would like to suggest, however, that wherever you end up, you find support in your BDSM community. You don't have to participate in the parties to find a network of people who can help you through tough times and who won't judge what you do together in the bedroom."

"If I do leave, it's going to take a while to get the ducks in a row."

"And I'm here. You can call any time. I'm happy to meet with you or Matty or both of you together. Hell, we could go on a double date. Dinner and a movie. Matty might like meeting Todd. If he's never truly met anyone who's part of the scene, he's probably a pretty lonely sub."

CHAPTER TWENTY-FIVE

MATTY SAT ON the stoop for a long time before he called Anja. He'd taken off the chastity device earlier after Rob had walked out. He hadn't even gotten hard when he removed it, which he wouldn't have thought possible before their fight. But his stomach was far too upset for him to be horny now. He'd put Rob's jeans back on and the t-shirt he'd been wearing and gone outside to wait for Rob to return. He kept thinking every shadow at the corner was Rob coming back. Rob had never done this before. He'd never just walked out on him and not explained what was happening. He'd never turned his phone off in the middle of a fight.

"Hey, Matty, what's up?" Anja's voice was kind but a little distracted. In the background, he could hear David Bowie's "China Girl" playing along with the clatter of plates and the splash of water. Rob obviously hadn't gone to her place, or she'd be expecting his call by now.

"Have you heard from Rob?"

"No. Why?"

"We had a fight."

"Oh." Anja was quiet for a second and then David Bowie's singing was cut off in the middle of a line. "Hold on a second." She spoke a bit more firmly when she said, "Ben, you'll concentrate better at the desk in your room. Finish your homework up there."

"Is something wrong?" Ben asked.

"Nope. Everything's fine."

Matty rubbed his eyes, still sore from crying, and hoped she was right.

Ben shot back, "Except that I'm grounded for the rest of eternity."

"You earned that, buddy."

Matty heard Ben's heavy feet storming up the stairs in their condo and the slam of a door.

"Teenagers," Anja muttered.

"Why's Ben grounded?"

"Didn't Rob tell you?"

Matty murmured, "Like I said, we had a fight."

"Oh." she sounded surprised. "I thought maybe it was about the situation with Ben and what I want to do about it."

A car alarm went off a block over, and some shouts echoed through the street.

"No. It was about...stuff."

"Ah. Fights about stuff always suck."

"Tell me about it."

Anja chuckled. "Well, our sweet teenaged-idiot, Ben Lovely, was caught skipping summer school to help his troublemaking friend Cardew hang out with college boys."

Matty gasped. "What?"

"Yes. Ben says it was his duty to skip school." Anja sounded beyond exasperated. "Apparently, Cardew wanted to meet his latest online boyfriend—a college boy, much too old for him—and Ben wanted to go with him because he didn't trust the guy."

"Was he right not to trust him?"

"He doesn't know. Apparently, Ebru coincidentally showed up at the campus deli they were meeting at. But there's no doubt the boy is far too old for Cardew to be messing around with."

"Then it's probably a good thing Ben went."

"Not if he's skipping school to do it. I don't like the precedent this sets. We don't need rumors getting back to the Federation that Ben isn't taking his school life seriously or that he's out 'partying' with Cardew and boys. The Feds hate Cardew. This friendship could jeopardize his skating career."

The threat of getting on the bad side of the Federation loomed in his mind. Ben had worked so hard and come so far. But could they really ask him to turn his back on his friend?

"Is he sorry? Did he say he understands why this was a bad idea?"

"Yes, and I believe him. But it was a stupid choice regardless." She sighed. "I'm wondering if we shouldn't pull him from this New Jersey program and move him to a different coach."

"Because he skipped school? Isn't that a little extreme? I'm not a huge fan of Greg's, but he and Ben work well together."

"No, to get him away from Cardew. I'm telling you, that friendship is going to cost Ben more than he realizes."

Matty noticed a fat piece of orange chalk on the stoop next to theirs. It probably belonged to the little girl who lived there. He stood up and opened the gate, going over to pick it up. He'd buy her a new one. A whole set of new fat chalk, actually.

"So am I missing something? Is Ben into this Cardew guy romantically?" Matty sat down on the sidewalk and started drawing in the light of street lamp. Orange lines that he colored in mindlessly.

Anja laughed. "Ben is straight."

"I thought so too, but are you sure? I mean, sometimes people do crazy things when they're in love."

"Oh, Ben's in love all right. But not with Cardew." Anja sighed. "Cardew's older sister, though, is another story."

"Wow. I feel like I'm coming to the soap opera late."

Anja chuckled. "I guess you are. You haven't been around a lot this year. Sabrina took up a lot of your time. Anyway, I've been thinking that getting him away from the both of them would be best for him."

Matty stopped drawing for a second, wiping his chalk-covered hand on Rob's loose blue jeans, leaving a streak. "Is he losing focus on the ice?"

"Of course! He's a teenager and he's got hormones coming out his pores and a best friend who has terrible ideas." She sighed. "I'm thinking we should take him to Colorado. Get him in with Forenza, maybe. Ira Mosely with the Federation has been advocating for that, actually."

"Forenza," Matty echoed. Then he was silent, looking down at the corner, checking the shadows again for Rob.

"What do you think of him?"

He went back to drawing with the chalk. "Sabrina's out there, of course. She likes him." Except for his scary chest hair, he remembered. "It's a great facility, and she says he's a strong coach."

"Yeah? You're still in touch with her?"

"She's my girl. Always will be my girl."

Anja made a soft sound. "You've got a sweet heart, Matty."

He didn't know what to say to that. He was pretty sure he had a selfish heart, actually, and nothing in the conversation so far had told him otherwise.

Anja said, "So you didn't call about any of that, though. You called because you and Rob had a fight."

Matty looked down at the shadows again. There was no movement. "I mainly just wondered if he'd gone to your place."

"Nope. He's probably halfway to Montana by now."

Matty dropped the chalk on the sidewalk. It broke in half. "Are you serious?"

"I hope not." After a few seconds, Anja went on musingly, "He always liked to go out in the fields when he was upset. He'd wander around out there for hours. Sometimes he'd head into the federal lands. Anyway, he's been pretty stressed lately. I'm sure you've noticed."

Matty felt like crying again. Rob never broke down. He never needed help. He was the rock, and Matty was the bird who flew. It was the way it worked. But as it turned out, Matty was the bird that broke the rock's back.

Anja went on. "I knew something wasn't right with you guys the other night. Rob was exhausted, and you were—well, I don't know what you were. But it was weird."

"Sorry. I was, I mean, it was… It's hard to explain."

"I think it was a sex thing so I really don't want to know."

Matty's chest felt heavy, and breathing was hard. "Okay."

"So it was a sex thing." She cracked up. "Jesus, you two. And you think he's going to leave you?" She laughed some more.

He colored between some curved lines until she quieted, and then he whispered into the phone, "I don't know what to do. I really screwed up."

"Did you cheat on him?"

"No!"

"Well, then you fought. So what." Anja had clearly gone back to the dishes. Water sounds and silverware clatter came over the line. It didn't escape Matty that she hadn't asked if Rob had cheated on him. Apparently, that was outside the realm of things Anja could imagine about Rob. "He'll get over it. He loves you."

"I don't know. He said he couldn't do this anymore and walked out."

"He said that?"

"Yeah."

"Matty, the man thinks you hung the moon and the stars. He'd probably commit a felony for you. At the very least, he'd drive your getaway car. Whatever he 'can't do anymore,' believe me, it's not you. He'll be back."

Matty picked up a piece of the chalk again and started swooping it back and forth, filling in the lines with zigzags and patterns. "What if the thing he can't deal with is part of me? Something I can't get rid of, and he just can't stand it anymore?"

"Well, sure. I imagine there are plenty of things about you that drive him batshit crazy. That's called being in a relationship." Anja snorted softly. "Or, you know, so I've heard from my friends. I've never really managed to be in a relationship myself, so I can't speak from experience."

On another day, Matty would have taken that opening and ran with it. He'd always wanted to know why Anja had never dated anyone after Ben was born. He'd sometimes wondered if she was actually in love with Rob, but she didn't behave like she was. He never understood it. She was a beautiful woman, but seemed completely disinterested in men or women.

But tonight he needed all the reassurance he could get, so he didn't ask.

"He puts the toilet paper on the wrong direction, and I want to murder him," he murmured, stroking some lines out from an orange ball.

"Exactly." She was loading the dishwasher now. Matty could hear the different bright sounds of the dishes clanking together.

"And he pretends like he's listening when I talk to him about accessories."

"Hey, pretending to listen? I call that a Grade B for Better than Most Guys I Know."

"But the ways I'm annoying are a lot bigger than that."

"Oh, no doubt."

Matty laughed in shock and she laughed too, before she went on to clarify, "I just mean that Rob's a pretty dull guy. You've got all that pizzazz going on, so I imagine you're creative with your annoyances too."

Matty leaned his elbows on his knees and pressed his phone closer to his ear. Three teenage boys bounced a basketball down the street, throwing it to one another and dribbling it from hand to hand before passing.

"Cool drawing, dude," one said as they passed him. Then one punched the other and they laughed, heading into the shadows at the end of the street.

Matty gave a half-hearted smile and looked at what he'd drawn. A mountain, a sun, and a lake. All orange, but still obvious and representational in a childish way.

"Hmm. How long has he been unhappy in general?" Anja mused. "I mean, I first noticed he was struggling a little over a year ago. It's escalated a lot since then."

"What do you mean?" Matty's pulse rushed in his veins, effervescent with anxiety.

"I mean, the guy is *not* happy. You haven't noticed?"

"No?"

"Oh. Well, I don't know what say about that." She was clearly judging him. He didn't blame her.

"It's been a busy year for me."

"With Sabrina's success, I'm sure it has." She was quiet a moment and Matty heard the soft purr of Margot Meow-Pants, her snooty cat that always tried to bite Matty if he walked past her on the way to their condo bathroom. "Sorry, she thinks the phone is a toy and likes to rub her face on it. Do you want to know my take on him?"

Did he? It was annoying how Anja seemed to think she knew Rob better than he did. She'd always been that way. But at the same time, she did seem to know things Matty didn't, so he supposed he should listen.

He tossed the chalk down and wiped his hands on Rob's jeans, heading back toward their stoop. He shut the gate behind him and plopped down on the concrete steps. "Yeah, sure. Tell me what you think."

"It's the city. He's always wanted me to think he loves it there, but I know him. He hates it."

Matty blinked and stared at the light in the lower window of the brownstone across the way. "He hates New York?"

"Yeah. It's pretty obvious that he doesn't fit in there. Don't you think? He's a country boy."

"I thought you used to say he needed to sell the ranch and move on with his life."

"Well, yeah. Move on to Missoula and become a PT there, not move on to New York City. He's not cut out for it. To be honest, I'm not sure you are either. You've both been spiraling for a while, and you've been a massive wreck this year especially. Both of you, but mostly you, Matty."

"I'm flattered."

"Well, I'm not trying to be nice. I'm trying to be helpful."

"Oh." Was that what this was called?

"When he came east with me and Ben, I encouraged him to find a place in New Jersey closer to us. After all, Jersey isn't known as the Garden State for nothing. He could have chosen to live somewhere a lot greener. But we all know why he chose Park Slope."

Matty looked up at the dark limbs moving across the glowing

night sky. It was never pitch black here, always a navy or dark gray color. "He was hoping to find me."

"And he did. Or, well, I guess you found each other. The city served its purpose. But for whatever reason, neither one of you has admitted that it isn't working out long term for you."

"Yeah. I don't know. It's been a rough year." Matty's head spun. He thought of all the little things he'd ignored or dismissed. The way Rob flinched when the neighbor kid used her pogo stick in front of their apartment. Or how he seemed so tired most days after work. Or the way he'd lingered longingly over travel magazine photos of mountains.

Why hadn't Rob ever said anything? Why was Anja the one telling him this?

Why didn't you ever notice?

Anja said, "I figured Sabrina was the main reason you stayed as long as you have. But rumor is she's going to transfer to Forenza's program, so maybe the two of you need to start looking at a change."

A change. Maybe that was exactly what Rob had left to find tonight, and maybe that change didn't include Matty.

No, Rob loved him. He knew he did. Sure, he was angry right now, and he'd walked out, but after all they'd been through and all they'd shared, there was no way Rob had suddenly stopped loving him. No matter what Control said, no matter what his worst fears told him. He knew that. He knew it so deep in his soul that he burned with it.

Still, the fact was he'd failed to be what Rob needed. Instead, he'd tried to solve all of his personal problems by using what Rob gave him—reset scenes and chastity and more patience than anyone deserved—and it hadn't worked. In the end, he'd pushed Rob past his limits with his endless need. There had to be a solution to Matty's problems that didn't involve pushing Rob until he had to use his safeword.

What was it that Rob was always saying he needed? Therapy.

"Maybe we do need a change."

"Maybe we all do. We could choose a new place together. Get

Ben away from Cardew and get the two of you out of the city." She sounded pleased with herself. "This could work out for everyone."

"Leave New York..." It wasn't a question so much as something he'd never seriously considered. He loved the city. He loved the beat and the pulse and the life. But it was killing him, too. He was never enough here. Never satisfied. He didn't know if he'd be happier somewhere else but he supposed he owed it to Rob to try.

"Colorado isn't Montana, but it's a great place for PT and figure skating."

A shadow broke free from the corner and the height and gait gave it away as Rob. Matty exhaled in a rush.

"He's home. He's walking up the street. I see him."

"Good. I knew he'd come back. Now, just keep calm and don't expect to solve everything tonight. It's late and you should both get some sleep before you discuss anything too serious. Like moving across the country with me and Ben." She laughed.

"All right."

"Night, Matty. Don't worry. Everything will be okay."

She hung up, and Matty watched Rob approach. The concrete stoop felt hard on his ass and the evening air had a chill in it, but the streets were still releasing the warmth they'd absorbed all day. His t-shirt and jeans didn't feel too light at all, but there was a cold weight in his gut.

Rob stood by the gate without opening it. His golden hair glowed in the light from the streetlamp and his shoulders rounded sadly. "Hey," he said.

"Hi," Matty answered, passing his phone from one hand to the next and waiting.

"We need to talk."

"Yeah, we do."

Chapter Twenty-Six

ROB LOCKED THE door behind him and noted how Matty's pale arms were wrapped protectively around his chest, fingers digging into his triceps as he watched Rob warily.

"Okay, I just need to know for sure," Matty said, his voice tight and high. "Are you leaving me?"

Rob shook his head, smiling tiredly. "Matty, that's absurd."

"I thought so too." Matty stared at him with wide eyes. "But you walked out. You scared the shit out of me."

Rob let out a slow breath. "I'm sorry." He hated to say it, but Sato was right. He had to be honest with Matty. "Frankly, Matty, you scared me too. The choices you've made lately, even choices I made with you, have been more and more chaotic. I'm exhausted. I can't do it anymore. Something has to give. And I guess it's me."

A pale purplish-red surrounded Matty's eyes, and Rob knew he'd been crying. "I took it off. Like you said."

"Good." Rob remembered the rest of his instructions. "Did you jerk off?"

Matty scoffed and threw his hands wide. "Like I could? Like I even wanted to?" He shook his head. "No. I called Cowbell too, remember?"

Rob nodded. "I'm sorry. It was too much for both of us."

Matty sat on the sofa, elbows on his knees, and covered his face with his hands. "I threw it away. I'm done with it." He looked up at Rob, and the darkness in his eyes was frightening. Rob didn't know what Matty might do with feelings like that.

"Sweetheart—"

"No, listen to me. I threw it in the trash, and I'm sorry I made you miserable with it."

Rob put his hands in his pockets, gazing down at Matty's earnest face. "I wasn't miserable. Well, not the whole time. Sometimes it was hot."

Matty snorted. "Great. Fine. It's done." Matty waved his hand toward the kitchen trashcan. "I'm never wearing it again. Ever."

"Okay. A hard limit then."

Matty rolled his eyes, and Rob sat at the kitchen counter. He noticed there was a plate with the takeout from Rachel's on it. "Did you eat?"

"I tried. I thought if I choked it down you'd be happy."

"I am. Thank you for eating." He looked at the plate again. "Two bites, apparently."

"I tried. I can't eat when I'm upset."

Rob sat the book Sato had given him down on the counter and tapped the cover.

Matty's next question was quiet. "Where did you go?"

"I met up with a friend."

"Arjun? Susan?"

"No, that guy Sato I told you about."

Matty's chin went up, a flash of doubt in his eyes. "The BDSM guy."

"Yeah."

Matty stared at him. His mind clearly whirring with thoughts that Rob needed to nip in the bud.

"He's a sports psychologist with a specialty in eating issues, and he's offered to help us."

Matty's eyes narrowed. "What does that mean?"

"He said he'd meet with you pro bono to help get you on track."

Matty looked even more skeptical, his hands clasping together on his knees and tension in every line of his body. "What's in it for him?"

"Nothing, sweetheart." Rob moved over to sit next to Matty on the sofa. "He's a nice guy."

"Are you going to sleep with him?"

Rob's stared at Matty, taking in his trembling lips and the way his fingers twisted together anxiously. "Wow. Amazing." He swallowed and shook his head. "I'm going to pretend you didn't ask that."

Matty looked at his feet. "I need to be able to trust you, Rob."

Rob's mouth fell open. "Excuse me? When have I ever given you a reason not to trust me?" It took a lot of effort to point out that the same couldn't be said for Matty.

Matty met Rob's eyes. "You don't tell me things. Important things, Rob. I'm sorry I've been so selfish that I haven't noticed it before now, and that it took someone else pointing it out for me to see it. But now that I have, I'm scared. I mean, what else aren't you saying? What other things do you want out of life that you haven't told me about?"

"What are you talking about, sweetheart?"

Matty's jaw clenched. "I was talking to Anja while you were gone."

Rob studied his face. He was serious. "You talked to Anja?"

Matty had always had a fraught relationship with Anja. It was a strange mixture of jealousy, mutual attachments, and respect—and that went both ways. The thing that always stuck in Matty's craw, aside from the fact that Anja had never truly fallen for Matty's charms, was that she insisted she knew Rob better than anyone and pretty much did. His stomach twisted.

"Yeah. I was trying to find you, and I thought you might have gone to her place."

"Usually a good bet." Rob cleared his throat, anxiety beating in his veins. Matty was clearly hurt and definitely scared. "What did she say?"

Matty looked at him with a wounded expression. "She said you hate the city."

Rob swallowed.

"She said you've been unhappy for over a year."

Rob briefly closed his eyes.

"She also said you'd drive my getaway car and commit a felony for me and not to worry because you'd never leave me. She said you love me." Matty waited for him to answer, tension around his mouth.

"She's right about all of those things. She's also very annoying," Rob said. "Rob, become a physical therapist, you'll love it. Rob, stop trying to please your dead daddy. Rob, you're gay."

"She informed you of your gayness?"

"Yeah. I mean, I knew, but yeah."

Matty laughed, and something in Rob's gut unwound. They'd be okay. Matty was still laughing. It was going to be fine. It had to be.

Matty said, "I still have no idea how you guys made Ben."

Rob felt his face scrunch up involuntarily. "It was weird. Let's not talk about that."

"Is she in love with you?"

Rob smiled. "I've waited years for you to ask that question. No. She's not. She's aromantic and asexual."

"Wait, okay...listen this fight is not over, but wait." Matty held up his hand, his gaze darting between Rob's eyes like he was trying to find the joke. "You're telling me that you're gay and you knocked up an asexual."

Rob laughed. "It's really absurd isn't it? Of course, we had no idea what an asexual or aromantic was back then. We just knew she'd never wanted to sleep with anyone. We were drunk. She didn't want to be a virgin anymore because she was a college kid who still thought labels like that mattered. So we took care of her virginity while we were so out of it on shots of Jägermeister that I'm surprised I didn't fuck her in the ass out of habit. Worse, no condom. Boom, pregnant."

Matty started laughing again. "Holy shit. That's actually terrible luck. Like unbelievably bad. Well, except for the Ben part."

"I know."

"But everything she said tonight is true?"

"Anja knows me too well."

Matty shook his head and looked at the floor, a bitter twist on his mouth. "Better than me, apparently."

"If that's anyone's fault, it's mine."

Matty covered his face with his hands. "I guess I'm supposed to say no, it's all my fault since I've been such an awful, selfish shit lately."

"Matty, that's not what I want to hear from you."

"Good, because you're right that you share some of the blame here." He looked at Rob, his hands falling over his knees and hanging limply. "All this time, I thought we both wanted to be here in the city. But it turns out you haven't told me how you really feel about our life together."

He hadn't told Anja either—she'd just known. But that was Anja and it wasn't something he necessarily enjoyed about her.

"I wanted to love the city for you. I wanted to be happy here. I'm just not."

Matty pressed his lips together. "When did you know?"

"It snuck up on me. I guess I just realized recently what all of this meant."

"All of this?"

"The depression, the mild panic attacks, the claustrophobia." Naming it all made him sweat, and he wanted to stand up and shake himself like a dog. He needed to get free.

"Why didn't you say anything?"

"You've been kind of a mess, Matty. I wanted to get you on solid ground again. I thought we could do that here. That if we just found the magic formula, then you'd be happy, and I'd realize that dealing with everything else—the city, the fact that I'm so unhappy here— was worth it."

Matty held very still and whispered, "I swear to God, Rob. I'm going to be less of a mess."

Rob closed his eyes and ducked his head.

"You don't believe me!"

Rob shrugged. "I'm glad you want to get well. But what's happening with you isn't your fault, Matty. It's an illness and you need help dealing with it."

Matty stood, pacing the length of the counter before leaning against the wall. "So you want me to meet with this Sato guy?"

"Matty, it's not about what I want. It's what I think we need. We both have to admit you need help."

Matty gritted his teeth together, but then he nodded sharply. "I do need help. I can't put this on you anymore." He bit his lip and said quietly, "You hate resets. I made you do them—pushed you into it, and you hated it. I'm so sorry, Rob."

"No, Matty, that's not it." Rob sighed and stood, wanting to go to him and put his arms around him, but feeling like Matty needed to stand on his own two feet for this conversation. "I just can't do them as often as you needed them. I can't hurt you like that without…" He trailed off and sat back down on the sofa, putting his head in his hands. "I don't have the headspace for it, Matty. Not here in the city."

"It's that bad? You hate it here that much?"

Rob lifted his head. "Matty, I need a different life. I think you do too."

Matty stared at him like Rob was saying something he didn't entirely understand. Then he walked into their bedroom. He opened the closet and stared at the contents as Rob walked up behind him.

"What are you doing, sweetheart?"

He pulled the humbler off the wall and stalked past Rob out the back door. Following him, Rob watched as Matty threw it on the hibachi and doused it with lighter fluid. Then he just stood there and stared at it.

"Well?" Rob asked.

"I don't have any matches."

"I can get them from the kitchen."

Matty nodded, and when Rob returned with the box, he hadn't moved at all. He just stared down at the humbler with a white face and dark eyes. He took the box from Rob, his fingers ice cold. He threw the lit match and when the flame caught, he turned his back on it, returning into the apartment and closing the door.

Rob watched the humbler catch fire, the metal pieces growing hot and blackening the wood around them. Then he left it behind too.

Back in the apartment, Matty was on the bed, his eyes closed and his body very still. Rob sat by his feet and waited in silence.

Finally, Matty murmured, "I'm done with needing resets. I'm going to stop being that person."

Rob laughed but it was a half-sob.

"And I'll get help. Like you want."

"Help I can't afford to give you."

"*We* can't afford." Matty sat up. "You've got to let me shoulder some of it, Rob. I can handle it. I was an Olympian. I can be strong."

"I know you can."

"Then let me. Trust me. Let me prove to you that I can be what you need for a change. I can be your partner, but only if you let me."

When Rob met Matty's earnest gaze, something inside broke. Small, choked sobs clogged his throat, and he couldn't breathe.

"Shh," Matty murmured, pulling him into his arms. "It's okay to cry. You should cry more often, Rob."

Rob snorted. "Like you?"

"Yeah. Like me. There are some things I'm better at than you, and admitting that I'm a broken fuck-up is one of them."

Rob laughed again, tears still prickling his eyelids. "I wanted to give you everything you ever wanted, Matty."

"Well, fuck you, then."

Rob pulled back, confused.

"I could start my big long list of all the things I wanted that I never got, but we both know the only thing I've ever needed was you. So fuck the rest." Matty gazed into his eyes.

Rob wiped his face with his fingers and pulled Matty into another hug.

Matty whispered, "Why didn't you tell me you were so unhappy? Why, Rob?"

"I wanted to take care of you."

"Fuck that. I want to take care of you when you need me. This relationship can't be all about me all the time."

Rob chuckled, his breath ruffling Matty's hair. "I think I need to get my hearing checked. Did you just say this relationship can't be all about you?"

Matty punched his shoulder lightly. "I'm an asshole, I know."

"No, you're just a very complicated man." Rob smiled. "And, well, truth be told, I'm not."

They sat quietly for a few moments in each other's arms, and Matty finally said, "What do we do now?"

"I need a shower. Gotta get this city grime off me."

Matty turned his face so they were looking at each other again. "You miss home."

Rob smiled sadly. "Yeah. I do. Not Montana necessarily, or even Whitefish, but I miss open spaces, and I miss living where there are a hell of a lot fewer people."

Matty nodded. "Okay."

Rob crinkled his brow. "What does that mean?"

"It means okay, we'll leave. We'll go. As soon as we can, we'll leave the city."

"Matty…"

"Come here." Matty stood, and Rob let him tug him up too. "This way."

Rob held Matty's hand as they walked out to the garden in the humid night. Trees rose up between the buildings, defiant and determined in their tiny plot of land.

Matty came to a halt in the middle of the path out to the back fence. He pulled Rob close and twined their hands together tightly. "Look up at the sky." Matty's face lifted, and in the shadow the moon fell on his features, making him look even more pale and beautiful. "Look up. See the sky?"

Rob tilted his head back. "I think I see a little square of it right there between that tree and those buildings."

"Good." Matty took a deep breath. "See the North Star?"

Rob squeezed his hand. "No."

"Well, it's up there. And you told me once to always remember."

Rob swallowed hard and took hold of Matty's chin, bringing his gaze from the sky to meet Rob's own. "I remember, Matty."

"Well, good. Don't forget."

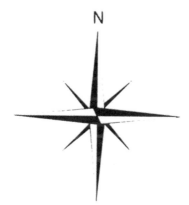

PART FOUR:

OUT OF A BLACK AND WHITE WORLD

CHAPTER TWENTY-SEVEN

T HE GUTTER WAS in an area of Brooklyn that made Matty feel sure they were going to be jumped if they didn't get inside quickly, but first there were greetings to get through.

"So, you're the Matty that makes Rob's eyes light up," Sato said, sticking out his hand with a confident grin.

Matty gripped his palm and slapped on his most charming media smile. "You must be Sato. It's a pleasure to meet you."

The redheaded young man standing with Sato smiled warmly at Matty and stuck out his hand. "Hi, I'm Todd."

Matty took in Todd's green skinny jeans, white-and-green Jefferson Natives, and pink lips that spread in a wide smile like bubblegum. It looked like Sato was a cradle robber, but who was he to judge? He took Todd's hand. "Nice to meet you."

"You too. Sato thinks we might be friends."

"I hope so," he said, and he found that he did. The kid seemed comfortable and relaxed in a way that made Matty envious, and if he could show Matty how to find even a little bit of that kind of peace, he'd feel lucky.

"Should we go inside?" Rob asked, putting his arm around Matty's shoulder. "Matty's probably hungry."

He was too anxious to be hungry. But Rob was all about "refeeding" him. He'd gobbled up the book Sato had given him in less than a day, apparently reading it during his breaks at work and on the train home at night. Now he was adding all kinds of "nutrient dense" powders he'd picked up at a health food store to Matty's meals. And making him eat every couple of hours. It had only been a few days, but Matty had to admit, he was already feeling a little better.

Rob had also removed the scale from the bathroom and taken it down the street to put directly into a garbage dumpster. Matty had sneaked and weighed himself on Wednesday at City Ice when he'd met secretly with Huxley to go over her program. He'd been proud of himself for not passing out when he saw how the numbers had already climbed. He also hadn't skipped his breakfast or lunch. He wasn't going to let Rob down. He'd get well, and he'd find a way for them to leave New York City. If that's what Rob needed, then that's what Matty was going to do. No more being a selfish ass. From now on, he was going to focus on Rob's happiness.

"Do they serve food here?" Rob asked anxiously, his arm squeezing Matty's shoulders.

"They have some really great spicy jerky, but otherwise, I'm sorry, no." Sato looked worried. "I should have considered that. We should go somewhere else."

Matty lifted his purse. "Don't worry. I brought my own." He smiled at Rob. "You know how I am about bar food, so I planned ahead. I used some of your wonder powders in the dressing."

Rob nuzzled him. "Great. I'm glad to hear that."

Sato grinned. "I like a guy who plans in advance." He led the way toward the entrance. "They have a great Smuttlabs beer selection. Todd's very fond of the Finklestein."

"Though the fifteen dollar price tag makes me balk at having more than one," Todd said, holding the door open. Music blared out, along with the sound of laughter. Rob winced but seemed to shake it off.

"I think they're going to hate me," Matty murmured to Rob as they followed inside the dive, letting the live acoustic music in the corner cover his words.

"They'll love you."

"Oh God, how many times have I heard that before?" He pulled Rob's arm around his shoulder. "You say that so often about people and it's so rarely true."

Sato chuckled, obviously having overheard at least part of what they were saying, and Matty wanted to hide under Rob's arm even more. There was something about Sato's calm, appraising gaze that made Matty feel like Sato knew everything about him—all of his flaws, all of his weaknesses, all the ways he'd let Rob down. And it was embarrassing as hell.

But he wasn't going to let that get to him. He was going to win him over. Somehow, someway, because it was important to Rob, and because Matty knew he needed help, and this Sato guy was their only hope on that front.

The Gutter Bar and Bowling Alley was a dive by design. Kitschy decor and old-school brown and red leather bar stools lined the wooden bar. Metal and vinyl diner chairs surrounded long, cheap-looking tables, and the eight vintage bowling lanes were visible through the windows along the far wall.

Everyone in the place had a hipster beard or looked like they were growing one. Matty, in his Alexander McQueen mesh-panel stretch jersey top and Rag & Bone Goa pleated leather shorts, felt pretty out of place. But Rob had his arm around him possessively, and he was the prettiest guy in the room by far, even prettier than Todd, so everything was going to be just fine.

Rob kissed Matty's cheek as he pulled the chair out for him at the table Sato led them to, and put his hand on Matty's knee when they sat down.

"Can I put in an order for you too?" Todd asked before he went to the bar.

"Thank you, Todd," Rob said. "I'll take a bottle of Righteous Ale and so will Matty."

Matty reached under the table and pinched Rob's leg but kept his smile firmly planted on his face. Rob covered his hand and squeezed. "Beer?" Matty asked under his breath. He wasn't a big beer drinker. He reserved his alcohol calories for things like delicious cocktails and wine.

"Beer."

Matty smiled and squeezed Rob's hand, a familiar pressure starting in the back of his head. He wouldn't listen to it, no matter what it said. He would do what Rob told him, and the refeeding would work. *Please don't come back.*

"So, Matty," Sato said after Todd returned with drinks. He paused to watch Todd fold his long legs up under the table with some difficulty. "Like a colt, this one."

Matty wondered just how many years difference there were between them. Sato looked to be in his late thirties or early forties, and Todd couldn't be twenty-five yet. "Yes?"

"I understand you're a figure skating coach." Sato tilted his head and smiled nicely.

Rob placed his hand on the small of Matty's back.

"I am." Matty cleared his throat.

"Has it been a difficult transition for you, going from a skater to a coach?" Sato smiled warmly, and Matty's stomach knotted up.

"It's had its challenges." A fine sweat broke out and the bees in the bonnet feeling grew. "I'm sorry. I'm just...I need to find the bathroom."

Sato glanced at Rob as Matty stood up.

"Sweetheart?" Rob rose too and followed him to the bathroom. Matty could feel the eyes of the other patrons on him. His hands were shaking. He didn't know what had triggered him.

The bathroom was a one-seater, and Rob caught his hand as he opened the door. "What's going on? Should I come in too?"

"I'm...yeah, come in." Matty shut the door behind them and then turned on the faucet. "I'm freaking out. I can feel Control coming. I feel really nervous. I hate this. Fuck, I'm sorry. I'm probably embarrassing you in front of your friends."

"No, it's okay." Rob rubbed his back as Matty used a wet paper towel to wipe down his face, trying not to smear his makeup. "Have you eaten enough today? All the calories we agreed on?"

Matty ignored the question. "I just feel exposed. Like he can see me and it's humiliating."

"He's a good guy, Matty. He can help you. Maybe you should talk to him about this. Did you eat before we left the house?"

Matty swallowed and almost lied. "No. I was nervous and I figured I'd just eat what I packed once I got here."

"Matty, you know how refeeding works. Enough calories in means less-intrusive thoughts. Not enough calories means the voice comes back. The way to defeat it is to eat."

"I know. I'm sorry. Let's just go back out there and act like I'm not insane, okay?" Matty pressed his lips together, trying to keep the rising fear from coming out in a sob. He could feel the hissing insults swirling at the back of skull.

"Matty, you're safe. I'm here with you. It's okay to eat and have a beer or two. I'll be right here with you."

Matty laughed hysterically, wobbly and tearful. "Do you hear yourself? I'm so fucking crazy, Rob. I am *fucking* insane. Why do you stay with me? Why do you love me?"

"Because you're strong, loyal, surprising, funny—"

"Stop, you'll just go on all night." Matty waved his hand at him, but just hearing him say the words lifted a little weight. "So, what do we do now?"

"We go back out there and sit down. You can ask Sato about refeeding if you want, or we can just have a night out with friends."

"Fuck knows we need that," Matty said. "A fun night out that isn't ruined with trips to the bathroom because I'm freaking out." He rolled his eyes. "Oops, blew that already."

Rob hugged him, and when Matty was ready, they left the bathroom, joining Sato and Todd at the table again.

"Everything all right?" Sato asked.

"Great," Matty said, smiling widely and a little desperately.

"All good," Rob agreed.

"Fantastic." Sato turned his attention to Rob, seeming to respect that Matty needed some space. "Rob, I was telling Todd that you were from Montana originally."

"Did you ski a lot?" Todd asked. "I've wanted to learn how to ski, but I haven't had the chance yet."

As Rob discussed the ski resort in Whitefish where he'd done plenty of skiing over the years, Matty pulled lip gloss from his purse and put it on. The action soothed him, and he felt a little calmer about the idea of eating in front of everyone.

Todd's eyes went a little wide, and Matty showed him the tube. "Who Swallowed a Star. Shiro Cosmetics. My current favorite."

"It's nice."

"Thank you."

"Matty, how do you feel about Marina Swanson's comeback chances after that injury at Nationals?" Sato asked.

"I think they're pretty good. I've talked with her mother—or rather, my mother talked with her mother—and she's not going down without a fight." Matty smiled again. "It all depends on her, doesn't it? Whether she wants to work for it or if she's tired of competing."

Sato nodded thoughtfully. "When did you know you were through with competition?"

The beers arrived and Matty stuck his Righteous Ale bottle in his mouth and drank several large gulps. He hated beer. But he was going to drink the entire bottle and order a second. Not just because he needed calories, but because he'd rather consume thousands of liquid ones until he passed out, if that's what it took to keep Control from waking up in his head again.

He smiled at Sato, feeling the warmth of alcohol in his belly. "I knew I was done when everything about competing hurt in the bad way and safewording was the only option left."

Sato nodded and lifted his bottle. "Good answer."

"Matty was a two-time Olympian," Rob said to Todd, his voice stuffed with pride. "He's still an amazing skater. You should see him perform sometime. Or just come to a practice."

Matty smiled at Rob and took his hand. "I'm going to Asia at the end of summer. I'll be performing six shows there."

"Are you excited about that?" Sato asked.

"Sure! I love performing. And in Asia, they take figure skating much more seriously than most Americans."

Rob looked toward the window to the bowling alley with a small frown on his face. He squeezed Matty's knee. "The city will be hard without you in it, but the money will be nice."

Matty hadn't considered that Rob would be even less happy in the city without Matty in it. He felt torn. He wanted to go—no, he needed to go, but now he wanted to stay too. Did they really need the money? *Yes.*

"Will you enjoy performing for an audience again?" Sato asked.

"I've missed it. It'll be nice to skate without any worry about scores."

His phone buzzed and he dug it out of his purse. It was Elliot.

In Prospect Park for show. Can I stop by after? Guy trouble. Need an ear.

Sorry. Wish I could. We're bowling with a BDSM master and his slave.

You have a weird life.

Speak for yourself, Orgy Boy.

When he looked up from his phone, Rob and Sato were talking about Dr. Joiner's new car, but Rob paused to say to Matty, "Didn't you bring something to eat?"

"Yes, thanks." Matty got into his purse again, pulling out the three Tupperware containers. One had the fruit he'd diced up, the other a salad with high-calorie protein flakes mixed into the dressing, and the third was cubed chicken smothered in olive oil. Matty felt Sato and Todd looking at him, and the eyes of other people in the room too. He reached into his bag for the fork he'd packed and felt another cold sweat break out on his neck.

Don't eat. It's not safe.

Panic roiled inside him, and he felt like he might puke. He cleared his throat and started putting the lids back on. "Oh. It looks like I forgot a fork. I'll just wait."

"I'll get a fork from the bar," Todd said, hopping up and crossing the room before Matty could stop him.

Rob held his gaze, and Matty flushed. But Rob said nothing about his lie.

Todd dropped into the chair again, squeezing his legs under, and passed Matty a plastic fork. "It's all they had." Then he picked up his jerky and took a chewy bite of it.

"All right," Matty whispered. He was going to do this. For Rob.

So he could get well and Rob would be happier until they could find a way out of the city. And he was going to do it for himself, so he wouldn't have to hear the voice of Control ever again.

He started to eat. The voices around him rankled. But he refused to give in to his sickness. He drank his entire beer as quickly as possible, hoping it would take the edge off. It did, so he asked Rob for another. Todd jumped up to get it before the words were fully out of his mouth.

When Todd returned, Matty smiled gratefully and took another swig. It tasted like fizzy rainwater with a splash of piss, but he drank it anyway. Rob rubbed between Matty's shoulder blades and watched him eat more of the salad.

Time seemed to turn to honey as Matty drank and ate. The alcohol in the beer draped him with a gauzy cape of relaxation, and when a third was delivered to him by a happy Todd before he'd even asked for one, Matty smiled goofily and thanked him. "I like beer. Beer is good."

Rob kissed his temple.

Soon, Sato and Rob were talking about baseball, and Todd and Matty were talking about movies.

"But the alien twins were clearly in love with each other," Matty said, his hands waving around. "And the costumes. The beautiful costumes!"

"Were they twins or just siblings?" Todd asked, tilting his head. "I couldn't figure that out. I think I missed that part of it when I went to get Sato more popcorn."

"I don't know, but does it matter? All I know for sure is that Channing Tatum can hop in my bed any night."

"Only after he visits my bed!"

Sato put his hand on Todd's chair and interjected with a chuckle, "Apparently the man is everyone's type."

"Damn straight, he is." Matty's eyes went wide and he laughed at himself. "Oh my God, I sound like my dad. He'd be so proud. Did you hear that? I might have been mistaken for a heterosexual for a second."

"Not in that outfit," Todd said.

Matty grinned. "True. You know what I learned from beer, Todd?"

"No?"

"I learned that I like you. You're pretty cool. And I think my friend Elliot would like you too."

"Elliot would want to dress him up," Rob said.

"Exactly! He'd make him so pretty! And then he'd want to take pictures of you, Todd! Would you like that? Have you thought about being a model?"

Todd's eyes gleamed. "Really? You know someone who works with a modeling agency?"

"Oh, no. Just a fashion photographer's assistant. But he knows people who know people who know—how many knows is that and how many beers did I have?"

"It really didn't seem like that many but I'm realizing how wrong I was," Rob said.

Matty put his elbow on the table and leaned his chin against it. "Yes, well...yes."

"You're such a lightweight," Todd said, laughing.

"Am I? I think I need something more than salad with protein powder dressing to go with my beer."

"Want some jerky?" Todd offered, holding out a piece.

Matty shocked himself by accepting. It was chewy and reminded him of going camping with his family when he was nine. His dad had fed them a pound of jerky each. He moaned a little as the oily, spicy taste rolled around on his tongue. "So good."

Eventually, Rob and Sato decided to bowl, but Matty declined, citing a recent manicure. Todd opted to stay behind too. As they looked at their guys through the window, picking out balls, they chatted over another plate of jerky.

"Those balls look like they came from the Flintstones or something."

"Or a garbage can," Todd added.

Matty eyed him. "Do you know who the Flintstones are?"

Todd shook his head. "Are they like comedians or somethings?"

"No." Matty sighed.

"Are you going to explain it to me?"

"No."

Todd sat back in his chair and after a thoughtful moment asked, "Were you serious about the modeling thing? I could really use some extra cash. I'm living with my dad and I could stand to get out of there."

"You don't live with Sato?"

"We aren't at that point in our relationship yet. But I do stay with him a lot."

Matty was surprised to hear that. For some reason, he'd imagined that a slave must live with his master. "Oh, well, sure. I'll introduce you to Elliot. He might help you with a headshot."

"Really? Matty, that would be amazing. Thank you so much." Todd shifted in his seat, and Matty glanced down at his crotch. He tilted his head, looking again. In the past, he never would have noticed, but after his own experience wearing a cock cage, he could tell Todd had one on. He looked up and saw that Todd had caught him looking.

"Sorry. I didn't mean...well, whatever. Let's get real. So, how do you like it?"

"I love it. Have you ever tried one?" Todd asked.

"It was an unmitigated disaster."

Todd's nose wrinkled when he smiled again. "Yeah. It can go that way. Especially the first time."

"You're not out-of-your-mind horny?"

Todd's face grew serious, and he looked like he was seriously considering Matty's question. "Well, I could be, but I choose not to be."

"Is that like a Buddhist mind-over-matter kind of thing?"

Todd shrugged. "You were an athlete, right? I'm sure you know more than I do about focus. I just focus on something else so I'm not out-of-my-mind horny. It's part of my service to Sato. I'm only horny when he wants me to be."

"Okay, wow." Still, what Todd had said about focus was true. He'd been selfish. He hadn't even tried to apply his athlete's focus to his libido when he'd been on lockdown. "I never thought of it like that."

"Why?"

Matty let the question sit with him for a few moments, and Todd didn't push. Finally, he said, "I've been a little self-centered lately. I wanted what I wanted for my own reasons. It helped me block out something else I didn't want to deal with, but it ended up being almost as bad as the problem I was trying to wipe out."

Todd nodded. "I call that being out of your place. You know, when you're not serving your dom, but doing what you want for your own reasons? Basically you're just making problems for him instead of making his life easier."

Matty looked through the window to where Rob was picking out a new bowling ball, returning the one he'd chosen first, and laughing with Sato. The sound of other players' balls hitting pins, and the smash of them falling, rattled underneath the acoustic guitar and keyboard. Had he ever considered the idea that maybe his role should be to make Rob's life easier? And not only the other way around? Maybe if he had, Rob would have leaned on him and told him the truth about his own pain.

"Anyway, it seems like maybe your dom is having a hard time right now," Todd said gently. He put his hand on Matty's shoulder. "It's not your fault. That happens sometimes."

Matty swallowed hard. How sweet that Todd didn't think it was his fault. Matty knew better.

Todd went on. "The way I see it, if your dom is having a hard time keeping you in your place because he's struggling with other things in his life, then you kind of owe it to him to just, you know, stay in your place." Todd smiled kindly. "Because if you step out of it, he'll just struggle more and things will fall apart."

Matty had been an asshole to think Todd was just a baby. He knew more about being a partner than Matty did, it seemed. "So, sometimes you have to do that for Sato?"

"Sure. When he took me on, he was still getting over his last slave, Josh. I served him like it was all I had going on in my life. I didn't make it hard for him to let me serve him. And I think it helped him heal."

"How did that work? Getting together with him?"

Todd shrugged. "It wasn't easy. He thought I was too young and didn't want to risk it with me. But I didn't want to go with some inexperienced master my own age." He rolled his eyes. "And I was totally done with basic bitches who thought all I needed to throw my legs in the air for them was a caramel latte and a day at the beach."

Todd's eyes glowed. "Sato had everything I wanted: age, experience, kindness, gentleness, respect for subs. I feel like I owe him so much for taking a chance on letting me be his slave." Todd smiled, and his freckled nose wrinkled cutely again. "So when he's having a rough time and doesn't have the energy to take control, I just fall back harder and serve him more, because I don't ever want him to regret trusting in me."

"Are you in college or...?"

Todd shook his head. "I work for my father. He owns a convenience store on Coney Island."

"Is he okay with you being with Sato?"

"He's not happy about it, but so long as I don't bring Sato around, it's okay." Todd's plump mouth went sad at the edges. "But you know what they say. You can't have everything."

"No," Matty murmured, turning to watch Rob and Sato through the window. He noted that Rob's smile still looked tired and his eyes a little sad. That was what the city had done to him. What Matty had done. "No, I guess you can't."

***

AS SATO PULLED down 7th Street, Rob could hear Matty in the backseat instructing Todd on how to blot his lips. Rob smiled to himself.

"You just put the tissue between and go like this." There was the sound of lips coming together and parting. "Didn't your mother wear lipstick?"

"She left me and my dad a long time ago. So I have no idea," Todd murmured.

"Well, now you know how to blot. Let me see your mouth." Matty clapped. "Holy shit. That's amazing. Here, let me take a picture with my phone."

A flash in the backseat left Rob rubbing his eyes and Sato braking slightly until his eyes adjusted.

"He's enthusiastic," Rob said by way of apology for whatever Matty had done to Todd's face. "And actually pretty good at this stuff."

"He's charming," Sato said, and Rob glowed to hear Sato describe Matty kindly.

"Oh my God!" Matty called gleefully from the backseat. "You have to see his mouth." Matty thrust his phone in Rob's face.

Rob glanced down at the picture. Todd really did have a very pretty mouth. Sato was a lucky guy. Sato pulled up to the curb in front of their apartment, and Rob handed the phone over to him. Sato's expression was priceless and Rob chuckled as Sato murmured, "Yes, he looks very..."

Todd started laughing again.

"You don't like it?" Matty asked. "How can you not like it?"

"It's..."

"You've left him speechless," Todd crowed. "I've never seen that happen before."

"Oh, it wasn't me. It's your mouth." Matty took the phone back from Sato. "Well, goodnight. Thanks for the hipster bowling and crazy expensive beers. Next time, though, we should grill in our backyard, because otherwise we'll never be able to afford to leave New York." Matty climbed out of the car after kissing Todd's cheek.

Rob turned to Sato. "That's an actual invitation by the way. We'd love to have you over."

"I'll have Todd text Matty and we'll work something out."

"Sounds perfect." Rob got out of the car with a wave. Putting his arm around Matty's shoulder, he guided him toward the gate to their stoop as Todd climbed in next to Sato and they started down the street.

"Did you end up having fun after all?" he asked Matty.

"I did. Once I ate, I felt better. I know it should be obvious, but it's just not to me, okay?"

"I know, sweetheart. Did you like Sato?"

"He was nice. I liked Todd a little better, though."

"Why's that?"

Matty shrugged. "I don't know." He hung back as Rob opened the gate, and Rob turned to see what he was doing. Matty dug around in his big blue purse and pulled out a package of fat colored chalk. He put it on the stoop next to theirs, and then slid beneath Rob's arm again.

"What was that about?"

"Paying an IOU."

Rob released him to pull his keys from his pocket, fitting one into the door.

Matty murmured, "Sabrina told me the other day that Chuck Forenza has too much chest hair."

"What's she doing seeing his chest hair?"

Matty laughed. "It's not like that!" Then he frowned and pushed a dark lock out of his eyes, tucking it behind his ear. It really was getting shaggy and long. Rob kind of loved it that way. "It's the same with Sato."

"I don't think the man has much chest hair at all if memory serves."

"No, he has too much something. I don't know what. I'll let you know when I figure it out."

"All right. You do that."

Matty pushed past him into the apartment, and Rob locked the front door behind them before closing the door to their apartment and locking it too. He turned around to find Matty on his knees.

He put his hand in Matty's hair and was surprised when Matty leaned forward and put his hands on Rob's shoes.

"Let me take them off."

Rob complied, and then Matty unbuttoned his jeans, working them down over his hips. "Step out." Matty folded them neatly on the chair and started on the buttons of Rob's short sleeve H&M shirt that Matty had picked out for him. "Let me have this too."

"What are you doing?"

"Taking care of you." He batted his lashes coyly. "Serving you. Master."

Rob chuckled. "Oh, I see." He let Matty slide off his shirt. "How else are you going to serve me tonight?"

"I'm going to wash you and dry you and put you to bed."

Rob grinned. "Do I get a goodnight kiss?"

"You get whatever you want."

He guided Matty toward the bathroom. "How about a goodnight fuck?"

"If it serves you, Master."

Rob smirked. "Oh, this is kind of fun."

"It is, isn't it?" Matty grinned as he adjusted the water in the shower and started to take off his own clothes. "I can be a good servant. You'll see. I'll be the best servant you've ever seen."

"I'm sure you will, sweetheart. You're always the best."

***

SATO PUSHED MATTY'S knees up to his chest and drove into him.

"Please, sir, may I come," Matty gasped, the urgent coil of orgasm beginning his pelvis and tensing in his balls.

Sato smiled smugly and pushed Matty's sweaty hair off his forehead. "No, you can hold out a little longer, I think."

Matty squirmed on Sato's cock, trying to find a position that didn't force Sato's dick against his prostate exactly right, but it was no good. The constant, drumming pleasure continued. He struggled against Todd's hold on his arms and looked desperately around for Rob. He was here somewhere. He knew he was. He just needed to find him.

315

Sato's dick was too distracting, though, and before long he was begging again. "Please, sir, I need to come."

"No," Sato said with a good-natured laugh. "Unless you enjoy being a failure? Then go ahead. Fail again."

Matty moaned and tossed his head, sweat in his eyes and his hips stuttering, his asshole flexing and his nipples peaking hard and tender to the cool air in the room.

"You're an athlete, Matty. An Olympian," Todd said. "Surely you can focus on something else."

"Fuck, fuck," he whimpered, heat pooling in his pelvis and the undeniable pull of pleasure dragging him to the point of no return. "Please! I'm trained to come like this! Please!"

Sato said calmly, "Then untrain yourself. It's not that hard. Use your strength of mind to unlearn your bad habits."

Matty flexed his toes, fighting the constant beating pleasure of Sato's stroking cock. He squeezed his eyes shut and struggled against Todd's strong hands. "Stop. Stop. I'm gonna—"

"Do it," Rob said in his ear. "Come for me."

Matty cried out, opening his eyes to their sun-drenched bedroom, his cock jerking helplessly as hot come spattered his chest and neck. His hips twitched and jerked as the orgasm gripped him again and again, pumping him dry. "Oh fuck," he moaned.

"Wow. What a thing to wake up to." Rob laughed softly.

Matty blinked the sweat out of his eyes and found Rob rolled up on one elbow, looking down on him, his eyes sleepy and cheeks flushed. He leaned down and licked the come from Matty's neck and then kissed his lips. "Good morning, horndog. That must have been a really hot dream."

Matty's heartbeat roared in his ears, and his dick jerked again, a last, sweet dribble of come oozing out. "God, it was…fuck."

"Yeah?" Rob laughed again and sat up. His cock was hard, and the tip glistened in the morning light coming from the windows. "Can I…?"

Matty nodded, his body still raw from the intense orgasm, and his words missing as his brain scrambled to separate the too-realistic dream from the truly real morning. Rob slid between Matty's legs, kissing his neck and still-heaving chest before scooping Matty's come up from his belly. He slicked the head of his cock with it and pressed his come-slick fingers against Matty's hole.

"Are you too sensitive from coming for me to put fuck you?"

Matty bit down on his lip and murmured, "S'okay."

Rob pressed his dick inside, and a flurry of visuals from the dream flitted through Matty's head as his girth put pressure on his prostate. Rob bent with the head of his dick just inside Matty's sphincter and licked the remaining come from Matty's abs. Then he kneeled up and thrust in slow and hard until he was balls deep, gazing tenderly at Matty.

"You're so beautiful, sweetheart. I love you so fucking much."

Matty reached up for him, and Rob fell forward, rutting into Matty's body, pushing against nerves already overstimulated and tender. But Matty wanted him inside, closer and harder—wanted him to make the dream go away.

"I love you too."

"This with you is all I need," Rob whispered, romantic in his sleepy arousal. "You and me. I love you."

"Come for me. Fill me up. Mark me."

Rob turned his head, kissing Matty's ear, his jawline and his mouth. Just as Rob's back broke out with sweat and his cock jerked hard inside Matty's body, he latched on to Matty's collarbone, leaving a lovemark Matty hoped would last a few days.

"Yes," Matty moaned, his ass milking the come from Rob's trembling body. "Come in me. Make me yours."

"Always mine."

Matty dug his heels into Rob's ass and held him inside, feeling the pulse of Rob's orgasm deep inside and feeling his groan hot against his throat. Rob kissed Matty's mouth and then carefully pulled his cock free. Matty felt his come slide out, and Rob scooped it up with his fingers and pushed it back in. Then he pressed Matty's knees to his chest and kissed his hole. As he licked him clean, fireworks tingled up Matty's spine as Rob's tongue teased the tender skin and stretched sphincter.

"Love the way I taste in you," he whispered, and Matty's cock made a valiant effort to get hard again, but it was too soon.

"So good," Matty moaned, his legs shaking and his fists knotting in the covers. "Don't stop yet."

Rob tongued his asshole and kissed it until Matty was groaning. Then he pressed his fingers deep inside, massaging his sensitive prostate until Matty had to beg him to stop. It felt too good, but too much.

"Refractory periods suck," Matty grumbled, rolling over to get away from Rob's fingers.

"Well, you came pretty damn hard, so it'll be a while, I'm sure." Rob smiled knowingly at him. "What were you dreaming about anyway?"

Matty felt his face go hot, and he looked out the window. "Fucking."

"Who were you fucking? Because it definitely wasn't me." He laughed, and Matty checked to see if he was upset but his eyes were clear and good-humored.

"Yeah. I don't know. You were there too." Somewhere. Matty had known Rob was in the room; he just hadn't been able to find him. "It was dark and I was being held down—"

"Oh, restraints. Your favorite."

"And the guy kept telling me not to come; to unlearn bad habits. But then you told me to come for you and..." Matty gestured helplessly at his still sticky chest. "I did."

"Hot," Rob said, kissing him on the mouth again. "And it was just a dream, Matty. It doesn't mean anything. Don't worry about it, okay? Let's get cleaned up. We should hit the road for our trip soon, or we'll get stuck in weekend exodus traffic."

Matty's legs felt weak like a newborn lamb as he tottered after Rob to the shower. As he climbed beneath the hot spray, Rob pulled him into his arms, kissing his cheek and neck. "Hey, listen, it's okay to fuck Sato in a dream. Because it will only ever be a dream."

Busted. Matty pressed his nose to Rob's neck and closed his eyes.

"How did you know?"

"You said his name a few times right before things got intense and you came."

"I'm not into him. I don't even know what that was about."

Rob kissed his shoulder. "He represents things. It's no big deal."

"Are you sure?"

Rob chuckled. "Of course, sweetheart. I'm sure." He let go of Matty and reached for the shampoo. "I can't wait to get out of the city. This vacation is going to be a whole new start."

Matty swallowed hard. Rob's shoulders were less tense and his eyes less tired than they had been in a long time. The promise of getting out of New York for even a weekend seemed to have taken a huge weight off his shoulders, and yet Matty couldn't help but feel a little sad.

Living in New York had been Matty's dream his whole life and, much like every other dream he'd cherished since childhood, it hadn't turned out the way he'd wanted at all.

Rob started to hum an old Matchbox 20 song from his college years, and Matty leaned against the cold tile wall, waiting for his turn to shower. Rob's abs were glorious and his cock hung thick and heavy with water running off the end of his dick. His voice wasn't bad, but it wasn't good either, and Matty smiled as Rob started to sing the chorus.

He'd learned a long time ago that dreams change, and this time he wasn't going to mess up his life by clinging to a dream it was long past time to let go.

CHAPTER TWENTY-EIGHT

"YOU'RE AWFULLY QUIET," Rob murmured.

The city had disappeared into the distance of their rearview mirror an hour earlier. It was their first vacation outside the city since they'd gotten back from Vegas three years before. Matty was still a little nervous that Rob might have arranged to stay at a dodgy hotel, but he was looking forward to some alone time with Rob and to figure out what their next steps were going to be in life.

Control was blessedly silent, though Matty didn't understand why. He thought that putting Rob's needs first might have switched something in his head from self-loathing punishment to determined empowerment. He didn't have to try to make his life in New York City work anymore. He wasn't giving up or being weak by walking away from being not-the-best-at-anything. By deciding to leave New York City, he was being strong for Rob, and that was better somehow.

Rob touched his knee. "What's on your mind?"

"Lots of things, but just now I was thinking about Sabrina." The jump clinic had ended the day before and he expected a call.

"Have you heard anything official yet?"

"No."

"Well, whatever happens, you're going to be okay. We'll make it work."

"Maybe."

Matty didn't know what to want anymore. If Sabrina came back, then how would that impact their new plans to leave New York? During their trip, he wanted to talk Rob into looking for PT jobs in

Missoula, and Matty had already put a call through to Margaret Page about looking quietly into a potential coaching situation in the area for himself.

Rob flicked a finger against the bag resting on the gear shift between them, still full of barely touched French fries. "Eat."

Matty grabbed two fries. They were terrifyingly delicious and he could practically feel his fat cells screaming in delight at the promise of starch and salt.

"Thanks, sweetheart," Rob murmured.

Matty tingled with the praise. Laying his head back against the headrest, he took a moment to enjoy it. Rob placed his hand on Matty's knee only to remove it to shift gears as they pulled off at the New Paltz/Poughkeepsie exit. "Listen, no matter what happens, we're going to be okay. I can handle you. All of you."

Matty felt the squirm of doubt in his gut, but he looked out the window, took a few deep breaths, and let it pass through him. They could both do this. They were committed and devoted. "Hey, Rob?"

"Yeah?"

"I can handle all of you too."

Rob went quiet, taking another turn onto a road shaped like a snake, twisting and hilly. He rubbed his hand up Matty's thigh and smiled at him tenderly before returning to the gear shift again.

Matty looked out the window and wondered just where Rob was taking him. It was very far off the main road and he doubted there was a La Quinta Inn up this way.

"Are there any special plans for this trip?" Matty fished. Elliot had planted a suspicion during a call the day before. It would be weird timing of course, given how difficult their last few weeks had been, but if Rob had planned it before everything went dramatic and miserable, maybe he still intended to follow through.

"I'm sure you packed plenty of different clothes for whatever occasion might arise."

"What if I didn't, though, and we need to make an emergency run for tuxes?"

"You won't need a tux where we're going."

Matty frowned. "Should I prepare myself mentally for anything in particular? A proposal maybe? During a hot air balloon ride?"

Rob tilted his head and seemed to consider the question before winking at Matty. "Nope. No hot air balloon rides and no proposals. But I'm definitely going to tie you up and hurt you." He laughed. "That didn't sound quite as romantic as it did in my head."

"Oh God! It's like you don't even know me." Matty scoffed. "Tie me up? Hurt me?" Matty fluttered a hand to his chest and fell back against the seat in a faked swoon.

"Ah, yes, exactly your brand of romance."

"But there's nothing else? Nothing *special*?"

"No. Let me guess, you talked to Elliot."

"Maybe."

"It's not a proposal."

"Are you sure?"

"Yes. I'm sure." After a pause Rob murmured, "Hot air balloon, huh? You've got some very definite ideas about what you want. Should I pump Elliot for your ultimate fantasy before I royally mess it up?"

"I can email you an outline of five different proposal scenarios to choose from if it would make it easier for you."

Rob snorted. "Yeah. Okay. You do that."

Matty wrinkled his nose. "But then you'll surprise me with something totally different, right?"

"Of course."

They traveled around the curves in smiling silence for a few minutes until Rob turned down a driveway that came out of nowhere and seemed to lead to nowhere too. "This is the place. It's pretty isolated."

Matty leaned forward, trying to see through the woods all around them. "So we'll be alone?" He'd been assuming they'd be at a hotel or B&B of some kind, but this looked like private property.

"Absolutely alone."

His breath quickened. "No one will hear my screams?"

"Not a living soul."

Matty groaned and shivered all over, his cock going hard and his pulse pounding. "Fuck."

Rob chuckled.

Matty was definitely back on the horny-as-hell roller coaster. Adrenaline rocketed through him and an anticipatory sweat broke over his skin. "Did you bring the whips?"

"Maybe."

"My heart! I can't take it!" Matty moaned, rubbing a hand over his crotch. "How much longer until we're there?"

Rob patted Matty's leg again as they pulled out into a clearing in the trees and the place they were staying came into view. "We're there now."

"I really do love you, Rob," Matty said, his voice coming out strangled and hoarse.

"Breathe, sweetheart. Just breathe."

***

Mr. Lovely,

We are happy to have you here at Blue Walnut Bed & Breakfast. As you requested, the entire house is yours for the next three nights. We pride ourselves on discretion and privacy, and we have no doubt that you will be satisfied on this front as well.

SO BEGAN THE note that was taped to the front door of the small, two-story stone and blue clapboard cottage with a wraparound porch and a vibrant English garden blooming all around the front and side of the house. The note went on to tell them that the refrigerator on the screened-in porch by the back entrance would be stocked each morning by six-thirty a.m. with the breakfast, lunch, and dinner options Rob had chosen in advance, and that management was just a phone call away, twenty-four hours a day, should there be any problems. Other than the morning food drops, they would have the property completely to themselves.

"You rented this whole place?" Matty asked. His eyes were wide and his neck flushed as he gazed around with an open mouth. He was obviously still aroused and in shock. "It's so beautiful, like a fairy tale or something."

"Yep." Rob opened the trunk and started lifting out Matty's many bags. How many bags did one guy need for three days spent mostly naked with his boyfriend? Six apparently.

"Seriously, though, Rob. We can't afford it. How much did you spend?"

"Nothing. Zip. Zero." Rob shot a wink his way and shrugged. "It was a gift to me from a patient—that basketball kid I mentioned?"

"The one with the Texas city name who wanted to get back to playing for NYU by this upcoming fall? Austin?"

"The very one. His name is Dallas, though."

"He owns this place? I thought he was a regular college kid."

"Dallas's dad owns it. Apparently everyone in that family was pretty grateful for my help in making sure Dallas got back on the court."

"Well, I'm grateful too. I mean, look!" Matty's voice ratcheted up with glee and Rob felt intensely gratified at witnessing his pleasure. Matty waved his arm dramatically toward the cottage. "It's amazing!"

"I can't take all the credit, though," Rob said. "I found out that Dallas's mom is a pretty big skating fan and I might have named dropped you and Ben during a conversation."

Matty beamed. "A fan? Seriously?"

Truthfully, she'd been more interested in Ben's career than in Matty's, but she hadn't been indifferent to Matty's former fame in the sport either. "Pretty cool swag you get for being your talented and amazing self, sweetheart."

Matty shrugged, but his lips twisted in a pleased, smug smile and Rob grinned to see it. "I will write her a very special thank you note when we get home."

"I'm sure she'd like that." Rob hefted the bags onto the side porch and took the key out from under the mat. "Also, there was a cancellation for these dates. They got to keep the deposit so they aren't out an entire three night's income. Come on, let's unload this stuff and then we'll look around."

Rob was pleased with the accommodations, and Matty was clearly impressed too. The property was set so far back from the main road that he couldn't see or hear the cars passing through the dense forest. The back of the house was all gardens and stone paths that led to arbors and a gazebo with an extra-large hammock suspended from the ceiling in the middle of it, and even more forest beyond that.

Inside the house was clean and decorated a little fussier than Rob would have liked, and definitely a little more country-chic than Matty preferred, but there was no doubt it was quite posh and everything from the fixtures to the furniture was of the highest quality. The kitchen was outfitted wonderfully and a wide table graced the middle of the room with enough chairs for a party if they'd wanted to have one. The living room featured a comfortable-looking sofa, a television, and a large ottoman. Along with the meal delivery fridge, the large screened-in porch attached to the back of the house featured a bed positioned diagonally so that the sun fell on it from the south. It was full of plush pillows, and the brochure had described it as a reading nook, but Rob thought he had better plans for that particular surface.

The bedroom was upstairs in the back of the house. It had a king-sized bed with wrought iron head and footboards perfect for ropes and cuffs. A shaft of light fell in from the western window and landed on the bed. The blue and white coverlet shone invitingly, and Rob wanted to see Matty on it naked and begging. But all things in their own time.

Matty followed Rob back outside to help carry the last of the bags in from the side porch.

"So, do you want to play a game this weekend?" Rob asked.

"What kind of game?"

"Master and servant."

Matty's cheeks pinked up and his eyes took on a glow. He licked his lips and whispered, "When do we start?"

"We can start now."

"Okay." Matty's voice was breathless and raw with excitement.

Rob dropped to his knees in front of him, unzipped his pants, and grinned at the sight of Matty's desperate dick.

"Look how badly you already want to come for me," Rob murmured, working Matty's leggings down to play with his balls, licking them and then moving up to tongue at the head of his penis.

"Oh God," Matty said, his knees shaking and giving out a little. He looked around like he expected someone to jump out of the bushes at any second. "We're outside, Rob."

Rob took hold of him by the hips and mouthed the tender, ticklish place where thigh met groin.

"Rob," Matty moaned.

"Mmm-hmm."

"We're outside."

"I know. There's no one around." He kissed Matty's quivering thighs and then stood up, slapping his hip. "Take off your clothes. You won't be needing them."

Matty jerked his shirt over his head and let it fall to the porch, still looking around nervously. "You're sure we're alone?"

"Yes." Rob explained the game. "So long as we're on the grounds, you'll be naked and available to me at any time."

Matty's chest flushed as he kicked off his shoes and pulled his pants and underwear down. He was naked in the summer sunshine, his skin pale brilliant enough to make Rob blink as his eyes followed the small trail of dark hair down Matty's chest and below his belly button.

"Beautiful." He motioned at the clothes, and Matty picked them up, clutching them to his chest. "You'll put those away when we get upstairs."

"Yes, sir."

"And these are the rest of the rules. Are you listening?"

"Yes, Master."

Rob had to stop a snort from escaping. It might be fun to play this for now, but he'd probably have to demand Matty cut the sirs and the master business before the day was up. But for the moment, it was perfect.

"Rule number one: you will not ask me for anything. You won't ask me to suck you, fuck you, or eat your ass. You'll offer to do any and all of that to me, however. And if I decide to return the favor, that's my decision."

"I understand."

"Safeword is the same as always and you can use it at any time."

"Of course."

"And be patient, Matty. It's going to be a long, fun, good few days." Matty's eyes dilated and he bit his lip, weight shifting slightly from foot to foot. "Have you ever been naked outside before?" Rob asked.

"No. Well, not since I was a little kid, I guess."

"All right. Go upstairs. Shower. Get prepared and I'll meet you in the bedroom when you're done."

"This anniversary is already amazing." Matty grinned as he opened the door and hurried into the house, his skater's butt flexing as he went.

Rob followed him in and waited downstairs until he heard the water running for Matty's shower. Then he went back out to get the final bag from the car—something he'd packed secretly, and full of the toys he planned to use.

He already felt better just being in the country. The rolling fields and flowers they'd seen on the drive had set his senses reeling, and a buzzing freedom rolled through his body. He'd breathed easier with each mile out of the city, and the comfort that filled him at the sight of mountains—puny and hillish as the Shawangunks seemed in the face of memories of his Montana home—almost made him tear up. He'd missed the land, the space, and the quiet. It was painful how good it felt to finally be back in what he only now realized he thought of as the real world.

He closed his eyes and listened. He could hear insects outside, cicadas already starting their mating song, and farther off came the rhythmic belching of frogs. It was all topped with the trilling sweetness of bird song. Turning to the kitchen window, he adjusted the curtains and gazed out at the green leaves and wide flower-filled garden out back. The sun was lowering, glinting from the west, and Rob checked the sky for clouds. Clear as a crystal blue bell.

He went upstairs and finished unpacking. He put most of the toys in a drawer so Matty wouldn't see them. Rob's throat clicked as he swallowed, fingering the blindfold and the ties. He laid them on the bed, smiling when the sun fell on them.

Anticipation was half the fun.

CHAPTER TWENTY-NINE

M ATTY'S THIGHS ACHED like he'd been fucked for hours by the time he slid down off Pearl Whiskers, a lovely mare who'd been very patient with his very out-of-practice riding skills. Of course he *had* been fucked for hours the night before, so that might have contributed to his shaky limbs and his sore ass.

The ride had only been an hour and a half up some winding trails, and down to a waterfall they'd played in before heading back up the mountainside again. But he felt like his legs and ass had been hit with sticks. Which wasn't a feeling he hated, exactly, but he usually preferred it when Rob did the hitting.

"Okay, now keep your eyes closed." Rob said, putting his hands over Matty's face before he could turn around and see what they'd come all this way for. "Oh, and this is not a proposal. So don't get excited."

"Too late," Matty said, letting Rob steer him around Pearl Whiskers and Elvis, the stallion Rob had chosen from the stables.

"Sorry," Rob said, kissing the side of his head. "One day, sweetheart. But not today."

"S'okay," Matty said, feeling a little delirious after a day in the woods with the wind in his hair and Rob's beautiful smile lighting up the trail more than the sunshine. "I know you love me."

"I do. Which is why..." Rob removed his hands.

The sight that greeted him was amazing. A bottle cooled in an ice chest, and a filled-to-the-brim picnic basket sat on a picnic table overlooking a wonderful mountain view.

"Well, you could propose. I mean, this would be an acceptable location."

Rob chucked his chin and kissed his lips. "I'm not proposing. Here, sit down and let's be romantic."

Matty chose the side of the table with the best view of the mountains, and Rob sat beside him. "The horses won't run off?"

"No. They'll be fine."

Matty watched as Pearl Whiskers and Elvis set about eating their own early dinner, chewing at the longer grass several yards away. "She's a good horse. When I was a kid, I never thought I'd go almost ten years without riding."

"Me either. Four years since I've been on a horse." Rob shook his head. "I had no idea how much I'd missed it."

Matty noticed the way Rob's eyes soaked in the landscape, the gentle way his body had unwound in just a day away from the city. His hair even looked more relaxed, flopping around on his head in the breeze, and the lines around his eyes had disappeared. He actually looked younger as he opened the bottle of what turned out to be sparkling grape juice and poured a glass.

"It's a shame it couldn't be wine, but it wouldn't be safe to ride back after drinking."

Matty accepted the glass and raised a toast. "To a new start for us. As soon as we can afford one."

Rob clinked and drank. "So, if you're going to do shows with Julien in Asia, do you have some ideas for a new routine or two? Or are you going to do 'Applause' day in and day out?"

"Oh, I've got ideas." His stomach growled, which surprised him and made Rob grin.

"The book says you'll feel hungry again, the right kind of hungry, when the refeeding is working."

"Well, it must be working because I'm starving."

"Then let's eat."

The golden early afternoon light played in Rob's hair, and Matty wallowed in Rob's physical beauty as they ate and discussed some of his plans for show programs. "And I was thinking I could ask Donna to ship my old costumes up. I'll still fit in them. I basically weigh the same..." He cut off. "It doesn't matter what I weigh." He bit into his fancy meat-and-veggie sandwich and chewed. "I'll fit in them."

"Won't the fans notice if you're recycling?"

Matty waved a hand. "What's a girl to do? I can't exactly order up a bunch of new costumes when we're saving for a new dream life. You know how much those fuckers cost."

"That's true."

"It's a good thing I've got shows lined up. If I got back on a regular performing agenda, like Julien, then I could spend most of my time working on my own things and choreographing for the occasional skater who wanted my input. If we lived outside of the city that would probably be enough to get by."

Rob shrugged, not meeting his eye.

"What? Is this about traveling with Julien?"

"No. It's not about him. I promise you, nothing is ever about Julien."

"Then what's it about?"

Rob flushed a little, his cheeks going red. "I miss you when you travel. It's selfish of me to admit that. I know you love the attention, and you're beautiful on the ice. But I hate it when you're gone for a month."

"I hate being away from you too." Matty did love skating for a crowd, but he still remembered the aching pain of coming home to a hotel room without Rob every night. "But there's FaceTime now and all kinds of good ways we can still see or talk to each other every day."

"Of course." Rob smiled at him. "Did I tell you I got an email from Margaret?"

"My number one fan, Margaret Page of Whitefish Montana?" He hoped she hadn't told Rob about Matty's phone call. He didn't want Rob to think he was pressuring him one way or another. Especially if her search turned up a lack of interest in his coaching skills.

"The very one." Rob smiled. "Thank God for her, huh? We'd never have met if she hadn't offered you that job house sitting."

"It was a plum position with many, many benefits. You being the biggest one of course."

Rob kissed him softly. "Anyway, she says Bing convinced her husband George to invest in the goat ranch too. Between Bill and Angus investing, and now George, we should be able to buy a lot more goats this year. And do you know what that means?"

"Nope."

"It means we should see some really good money this spring and next fall. We just have to hold out until then."

"Hold out for what?"

Rob grinned. "Hold out to move out of the city."

Matty shook his head, frowning. That wasn't acceptable. He wanted Rob happy, and he wanted him happy *now*. Just the sight of the mountains had erased a year's worth of Rob's worry lines. It made Matty feel a little sick to think of forcing him to go back to New York in just a few days. He wished somehow they could just stay here.

"That's a long time to keep living somewhere you're not happy." Besides, now that he'd decided they were leaving, Matty wanted to just do it. Patience had never been his best event.

Rob shrugged. "I'll be okay. Just knowing we've agreed to leave makes it easier to deal with. I know it's temporary at least."

"Are you thinking that we'll head back to Whitefish? Or Missoula?"

"I don't know. Anja said she talked to you about the idea of taking Ben out to Colorado to work with Forenza."

"She mentioned that, yeah."

"Well, she says there are a lot of physical therapy jobs available out there, especi ally for a generalist. Obviously, there's no way to tell if Forenza might be a better coach for Ben without giving him a try, but I suspect he's got more to offer than Greg Simon."

"Probably."

"So, what do you think of the Colorado idea?"

Matty picked at his lunch. The book had said not to have intense conversations over meals, because food shouldn't be associated with stress. But he wasn't going to say anything about that. He was just going to put his food in his mouth and be a fucking grownup about it.

"Well?" Rob asked again.

"What would I do out there?"

"Coach."

"I can't just walk into the Colorado training facility and say, 'Hey, give me a job coaching.' And even if they wanted to interview me, Valentina probably wouldn't give me a good recommendation after all the fights we've had lately."

"She might. I don't think she'd want to say anything bad about you, anyway. It'd say something about her own coaching skills if she did."

"Maybe." Matty sighed. "I don't know. If Ben goes to Colorado, obviously that's where we should go too." He forced another bite down. He couldn't really taste it, but it didn't matter. He just needed to eat it.

Rob ate in silence for a few minutes and then asked something that had obviously been on his mind, based on the overly nonchalant way he threw it out. "Do you think you'd like to meet up with Sato when we get back?"

"Why?"

"For a counseling session. I'd like to talk to him about the refeeding process we've been doing, and how it's working. I'd like you to talk to him. I need to know if you feel good about it."

"Well, first of all, I do feel good about it. I promise. As for meeting Sato, I don't know. He makes me nervous."

"Because you're attracted to him?"

"That's—I'm not—no."

Rob lifted his brows and laughed. "Matty, it's okay. He's an attractive man."

"He's bald. And sleeps with barely legal babies."

"When I met you, you were a barely legal baby."

"Well, you were younger than you are now. Todd's barely older than Ben."

Rob laughed. "Actually, he's a few very important years older than Ben."

"Maybe."

"Okay, does that mean you're not interested in letting him help you?"

Matty didn't want to let Rob down. "I just mean that he obviously has his own issues, but I'll listen to what he has to say about refeeding and I'll go out with them as friends, but I'm not going to start spilling my deep dark secrets to him."

"Deep dark secrets?"

"Yeah. I won't be crying to him about how Donna put too much pressure on me as a kid, and maybe I didn't need to know she'd emptied her retirement accounts for me." Matty shrugged. "Maybe I didn't need to know they'd mortgaged the house."

Rob nodded and twisted his lips up thoughtfully.

"What?" Matty asked.

"I think I need to tell Anja that no matter where you and I end up, Ben should stay in New Jersey."

"She won't like that."

Rob sighed. "I know."

"She'll say that there's a better coach in Colorado, and that Cardew is trouble and Ben's too young to know what's important."

"But he's not. He's a good kid. And he'll be eighteen in a year anyway. He wanted to do the right thing by his friend by going with him to meet a stranger he'd met online. When Ebru caught them, he was mortified because he wants to impress her." Rob furrowed his brow. "What you just said about pressure... If Ben is going to be an Olympian it's going to be because Ben wants it, not because Anja is overly invested, or because we got him away from bad influences, or because we've all sacrificed for his costumes and coaching fees."

Matty wasn't so sure. "Well, isn't there a line you have to walk as his parents? You have to decide what's too much pressure, and what's making sure he doesn't throw his chances away."

"True."

Matty's phone vibrated in his pocket and he pulled it out, frowning. "I can't believe we get reception out here." He looked at the screen and swallowed hard. "Oh."

"Who is it?"

"Sabrina's dad."

Rob's eyes went wide. "You should answer."

Matty was frozen. He didn't want to know.

"Matty, answer the phone."

Matty's stomach flip-flopped. "Hello? Mr. Miller?" Rob's hand on his back made him feel a little stronger. Whatever happened, they'd figure it out together.

He held his breath and listened, as Sabrina's father spoke, murmuring responses when necessary. When he finally said goodbye and hung up, Matty stared at the phone in a daze.

"She's going to stay?" Rob asked, one hand on Matty's knee and the other still on his back.

"Yeah." Matty blinked slowly.

"And? What else? That was a long conversation with a lot of confusion on your end."

"He said that tomorrow I should expect a call from Chuck Forenza."

"About Sabrina's coaching?"

"Kind of, but no, about me. About me flying out to interview as an assistant coach for him."

Rob's mouth fell open. "What? Are you kidding?"

"No. But maybe he was? I mean, this is impossible." Matty stared at the phone still in his hand. "People don't just call me up and say, 'Hey, come interview to work for me.' What happens is I grovel and flash the pretty eyes, and they say, 'All right, fine, you not bad ex-student. I will hire and hold this job over your head until the day you die. So you kiss my boots and agree that I am the coach of all coaches or I'll hit you with meat sticks.'"

Rob rubbed Matty's shoulder. "Sweetheart, you have PTSD from Valentina."

"I should sue her for emotional distress and psychological damages."

Rob took the phone from Matty's grip and put it on the table.

"An interview, huh? Did Mr. Miller say anything about what Forenza might be looking for?"

"He said Sabrina told Forenza I was the best coach in the world." Matty's voice grew tight. "Can you believe that?"

"Of course. You guys have a special bond." Rob rubbed his shoulders again.

"I don't know what to think. Mr. Miller told me that when Forenza sat them all down to discuss the coaching contract should she choose to stay, she made a compelling argument that I would make an excellent addition to Forenza's team. She said there was no one like me in terms of coaching style or personal history, and that she knows a lot of skaters of all ages who could benefit from what I bring to the table." Matty's throat was tight. His girl. His Sabrina. He couldn't believe she'd gone to bat for him like that. And she hadn't even known that he'd want her to. It was amazing. Unreal. So fucking sweet.

Next to him, Rob was vibrating with excitement as he packed the picnic basket. "Did he by any chance mention anything like the possible salary?"

"No. I have to fly out and meet with Forenza first. He wants to see me in person to make sure that I'm 'the right guy for his team.' Whatever that means."

Rob took Matty's hands. "How do you feel about this? What do you want to happen?"

"I don't know. I wasn't expecting this opportunity. I mean, I should obviously interview, right?"

"Absolutely."

"But the airline tickets will be expensive. And if I don't get the job, it would be a giant waste."

"We have credit cards. It's worth it. You're flying out there. When do you have to go, did he know?"

"Monday. Valentina won't be impressed with the timing."

"She'll live."

***

THE NEXT AFTERNOON, Rob returned from a walk around the grounds to find Matty still on the phone with his mother. It'd been over an hour, but that wasn't unusual for them. Donna clearly had a lot to say about the cruise she and Matty's father had just returned from, though Rob wasn't sure what exactly those things might be. When he'd left the house earlier, Matty had been deeply engaged in a discussion of whether or not it was acceptable to go dancing in flip-flops in St. Maarten. Matty said no, but Donna said yes, and right as Rob had had enough, it'd descended into caveats regarding sequins sandals versus plastic flip-flops.

The tour around the gardens and onto the wooded path that led somewhere up the mountain had been restorative, and Rob hummed under his breath, full of sunlight and plans as he came back inside. His heart clenched at the sight that met him. As Matty paced the kitchen, the light from the windows stroking over his naked skin and dark hair, making him look like a living oil painting. His ass flexed and his powerful thighs moved beautifully as he passed by the kitchen table and then turned to walk the other way. His cock bounced, and his pubic hair glowed in the lowering sun.

During their horseback ride the day before, Matty's ass had been very distracting. It'd looked so amazing perched on the back of Pearl Whiskers. Rob hadn't expected to be so undone by the sight of Matty on a horse, but he hadn't expected to be moved to throat-tightening heights by all the open space and the rhythmic, familiar feeling of a horse between his legs either. After the emotional shock of the possible offer from Forenza had worn off, he'd fucked Matty on the screened-in porch bed, taking his time and enjoying the sensation of Matty's hot body around his cock, loving the little breathy moans he let loose when Rob hit his prostate just right.

Getting hard remembering it, Rob moved to stand by the bay windows. Looking outside at the English garden surrounding the little man-made creek and bubbling fountain that ran by the back of the house, he decided he would give Matty exactly two more minutes to end the conversation before pulling rank on his weekend slave. He stroked his dick through his loose shorts and gazed at

Matty's ass and bobbing cock.

Matty rolled his eyes at whatever Donna was saying. "No, we didn't gallop. No, Donna, I know. My body is my career. I know that. Listen to me." He threw his hands up and shook his head, like she could see him. "Yes, I heard you. Of course I was careful, Donna!" He groaned. "What do I mean by 'careful'? I mean I didn't attempt to stand on my hands in the saddle or to reenact the rumored circumstances leading to Catherine the Great's demise." He rolled his eyes "I'm not being disgusting. I'm pointing out how ridiculous you're being."

He stopped walking and caught Rob's eye. His gaze widened seeing Rob's dick straining against his shorts and he said, "Mother, stop. I'm a grown man. I can ride a horse with my boyfriend on our vacation if I want. Look I need to go. Rob has dinner plans for me or something. Yeah, I've missed you too. Yes, I'll tell him."

He threw the phone on the counter and turned to Rob, his cock jiggling as he mimed strangling the air. "My mom says hi."

"Hi back at her."

"She also says that I'm lucky I wasn't beheaded by a low-hanging limb while we were out gallivanting on horses."

Rob chuckled and motioned for Matty to come closer. "Well, that would've been a big bummer." Rob pulled his dick out of his shorts and held it. "I think this is the 'dinner plans' you were referring to."

Matty bit his lip. "All that for me, though? It's such a big portion."

Rob snorted. "See how much you can eat."

Matty dropped to his knees, and Rob admired the length of his back and his juicy ass jutting out, begging to be slapped. Matty cupped his balls and licked up the side of Rob's cock, gazing up between his lashes with a small smile. "If I can't eat it all, what will you do with the leftovers?"

Rob chuckled. "Oh, I have a plan for anything you can't handle."

Matty's eyes sparked and he opened his mouth wide.

"Oh, fuck, sweetheart. Have I ever told you that you're a Grade A cocksucker?"

Matty took him in deeper, opening his throat and letting Rob slide in. He pushed his ass up as he did, and Rob bent forward, sliding his hands down Matty's back and then kneading his ass cheeks. "Mmm, love all this you've got for me."

Matty gagged a little, and Rob straightened, gripping Matty's hair in his hand as he looked down at the thick root of his cock spreading Matty's mouth wide. "That's a good slave."

Matty moaned and shifted on his knees, gasping wildly when Rob pulled free of his mouth. His chest was flushed a bright pink that creeped up his neck, and he came after Rob's cock eagerly.

"Such a good little slut."

Matty's breath jittered at the dirty name, and he sucked the head of Rob's cock into his mouth, batting his lashes and running his hands up and down Rob's thighs like he couldn't get enough of the feel of them.

Rob took hold of Matty's chin and pulled his dick free. "I've got another plan for you."

"Oh, God."

"Up." He helped Matty stand and pulled him tight, enjoying the slide of their bodies together. His chest hair brushed against Matty's smoother torso and Matty's crinkly bush and hard cock rubbed against his thigh. "Fuck, I could fuck you right here."

"I'm okay with that."

Rob chuckled and took hold of Matty's hand, pushing him slightly away before he decided to forego his plans and screw him up against the wall. "Come outside. I want to show you something."

Matty flushed even more prettily. "But I'm naked. And hard."

"I know. I want to see you outside in the sunlight again." He grinned. "I've always wanted to see that. But it was so fucking cold that winter in Montana. And in the city, well, we know you can't go naked outside there."

"What if someone comes up here for some reason?"

"No one will. There's no one around. Not for miles actually."

A smile spread slowly over Matty's face. "Okay, but you take your clothes off too."

"Uh-uh." Rob smirked. "You're my dirty sex slave and I'll use your body however I want."

"Yes, sir." Matty looked up from under his lashes. "I forgot."

Heat pooled in Rob's gut, and he nearly turned Matty around and spanked his round ass right there over the kitchen table. But he wasn't ready to give up on the plan he'd carefully crafted the day before while watching Matty's ass bounce on Pearl Whiskers.

"I guess I'll have to punish you for forgetting your place."

Matty's breath came in sharp. His eyes dilated and his cock flexed, a bead of pre-come forming at the top. Rob reached out and took hold of Matty's dick and pulled, leading him across the kitchen to the back door. "This way."

The gazebo was set pretty far back from the house, obscured by a row of high-growing rhododendron and surrounded by blooming rose bushes. Their sweet-spicy scent wafted across the raised floor and perfumed the air. It was romantic and beyond secluded, and Rob intended to make it memorable.

A hammock made of soft floral material stretched from one sturdy plank in the ceiling to another. It was rather higher than most hammocks, but Rob had tested its strength earlier while out on his walk and found it sufficient. Matty let out a soft moan as soon as he saw it.

"You know what I'm going to do to you on that, don't you?" Rob asked.

"I hope so."

Rob grinned. "But I have another surprise first." His cock pushed against his soft track shorts, and he adjusted it before he walked over to the railing where he'd lined up three flexible and strong willow switches he'd picked up on his walk.

He held up the first light brown wand. Matty's cheeks went hot pink, his eyes dark and wild and the skin around his mouth a little pale. Arousal. Panic. Lust. Fear. It was all there and Rob's cock flexed hard.

"I promised you whips but if we play with these right now, we'll have to pass on those. So slave, you choose. These switches I made

340

for you now? Or whips later?"

Matty swallowed and his mouth opened as he made an obviously involuntary move to take one of the switches from Rob's hand. But he stopped himself, put his hands behind his back like a good boy and said, "Whatever Master wants is best."

Rob smiled slowly, heat rushing in his cock and making him so hard he ached. "Good answer." He approached Matty with one of the switches as Matty's eyes fell closed and he took a breath in and let it out, trying to relax but clearly riled into shivering anticipation.

"Are you shaking already, sweetheart?" Rob ran his hand over Matty's body, the sunlight playing over the muscles in his torso and back. "Oh, you're beautiful Matty." He wrapped his arms around him, rubbing the length of the switch over his ass in a slow circle as he hugged him gently and then took his mouth in a tender, lingering kiss.

Matty's cock pressed against his leg. Rob dragged him closer, deepening their kiss, tasting Matty's mouth and tongue, licking against his teeth and sucking on his bottom lip. He tossed the switch onto the hammock to grip Matty's ass in both hands. He squeezed and rubbed, and then spread his cheeks apart, exposing his tight hole to the air. Breaking the kiss, he bent and nuzzled Matty's neck, kissing his throat and down to his nipples before straightening up again. He tapped his fingers against Matty's asshole.

"Such a sweet hole for me. Love how hot it is." He pressed a finger to Matty's mouth, grunting as Matty sucked it in, eager and already lost in the trance of sexual submission.

"Get it so wet. That's good, so good. Use your tongue like you would on my cock." Rob pressed his dick against Matty's side and pulled his finger out of Matty's mouth, shoving it directly into his ass.

"Oh God," Matty moaned. "Oh, fuck."

"Yes, Matty. Yeah. You're getting me so hard."

He pushed Matty over the hammock ass up, steadying it as he kicked Matty's legs apart. He drank in the lily white, muscled butt cheeks dusted lightly with dark hair, and strong legs that led down to feet that were a little dirty from the walk in the dirt and grass. Rob ran his hands down Matty's back and bent close, breathing in his scent and whispering in his ear, "Still trembling?"

"Yeah," Matty whispered, his legs shaking and his breath coming in hiccups. "You're not going to be gentle, are you? Leave marks, please."

Rob slapped his ass so hard that Matty gasped. "I'll do what I think is best. Because who's the master here?"

"You."

"And who's the slave?"

"Me, sir." Matty's fingers twisted into the fabric on the opposite side of the hammock, clenching it hard. "I'm sorry, sir."

"You should be." Rob chuckled and kissed his neck, rubbing his shoulders and kissing each scapula and the knots of his spine. He was pleased they weren't as obvious under the refeeding weight he'd been putting on.

"You've been such a good boy lately, Matty. Eating and following the refeeding guidelines. Do you want your reward?"

"Yes, sir."

"Do you want your reward to hurt?"

"Please, sir."

"Do you want it to make you scream?"

"Ah, fuck. I mean yes, yes, sir."

"Good, good." Rob was enjoying the "master" and "sir" business more than he'd expected. He pulled off his shorts, tossing them and the T-shirt aside. Naked in the afternoon heat, he felt freer than he had in years.

He looked at Matty, his face buried in the hammock, ass up and waiting, and stroked his dick a few times. He grabbed the switch from where it had rolled next to Matty's body and swooshed it in the air.

Matty flinched, and his ass tightened as an anticipatory yelp escaped. Rob swished the wand in the air again but didn't land it, and then slapped Matty's ass with his palm. "Relax. I want to see those cheeks round and soft."

Matty fidgeted, trying to get his body to comply. Gooseflesh spread on his back, and Rob smiled. "Mmm, does the breeze feel good, sweetheart?"

A brief nod and a shudder was all he got as a response. Rob tapped the switch against Matty's ass gently to give him a taste of it and to warn him it was time now.

"Five to start."

The shriek of the switch in the air was thrilling and Rob noted that Matty seized up before the thin branch landed on his ass with a crack.

"Fuck!" Matty cried, his feet skittering as he shifted.

A vivid pink line bloomed across Matty's butt, and he whimpered when Rob reached out to touch it.

"Beautiful, Matty. That's one."

He stood back and raised the switch again. Three marks later, Matty was a mess of hitching breaths and very close to tears. The fourth strike brought a small sob.

"Five."

Matty wailed and lifted up, his ass clenching hard as though trying to get away from the pain.

Rob lay down over Matty, balancing on the hammock and feeling the heat of Matty's ass burn against his cock and hips. "That is one hot butt. Burning hot." He kissed Matty's shoulders, listening to him pant and struggle for composure. "You're doing a great job."

"Thank you," Matty murmured. "I love it."

"I know you do, sweetheart."

It was hard to pull away. Part of him wanted to stay put, sliding his cock between Matty's cheeks and using the friction of his muscled ass to get off. But he controlled himself. He wanted to make Matty scream. Want to hear it echo in the hills around them; wanted to experience the depth of freedom they could have in the country, away from the public anonymity of the city.

He stroked Matty's hair back and kissed his cheek. Then he stood again, took up the switch, and said, "Eight."

Matty squirmed as if he couldn't help it.

"Hold still. I don't want to miss." Rob touched Matty's hanging cock and balls. "There are delicate bits down there. And I'm not planning to hurt them today."

Matty took a deep, slow breath and relaxed his body. Rob tapped the switch against a still unblemished strip of skin, and Matty whimpered. He drew back and brought the switch down hard. Matty yelled.

"I want to hear screams, Matty. Show me how loud you can get. Let it all out. Everything." He leaned close and murmured in Matty's ear, "All your anxiety, and fear, and worry. Let it all come out. Just feel this moment and release all the rest."

Rob stood and touched the places he'd hit before feeling the heat against his fingertips. Then, carefully avoiding any strip of skin he'd already hit, he brought the willow branch down hard. Matty lurched and kicked, another wail launching from his throat. His struggle set the hammock rocking and Rob stilled it. Then he held the back of Matty's neck down and switched his ass five times in a row, hard and brutal. Matty screamed. He screamed like a newborn, terrified and shocked. He screamed like a hero going into war. And he screamed like a grieving man.

Rob finished out the eight blows and came around to kneel in front of Matty, kissing his face as he cried, telling him he'd been good. "You're so strong, Matty."

Their mouths touched, and Rob took a kiss, sucking in Matty's heaving breaths and touching his tongue to Matty's palate. He broke away, kissing his cheek and eyelids, his ear and shoulder. He rose and bent his knees just enough that his dick hung directly in front of Matty's open mouth.

Aiming as best he could, he swung the hammock a little, and as it came back, he pressed his cock into Matty's mouth. As the hammock moved away, he stepped forward so that Matty didn't pop off. He used the hammock as a swing to guide Matty's mouth up and down his cock.

"Good, yes, keep your mouth wide."

Tears smeared Matty's cheeks, but he didn't fail to stick out his tongue and take Rob deep into his throat and then let him slide right back out again. He moaned around Rob's dick, rolling his hips against the hammock, his striped red ass shining in the sunlight.

"Watch your teeth," Rob murmured, picking up the switch again. He watched Matty's breathing go through the roof and how Matty went very, very still. He hit him on the ass lightly, and Matty yelled around his cock, the sensation vibrating to the root of him and drawing his balls up tight.

"Fuck," Rob murmured and did it again, his hips twitching forward into Matty's vibrating throat. Letting it linger for a moment, he patted Matty's hair and then pulled out, strings of saliva hanging from his cock. "That's my sweetheart. Such a good boy."

He kneeled by Matty's head again and murmured, "I trust you, Matty. Do you trust me?"

Matty nodded, breathless and bleary-eyed, his face splotchy from crying and his whole body trembling until the hammock shook as well.

"Can you take some more pain?"

Matty moaned and shook his head.

"Willow branch switches are hard to deal with, aren't they?"

Matty's eyes met his, glassy brown and open only for him, seeing only him. Rob could tell the hammock was gone; the roses, the world around them. In Matty's eyes there was only room for one thing—Rob and his switch.

"Three more."

Matty's breath quickened and he keened.

"You with me, Matty?"

"Yeah," it came out a slow draw of hurt.

"Safeword?"

Matty shook his head and pushed his ass up, half-sobbing. "Three more, please, sir."

Rob ruffled his hair. "Brave boy. You're a good brave boy, Matty."

He took his position by Matty's ass and found the first two strike lines easily. He carefully laid the switch hard against the still-untouched spots, and then pulled back, striping each one. Matty writhed and screamed again, getting into the freedom of allowing the sound to rip out of his throat. Carefully, with enough strength to hurt like hell but not enough to break the skin, Rob laid down a swat diagonally across Matty's wounded ass, striking over the already welted skin.

The sound of Matty's scream echoed all around them, bouncing off the hills. Rob heard the joy in it, overriding the pain, and he felt lightheaded with adoration. When Matty collapsed on the hammock, a seemingly involuntary shaking taking over his otherwise limp body, Rob dropped to his knees behind Matty and pressed kisses to his red striped ass.

As the late afternoon light fell across the gazebo and the breeze stirred up the scent of the roses again, Rob's heart soared. He could handle this. He *wanted* to handle it. He wasn't doing this scene just for Matty. Calm arousal flowed in him, steady, and intense as a rushing river.

Rob could breathe in all the space around them. It was beautiful. They were beautiful.

"You're so amazing, sweetheart," Rob murmured, rubbing his hand gently over the marks on Matty's ass. "I want to be inside you. Do you want that?"

"Please!" Matty lifted his ass and spread his legs wider.

Rob fetched the lube he'd placed on the railing next to the two other switches earlier during his walk.

Matty reached back and spread his own cheeks, hissing at the contact of his palms on his flaming ass.

"You okay?" Rob asked.

"Yes. I love it."

Rob smiled. His heart quickened and his hands shook with desire. "You want it, sweetheart?"

"God, yeah. Want it hard," Matty said, shoving with his feet so that the hammock swung a little. "Fuck me on your dick."

Rob stepped between his legs and slowed the swing of the hammock. He bent his knees to get the right height, slicked his cock with lube and rubbed two fingers against Matty's pink, tight hole, exposed to him and framed by Matty's long fingers holding his cheeks apart. "Mmm, here we go."

Matty's cheeks were burning hot from the switching, and inside he was even hotter.

"Fuck," Rob moaned, going deeper. His hips twitched forward in a needy thrust. The thrum of Matty's pulse beat around his cock, and he wanted to be all the way in, rutting, rolling, thrusting until he was part of Matty forever.

"Fuck me, fuck me," Matty begged, gripping the fabric of the hammock tightly. "Please, I love it. I want it hard."

Rob wanted it hard too. He wanted it hard enough to lose himself, to sweat and moan, and bury himself in Matty's noises and body, to enjoy the privilege of being the man who was allowed this—who was given this gift.

The hammock worked perfectly as a swing, and he swung Matty nearly off his cock and let him drop back down on it, the function of gravity and the force of motion driving him hard and deep each time. Matty spread his legs wide, and Rob helped him get his knees up onto the hammock, allowing even closer access and a harder, more aggressive fall onto Rob's dick.

Each slam in pushed a shout from Matty's mouth, and when he slapped Matty's striped red ass as he plugged him deep, the scream bounced around the mountains and was absorbed by the dense woods.

"I love you," Rob whispered, letting himself fall against Matty's back, grinding his cock into him. "I fucking love you."

Matty reached back and brought their mouths together, kissing and swallowing each other's grunts and moans. Sweat built between their bodies as the afternoon sun slanted across them, adding heat to their passion, and the sound of their fucking was loud and slapping. Matty didn't hold back his cries of ecstatic pleasure, working his asshole around Rob's dick, and rutting back onto him.

"Gonna come for me?" Rob murmured, and Matty hitched his right leg up higher on the hammock so that Rob slid in even deeper.

Wanting to prolong the blissful, out-of-time sense of wonder and perfection, he kissed Matty's open, wet lips and lifted himself off and out. The air felt cool on his wet cock, and he moaned, biting his lip to keep from thrusting back in immediately. Matty whimpered in protest and reached back to spread himself open again, giving Rob a view of his open, starfished-shaped hole, already squeezing shut.

Rob fell to his knees and pressed his face between Matty's muscled cheeks to eat his ass.

"Oh God! Holy fuck!" Matty cried out, his hole squeezing around Rob's tongue as he pressed it inside, circling it as Matty pushed back. He worshiped Matty's asshole with his lips and teeth and tongue while Matty shuddered and broke into chills that Rob felt under his palms. He rubbed Matty's ass-cheeks and back as he ate him, soothing his welts and digging his fingers into his waist to hold him steady when Matty scrambled at the hammock, warbling about it being too good, too much.

"Oh my God, don't stop, don't stop," Matty muttered, clenching and unclenching his toes and trembling as Rob sucked his hole. "Don't ever, ever fucking stop."

Rob's cock ached and flexed, pre-come slipping down, and he wanted back inside. He wanted to see Matty's face when he shot his load deep inside him. He slapped Matty's thigh and stood up.

"No, no, no," Matty whimpered, his hole clenching in a seductive, beckoning way.

"Get on your back."

Matty rolled over and hissed as his ass slid across the fabric. It was soft but clearly not soft enough to not sting with pain from his welts.

"Knees up."

Matty pulled his knees up and open, exposing his hard cock and tight balls, and his red ass parted by the dark, beautiful cleft that Rob wanted to dive into and never leave.

"Oh, sweetheart, look at you." Matty's eyes were wild and dark, his pupils blown and his expression a haze of lust and love. Rob added more lube to his dick, getting it slick again. "You're so fucking hot." He put two lubed fingers in Matty's ass and watched him twist on them. "Oh, fuck. You're going to make me come doing that."

Matty pulled his knees up higher and said, "Come in me, then."

Rob plunged in, driving deep and hard, wrapping his arms around Matty and surrendering to the swing of the hammock. They grappled together, fighting for a rhythm, and then Matty yielded, turning his mouth to Rob and kissing him passionately. They lay locked together with Rob's cock deep inside and Matty's asshole clenching around him until Rob couldn't take it anymore.

He found purchase with his feet and fucked into Matty as hard and pounding as he could. "Gonna come, gonna come in you," he muttered in Matty's ear as he worked. "Gonna make you mine all over again."

"Yes. I want it. Do it." Matty's cock pressed against Rob's stomach and he deliberately dragged his torso against it. "Need you. Always need you."

Rob moaned and lifted up. Standing with his knees bent, he aimed his cock to nail Matty's prostate and fucked him firmly, sweat sliding down his back and the side of his face. "Come on. Show me how you come for me."

Matty grabbed his own cock and then gazed up at Rob. As Rob pounded his ass, he watched Matty's face shift and change, watched it grow tight and then wobble into a vulnerable mess—saw how he fell apart and then grimaced as the orgasm gripped him. He moaned as white jizz from Matty's dick landed on his chin and in his hair.

"Fuck yes," Rob said, driving past Matty's squeezing sphincter.

The orgasm ripped up through him, a pumping, wrenching sensation from the heels of his feet to his balls and cock, and up through his pelvis and spine, like perfect, unconditional love shooting from the top of his head and the end of his dick, and pulsing out of him and enveloping him all over.

He fell onto Matty and buried his face in his sweaty-sticky neck, shaking as he convulsed and pumped semen into his ass. "Goddamn. Oh, fuck." He trembled and felt a wild joy rush inside. This was them. It was everything.

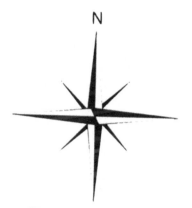

PART FIVE:

THE PEACE OF COMPLEXITY

CHAPTER THIRTY

WHEN MATTY ARRIVED at the training complex where Chuck Forenza served as head figure skating coach, his heart was beating a mile a minute and he felt a little ill. He'd arrived less than an hour before, driving straight from the airport to make his appointment time. He'd taken the red eye which meant a middle of the night layover in Atlanta, but it was the only way he could be sure to make it to Colorado Springs in time.

He'd freshened up in the airport bathroom, adding some makeup over the dark rings under his eyes. He wished to God he had time for a real shower at a hotel room, but a spritz of citrus deodorant and a touch of tangerine-scented product in his hair would have to do.

The cab ride from the airport offered some tremendous views of the Southern Rocky Mountains and Pikes Peak. He'd taken a few shots through the window for Rob but hadn't texted them. He didn't want to get Rob's hopes up, didn't want him to imagine them living there in the view of mountains so much like Rob's home if he wasn't going to get the job.

As he'd paid the cabby and tucked his wallet back into his orange purse, he realized he'd harbored a fantasy of his own. He'd hoped that he'd pull up and Sabrina would dart out from the building, hug him tightly, and tell him that he didn't have to impress anyone or do anything at all—he had the job.

But it was time to put dreams aside and make a real life.

Inside the bustling complex, the girl at the front desk took his ID and asked him to sign for a guest pass. She grinned at him in recognition but didn't say anything about being his biggest fan. He supposed that he'd been retired long enough that most young skating fans were past the squeals when it came to him.

After consulting a clipboard, she said, "You're meeting with Coach Forenza. He's on the ice with PJ Kataria right now and I've been instructed to deliver you to him when you arrive."

"Thank you."

"Hold on and I'll walk you out to the ice." She motioned for someone at the snack bar to come take her place, and then smiled brightly at him. "Are you going to be a new coach with us?"

Matty plastered on his media smile. "I'm just having a look at the facilities for now. Anything else would be very premature, I'm sure."

She led him into the rink area. The familiar scent of ice and the tingle of cold air against his face was home. His shoulders relaxed and his heart rate slowed. He could do this. Probably. And if he couldn't, well, he'd buck up and be a big boy. No matter what, New York City would be in their past before the year was up. Matty had decided that already. He supposed it was what came of falling in love with a rancher. If he'd been smart, he'd have fallen in love with a Wall Street tycoon. And been miserable and sick the rest of his life because no one would ever love him the way Rob did.

Chuck Forenza was a man's man, with bulky muscles and paw-like hands. Matty had always wondered how Forenza managed to coach the most graceful and delicate skaters around when he was such a massive bear himself. Forenza looked out over the ice to where PJ Kataria was skating in tight circles, his hands behind his back and his face set in a dark scowl.

The front desk girl took him directly over to Forenza, who greeted him with a smile and a hearty handshake. He was taller than Matty but not as tall as Rob, and Sabrina was right—he had tuft of hair that popped out of the open collar of his polo shirt.

"Good to meet you, Coach Marcus—"

"Just call me Matty."

"Okay, Matty. And you call me Chuck." Forenza smiled again, his blue eyes crinkling and his gray-sprinkled, soft-looking beard spreading around white teeth. "I was always a big fan of yours."

Matty blushed. His hand in the man's big paw and those eyes on his left him with his tongue suddenly sticking to the roof of his mouth. Now he understood Sabrina's problem with Chuck Forenza. He wasn't conventionally handsome but he was incredibly sexy. He had charisma and something indefinable that made Matty want to please him. Not being a pubescent teenager, he wasn't entirely flummoxed by the commanding, confident attitude combined with muscles and chest hair, but that didn't mean he wasn't momentarily flustered. Truth be told, if he wasn't insanely in love with Rob, he'd be gagging for it.

Chuck nodded toward Kataria and said, "Are you ready for him?"

"Me?"

"You."

"Uh, yeah. Sure."

PJ cast a half-glare at Forenza, his heavy breath coming in white puffs as he skated in small circles.

"Great, get your skates on."

Matty sat down on a bench and watched Kataria out of the corner of his eye while he laced up and pulled on his gloves and hat. Chuck stood beside him and asked, "I don't suppose I need to fill you in on him."

"No, I've got the four-one-one."

Chuck slapped Matty on the back when he stood up in his skates and called Kataria over.

Matty knew all about PJ Kataria. He was after all one of Ben's strongest competitors. Nineteen years old with a ton of a potential but a terrible tendency to psych himself out during competitions. Everyone knew PJ could be at the next Olympics if he just learned to get out of his head when it counted.

Chuck squeezed PJ's shoulder. "Peej, Coach Marcus is going to work with you today."

"Sure, Coach. Sounds good." PJ stared moodily at Matty through his over-long bangs. It wasn't exactly the reception Matty would have liked, but it was what it was. Teenagers didn't follow the rules.

Especially not bratty, entitled ones with chips on their shoulders.

"You've got the floor, Coach Marcus. Do with it what you will." Chuck indicated the stands. "I'll sit over there with my coffee. Just do your best with him. I'd like to see your technique."

Matty blinked at Chuck and then smiled at PJ with what he hoped was extreme confidence. His pulse rushing in his ears and the sweat prickling his forehead, though, told a different story.

Next began one of the longest forty-five minutes of his life. As it turned out, PJ Kataria was in the middle of a massive pity-party and was determined to invite the world. Matty quickly found himself at his wits' end to get much out of PJ except glares and half-assed attempts at his jumps.

"You're dropping your right side," he called out for the third time. "You need to stay in the circle."

PJ skated around the rink a few times, shaking his head and shooting dirty looks to both Matty and Chuck. Matty glanced over see what Chuck was doing; if he was frowning or smiling and judging Matty a failure already. He looked on impassively.

Matty's hands were sweaty in his gloves, and he took off his hat, tossing it onto the bleachers behind him.

He took a slow, calming breath and closed his eyes. This was a test. Chuck had put him with this recalcitrant little shit because he wanted to see what Matty would do and how he'd handle it. If PJ was five or six years younger, he'd go into his Yuliya Yasneyeva routine and shock him out of his mood. But PJ was too old for that kind of game.

"Keep it tight. Suck in your stomach." He shook his head as PJ fell again, laying on the ice for a long time instead of getting back up. "Shake it off."

PJ hauled himself up and stood with his hands on his hips, almost daring Matty to give him another command.

Matty pushed off the boards and skated to middle ice. "Look, I don't know why you're pissed off today, but don't take it out on me. If you want to learn to dominate on the ice and not cave in to panic, then believe me, I have experience and advice to offer you."

PJ rolled his eyes.

"But if you want to pout about it, go ahead. It feels awfully good, I know. I do that often enough myself. But it won't get you any-where."

PJ shrugged and snorted some snot. It was pretty disgusting.

Matty looked over to where Chuck was watching them closely. He was failing at this harder than he'd failed at chastity or the Olympics. Here he was so close to having the answer to their problems in the palm of his hand and this little shit was pouting him out of the job. It made him want scream.

He smirked. Oh, well. What did he have to lose?

"Fine, you're pissed. I get it. Sometimes I get pissed off too. Sometimes I want to shout until the world is obliterated."

PJ stared at him like he was crazy. It was a look he was familiar with.

Matty swallowed. What the hell? Why not? "So, how about this? Let's pitch a fit together. I'll start."

"What? I don't understand."

Matty threw back his head and yelled, the sound echoing around the rink and vibrating against the ceiling. When his throat hurt, he stopped, adrenaline pumping through him at what a stupid, stupid, stupid idea that had been.

In the ringing silence, PJ stared at him with wide eyes and an open mouth. A quick look around the rink showed that everyone else was frozen, staring at Matty too. Chuck had risen from his seat in the stands, frowning.

"Dude, you're crazy."

"I hear that a lot." Matty nudged him, his pulse thudding in his throat, and his scream still echoing in his ears. "You try it."

"You're going to get me trouble."

"Maybe. Are you scared of getting into trouble?"

PJ bit into his lower lip, shot an angry look toward Chuck again, and then threw his head back and yelled, too. It was awesome and powerful and came from his gut. The sound filled the entire rink, and people rushed from the lobby area to see what was happening.

Chuck moved down the stands toward the ice, and Matty started laughing as the scream went on and on.

He'd blown it. He'd blown the whole thing.

But fuck if he hadn't done it his own damn way.

Matty did a little skate around PJ, dancing to the sound of his yell, waving his arms delicately even as the yell became rough and hoarse. Chuck stepped onto the ice just as PJ bit the sound off and stood with a sloppy, satisfied grin. The echo bounced off the walls in diminishing repeat.

There was an absolute stillness from the rest of the rink. Chuck waited by the boards.

"Feel better?" Matty asked.

PJ's chest heaved up and down, and a silly smile spread over his face. He shoved his hair out of his eyes and met Matty's grinning gaze. "Um, yeah?"

"Cool." Matty squeezed his arm, feeling the muscle beneath the Under Armour shirt. "Then let's do this thing. Start at the beginning. And this time? Keep in the circle."

When he reached the boards, Chuck had moved back to the stands again. Feeling shaky with an insane relief, Matty started to work with PJ again from the top of his program. PJ was more relaxed, and when he went up for a triple Axel he didn't drop his right side. He stuck his tongue out at Matty and laughed when he landed, crossing the rink for the speed to tackle the next jump.

Matty called, "Good. A definite improvement. Keep going. Lift, lift with your legs not just your chest—yes! That's it!"

Twenty minutes later, PJ's lesson was over and he skated over to Matty with a satisfied and sparkling grin on his face. "So, Coach, where'd you learn that scream thing?"

"I made it up."

"Just now?"

"Yeah."

PJ laughed. "Cool. You're totally crazy. And, I don't know. Cool."

Matty shrugged. "It seemed to help. But, you probably shouldn't do it here again. I have a feeling they'd kick you out."

"I'm surprised they didn't do it today!"

Matty laughed. "Me too."

"But it felt great. What if I do want to do it again?"

Matty took both his arms in his hands and shook him a little. "Well, if you want to, maybe you can do it in your car before you come inside. Or if you live somewhere the neighbors won't get spooked, you could try going outside. Scream in your yard. See if you can fill the sky with it."

"You are the weirdest coach ever. I like it. Thanks." He clomped off toward the locker rooms, and Matty let out a long breath before turning to see what Chuck Forenza had to say about his performance.

He walked toward Matty. "That was quite a spectacle you made out there, Coach Marcus." He raised a brow at Matty and looked him up and down. "Tell you what. I'll meet you in my office. Callie at the front desk will take you there." Then he walked purposefully toward the locker rooms, heading after PJ.

Matty was dizzy with fear, relief, anxiety? He didn't know. It was a whirlwind inside and he half wanted to laugh and half wanted to cry.

Forenza's office was lined with photos of his students on the podium. Bronze, silver, and gold medals hung from their necks, proclaiming them winners and Forenza a winning coach. Matty stood examining them, waiting for Forenza to finish talking with PJ in the locker room so he could come render his verdict.

When the door opened, Matty wasn't ready. His hands shook and he felt sick. He'd been an idiot to do something so socially unacceptable as scream in the middle of a busy training facility and encourage his student to do the same. There'd probably been a better solution, but there was no room for regrets now. He'd done what he'd done, and now there would be consequences for that. Hadn't he learned how that worked by now?

He tried for a genuine smile but figured his face betrayed him. His stomach was a ball of nausea. He'd have a hard time eating tonight if he didn't get this job, and truly, Chuck would be crazy to give it to him.

"Well, you're everything they say and more, kid." Chuck tossed his rink jacket on his desk and sat down against it. "Have a seat," he said, motioning at the chair in front of him.

Feeling like a child, Matty dropped into it and cleared his throat, ready to make an apology, but Chuck stood up and walked around his desk, sitting down on it, gazing down at Matty.

"So, you wear makeup and carry a purse. And you scream in the rink during your lessons—"

"Not usually. That was new."

"Ah, well don't I feel lucky that you tried it out on my pupil first?"

"Chuck, listen, I'm—"

"No, Matty, you listen."

Matty swallowed back his fumbling, inept apology and used his fingers to zip his lips.

Chuck laughed under his breath. "Well, Christ, you'd bring some life to the coaching staff around here, wouldn't you?" He cracked his knuckles. "Matty, I'm glad you could make it out for an interview on such short notice. Frankly, I'd have given you more warning so that you could plan a proper trip with your partner to check out the town too, but Sabrina waited until the camps were almost over to make her suggestion that I look into what assets you might bring to our team."

Matty couldn't believe what he was hearing. His lips trembled as he smiled at Chuck. "It was a very unexpected call. I was shocked but very happy that you'd be interested in talking with me."

"Shocked? I don't know why you would be. Anyone who saw what Sabrina accomplished over the last year and a half knows it's because of you. I was actually worried she wouldn't agree to leave you." He raised his hand. "But you need to understand this: she's coming with me whether or not you come on board. She's made up her mind on that front."

Matty's heart clenched but it was what he expected to hear. "I understand."

"I've followed her career closely. She's got a certain grace and regality that you don't see with every female skater. I saw videos of her work under Valentina and was disappointed that she'd taken such a turn for the worse under her guidance. But within weeks of you taking over, the practice tapes I saw showed a whole new skater." He smiled and leaned across the desk, his hands relaxed and loosely clasped together. "That's a marketable skill. We have plenty of skaters who need a softer approach; a more patient or, like today, *creative* hand—and they need it from someone who can commit to their daily development at a level that I sometimes just don't have the time for. Not for every student. Not every day. I need a man like that on my team."

Matty's skin buzzed. He felt like he'd been covered in joy juice and he was going to burst into tears or start clapping like a seal any second. "I should warn you that I'm not a punitive coach. I don't let them get away with failing to live up to their potential, but I also don't rant and rave, or insult them."

"I prefer a more respectful approach myself."

Matty nodded, trying to keep his excitement from showing. "Valentina...I'll never be able to express what she did for me, both as an athlete and as a new coach. But I feel like my skills have outgrown my position there."

That was a line that he and Rob had worked out carefully. They didn't want to call Valentina out in front of a competitor, but they also wanted to make sure Matty came across as someone who had something of value to offer and a desire to see that asset used in a more fulfilling way.

Chuck nodded. "I agree. And now that I see you, man-to-man, I'd like to formally offer you a position on my team." Matty opened his mouth to say yes, but Chuck held up his hand. "Before you accept, you should know there are some strings attached."

He swallowed and waited for the inevitable. He could guess what Chuck was going to say next. He'd heard it his whole life. He needed to stop wearing makeup—needed to butch it up, drop the purse and the lip gloss, and the glitter and eyeliner. He was about to be told that he couldn't be himself.

A memory of Rob's smile in the sunshine as they'd snuggled together in the hammock flashed across his mind.

Fine. He'd still accept. He'd sacrifice being his true self if it meant getting Rob out of the city so he'd smile like that again every day, and if it meant getting himself off the path of hunger and hopeless mediocrity. Some things were worth the sacrifice.

Chuck ticked off the rules on his fingers. "First off, it's imperative that you set a good example for the students. I won't have any coach work with me who lives in such a way that it impairs the mental, emotional, or physical health of my skaters."

"I understand."

"I can tell just by looking at you that the rumors are true, Matty. And so we need to address this particular problem from the start."

"What rumors?"

"That you struggle with disordered eating."

Matty blinked and clenched the arm of the seat with his fingers. "Oh..."

"As a coach, I know you're aware that eating a nutritious diet is an important part of being a successful athlete and a healthy person. But you also know, as a former skater yourself, the immense pressure these kids feel to be slender, to always weigh a little less. Well, I lost a kid to that disease twelve years ago and I won't lose another."

"No, sir."

"Matty, it's important that you don't set a bad example."

"Of course. I'm improving already and I think getting out of New York will only help with that problem." He wondered if Chuck noticed his blush.

"Good. But that's not enough. I'll require an initial appointment with our dietician and we'll arrange a weekly weigh-in to begin with. She'll set a maximum lower limit for your weight, and if you go beneath it, we'll be looking at immediate suspension and possible termination. I know that's harsh, but I can't allow that disease to get another one of my kids. Ever. I wouldn't be able to live through it again."

Matty's throat went tight, and he was horrified as his eyes filled with tears.

"I'm sure gaining weight is a scary proposition for you, but—"

"No. No, sir. That's not it. I just—I want to thank you."

Chuck looked surprised. "Thank me?"

"I can't explain how much this means to me. What I mean is...I appreciate the help. Very much."

Chuck gazed at Matty, long and measuring. Just before Matty started to wriggle under his appraisal, Chuck slapped his hands on the desk. "Then that's settled. You'll start in two weeks."

Two weeks? That was fast. They didn't have a place to live, they had to sort out their life in New York, and there were shows he'd scheduled with Julien for August.

Matty cleared his throat. "Chuck, I'd scheduled some shows in Asia later in the summer."

Chuck frowned. "Hmm. Well, I don't mind coaches doing the occasional show, but if it's a tour, that cuts into things for me. See if it's too late to get out of it. If it is, we'll work around it this year, but I'd rather not."

Matty scrambled, his mind insisting that there was more he needed to know before he shook hands on the deal. "Salary? Benefits?" He laughed. "I can't accept until I know a little bit more."

Chuck opened his desk drawer and pulled out a legal-sized white envelope. "Employment proposal and contract. Look it over. If you have questions or want to negotiate anything, just ask. I'm happy to have you on our team, Matty." He came around his desk and shook his hand. "And little Sabrina will be thrilled."

***

"HOW MUCH?" ROB asked, unable to believe his ears. "Are you serious?"

"I know it's not much in New York money, but in Colorado Springs money, I think we could afford to rent an actual house. Maybe even buy one." Matty babbled on, pacing their living room floor, his hands flitting around wildly. "Especially if you find work in the PT field, which Mr. and Mrs. Miller think won't be hard at all. They said they've both seen advertisements for physical therapy positions at clinics in town."

Rob sat on the sofa watching him go back and forth, a grin spreading over his face as warmth tingled through him. "I should start looking now if we have to be out there in two weeks. You might have to go on ahead while I close up shop here and figure out what to do about our lease."

"The benefit package isn't that great, so hopefully that's another thing you can make up with your PT job. But like I said on the phone, I do have to see a sports psychologist every two weeks and do a weekly weigh-in. Apparently rumors of my imminent starvation had reached Forenza's ears and seeing me didn't make him feel any better about it."

"Wow." Rob felt a strange lightening in his chest, the heavy, rock-like burden finally lifted away. He wasn't the only one fighting this with Matty anymore. They were going to have help. Real help. From people who cared. "How do you feel about that?"

"Relieved!" Matty was breathless but serious. "He said if I don't meet certain weight parameters assigned by my dietician, I'm out of there. There's no room for slip-ups."

"What about the shows in Asia?"

"Julien said Hank Babikov had been gunning for the slots assigned to me anyway, so he's more than happy to step in. Looks like I'm out of show business again."

"Sweetheart, you'll do more shows someday. I know you will."

Matty shrugged. "We've got a lot to do to get ready for the next season. I'm supposed to work with PJ Kataria, and Chuck is going to assign me a couple of other skaters as well. And I get to see Sabrina twice a week with Chuck. We're going to work together with her."

Rob didn't want to say anything, but he hoped the stars had finally aligned to put them on the right path. He hadn't ever been to Colorado Springs, but he'd done some internet research while Matty was away and he already had his heart set on a little farmhouse with a good-sized barn and a view of the Rockies. It was for rent, and Rob had sent an email to Bing asking how he might feel about expanding the goat business to include a second ranch.

"Two weeks ago, I couldn't have seen this coming."

"Me either." Matty laughed. "I need to call Donna. She's going to flip out." His smile faded. "I'm not sure she'll be happy, actually."

"She'll be fine."

Matty jumped on him on the sofa and kissed all over his face, and then Rob took command, kissing Matty's mouth hard and taking him down to the floor of the living room, tongues and teeth coming into play as they rolled on the rug and moved together.

"I love you. I know you're giving up a big dream, Matty."

"I don't care. We're going to have a great life."

"We'll be able to see the North Star almost every night."

Matty kissed Rob's chin. "I see it every night now. I see it whenever you look at me."

Rob cupped Matty's face, gazing into his eyes. "I see it too."

CHAPTER THIRTY-ONE

MCNULTY'S RARE TEAS and Choice Coffees was small, tight, and packed with teas, bags, boxes, and people. It smelled like an orgy of coffee and oolong had resulted in the wild offspring of black and green tea blends. Sato appeared to be in heaven, smelling the various teas in a multitude of glass jars that a small, older Asian man opened for him.

"Rob, you'll like this chai."

Rob bent to smell the leaves and was warmed by the familiar spicy scent. "It smells good."

"A quarter pound for us both," Sato said and smiled at Rob. "A good luck present for your move."

"You'll have to come visit and share some with me."

Sato put his hands in his pockets, watching the man weigh the tea on a quaint, old-fashioned scale. "Todd and I would enjoy that. I've been meaning to teach the boy to ski."

"Colorado is a great place for that."

After taking the small, tight packages of tea and paying for them with cash, Sato hooked his arm through Rob's, steering him toward the door and the commotion of Christopher Street. "Before we meet our significant others at Slap & Tickle, why don't we grab a few quiet minutes over here?"

Rob let Sato guide him toward Christopher Park. They passed the Gay Liberation Monument to sit on a bench.

"How did my cousin take the news that you're leaving?"

"Without much surprise, actually. She said she'd be happy to provide a suitable recommendation and wished me luck. Then she shooed me out, saying I'd made a lot of work for her now that she'd have to reassign all of my patients. I need to work out my two weeks, of course, and I regret having to let so many of my patients down by not seeing them through to full recovery, but they're in great hands with Dr. Joiner and the rest of the gang."

"Have you found a place to live?"

Rob smiled. "We have. Matty's chosen a small apartment for now, but it looks like the goats I was telling you about are ready to pay off. My partner Bing let me know last night that the yearlings are looking perfect for Eid al-Adha, the Feast of the Sacrifice. By the lunar calendar, that means big money for us at the end of August. I think we'll be able to look into renting a ranch actually. There are a few we've been looking at online, and while Matty thinks the houses are abominations, he's pretty happy with the views."

"You can rent ranches? I had no idea."

"Sure. People sometimes have more land than they can work alone, or maybe they're older and don't want to deal with the whole property. And others just own the land to rent it. I saw one I liked a lot and it looks like a rent-to-own situation, which would be great if we're happy out there. If we moved to a ranch this fall, then Bing could send some of the herd my way and I could set up a second operation."

"It sounds like things have come full circle for you."

"It's all happened so quickly." Rob laughed. "I'm having a hard time believing it myself."

"And Matty? He's happy with the change?"

"He's over the moon! I think he has a little bit of a crush on his new boss. It's 'Chuck said this, Chuck said that,' all the time. He and his Sabrina are on the phone every night making plans for next season. The day he quit his job with Valentina I thought he was going to fly into the sky powered by his sheer relief."

"And eating? He's doing better?"

"That's interesting, honestly. I've seen him struggle with it a lot more this week than I expected. You know how some people will binge eat before starting a diet? I think Matty's tempted to binge starve before he's forced into something sustainable once we're in Colorado. But he's fighting it off. In fact, our appointment this afternoon is for something he thinks will help with that."

Sato smiled, his eyes crinkling with amusement. "Not another chastity device?"

"Oh, hell no!"

Sato threw back his head and laughed.

"Not a collar either, before you ask."

Sato held up his hands and chuckled more. "I never assume."

"You're good at that. Listen, I wanted to tell you how much I appreciated everything you've done for me in the last few weeks. We barely knew each other before, and hell, you didn't have to be so generous, but you were. It helped a lot. So thank you."

Sato patted Rob's knee. "You needed a friend and I was happy to be one to you."

"Todd's been good for Matty too. He's inspired him to try to focus on service instead of control, and so far, it seems to be working to calm his mind."

"I'm glad to hear it. Matty will probably try to buck the responsibility of service sometimes, but I think he'll find it soothing and return to it easily enough with a small correction."

Rob chuckled. "You've pegged him pretty well."

"He's easy to read." Sato smiled at Rob. "It's clear that he loves you."

"He does. I'm working on making sure all of my feelings are up front too. I don't need to shield him from my problems. He's not a child even if he likes to be punished like one."

"He's not punished like a child. He's punished like a grown man who makes the choice to experience pain. Children never have a choice. The power dynamic is wrong."

Rob smiled and nodded. "Thanks for the correction."

"Was it small enough? Painless enough?"

"It was. I'm going to miss you and I only just got to know you. It's a shame."

"One of the only shames of this move," Sato agreed. "But of

course our friendship isn't over. As you said, Todd and I can visit. And maybe you'll miss the city once you're stuck in Colorado with all that horrible, fresh air."

Rob laughed. "Maybe I will."

"You're welcome to stay with me if you ever want to come visit."

"Oh, I'll definitely be back. The biggest dangling thread right now is my son. His mother wants to move to Colorado too, but Ben's almost eighteen and not interested in moving. He's got a life here — friends, a girl he likes. It doesn't seem right to uproot him."

"That must be a hard choice."

"Yeah. I'll need to come back here to see him a couple of times a year." Rob winced. "God, that's going to suck. I've never been away from him for that long. At least we have FaceTime now. And Skype."

"Children grow up, grow wings, and fly away."

"I think I'd actually feel better about it if that was what was happening." Rob sighed. "Instead, I'm leaving him behind."

"What does he say about it?"

Rob snorted. "He tells me to stop being a worry wart and follow my man to greener pastures. Then he hugged me and cried a little, but he said it was just allergies." Rob sighed. "He's a good kid. Full of love. Strong."

"You mentioned before that his mother wanted him out in Colorado to get away from a problematic friend? Do you think it's best for him to stay here?"

"Well, his friend isn't that problematic. I think Anja is mostly afraid that Ben will be smeared in the Federation's eyes by his association with an openly gay and flamboyant skater. But I'm not going to teach my kid to abandon a boy he cares about to get ahead in life. And to be fair, I really don't think the Federation will do that. They want their skaters to succeed. At the end of the day, we all want the same things."

"And wasn't there a coach your ex thought he'd be better working under?"

"Yes. Chuck Forenza is a better coach, but success isn't always about working with the so-called 'best' coach. Look at Matty and

Sabrina. She succeeded because of their relationship, not because of his experience and skills. Ben and Greg have a bond. Personally, I think Greg's a dick, but Ben likes him and they've gone far together. I'm not sure messing with his momentum by starting over somewhere fresh is what's best for his Olympic aspirations."

"What does Matty say about that?"

"He agrees with me, though he hates Greg. Thinks he smells like IcyHot and cigarettes."

Sato chuckled and shook his head. "It seems smart to go with what the coach in the family thinks is best, so if Matty thinks Ben should stay..."

"Yeah." Rob grinned again. "Matty's excited about coaching with Forenza. There are so many more opportunities for him there. So much more support for his eating issues and his psychological needs. I'm pretty fucking thrilled about that."

"And you're excited about possible future ranching. I'm happy for you, Rob. It seems that you're being given a second chance here. It couldn't have happened to a better man." Sato glanced at his phone and stood up. "Surely they should be done buying sex toys, or whatever they're doing for this photoshoot, by now, don't you think?"

"Well, with Matty's friend Elliot along for the ride, it could take a few more hours." Rob followed Sato from Christopher Park and added, "But Matty and I have an appointment to keep, so even if they aren't done, we need to head out."

"This Elliot? You're sure he's not into porn? Todd thinks this is for fashion modeling."

"Oh no, Elliot's into a lot of things, including porn stars, I'm sure, but he's not a porn photographer. His boss is the real deal, and Elliot is a pretty talented with a camera himself. I've seen his work. Todd's in good—if really bitchy—hands." Rob smiled.

"Oh, my favorite kind." Sato chuckled and they walked for a while together arm in arm.

Rob felt a warm affection for the man beside him. He wished somehow they'd known each other longer and decided that Sato was right: he would seek out some BDSM acquaintances in Colorado. He and Matty both needed community support, even if they didn't play in groups.

"It's been good for me as well, meeting up with you again, Rob," Sato said, releasing Rob's arm and stuffing his hands in his pockets. "I've learned a lot from you."

"Oh, yeah? Did you learn never fall in love with a complicated, anorexic but amazing figure skater?"

"No, you've inspired me."

Rob looked down at the sun glinting on Sato's bald head. "How's that?"

"I'm going to take the next step with Todd. Maybe you've catered too much to Matty, but I haven't catered enough to Todd. I've held back out of fear of his youth and my past hurts. But watching you throw it all in for Matty, even when you came up raw and short, was admirable and obviously worth it."

"Thank you."

"So, yes, I'm going to commit to him and ask him to move in with me. If my heart gets broken one day because, to use my metaphor from earlier, he's a child who grows up and flies away, at least I loved him with all I had, right?"

"He's not that much of a child. I think he knows what he wants."

Sato nodded. "Yes, and that, my friend, is the key to everything."

***

TODD FOLLOWED ELLIOT upstairs to the leather sale area of Slap & Tickle, listening with his usual smile as Elliot explained his idea for the photoshoot. He'd borrowed some of Guyton's less-expensive equipment and thrown himself into the project of getting some good photos for Todd to start a lookbook to take to modeling agencies. He claimed it was a way to distract himself from the misery of Matty leaving.

"Todd, you've got that boy-next-door thing happening and we need to slut that up."

Matty followed behind, his attention split between his friends and Clem's new bright pink and green hair. She was helping a customer, but when she'd seen them come in, her eyes had lit up and she'd waved cheerfully. Now she chomped her gum as she demonstrated the vibration strength of a rabbit vibe for a couple of college girls.

"So, I don't know if things are going to work with him," Elliot said. "Are you listening, Matty?"

"I always listen to you."

Elliot rolled his eyes as he held up a pair of leather pants to Todd. "These are on sale for half off. Hmm." He put them back on the rack, shaking his head, and continuing his lament about Ulysses. "I mean, he's dreamy-looking and kind and smart, but he won't have sex with me!"

"I thought you said he wanted to take it slow?" Todd said.

"I don't do slow." Elliot's cheeks stained pink and his eyes darkened with hurt more than anger. "I need to know upfront if it's going to work in the bedroom. Why get my heart involved if he's going to end up a dud in the sack?"

Todd shrugged. "Okay, if he's not interested in doing it until his heart is involved, and you're not interested in getting hearts involved until you've done it, then it sounds like it won't work out."

"Just like that? I mean, Uly is..." Elliot trailed off and sighed. "He's definitely hung. I managed to cop a feel of his cock while we were dancing at his apartment. Slow dancing, mind you. To some Taylor Swift song. What the fuck, right? So weird."

"Taylor Swift?" Todd asked.

"Yeah."

"I love her," Todd murmured.

"I didn't get laid, though. Slow dancing at his apartment, after a romantic dinner, great conversation, and some wine, and then *nothing*."

"You got a grope of his dick. That's something," Matty said.

"And that something might be assault," Todd said, laughing as he grabbed a pair of red leather pants from the more expensive rack on the wall. "What about these? I could channel a redheaded demon vibe?"

"With that angelic face?" Elliot narrowed his eyes and considered. "Actually, that's perfect. Hold these, Matty."

"At your service," Matty murmured, and Todd winked at him.

"Speaking of, how's service going for you?" Todd asked quietly when Elliot darted across the room to examine a trashy silver see-through top that he thought would play up Todd's pale skin and freckles.

"I'm doing better with it. So far, I like it. It's calming." Matty swallowed hard, remembering that before long Rob and Sato would be joining them, and then he and Rob would head off alone to seal the deal on Matty's commitment to service. He shivered, excitement and nerves prickling his skin. "It's only been a few days, but I'm learning."

"Does Rob like it?"

Matty felt his cheeks heat. "He's amused, I think. But he isn't complaining."

Rob liked it but Matty thought what they enjoyed the most was the way it helped Matty stay calm. Even amidst all the changes and madness of their impending move, focusing on ways to help improve Rob's day in small but important ways put everything else into perspective.

It made Matty feel safe. It was a choice about where to put his focus. He could choose to panic about the move, sure, but that wouldn't improve Rob's life, so instead he chose to make brownies and even eat one. He could choose to dissolve into anxiety about his fear that they might make this massive life change, move across the country, and he'd still somehow fail—either with his weight or as a coach—and get fired.

But those fears didn't make Rob smile.

So Matty rubbed Rob's feet and sucked him off while he watched *Lord of the Rings* or something equally long and boring. As soon as Rob shot, Matty wiped his mouth, kissed him, and didn't let his mind go back to his worries. Instead, he packed up their DVDs for the move so Rob wouldn't have to do it later.

That's a good boy. You're doing a good job for Rob.

Service had a much more pleasant voice than Control. Matty liked Service. Service could stay.

"Bitches, get over here."

Todd looked unimpressed. "You guys need to get new slang. No tea, no shade."

Matty snorted. "Yes, please teach me gay realness, Todd."

"Praise Beysus, look at this hot bitch," Elliot said, holding the silver shirt up against Todd's chest. "Is he a fucking sparkle-vamp or what?"

"How much is this going to put me out?" Todd asked, trying to get a look at the price tag.

Elliot waved his hand. "It's on my trust fund as a thank you for helping me build up my viewbook while you build your lookbook."

As Todd and Elliot headed to the checkout, Matty swerved over to where Clem was waving the college girls down the street.

"Hey, princess," Clem said, punching his shoulder gently. "How'd the anniversary gift go?"

"Pretty fucking awful."

She cracked up. "I figured it might. Blew your mind, didn't it?"

"A little." Matty chuckled. "Okay, a lot."

"Well, that was to be expected. I did warn you."

"You did." Matty trusted Rob's judgment, he did, but he still wanted to check on something just to be sure. "So, I was wondering, do you know anything about a guy named Sato?

"In the BDSM community?" Clem's eyes strayed over to Todd, and she shrugged. "A little. He's a well-respected dom. Treats his subs well. Good at what he does."

"So you think my friend is safe with him?"

She smiled. "If he's with Sato, he's safe as houses."

"Houses can collapse and burn in fires and all kinds of things."

"Such is life, princess." She patted his arm. "Anything else I can help you with today?"

"No. I'm good." Matty barely knew her but he somehow felt like he'd shared an intimate part of his life with her when she sold him the chastity device. He wanted to hug her but instead he just said, "Hey, I'm moving away. Like in two days. So if I don't see you again, thank you so much for taking my sex toy purchases seriously."

Clem snapped her gum and laughed, tugging Matty down for a fast embrace. "Oh God, that review on Yelp. I'm never gonna live it down!"

Matty shrugged and gave her a saucy wave as Todd and Elliot joined him.

Rob and Sato waited outside the shop. After introducing Elliot to Sato, they stood around and chatted for a while. Todd showed off his red leather pants, much to Sato's amusement, and Matty, listening to the murmur of Service, asked Rob if he was hungry or needed anything.

"I'm fine. But we'll get a snack for you before we head over to Williamsburg."

"It's okay. I've got something in my purse. I'll eat it on the way there."

Sato shook Matty's hand and offered congratulations on the new job. "I was thinking Todd and I might come visit this winter."

Todd grinned and slipped his arm around Sato's shoulder. "Really? You've never taken me anywhere before."

"Well, I think a vacation with you sounds nice. Besides, you mentioned learning to ski. We might as well get that done so you'll know how when I take you to Japan next year."

Todd's eyes flew wide and he kissed the top of Sato's head, looking as eager as a puppy. Matty thought he might actually lick Sato in his joy.

"Japan's nice," Elliot murmured, wrapping his arm around Matty's waist and squeezing. "When do you leave?"

"I'll see you again before I go."

"I *hate* you for leaving me, bitch," Elliot said, his eyes expressing his inner turmoil. "But never forget I'll always love you. I want you to be happy."

"I think I'll be happy in Colorado, Elliot. I really do." He kissed

Elliot's cheek. "I love you too. You can always come visit me."

"Let's not do the 'collapse in each other's arms' thing and sob about how we'll see each other all the time."

"Why not?"

"Well, okay." Elliot wrapped him up hard and Matty had to stand on his tiptoes to get his arms around Elliot's neck. They didn't cry but they did hug for a long time. "That's enough of that," Elliot said, pulling away. "We have to save something for our real good-bye." He fanned at his face and lifted his chin imperially. "We have photos to shoot, and you guys have some secret appointment to keep."

After waving them off, Rob hailed a taxi and they crawled into the hot back seat. Rob reached across for his hand after giving the address. "Are you ready?"

"I'm more than ready."

***

SITTING AT THEIR kitchen table that night, Rob peeled the plastic wrap away from Matty's wrist. The skin was pink around the edges of the North Star that rested on his wrist just beneath the palm of his hand. "The white ink looks great with your pale skin."

"I like that it looks like a brand," Matty murmured, gazing down at it with calm eyes.

"You were beautiful when they put it on you. Flushed and determined. So hot, sweetheart."

"Thank you for going with me and holding my hand. It wouldn't mean the same thing without you there."

"Of course. This is your reminder: North Star—our words for 'everything's okay'."

"Forever. A serenity prayer on my body," Matty said in a hushed voice like he hoped it would invoke some sort of magic.

Careful of the tender new tattoo, Rob pulled Matty into his arms, holding him tight and breathing him in. "I love you."

"I love you, too."

"It's easier than I thought," Matty murmured as they clung together.

"What is, sweetheart?"

"Leaving New York."

"Yeah?"

"Yeah. I'm excited to see what the future holds for me somewhere I can really shine. I'm excited to see you in your element again. This is a good change, Rob."

"It is."

"I'm so ready to let go of that old dream and build a new one that's all about me and you."

Rob kissed Matty, loving the way his soft lips felt against his own. "Me too, sweetheart. Me too."

EPILOGUE

"**B**EANY-BABY, YOU WERE fantastic today! Did you hear how proud Chuck was when he came in to see your run-through?" Matty turned up the volume on his Bluetooth so he could hear Sabrina's soft voice a little better.

He was less than two minutes from home and out in the middle of nowhere. Snow-covered fields rolled around him, rising up to snowcapped mountains and blue skies.

"I did! He was so happy with our work!"

"I know! I almost peed myself."

"Matty!" She laughed, and then he heard Mrs. Miller in the background.

"Let me guess, piano practice?"

"Nope. Homework. I'm behind from our trip to Dallas."

"All right. You get on that."

"Tell Rob I said hi."

Disconnecting the call, Matty slipped on his sunglasses. The land out the driver's side window was part of the ranch they were renting. The older couple who owned it were retiring to a beach in Texas, but neither of them had been ready to give up the place for good. Rob had been their dream come true, and now Rob was negotiating to buy the property from them little by little, providing a kind of annuity for them to live on and allowing Rob the time to come up with the money over the course of years instead of months.

The ranch land wasn't all that much to look at right now. It was the middle of December and everything was brown and white, or white and brown. As he pulled down the drive, Matty took in the one story, brown-and-bland three-bedroom ranch house. He would be miserable about that except that the mountains rising up behind it were stunning. They shone in the sunlight with new-fallen snow and commanded the eye to admire them. A fancy-looking house would be an embarrassment beside such beauty. The little brownish-beige rancher blended into the trees and kept everyone's gaze where it belonged: on the scenery.

But the inside of the house was Matty's domain. He'd decorated it carefully over the last six months, and though it was far from finished, he loved the cozy kitchen with its pretty little nook that looked out at the mountains. He loved their living room, though he couldn't wait to replace their IKEA couch with something a little nicer. The bedrooms all had views of the mountains. Between his mother and father, Ben and Anja, Bill and Angus, Sato and Todd, and Elliot when he deigned to leave the city, the guest rooms were in regular use.

And of course Matty's favorite room was his and Rob's bedroom.

It was almost as big as their entire apartment in New York and, with the curtain-less windows emphasizing their complete isolation, many amazing nights had been spent in their enormous bed. Their room was safety and pleasure rolled together with green walls and beautiful views.

All in all, it was a pretty great house.

As the driveway curled away from the road, Matty noted that Rob had made it home from his PT job early. Their Christmas tree was on and it dazzled from the wide picture window in the front living room. It was covered in silver ornaments and white lights, and Matty was inordinately pleased with it. He and Ben had done it together while Anja and Rob had watched from the sofa, discussing the future and Ben's skating plans. It looked like they were going to stay in New Jersey. In a surprise to Matty, but not to Rob, Anja revealed that she'd spoken at length with Ben's friend Cardew's sister, Ebru, and she'd agreed it would be helpful to everyone if Anja allowed Cardew to live with her and Ben for a while.

"I think he'll do better with an older mother figure to take him in hand," she'd explained.

"It'll be like having a brother. A really shiny brother," Ben had said, smiling happily.

"Oh, you should ask Joey about that," Matty had replied. "It's not all it's cracked up to be."

Ben had kissed Matty's cheek. "I think I can handle it."

Matty smiled as he pulled into the garage and clicked for the automatic door to drop behind him. Joey and Chelsea had gotten married in September and it'd been a beautiful wedding. Matty and Rob had flown down to Atlanta for it, and he'd enjoyed being Joey's best man. During the reception toast, he'd managing to piss off Joey while simultaneously making him cry. Rob agreed that it'd been a smashing success.

Matty's hip felt a little stiff as he climbed out of his blue Subaru Forester, and he made a note to ask Rob to work on it that night. As he reached into the backseat for his duffel, his eyes fell on the white tattoo on his wrist and he touched it softly. He still loved it. He looked at it dozens of times a day and never got past thinking that it was beautiful and subtle; classic and perfect.

The tattoo served as a reminder, and Service murmured in his head. *Ask Rob how his day was. Find at least one way to make his evening relaxing and calm.*

Hefting the bag on his shoulder, Matty went into the house through the connecting door to the garage and called out, "Rob, I'm home!"

He was met with a silence that meant Rob was out in the barn with the goats. That was the norm these days heading up to the holidays. He was preparing some of the male suckling kids for sale at the market in time for the Christmas holiday feasts. It was Matty's first experience with the discomfort of selling animals he'd helped bring into the world, but he was trying to be strong about it. He hated to admit it, but he kind of loved the goats. They were always so damn cheerful and eager to see him, bleating madly whenever he came into the barn.

Matty dumped his duffel on the kitchen table, grabbed a fruit and nut bar from the bowl on the counter, and then stopped in the mud room to pull on his big rubber boots and a heavy barn coat before heading across the yard toward the russet-painted barn to find Rob.

On the way there, he was greeted by Patches and Chuckles, two dogs that Rob had brought to the farm in November. They were a gift from a new neighbor who had more than his fair share of herding dogs. Matty patted both of their heads and walked more rapidly in the frigid air toward the warmth of the insulated, heated barn. Neither dog had wormed his way into Rob's heart the way Lila had, but Matty had a great plan for an anniversary present this year: a golden retriever puppy. He'd already been in contact with a breeder and felt sure that Rob would fall head over heels in love with it. The real struggle would be allowing Rob to come up with the name because, boy or girl, Matty really wanted to name it Peaches Glittershine.

The baby goats were in their pen, bleating, hopping, and climbing on top of each other in their rush to greet Matty.

"Hey, sweetheart," Rob said from the back of the pen. He was wearing a red canvas barn coat and blue jeans. His blond hair glowed in the light from one of the south-facing windows, and he smiled happily at Matty. "Little Rhoda grew overnight." He nodded toward the tiny white goat Matty had delivered himself and declared his own. "She was kicking her brother's butt with her back hooves earlier."

Matty finished off the fruit and nut bar before carefully unlatching the gate and stepping into the pen. The goats surrounded him joyfully, and he snatched Rhoda from the middle of them and held her against his chest. She *was* getting bigger, and fast. Soon he wouldn't be able to hold her anymore. "My sweet, violent baby," he crooned. "Beat those other goats up all you want. You're the queen of the herd, aren't you?"

Rhoda bleated and chewed on the edge of his barn coat sleeve. Matty let her.

"How was work?" Rob asked.

"No, me first. How was *your* work?"

Rob smiled at him. "It was fine. Another ski injury and a hip injury in a certain figure skater from another coach, but I'll let that news come to you from the grapevine if it hasn't already."

"Darren Mathis. Heard already. Don't patch him up too well, though, he's PJ's main competition."

"Aside from Ben."

Matty smiled. "Well, we know Ben will beat his ass when it counts, don't we?"

"With you as PJ's coach, there's no telling." Rob stepped forward and took Rhoda from Matty's arms. "Now, how about your day?"

"All good! Awesome, actually. Sabrina is nailing the new triple toe combination we've been working on and I think she's got a chance for gold this year at Junior Worlds. Chuck came to see her do a run-through this afternoon during my time with her, and he was really pleased with her work. And mine."

"Does his pleasure result in a raise?"

Matty laughed. "Not yet. But maybe if we do prove ourselves at Worlds. We'll see. Chuck's been really generous."

"He has."

"I talked to Sato today," Matty said, taking Rob's hand and pulling him out of the goat pen and toward a sunny window.

"You did?"

"Yeah, he asked me when they visited to give him a call to talk about how things are going with Jack and Bea." Jack was the sports psychologist Matty was seeing once every two weeks as part of his commitment to Chuck, and Bea was the dietician who took his weight and helped him feel more secure in his food choices. He liked them both and, in general, felt emotionally stronger and healthier than ever.

Control hadn't made a peep in a long time. He wasn't foolish enough to think he'd beaten it, though. It was probably going to be a lifelong battle. But he was strong—a former Olympian. He was Matty Marcus. He'd come out on top. With Rob's help, and the help of his team, he hoped that on his death bed, this would be one challenger he hands-down defeated.

"And what did you tell him about how things are going?"

"I told him they're good."

"Are they good?"

"Well, today I had a hard time eating when I realized Chuck was going to observe Sabrina this afternoon, but I got my portion down. It wasn't easy but I just kept looking at this every time I thought I might give up." He lifted his wrist, and Rob took hold of his forearm, sliding up his coat sleeve to bring Matty's tattoo up to his mouth, kissing it softly.

"You're so brave, sweetheart."

Matty laughed. "Yeah, I ate some lunch. I'm a fucking hero."

"You are."

Matty rolled his eyes. "You're my hero."

"You're mine."

"Oh my God, what is going on with you? Are you drunk?"

Rob laughed. "No. Just happy. So was Sato satisfied with what you told him?"

"Yeah, but he was happier when I said we'd gone to another munch to meet some more people in the scene. He's really into us having support for our 'lifestyle.'"

"He's not wrong. Look how nice it's been to have him and Todd in our lives. We don't have to explain anything to them."

Matty nodded and shivered as Rob kissed the inside of his wrist again and pulled him flush against his body. "Do you need me to help with anything out here?" Matty asked.

"Well, if you'd do me one small favor, that'd be great."

"Sure. Anything."

"Come here." Rob led him back into the goat pen and over to another sunny window. "Look out there a second and I'll tell you what I want you to do next."

Matty frowned, but did as he was told. Outside, the mountains rose up, and he thought about how they'd need to completely insulate these windows very soon for the winter, but for now they provided an amazing view. Matty could hear the goats going wild behind him, and wondered why Rob wanted him to look out the window. Had Rob changed his mind and gone back to the farmer's market to purchase the little red crocheted vest Matty had wanted to buy for Rhoda? Matty had insisted Rhoda would look adorable, but Rob had countered that the other goats would eat it off her in ten seconds flat.

"Okay, turn around."

Matty did.

Rob was down on one knee.

"Oh my God."

"What do you think? Is this romantic enough?" Rhoda jumped onto Rob's shoulder and hopped back down again, but Rob didn't flinch. He grinned and held open a black box containing a shiny circle of diamonds. The goats were milling around, dangerously close to eating the ring in Matty's wildly overwhelmed opinion. "I bought this with an advance on our goat money, so I thought this was an appropriate place to ask. What do you say? Want to be my husband?"

Matty's eyes prickled, and his throat went tight. "Are you really proposing to me right now?"

"Yes. Want to hitch our stars together? Want to be with me until we die? Live in whatever insanity we make our lives into and have the whole world know we chose it together?"

"Oh my God! You can't do this to me! Why didn't you ask me when we were at that amazing picnic in New York?" Matty wiped at his wet eyes, his hands shaking and his heart pounding. His knees even felt wobbly. The goats were bleating and milling around him, nearly knocking him over in their desire to comfort his distress. "Why didn't you ask me then?"

"Because I couldn't do it until right now. Until right this moment when our new life has truly started." Rob laughed. "You should see your face." He laughed even harder. "This will make a great story, sweetheart."

"For you!"

"For you too."

Matty stared at Rob—at his blond, green-eyed Rob Lovely-ness lighting up the barn. Even the ridiculous goats knew Rob was special. They climbed all over him, or tried to, and before they could knock the ring out of his hand and eat it, Matty had to say something. "Yes! Yes! I'll marry you!"

Matty flung himself on Rob and kissed him hard. As Rob stood, Matty jumped up and wrapped his legs around his waist. Rob held him tightly, and goats bleated all around in a joyous melody of congratulations. Somewhere between the bleating and the kissing, Matty got the ring on his finger, and he held it out in front of him. "Wow. It's beautiful."

"I had Elliot's help."

Matty laughed. "It's perfect. I love it so much. And I love you. And I love this barn. And I love this ranch. And I love our ugly rented house. And I love these cute fucking goats. And wow. I love our whole damn life."

"Me too, sweetheart. This new life goal of happiness is going pretty well, huh?"

Matty laughed and cried at the same time. Rob kissed him again, and when they finally left the barn to walk home in the evening gloaming, Matty turned his head to look at the mountains in the distance, snowcapped and eternal against the night sky.

THE END

N

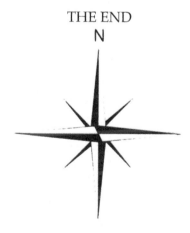

Author Notes

First, I'd like to thank all of the BDSM experts that I've interacted with over the last four years. Their advice and input has been invaluable.

Second, I'd like to acknowledge the heavy burden of eating disorders and disordered eating. My research into the topic was extensive, and, unfortunately, a bit personal. Seeing a family member struggle has given this topic a lot of emotional power for me, and it's possible that some of those demons needed to be written out. I don't pretend that this book reflects every anorexic's experience or that any kind of recovery is easy, but I hope my research and personal experience shines through.

Thank you to first and foremost to the fans of *Training Season*. I'm so incredibly grateful for your enthusiasm and devotion to Matty and Rob.

Thank you beyond measure to Darrah Glass, Ajax Bell, Keira Andrews, and Indra Vaughn. Thank you so much to Frances for her fast and insightful beta read, and especially for her dedication to making this a better book! Thank you to Kim forever and always. Thank you to Liza, Rachel, and my sister-in-law Cindy. Thank you to my parents for believing in and supporting me. Thank you to my in-laws for their wonderful help. And thank you to my daughter for telling me to go write more books. Thank you to my husband for his love, faith, and unfailing encouragement.

Again, thank you to any and all readers of this work. No book is complete without a reader and you hold a dear place in my heart.

All my best,
Leta Blake

Letter from Leta with the 2nd Edition

Dear Reader,

Thank you so much for reading *Training Complex*!

After the release of *Training Season* I realized that Matty's eating disorder had been glossed over, and, after thinking it over, the character wanted a chance to explore that. The misapplication of BDSM was also something I wanted to explore, since it's so rarely done in novels. It's possible for otherwise good practitioners to run into issues with their practice and need to reevaluate it. And it isn't always an abusive Dom who changes the dynamic...

Extras and deleted scenes for the *Training Season* series, as well as other book universes, can be found at my Patreon. Be sure to follow me on BookBub or Goodreads to be notified of new releases. And look for me on Facebook for snippets of the day-to-day writing life, or join my Facebook Group for announcements and special giveaways. To see some sources of my inspiration, you can follow my Pinterest boards or Instagram.

If you enjoyed the book, please take a moment to leave a review! Reviews not only help readers determine if a book is for them, but also help a book show up in site searches.

Also, for the audiobook connoisseurs out there, *Training Series* is available narrated by the amazing Michael Ferraiuolo. I hope to eventually add my entire backlist to my audiobook roster over the next few years.

Thank you for being a reader!
Leta

Book 1 in the Home for the Holidays series

MR. FROSTY PANTS

by Leta Blake

Frosty former friends get a steamy second chance in this Christmas gay romance!

Can true love warm his frozen heart?

When Casey Stevens went away to college four years ago, he ghosted on his straight best friend, Joel Vreeland. He hoped time and distance would lessen the unrequited affection he felt, but all it did was make him miss Joel more.

Home for the holidays, Casey hopes they might find a way to be friends again. But Joel's frosty reception reminds Casey of just how hard he had to fight to be Joel's friend in the first place. It's going to take a Christmas miracle to get past that cool façade again.

Joel isn't as straight as Casey believes, and his years of pining for Casey have left him hurting and alone, caring for his abusive father and struggling to get by. Unable to trust anyone except his rescue dog—and with no reason to believe Casey is interested in him for more than a holiday fling—Joel's icy heart might shatter before it can thaw.

Can Casey and Joel's love overcome mistrust, parental rejection, class differences, and four long years apart? *Mr. Frosty Pants* is a stand-alone, Christmas gay romance by Leta Blake featuring a virgin hero, childhood friends-to-lovers, second chance romance, and steamy mm first times.

Standalone novel featuring winter holidays

SMOKY MOUNTAIN DREAMS
by Leta Blake

Sometimes holding on means letting go.

After giving up on his career as a country singer in Nashville, Christopher Ryder is happy enough performing at the Smoky Mountain Dreams theme park in Tennessee. But while his beloved Gran loves him exactly the way he is, Christopher feels painfully invisible to everyone else. Even when he's center stage he aches for someone to see the real him.

Bisexual Jesse Birch is a single dad with no room in his life for dating. Raising two kids and fighting with family after a tragic accident took his children's mother, he doesn't want more than an occasional hook-up. He sure as hell doesn't want to fall hard for his favorite local singer, but when Christopher walks into his jewelry studio, Jesse hears a new song in his heart.

Smoky Mountain Dreams is a heartfelt gay romance with a single dad, winter holiday highlights, found family, and steamy scenes to warm even the coldest heart!

COWBOY SEEKS HUSBAND

by Leta Blake & Indra Vaughn

Can two men who are just in it for the money fake their way into real and lasting love?

Walker Reed's Louisiana cattle ranch is in debt after costly repairs from hurricane damage. To get the money, his family schemes to make Walker the star of a new bachelor reality series: *Queer Seeks Spouse*. How hard can it be to fake interest in a dozen handsome men for a few weeks in exchange for enough money to solve all of their problems?

Roan Carmichael never got his Masters degree after his mother was diagnosed with cancer. With medical bills piling up, and a costly experimental treatment available, Roan signs on to be a suitor on *Queer Seeks Spouse*. While he hates having to leave his sick mother long enough to win the cash for her treatment, he's willing to do whatever it takes.

Cowboy Seeks Husband, the latest book by *Vespertine* authors Leta Blake and Indra Vaughn, features a cowboy, a hipster, opposites attract, steamy scenes, and heart tugging moments that culminate with a lovely happy ending for the couple.

ANY GIVEN LIFETIME

He'll love him in any lifetime.

Neil isn't a ghost, but he feels like one. Reincarnated with all his memories from his prior life, he spent twenty years trapped in a child's body, wanting nothing more than to grow up and reclaim the love of his life.

As an adult, Neil finds there's more than lost time separating them. Joshua has built a beautiful life since Neil's death, and how exactly is Neil supposed to introduce himself? As Joshua's long-dead lover in a new body? Heartbroken and hopeless, Neil takes refuge in his work, developing microscopic robots called nanites that can produce medical miracles.

When Joshua meets a young scientist working on a medical project, his soul senses something his rational mind can't believe. Has Neil truly come back to him after twenty years? And if the impossible is real, can they be together at long last?

Any Given Lifetime is a stand-alone, slow burn, second chance gay romance by Leta Blake featuring reincarnation and true love. This story includes some angst, some steam, an age gap, and, of course, a happy ending.

Gay Romance Newsletter

Leta's newsletter will keep you up to date on her latest releases and news from the world of M/M romance. Join the mailing list today and you're automatically entered into future giveaways.
letablake.com

Leta Blake on Patreon

Become part of Leta Blake's Patreon community in order to access exclusive content, deleted scenes, extras, bonus stories, rewards, prizes, interviews, and more.
www.patreon.com/letablake

Other Books by Leta Blake

Any Given Lifetime
The River Leith
Smoky Mountain Dreams
Angel Undone

The Home for the Holidays Series
Mr. Frosty Pants
Mr. Naughty List

The Training Season Series
Training Season
Training Complex

Heat of Love Series
Slow Heat
Alpha Heat
Slow Birth
Bitter Heat

'90s Coming of Age Series
Pictures of You
You Are Not Me

Co-Authored with Indra Vaughn
Vespertine
Cowboy Seeks Husband

Co-Authored with Alice Griffiths
The Wake Up Married serial
Will & Patrick's Endless Honeymoon

Gay Fairy Tales
Co-Authored with Keira Andrews
Flight
Levity
Rise

Leta Blake writing as Blake Moreno
The Difference Between
Heat for Sale

Leta Blake writing as Halsey Harlow
Stay Lucky
Stay Sexy
Omega Mine: Search for a Soulmate
Bring on Forever

Audiobooks
Leta Blake at Audible

Free Read
Stalking Dreams

Discover more about the author online:
Leta Blake
letablake.com

About the Author

Author of the bestselling book Smoky Mountain Dreams and the fan favorite Training Season, Leta Blake's educational and professional background is in psychology and finance, respectively. However, her passion has always been for writing. She enjoys crafting romance stories and exploring the psyches of made up people. At home in the Southern U.S., Leta works hard at achieving balance between her day job, her writing, and her family.

Made in the USA
Coppell, TX
19 July 2020